From Anastasia

Jordi Burton

Copyright © 2019 by Jordi Burton
Cover Art by Aaron Lambert

ISBN: 1-7336110-0-2
ISBN-13: 978-1-7336110-0-8

To Morrie
the most passionate person I've ever known

We miss you

ALSO BY JORDI BURTON

The Anastasia Series

Call Me Anastasia

Her Name Was Anastasia

From Anastasia

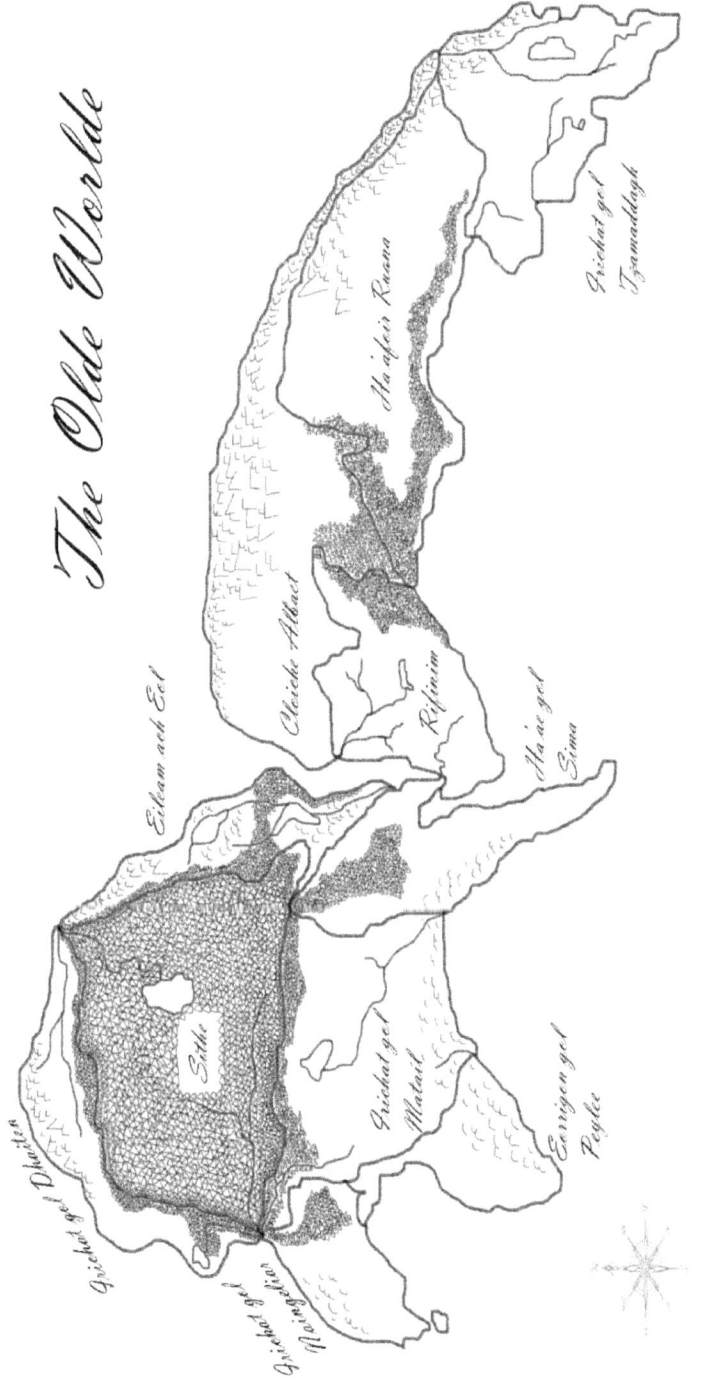

The Olde Worlde

Dramatis Personae

The Jacquelinian Royal Family
Analie Astor………………..Queen of the Nadmilise
~~Brock Astor…………………….King of the Nadmilise~~
Bale Astor………………………………..A Lord
Calla………………………….Mother of the Sterata
Anarose Piliar………………….Queen of the Nadmilise
Elliot Piliar…………………….King of the Nadmilise
Anastasia Piliar Moneth……………..Crown Princess of Jacqueline
Celia Rowan……………………………..A Lady
Graham Piliar…………………….A Diplomat

The Hullenian Royal Family
Tamo Moneth……………….King of the Werewolves
Aylen Moneth……………….Queen of the Werewolves
~~Aatu Moneth……………….Crown Prince of the Werewolves~~
Kanna Moneth………………Princess of the Werewolves
Niboki Moneth…………………Prince of the Werewolves

The Viirean Royal Family
Mateiv Roza…………………….King of the Vampires
Vlad Roza…………………….Prince of the Vampires
Ostana Moneth……………….Princess of the Werewolves

The Castavi Royal Family
Sona……………….Queen of the Sorcerers
Mohan………………Prince of the Sorcerers

The High Council
Euaristos Spiros…………………….King of the Demigods
Krag Rok………………….King of the Trolls
Dohate…………………….King of the Giants
Aguin Fom……………………………..King of the Elementals
Luana Lanana…………………..Queen of the Mermaids
Karmen Roth………………….Queen of the Ghosts
Valdon……………….Special Representative to Jacqueline

The Future Kings of the Realms
Zethus Spiros…………………….Prince of the Demigods
Rokker Rok……………………..Prince of the Trolls
Dammek……………………..Prince of the Giants
Nalin Eom……………………..Prince of the Elementals
Eala Lanana…………………..Prince of the Mermaids
Hugie Roth…………………..Prince of the Ghosts

The Dinas Family
Dolan Dinas………………… The Blacksmith
~~Victorya Dinas………………….Dance Master of Sehir~~
William Dinas………………….A Warrior Apprentice
Dani Dinas……………………….A Healing Apprentice

The Woodsman Family
Jelina Woodsman………………A Seamstress
Aleric Woodsman…………..A Knowledgist
Eleka Woodsman……………….A Musician

Chris Woodsman............A Royal Warrior
Alex Woodsman................A Knowledgist

Representatives

Murcy Zand.............................Of the City
of Talrom
Sophine.....................................Of the Isle
of Berysa

Warriors

Hayde Zand...........................Realm Guard
Ioan Moldovan...........................A Vampire
Firro Glude........................Warrior Master
of Sehir
Surreg Toldens.................Commander of
the Realm Guard
Kalgess Follant................Warrior Master
of Jacqueline
Durse Follant.............................An Outlaw

The Gods and Angels

Kristana.....................Goddess of Creation
Julieus...............................God of Creation
Razibelle.............................Warrior Angel
Humurse................................Warrior God
Lumise........................Goddess of Healing
Luke..................................Angel of Healing

Others

Lili Hadsun.............................Handmaiden
to Anastasia
Melina Hadsun.............................A Baking
Apprentice
Joey Surine ....The Sterata
Fairy Queen..............Queen of the Fairies
Turania Noul.......................The Keeper of
the Words
Miruna Tayna....................The Keeper of
Secrets
Jumba.............................The Soul Seeker
~~Adrian............................The Sterata~~
Deera Ros.........................The Mother of
the Sterata

Isidora Spiros.............................A Demigod
Ourla Emalia............................A Mermaid
~~Healer Dounin...............................A Healer~~

CHAPTER ONE

E arly morning sunlight filtered through the squat windows in the Council chambers of the Sehirian castle. Anastasia sat alone at the ancient round table, spinning her gold engagement ring over the wood. Branded inside were Aatu Moneth's initials, carved in the traditional werewolf language, Bashaa.

Six months. Six months had passed since the man with the black eyes, Adrian, had stabbed Aatu in the back and watched him die in Anastasia's arms. Six months since her best friend, Joey, had been kidnapped and held in the Shadow compound Adrian had controlled. Six months since Healer Dounin confessed to working to take away her premonitions so Adrian could go ahead with his dastardly plans. Six months since Aatu's sister, Ostana, had been outed as being a spy, resulting in her brother's death.

And yet… none of it mattered now.

A cool wind tore through the room a moment before the gilded outline of a portal appeared. Right on time. Anastasia slid the ring onto her finger, getting to her feet.

The portal opened to reveal a young woman wearing a tichel headwrap and conservative ankle-length, weather-worn dress. Lowering the cloth covering the lower half of her face, she offered Anastasia a humorless smile.

Anastasia couldn't help but think how much she looked like her brother, William.

"Dani."

Dani Dinas glanced over her shoulder, dropping into a quick curtsy. "Any news?"

"Not yet. The trial hasn't yet convened." Anastasia hesitated. "And you?"

"Nothing."

An awkward silence spread between them. Anastasia took the time to look over Dani. In the two months since they'd reclaimed Sehir together from the Shadows, she'd grown stronger, surer of herself. She still sported the three scars on the right side of her head, the flaxen hair around them completely shaved. The scars stood out against her tanned skin, unable to be healed due to the poison with which the Shadow's claws had been laced when it cut her.

Anastasia finally broke the silence. "A new warrior will be joining you in the Sand Isles."

"When can I expect her?"

"*He* will arrive around noon your time."

Dani nodded. "We can wait."

A knock sounded at the door to the Council chambers. Anastasia hurriedly reached through the portal and took Dani's hand.

"I will give you any news I have once I'm able."

Dani held her gaze. "And I you."

The portal vanished just as the door to the chambers opened. Anastasia smoothed down her hair as Valdon stepped inside. He wore his traditional drape-like sorcerers' robes that flowed behind him as he moved. His dark sapphire eyes, which matched the color of his vibrant hair, held a melancholy expression. It filled Anastasia with an acidic anger; bile coated her throat. She couldn't believe it had truly come to this. And yet here they were.

"Are you ready?"

She scoffed. "Would you be?"

She looked around the room to calm herself. The map depicting the ten non-human realms as one world looked pristine, scrubbed of all blood— Shadow and Nadmilise alike. It helped her believe that just maybe they could cleanse the realms of the bloodshed as well.

Holding her head high, she stepped out into the hall. Her guards, Gath and Mortam, took up their usual posts at her side, reminding her of when she'd first arrived in Sehir, nearly a year previous.

Pushing those memories from her mind, for fear of where they would lead her, she stopped in front of the side door to the throne room. Beyond the doorway, the people of Sehir, and the Representatives to the Crown of Jacqueline, gathered. Anastasia had only seen something like it once before. Then, she had sat with Joey and Ostana, watching a man as he was greyed out, the divine tattoos granted him by the Gods and Angels particular to his trade turned ashen by Valdon's powerful magic. Now? Now was an altogether different setting, and she wasn't sure she was prepared to handle it.

Valdon caught her arm. "Remember, you don't know him, either of them. You owe them nothing."

"I remember."

Pulling from his grasp, she marched into the room. The people stood as she entered, their eyes trained on her as she took the throne behind the long table of Representatives. After a wave of her hand, they sat. Silence pervaded the chamber.

She gripped the armrests of the throne to hide the trembling of her hands. Releasing a breath, she resisted the urge to run back the way she came. But she knew she couldn't hide.

"Bring them in," she commanded.

Two guards at the end of the hall opened the large doors. A moment later, four more guards led two prisoners between them. One was tall, even by Nadmilise standards, with long, unkempt raven hair, and a soiled length of cloth tied over his eyes. The other… the rough beard covering his jaw, and the intensity in his hazel eyes made Anastasia's breath catch.

Her mind took her back to that afternoon, the day before he'd been arrested, the last time she'd seen him:

"I was given a test, when I returned to this universe. It showed me everything I could've ever wanted, gave me my grandmother, Aatu. But I turned it down. And it wasn't to save my people, or rescue my family, or defeat the Shadows."

"What was it for?"

"You."

The sound of their chains clanging on the stone floor drew her back to the present. Both prisoners knelt before her, before the row of Representatives, before the people of the royal city. She tightened her grip on the throne, making sure her expression remained neutral, impassive, remembering what Valdon had said. She didn't know them. She didn't owe them anything. If only it were true, this whole process would go much more smoothly.

3

"Christopher Jay Woodsman, William James Dinas, you stand accused of desertion." Her voice reverberated loudly through the chamber.

Chris flinched. He looked pitiful, blinded as he was, with his hands chained behind his back. William stared defiantly ahead. She almost wished he would make eye contact with her, but she knew it wasn't best. Just being in the same room as him made gooseflesh erupt across her skin; she couldn't imagine what it would be like to look him in the eye and pretend he meant nothing to her.

Lili had been the only person to witness the moment between them. Every other moment they'd been together in the last six months could be explained away in a way that kept their scavenger hunt to find her grandmother, and the alternate universe she lived in, a secret.

"And who represents these men before the Crown and the Gods and Angels?"

Anastasia looked to William, but he remained expressionless. Good. It was better he didn't speak until he needed to.

"I do."

Murmurs erupted through the throne room as the Head Warrior Master of Jacqueline stepped through the doors to the throne room. Snow dusted her shoulders, puddled at her feet; she'd just portaled from a place where it was still winter. She shed her furs as she strode down the aisle, the bronze broadsword at her back glinting in the bright summer sun filtering through the high windows. Reaching Chris and William, she dropped her furs on the floor beside them, placing her hands on her hips.

"Mistress Follant."

The warrior inclined her head. "Your Highness, Representatives."

Anastasia resisted the urge to glance at William again. Mistress Follant had been at the Center Realm when she and William arrived together, and she'd seen her and Chris leave together to go to the Sky Temple in the elemental realm. She *knew* William and Chris were deserters.

"William Dinas and Christopher Woodsman are two of the finest warriors I've worked with. You will hear stories of their lack of regard for the law, but that is all they are—stories."

Representative Sirren, of the eastern city of Irroun, shook his head. "We are not interested in your pretty words, Follant. Either Dinas and Woodsman deserted the Realm Guard, or they did not. There is no gray area here."

"With all due respect, Representative, there is *always* a gray area, especially where warriors are concerned." Mistress Follant narrowed her flinty eyes. "If Christopher Woodsman had followed strict orders, young Melina Hadsun would be dead. He broke rank to get her to a healer when she had been possessed by the Shadows, which saved her life. And William Dinas defied orders to fight against a group of possessed werewolves, which saved nearly a dozen young warrior apprentices in the Small Hall. One of which, I believe, is your niece, Representative."

Anastasia kept a smirk from her lips, making sure her expression remained stoic. Representative Sirren, however, soured.

"That is all well and good, Mistress Follant. But if we do not have order, we shall have Chaos."

"Are you really suggesting that you punish every infraction to the greatest extent? For we shall surely have no warriors left."

The grandfatherly Representative of Talrom, Murcy Zand, chuckled. "Do not be so dramatic, Kalgess. This is not a witch hunt. We are making sure the realm is safe, protected, and we cannot rely on warriors who have shown to disregard the law for their own personal needs. You of all people know the realm, the Crown, must come first."

"Besides," Representative Sirren interjected. "By pruning the Realm Guard of deserters, we are giving the realms the best chance at survival once the Shadows break free of their stony enchantment. We must be able to trust those that guard us."

Murmurs of agreement buzzed through the room. Anastasia held her hand up for silence, hiding a frown. Many Nadmilise warriors had been brought to trial for desertion, but they had not faced the same scrutiny from the Representatives as William and Chris. What had brought on such a strong reaction? And how could Mistress Follant make it stop? She wasn't a knowledgist, she didn't study words and law. Was she capable of representing Chris and William, of making sure they were freed?

Mistress Follant pursed her lips. "Prune the plant too much and it dies, Representative."

All eyes turned to Representative Sophine as she cleared her throat. "If we may let Mistress Follant at least get through her opening statements?"

The other Representatives murmured their agreement, giving Mistress Follant the floor. Anastasia let out a breath, studying the back of Representative Sophine's head. For months, she'd been held captive by Adrian, tortured in the same compound in which Joey had been held.

Chris had personally carried the Representative from her cell, bringing her back to Sehir. Surely that would sway the Representative's thinking?

Could she be counted on to be more lenient, maybe? Understanding of Chris's actions, seeing as he'd been instrumental in saving her life? Or, perhaps, she would be understanding in that he was now as blind as she. Though hers was due to torture at the hand of the Shadows, and Chris's was from taking the List of Ancients from the Wishing Tree, they now had a disability in common.

Mistress Follant inclined her head to Representative Sophine. "Thank you." Motioning to Chris and William, she turned to meet the eyes of the people gathered in the stands. "Christopher Woodsman is a royal warrior. He studied under the tutelage of Master Glude while an apprentice, and then worked beneath Warrior Surreg Toldens as a Gate Guardsman, and as one of the select few who provided the cure to possessed werewolves. He rescued thirty-six innocent people held captive in Pousa, and then was a part of the group that destroyed the Shadow compound in the Wetland Line."

Anastasia turned her engagement ring around on her finger, memories of the compound flashing through her mind. Guilt tightened her chest.

"William Dinas," Mistress Follant continued. "At ten-years-old, he already surpassed many of his superiors in technical skill and ability. He was the only apprentice ever admitted to the Royal Guard, and was chosen to protect the Princess, herself."

All eyes flicked to Anastasia. She struggled to keep from looking at William. The ruse had to hold. She had to minimize any relationship she had with William, to distance herself, or else the Representatives could argue she was unfit to oversee this trial, and she would be unable to cast her vote in William's and Chris's favor.

Instead, she looked at the people. Were they truly listening to Mistress Follant's words, or had they already made up their minds about *the deserters*?

"During his time as an apprentice with the Royal Guard, William shielded Princess Anastasia from harm. He was the first to go after Lord Joseph when he was kidnapped by the Shadows, and he was part of the rescue team that found the royal family when they were taken captive by the coward, Adrian."

Anastasia shivered, remembering the way her family had looked when Valdon and William brought them back from the Shadow universe. Her mother still hadn't recovered from the months of torture, which explained why *she* was presiding over the trial instead of Anarose. Anger boiled through her. She wanted to tear Adrian apart for what he'd done to them. And yet, instead of going after him, instead of focusing on finding him and stopping the Shadows' reanimation, they were squabbling about deserters.

How did that make any sense?

"William Dinas and Christopher Woodsman are exceptional warriors that simply made a mistake. But their mistake saved the lives of the royal family, and that of countless warriors, Nadmilise and others, alike. All I ask is that you see these men not for this one indiscretion, but for who they are."

Representative Sirren frowned. "And just who are they, then?"

"Two men who disobeyed orders for the sake of saving millions of people."

"Don't make this sound so dramatic, Kalgess." Representative Zand chortled. "These two broke the law, and as a result, must face punishment for their actions."

Anastasia worked to keep from frowning. She didn't like the edge to Representative Zand's voice.

"We do not know what may have happened had they not disobeyed orders," he continued. "For all we know, they could have saved more lives. And you, yourself, mentioned that this is not the first time William Dinas has disobeyed orders. He was still an apprentice, and on probation, when he broke the law for the second time."

Silence grew through the room. Anastasia covertly watched William out of the corner of her eye. He remained stoic, unmoving, his eyes trained on the ground. Everything about his posture screamed passivity, but Anastasia could see the defiance in his eyes. If he had to, he'd do the same thing over again, dash the consequences. Together, they'd faced a kraken, a madwoman, threats from the Fairy Queen, and countless Shadow attacks. They had made it through. Anastasia had no doubt they would make it through this, too.

Representative Sophine broke the silence. "Do you have any further remarks, Mistress Follant?"

The Head Warrior Master of Jacqueline pursed her lips. "We can play a game of what-ifs, if it would please you. But the bottom line is that William Dinas and Christopher Woodsman are exceptional warriors. Yes, they broke the law. But their punishment for their actions should be one of lenience."

Was that it? Anastasia tightened her grip on the throne. Was that all Mistress Follant could say on their behalf? How was that supposed to get them out of this mess?

And yet… Just one hole in her carefully concocted story could lead them to the alternate universe, to her grandmother, to the premonitions, to the Shadows' plans of bringing all the universes together. And those were secrets better kept from the people. But was it worth keeping the secret if it meant ruining William's and Chris's lives? Could she live with that on her conscience?

William shifted in her peripheral vision. Glancing over at him, she found he was staring at her. Warmth flooded her body as she stared into his familiar hazel eyes. As though he knew her thoughts, he gave her an imperceptible nod. Her heart broke.

Representative Sirren got to his feet. "The votes shall be cast. Representative, if you please."

Anastasia hardly dared to breathe. The Representative of the city Menen got to her feet. Looking out across the room, she nodded once. "Guilty."

The other Representatives fired off their guiltys and not guiltys until, at last, Representative Zand got to his feet. "As a warrior, I understand the struggle to keep the balance between duty and love. But in times of war, they must be one in the same. Guilty."

Anastasia's heart sank. The "Guilty" had the majority. Even if she voted in their favor, they would still be held guilty. Gods and Angels, how had this happened?

"Your Highness, if you please," Representative Sirren interjected. She looked at him, confused. He wasn't supposed to speak after his vote had been cast. "We ask that you punish these men to the fullest extent, Your Highness. If you cannot depend on a Nadmilise to defend their home against the Shadows, our greatest foes, then you can count on them for naught. This is the highest affront to the Crown, and to the realm."

Mistress Follant frowned. "Does it matter not that William was the one to rescue the royal family?"

"Yes, how did a boy of seventeen manage to find the royal family and rescue them from a Shadow compound? Isn't it peculiar that Dinas was also one of the warriors to rescue the Lord Joseph from a similar compound six months prior, even though, as an apprentice, he was not to be on active duty?"

"We are not speaking of conspiracies, Representative."

"I should hope not, Kalgess." Representative Sirren turned to face Anastasia. "Your Highness, we request to try William Dinas separately from Christopher Woodsman."

Keeping her expression blank, Anastasia looked over the Representatives. William had already been found guilty of desertion. At the least it meant imprisonment. But she knew the Representatives wanted to try them to the fullest extent. What else could they possibly be charging him with? What else could they want to punish him for?

"What do you charge him with?"

Representative Sirren's expression grew grave. "Conspiracy to commit treason."

Gasps erupted through the room. Icy dread dripped down Anastasia's spine. Conspiracy meant they could gray William out, *and* throw him in prison.

She shook her head. "With what proof?"

But too late she realized the Representatives had already planned this. She saw the look of resentment flash through their eyes as they glanced up at her. She wasn't there to cast a vote, but to make a point to her family. She wasn't in charge of this any more than William was. They'd made her a figurehead and had run off with their own plot from the beginning. Could she really step in and stop it now? She shot Valdon a panicked look, finding that he, too, understood what had happened.

Valdon held her off with a barely perceptible shake of his head. But how could she remain calm? William could face the death penalty.

No one gave her an answer.

The Representative of Menen got to her feet. "Guilty."

In a line, the Representatives cast their votes. Only Representatives Sophine and Zand cast not guilty. Anastasia's throat constricted. Gripping the throne, she struggled to hear past the intense ringing in her ears.

"Your Highness?" Representative Sirren prompted.

With only two not guilty votes, Anastasia knew what the law commanded. But she couldn't bring herself to say the words.

William met her eyes. She wished for all the world she could have seen this coming.

"Christopher Jay Woodsman," she heard herself say as though from far away. "The Representatives of the realm of Jacqueline, and the Crown, find you guilty of desertion. As punishment for your crime, you will be fined one-thousand fisas, and are sentenced to prison."

Her throat burned as she turned to William.

"William James Dinas. The Representatives of the realm of Jacqueline find you guilty of desertion and conspiracy to commit treason. As punishment for your crimes, you are sentenced to prison, and are hereby stripped of your position as a Warrior Apprentice." She swallowed bile. "You will both serve out your sentences as long as the Shadows remain encased in stone."

Ignoring the murmurs of the people, Anastasia got to her feet and fled the room. Hot tears burned behind her eyes, but she refused to let them fall. She just sentenced William and Chris to prison. She took away William's chance of ever becoming a warrior. Just like that. And she could tell herself all she wanted that her hands had been tied, that there was nothing else she could've done. But that didn't change the fact that her words had been the ones to sentence them.

Gods and Angels, what had she done?

CHAPTER TWO

Anastasia sat at her mother's desk in the Queen's study. She refused to think of it as her desk, even though she had taken it over for the last two months. Parchments and scrolls covered the surface, begging her attention, but she simply stared at the far wall. A portrait of her grandparents sat in a gilded frame. They were young, a few years older than Anastasia, and illuminated with happiness.

Studying her grandmother's face, Anastasia frowned. Analie had already given birth to Anastasia's aunt Calla by then, and hidden the baby away with the mysterious father. This young Analie, even with her premonitions, didn't see the terror that would be brought into that baby's life, and the repercussions it would have for them all.

Leaning back in her chair, she brushed her fingers over her moonstone pendant. She was seventeen-years-old, just six months past her coming of age, and already she ruled over her realm, and presided over the High Council. But the only thing that seemed to matter was William's face as she declared him guilty. His expression, and the small gasp that had left Chris's lips, were burned into her senses. How could she move past this? For she would have to, in order to keep the realms afloat in the aftermath of the Shadows' Chaos.

Settling back in her seat, she closed her eyes and centered herself. Taking deep, even breaths, she focused on William's face, in the familiar turn of his mouth, and the deep color of his eyes.

The uneasy, gut-wrenching feeling of a premonition flooded through her. She gasped, as pain roiled through her stomach, clutching the edge of the desk. Holding onto the image of William's face, she pushed outward with her mind, and let the premonition overwhelm her:

I stand in the middle of a circle drawn in the dirt. Six identical copies of myself stand around me on the line of the circle. They're dressed strangely, in anciently-fashioned clothing, but that isn't even the strangest thing about them. No, they're all wearing my pendant, but the stones are different colors.

Blinding light surges around us. When I open my eyes, there are two rooms reflected as though on opposite sides of a window. Three of my doppelgangers stand in the Sehirian throne room on the left, while the other three stand in an ancient throne room, complete with a checkered floor and pale red walls. I'm in the center of it all, as though I am the window.

As one, the doppelgangers grab their pendants and smash them. The beautiful stones shatter, sending flecks of colored gemstone skittering across the floor.

Magic explodes forth, engulfing us. As it dissipates, the doppelgangers freeze like statues. Stone rises up their bodies, like that of the Shadow statues. They stare straight ahead, even as the blue-eyed sorcerer from my previous visions swoops in and gathers all the shards of gemstone.

I break free of my window and charge him, managing to take the shards back from him. Whirling, I drop them into a goblet of blood and shout words in a strange language. Light surges, once again, and the Sehirian throne room disappears, leaving us all in the ancient throne room. But when I turn, my doppelgangers are gone. It's just me, holding the six repaired pendants. But I'm unafraid by the sudden loneliness. Somehow, it gives me hope.

Anastasia jolted awake, gasping for breath. The deep colors of her premonition saturated her vision; the strange detachment of emotion clung to her.

This premonition left her even more confused than her previous ones. Why were there doppelgangers of her? And why all the different pendants? Did it have something to do with her premonitions? She had been trying to see a future containing William, and instead she'd been brought to some strange duality. Did that mean there was something wrong with her visions? And why had everyone turned to stone?

A knock sounded at the door. Anastasia didn't bother to look up as someone entered; anyone that came to the Queen's study just dropped some papers on the desk and left.

"Anastasia?"

The familiar female voice set Anastasia on edge, making the vestiges of her premonition fade. She turned, glaring at the young woman in the doorway. She'd grown even rounder in the month since Anastasia had last seen her, her pregnant belly swelling beneath her loose-fitting Viirean gown. Her curtain of dark hair, usually loosely strung with tiny bells, was twisted back in the Viirean fashion. She offered a timid smile.

Anastasia turned away from her, pretending to be engrossed in the papers on her desk. "What do you want, Ostana?"

"I wanted to see how you were." When Anastasia didn't respond she continued, "Vlad and I are staying with Mohan until things die down with our families. I can't quite believe my dad tried to arrest him for desertion—"

"King Tamo *did* arrest Mohan," Anastasia icily intoned. "You did us a great favor by ending Anistes Droun, Ostana, and if I haven't already, I thank you for it."

"You're welcome—"

"But we are not friends. Your actions caused the death of my husband, your brother. You sided with a man who kidnapped and tortured my family."

"I am *so* sorry, Anastasia. You can never know the remorse I feel. I can't have you hate me."

"I don't hate you; I just don't trust you."

Turning her back on the young werewolf woman, Anastasia ended the conversation. Ostana hesitated a moment, clearly wanting to say something else, before she slowly exited the room. When the door closed behind her, Anastasia let out a breath, slumping in her chair. It had been easy to hate Ostana before, back when she'd been a spy for Adrian, and had been the one to poison Anastasia and cause her premonitions to temporarily disappear. But now she was pregnant with Vlad's child, and had been instrumental in stopping the Shadows.

Did that really make up for what she'd done? Aatu was dead. He was never coming back. And his sister was the reason. And yet Anastasia kept Ostana's secret. She still hadn't told anyone that Ostana was the one who had let the werewolves into Sehir all those months ago. And why not? Because Ostana was pregnant?

Gods and Angels, she just wanted an easy answer for once.

Tiredly running a hand over her face, she looked down at the papers on her desk. The register of Nadmilise refugees sat on top, organized based on city of origin. But it was already two hours old, and therefore void. Everything moved so quickly, she didn't know how to get a grasp on it.

Beside it were the plans for construction projects through Sehir, and a rough map of the Shadows' positions throughout the realms. Lists of resources and requests for supplies were stacked a few inches high. Realm Guard deployment scrolls sat in a neat pile, alongside information about suspected deserters, criminals, and traitors. Somewhere in there was a blueprint for some gallows, the idea of which made Anastasia shudder.

Signing her name at the bottom of a grant for the Realm Guard, she sealed it with her mother's violet wax. She hesitated for the briefest of moments before stamping it with the royal seal.

"Lili?" she called

A moment later, her handmaiden stepped through the door, carrying a pile of scrolls and parchments. Just two years older than Anastasia, Lili looked as bewildered as Anastasia felt. But she was strong. She'd soldier on.

"Please make sure this gets to the Realm Guard outpost in the Wetland Line."

Lili curtsied. "Yes, my Princess."

When Lili hesitated, Anastasia frowned. "What is it?"

"You asked me to tell you if there was any change in your mother's condition."

Alarm shot through Anastasia. "Is she all right? What's happened?"

"She's fine, my Princess. But—well, she's fallen unconscious again. Mistress Miglune is concerned. She insists you take the signet."

Anastasia narrowed her eyes. "She *insists*, does she?"

Lili didn't respond. Anastasia slammed her hand on the desk. She was the Crown Princess, yet everyone made demands of her, made decisions without her, just as the Representatives had done that morning with William's sentence. Just as the High Council glossed over the fact that Tamo had mutinied and left the realms to die, imprisoning his own son, and declaring Mohan a traitor.

But none of that was the cause of her mother's illness. No, months held prisoner with the Shadows, tortured by Adrian, had done that. And Anastasia had been too focused on finding her grandmother, on saving the realms, to go and find her family.

She could never repay William and Valdon for rescuing them.

"I'll go and see her," she murmured, resigned.

Lili hesitated again. But this time, she took Anastasia's hand and squeezed. "She will be fine, my Princess. And so will William. He's strong."

"Thank you."

Curtsying again, Lili left. Anastasia pushed back from the desk and paced around the room. Feeling restless, she marched through the antechamber—where Lili had a small desk—and into the hall. Her guards, Gath and Mortam, immediately took up positions on either side of her, their bronze weapons glinting in the torchlight as they moved.

Collecting her traveling cloak in the foyer, she made her way outside. The warm summer sun conflicted with her stormy insides. All around her, people were rebuilding their homes, their lives, while hers just felt like an unsalvage-able wreck.

Mortam and Gath didn't ask where they were headed, and she didn't offer. They skirted the marketplace and residential areas, heading eastward. After a short trek, they came upon a pale green light. Anastasia let out a slow breath, looking up at the Earth Lake of Sehir. An emerald green waterfall cascaded over thick gray rocks, the top obscured by a canopy of vines and flowers. Dragonflies leisurely flitted about, touching down on the field of wildflowers circling the embankment of the shimmering waters. A large oak tree stood off to the right, vibrant with bright green leaves, thick sage vines, and soft pink summer runas flowers.

Anastasia reached out a hand. The nearest branch of the tree swung out to meet her, lifting her out over the water. Pulling herself up, she straddled the branch, settling back against the earthy trunk.

When had her life become such a mess? Usually, after you defeated the villain, you lived happily ever after. The fairy tales never explained what hap-pened after you won, all the damage you'd have to clean up, the people you'd lost. Was she even capable of handling it without her mother, or her grand-mother? Everything she'd done, she'd done with someone else's help.

She needed to get a grip.

Burying her hands in the soft, damp moss around her, she closed her eyes. The smell of rain and dewy grasses filled her nose, and she breathed deep.

During her time in the human realm, she'd studied the art of ruling with her mother, learning all the histories, the languages, the customs. Mostly, it was fun, a decent distraction from the fact that they were being hunted by the Shadows. But sometimes, when she stopped to really think about ruling, about how her becoming Queen of Jacqueline meant that her mother had passed away, it felt overwhelming. Those times, she always pictured the Earth Lake, or how she remembered it from her trips as a small child. It grounded her in her surroundings, and allowed her to really think.

Now was one of those times where she'd needed it, needed the sound of the waterfall, the smell of the earth and flowers to help her sort through the mayhem in her mind. As she sat, her thoughts became clearer. She sorted out her priorities, making a mental list in her head to add to all the others piling up on her desk.

"Mortam?" she called. His robust figure appeared immediately bellow the branch. "Can you draft a letter for me?"

He nodded. "Of course, my Princess."

Before she could tell him what she wanted, however, a flash of pale purple smoke appeared before her. She waved away the smoke, finding a scroll hovering in its wake. Anastasia plucked it out of the air, frowning at the cresting wave royal seal of the mermaids.

All letters addressed to her went through the appropriate channels in the castle. The sorcerer messenger, who sent the letter, would connect to her personally with magic, but Valdon's wards around the castle made sure every letter went through the royal messengers and pages. This letter, however, came directly to her from the royal city of Seathium. Opening the letter, she quickly scanned the hastily-written words:

> *Anastasia,*
>
> *I hope this letter finds you well. There has been a disturbing development in Seathium this morning. A young mermaid was found onland, upside down, her ankles nailed to a tree, the tips of her fingers burned. I would never want to share such a horrific happening with you. However, a parchment with your name on it was pinned to her chest. Just thought you should know.*
>
> *Yours truly,*
> *Eala Lanana*

Anastasia ran her fingers over her pendant, disgust flooding through her. How could someone do that to another person? And why was her name pinned to that poor mermaid's chest? Gods and Angels, she was glad the prince of the mermaids managed to write to her directly.

Reaching out a hand, she let the tree deposit her beside Mortam. Tucking the letter into her bodice, she turned her back on the lake and headed for the forest.

"Is everything well, my Princess?" Mortam questioned.

"We need to go to Seathium."

Neither guard responded, but rather took up their positions on either side of her as they returned to the castle. As soon as they strode through the front door, a young messenger raced up to them, holding a pile of letters.

"These came for you, Your Highness," the young boy squeaked. He'd been her page for nearly a month now, and was still too intimidated to look her in the eye.

"Thank you, Fommen."

He bowed and raced away, flushed embarrassment creeping up his cheeks.

Anastasia tucked the letters under her arm, making her way back up to her study. There, Lili had returned to her desk, and was whittling away at a block of wood. She glanced up, her brown eyes unfocused, as Anastasia entered. Tucking her vibrant red hair behind her ears, she got to her feet, forgetting her woodwork.

"What's wrong, my Princess?"

Anastasia waved away her concerns. "Would you please contact Seathium and let Prince Eala know I would like to meet with him?"

Lili bowed. "Of course."

Moving into the study, she dropped the letters onto the desk. Pulling out a fresh parchment, she crafted a letter:

> *I would like to extend to you a dinner invitation for the night after next, should the date work for you.*

Getting to her feet, she handed the letter to Lili. "Have the messenger make nine copies of this."

"To whom shall they be sent?"

"The Princes of the realms."

Lili nodded. "Prince Eala said he can meet with you right away. You can portal to Seathium and he will meet you at the Council Hall."

"Thank you."

Gathering her papers, Lili hurried from the room. Anastasia stepped out into the hall, collecting Mortam and Gath. Together, they made their way to the gardens, the best place to open a portal on the castle grounds. Pulling his portal tool from his pocket, Gath pressed the ashen triangular stone to the skin of his forearm. The runes on the face of the tool burned painlessly into his arm, before swirling up into the air and creating a golden doorway. When it opened, the pale skies of Seathium sat on the other side.

Striding through, Anastasia looked around. It had been many years since she'd been inside the Council Hall in the mermaid realm, the one place in Seathium that was made for visitors who couldn't breathe underwater.

They stood inside a series of opaque, bubble-like domes. Damp moss, wet with seawater, made up the floors, and curtains of dried seafoam hung like doors in curved archways. Bioluminescent fish flitted in bowled sconces, illuminating the dank halls. The air smelled brackish, and a thin, crusty layer of salt clung to every surface. The floor squished beneath them, water pooling around their feet. Anastasia removed her sopping slippers, letting her toes sink into the moss.

"Anastasia!"

She glanced up, immediately recognizing Eala Lanana, the Prince of the Mermaids. He looked as most mermaids did outside of the water: sickly gray skin, matted wet hair, pure black eyes, and rows of shark-like teeth. A tattered pair of trousers hung from his hips, bloated with seawater.

Anastasia grinned, despite his off-putting appearance. "Eala! It has been too long."

"I'm sorry that these are the circumstances that bring us together." He frowned. "But I felt you had to know what had happened."

"I am glad you told me."

He motioned back the way he came. "I shall take you to her."

Together they strode down the hall. Mortam and Gath followed closely, their hands on the hilts of their swords. When they entered the small chamber just off the main room, they found a young mermaid woman lying on the large sponge structure in the center of the room. A thin sheet covered her body, save for her face, hands, and feet. An older couple, who were obviously the young woman's parents, stood hunched over her unmoving form. They didn't so much as glance up as Anastasia and her guards entered.

Eala pulled Anastasia aside, a grim expression upon his face. "Her name was Ourla."

Anastasia gasped; she recognized the name. As she looked closer at the young woman's face, she realized she knew her. A memory flashed through her mind, from the Viirean Opera House in the alternate universe: *Vlad ran over, flipping his shaggy hair out of his eyes. A young mermaid woman hovered behind him, wearing a strange garment of torn lace and shreds of scale-like fabric.*

"Ourla," he said, "this is Princess Anastasia, Prince Aatu, and Miss Lili."

"Gods and Angels," Anastasia breathed.

Eala continued, "She is the only daughter of Cress and Greina, of a noble house in Seathium. We believe that was why she was targeted."

Swallowing her surprise—she certainly could not tell Eala that she knew this girl, for they had met in the alternate universe—she turned away from Ourla. "Are there any leads as to who did this? Or any idea why?"

"None."

Motioning to the body, she murmured, "May I?"

Eala nodded. Anastasia crossed the room, approaching Ourla's parents. They still hadn't noticed that anyone else was in the room with them. Nor did Anastasia blame them. They'd just lost their only daughter in such a savage and incomprehensible way. Forlornly, Anastasia remembered the Ourla she'd met, the one that alternate universe Vlad had been courting. That young woman had been romantic and kind. She wondered how much this Ourla differed from her counterpart.

Slowly, she reached out and gently touched Ourla's mother on the elbow. The mermaid glanced up and gasped, her eyes growing wide. Remembering the courtesies her mother taught her, Anastasia took two steps back and bowed. Ourla's parents woodenly followed suit.

"Princess Anastasia." Ourla's mother's voice came out rough and thick with sorrow.

"I am so very sorry for your loss."

Ourla's father narrowed his eyes. "Are you? For your name was tacked to her chest. Like an artist's name at the bottom of a painting, or, perhaps, as a warning to you. Either way, you are a part of this. Her death is on your hands."

Though his reaction wasn't unexpected, it still stung. Anastasia wrung her hands, saying nothing. Eala came up beside her, frowning.

"Anastasia played no part in this."

"I have many deaths on my conscience, sir," Anastasia said. "And if your daughter's is on mine as well, I shall take full responsibility. But I know nothing of this heinous attack."

Ourla's mother shook her head. "She was returning home from a stay with my sister in Oceanus. She stays there every spring to spend time with her cousins, as she has since she was a wee girl. Someone must've—I don't understand how—they captured my baby."

Unsure of what to say, Anastasia turned her attention back to Ourla. True to Eala's letter, the mermaid's fingertips had been burnt, and nails driven through her ankles. To be hung upside down, with that unimaginable pain…

19

it felt familiar, as though Anastasia had experienced it before. But how could she have? The only thing she'd had to fear was Adrian and the Shadows, and they'd never hung her upside down.

But what did it mean? Why burn the fingertips? Why nail the girl upside down? And why pin her name on the girl's chest? Was it just a warning? Or had someone been calling her out? Was this supposed to be some kind of message? The questions assailed her, without any answers. It just didn't make sense. It wasn't the Shadows, or Adrian—they had all been magically encased in stone. But the Shadows and their leader weren't her only enemies. Her own people didn't trust her and her family. She assumed many other realms felt the same way. Did that constitute murder, though?

Sloshing footsteps sounded a moment before a young mermaid hurried into the room. He approached Eala, averting his gaze from Ourla's body, and whispered in the mermaid prince's ear. Eala nodded, sending the young man away.

"Anastasia?"

She went to him. "What's wrong?"

"It seems you are being summoned back to Sehir." He shook his head. "Valdon is requesting you leave at once."

Stunned, she simply stared at Eala. Valdon was summoning her? Was there a Council meeting she'd forgotten? Had something happened to William? Her mother? She quickly turned back to Cress and Greina, bowing to them again.

"I apologize for my hasty exit, but—"

Eala cut her off. "You do not need to apologize, Anastasia. I understand the demands of ruling."

"Thank you."

Eala took her hand, pressing it to his lips. "May our interactions not be so far between in the future, yes?"

She smiled. "Of course."

Eala wordlessly escorted her to the main room of the Hall, where Gath opened a return portal to the royal city of Jacqueline. She waved to Eala before the portal closed, sealing off their realms. Drying her feet in the grass of the royal gardens, she ran up the steps to the castle barefoot, heading for Valdon's chambers. She found him in the hall just outside the Council chambers, pacing. He looked unnerved, his dark blue eyes narrowed, his mouth set in a hard line. Magic crackled between his fingers.

He rounded on her as she approached. "Where have you been?"

"I—what?"

"Never mind," he growled.

She stared at him. "What is going on?"

"The werewolves have ended their alliance with Jacqueline. They are pulling their warriors from the Realm Guard."

"*What?*"

He narrowed his eyes. "There was supposedly a letter that came this morning for you?"

Anastasia swore under her breath, pushing past him. The letters her page had given her—she hadn't even opened them, so preoccupied as she was with Ourla's murder. She took the stairs two-at-a-time, all but running up to her mother's study. Lili started as she burst through the door, dropping her whittling. Anastasia hardly noticed as she crossed to the desk, grabbing her stack of letters.

Shuffling through them, she found the one with the Hullenian royal seal. Ripping it open, she hastily scanned the official document. She swore again.

"So, it's true," murmured Valdon.

She turned to him with wide eyes. "What do I do?"

"There's not much you can do. But I would contact Mistress Follant and alert her that the alliance has ended."

Crumpling the letter in her hand, she glowered. "Call a High Council meeting. And the privy council."

She tossed the letter onto her desk, marching from the room. Lili darted after her, clutching a stack of parchment to her chest.

"My Princess?" Lili held out the parchments. "I have responses to your invitation for dinner."

Anastasia turned. "And?"

"They all said they were coming." Lili hesitated. "Should I rescind Prince Niboki's invitation, given the state of affairs between Jacqueline and Hullenia?"

Anastasia laughed darkly. "No."

She wanted to see what her ex-fiancé had to say about their end in alliance.

CHAPTER THREE

Dani Dinas paid for her food from the vendor, tucking the spiced meat pastries into the belt of her homely skirt. She'd long since gotten used to the rough material of her clothing in her month in the Sand Isles of Jacqueline. More conservative than her gowns back home, the skirt and tunic covered every inch of bare skin. Though it protected her from the harsh desert sun, she knew the modesty it provided was for more religious purposes. All the women in this part of the Isles dressed this way, their hair hidden beneath headwraps.

Turning, she kept her eyes on the ruby sand, heading back through the market. Hearing children laughing, she looked up. To her utter horror, they hung from a Shadow statue, swinging from its massive claws. She nearly ran to them and tore them off the Shadow herself, but she knew that wasn't her mission. Instead, she covered her face with her scarf and moved towards the dunes.

Reaching the edge of town, she headed east. A short trek across the sands later, she came upon her tent. Mira was already there, trying to patch a hole in her sock with magic. Her ruby-colored hair quivered with her exertion, until she finally gave up with a groan.

"No luck?"

Mira started, unaware Dani had returned. "Do you ever make any noise?"

"Not when you make that expression."

Frowning, the sorceress looked down at her foot. "I can open direct portals to other realms, but I can't darn a sock. I don't understand."

Settling back on her bedroll, Dani pulled out the pastries. Eating half of one in one bite, she replied, "Anastasia's sending a warrior our way. Should be here soon."

Mira pulled free a thread from her skirt, and created a needle with magic. She worked quietly for a while, fixing the hole in the sock. When she finished, she put it over her foot and wiggled her toes. The edge over her smallest toe was puckered and lumpy, and would surely irritate Mira's foot in her boot, but the sorceress grinned like she'd just defeated an army.

Cutting off the excess thread with her teeth, she settled back and looked at Dani. "It's so weird how you call your princess by her first name."

Dani shrugged. Was it? Anastasia had asked her to when they'd met. And after everything they'd gone through together, it felt natural. Calling her by her title just felt forced. But she remembered how odd it had been to hear William refer to her so informally.

Finishing her pastry, she stretched out on her bedroll. A hole was starting to form at the upper leftmost corner of their tent; little strands of fabric fluttered in the breeze. Dani stared at it, imagining what it would be like to pull on those threads, unravel the whole tent. She could picture herself standing in a pool of strings, lying beneath the harsh sun, surrounded by the ruby sands. For some reason, the idea brought her a sense of peace.

She blew out a breath. "Saw another statue in town today."

"I'll add it to the list."

"You really think we'll find them all?"

Mira pursed her lips. "We'll have to. Otherwise, when the Shadows unfreeze or whatever, innocent lives will be lost."

"I guess."

Taking a second pastry, Dani tossed the bag to Mira. They ate together in silence, keeping an eye on the entrance to their tent. Anastasia had said noon, but the sun was already high in the sky, heading towards the opposite horizon. Idly, Dani wondered who Anastasia was sending them. So far, they'd been fine just the two of them, locating Shadows and tagging them so they could be removed to an unpopulated location. Why did they need a third person, much less a warrior?

When the whooshing wind of a portal finally tore through their tent, Dani leapt to her feet, drawing her crossbow. Locking a bolt, she moved towards the entrance. Mira followed behind her, her hands raised defensively, alight with red magic.

The gilded portal doorway opened to reveal an evening sky, bringing with it the damp scents of the forest. Longing tore through Dani. She loved the summers of Sehir; they were her favorite time of year.

She shielded her eyes as a figure stepped through and the portal closed. Training her crossbow, she studied him. He didn't have the bronze dagger of a Sehirian warrior, but carried a bronze battle axe instead. Wearing boiled leather over his tunic, and thick leather boots, he was dressed more for a western or northern city, *not* the Sand Isles. But they could easily get him clothes. His long sandy hair and soft brown eyes were familiar, but she couldn't figure out why.

They assessed each other in silence. Mira stepped around Dani, a curious look on her face. "*You're* the warrior?"

He looked offended. "I was sent by Princess Anastasia, yes."

"You're so young."

"As are you."

Dani stifled a laugh. It was true, though. Mira was only a year older than Dani's sixteen years, and this warrior looked only a couple of years older than her.

Turning back to the tent, Dani said to Mira, "What were you expecting, a grandfather?"

"Well, someone who could handle himself, at least."

The young man trotted after them. "I can handle myself! I am a member of the Realm Guard—"

"Everyone is a member of the Realm Guard these days," Mira fired back.

Entering the tent, Dani glanced around. They might need to make more room. Hers and Mira's bedrolls sat head-to-head off to the left, while their makeshift kitchen sat off to the right. The rest of the tent was filled with provisions, mainly water. They could, perhaps, restack their sacks of food they used for bartering with the locals, but doing it the first time had taken forever with Mira's magic mishaps.

The young man cleared his throat, tearing her from her thoughts. "You're Dani Dinas?"

Dani nodded. Part of her wondered what he was thinking; he wore the same kind of impassive, unreadable expression William did. Did they teach all warriors to do that?

As always, thinking of William left a sour taste in her mouth. She hated leaving him when he'd been arrested. But Valdon had said it would be safer for William in the long run if she wasn't around. Besides, it felt good to keep moving. It gave her less time to think about her mother.

"I'm Hayde Zand." He held out his hand. "I fought alongside your brother and Chris Woodsman."

Dani pondered this. "Zand? As in Murcy Zand, the Representative of Talrom?"

He nodded. "He's my grandfather."

Pursing her lips, Dani didn't respond. After what William had told her about his time in the alternate universe with Valdon, she didn't trust the Representative. It was strange to imagine an alternate version of Representative Zand attacking William and knocking Valdon unconscious, much less working for the Shadows.

Hayde lowered his hand. "So, Princess Anastasia did not give me much information about our quest."

"We locate Shadow statues and mark them for removal," Dani explained. "But most importantly, we don't alert people to our presence. We do so to prevent the people from panicking."

"Why would they panic?"

Mira laughed mirthlessly. "Because the first Shadow statue cracked months ago."

"And?"

"They've begun to unfreeze?" Mira rolled her eyes. "Honestly, what kind of warrior are you?"

"What do you mean they've begun to unfreeze?" Hayde drew his battle axe and marched to the entrance of the tent. "The people should be panicking! The Shadows need to be removed as quickly as possible! We must do everything to protect the people."

Dani chuckled, flopping down on her bedroll. Mira mirrored her, returning to her darning. Hayde stood, glancing worriedly between the two of them.

"What are you doing?"

Sighing, Dani motioned for Hayde to sit beside her. "We have our orders, warrior. Calm down."

He frowned. "Why are you so nonchalant about this? The Shadows are returning, and we are nowhere near ready to fight them off."

"Anastasia and the High Council have given us their orders." She motioned for him to sit. "Do you really believe they would put us out here to do this job if they believed it to be moot? We must trust they know what they're doing."

25

"Besides," Mira glared at Hayde, "the sooner we get the statues removed to a remote location, the safer everyone will be."

"And the sooner we can all go home."

Reluctantly, Hayde sat. Dani passed him a pastry, relaxing back on her elbows. He inspected it before taking a bite. When his eyes started to water, Dani sniggered. She remembered the spice well. Nearly everything in the Sand Isles was spicy, even the desserts, tinted red with the hot peppers indigenous to the islands.

Looking him over, she measured his frame with her eyes. Getting clothes would be expensive, and draw unwanted attention. His tunic would pass well enough, if they dirtied it. But his trousers and boiled leather would have to go. And he'd need a headwrap.

Thinking quickly, she grabbed an older skirt from her bag. It was too stretched out to fit her anymore. But, if she altered it...

Pulling her knife from her belt, she set to work fashioning the cloth into trousers.

"How long have you been here?" Hayde questioned.

Dani thought back, glancing at Mira. "Maybe three weeks?"

"That long?"

"We are in charge of the southwestern part of Jacqueline. Once we clear the Sand Isles, we will move inland until all Shadow statues in our area of the realm are accounted for."

Hayde frowned. "Bit difficult for just the two of you, neither a warrior."

Mira scoffed. "Oh, yes, because we must all be ferocious, blade-happy soldiers in order to succeed."

"That's not what I meant."

Taking Mira's needle and thread, Dani interjected, "Anastasia and I grew close. She trusted me to go on this mission. Not to mention, I am less conspicuous than a group of warriors. As I said, we are to avoid a panic, but keep the people safe."

"I wonder, then, why I am here."

Dani shrugged. "Take off your trousers."

"I beg your pardon?"

She held up the makeshift trousers she'd fashioned. "I need to see if these fit you."

Looking again between her and Mira, he took the trousers and stepped outside the tent to change. Mira sniggered, lying back on her bedroll. When Hayde returned, Dani knelt in front of him, checking the waistline. Ignoring his protests, she altered the trousers to fit him. While they wouldn't have passed for proper clothing in Sehir, it was passable in the Isles, where most clothing was worn from the sand and sun.

Before too long, the sun dipped below the horizon. Dani and Mira readied themselves, Dani strapping her crossbow on her back, and Mira tucking her hair into a headwrap. Hayde stood by, watching them with heavily-lidded eyes. It was then Dani remembered the time change between Sehir and the Sand Isles. He must've been exhausted.

"Why don't you sit this one out?" she offered.

He shook himself awake, narrowing his eyes. "I'm fine. When do we leave?"

Tucking a handful of bolts into her belt, Dani stepped from the tent. Mira followed, her hands softly glowing with vibrant red magic, lighting their way.

"We tag the Shadows we've marked and move on, understand?" Dani asked of Hayde.

He nodded. "Understood."

As they headed for town, she blew out a breath. "Two things you must understand about the Sand Isles, Warrior Zand: one, the nights are just as harsh as the days; and two, it is illegal for anyone to be out after dark."

Mira's teeth flashed through the darkness. "If we are caught, we will most certainly be imprisoned."

"Great," Hayde breathed. "No pressure."

When they reached town, Dani pointed out the Shadow statue she'd noticed earlier. Mira stealthily moved across the sand, pressing her hand to the statue. When she moved away, a red stamp, the same color as her magic, pulsated.

When she rejoined them, they moved on to the next part of town. Dani and Hayde ran ahead, scouting the way, making sure Mira would be able to reach each statue unmolested.

Dani sighed. They'd have to move on, soon. She suspected in the next couple of days, they'd reach the northernmost part of the Sand Isles, which meant they'd need to move further inland to reach the Shadows nearing Jacqueline's southwestern border. Then they'd move around the outskirts of the Fire Desert, steering clear of where the Shadow statues were being collected in the uninhabited desert.

Though tagging the statues would go faster with Hayde helping them, Dani figured travel would be slower, what with all of Hayde's questions. Usually, Mira just muttered to herself, leaving Dani to her silence. But that silence usually meant she thought about her mother and William, which she got enough of in her nightmares. Every time she closed her eyes, she saw her mother leap in front of her, taking a crossbow bolt to the chest. Or, she watched helplessly as William was led through Sehir in chains.

Thankfully, walking through cities and sighting Shadow statues kept her mind busy enough.

Hayde cleared his throat and she started; he'd been so quiet, she'd nearly forgotten he was there. But then he opened his mouth.

"I wanted to express my apologies for what happened to your brother. He was a superior warrior."

"He still is a superior warrior," Dani hissed.

Hayde nodded. "Oh, of course. I didn't mean that—"

A scream cut through the silent night. Hayde jumped, whirling around. Dani merely rolled her eyes, a groan leaning her lips.

"Not again."

CHAPTER FOUR

Anastasia sat in her throne once again. This time, however, the room was relatively empty. Only her privy council looked up at her, their voices carrying through the room. They were short two members: her mother unable to attend due to her illness, and her uncle on a diplomatic assignment in Viire.

"We can still function without the werewolf warriors," her father was saying.

Her Aunt Celia shook her head, her white-blond curls bouncing. "It is not about functioning, but about the fact that the wolves can now declare war on Jacqueline."

"Or the other way around," her Great-Uncle Bale murmured.

"But they won't," her father said. "They know it is not wise."

Celia scoffed. "Since when have the werewolves ever done anything that is wise?"

"We have a much greater enemy we are fighting. Aylen and Tamo know this. They understand what we are up against."

"And yet they withdraw from the Realm Guard."

Leaning back, Anastasia pondered their words. What could the werewolves gain from withdrawing from the Realm Guard? What was the point? That morning, all their warriors had returned to Hullenia. But if they were not a part of the Guard, how did they plan to protect themselves from the Shadows once they unfroze from their magical encasement?

"Anastasia."

She looked over at her Aunt Calla, a pang going through her; she looked so remarkably like Anarose. They had the same light brown hair and noble facial structure, but her eyes were the color of sapphires, not the royal violet. "What?"

Calla raised a brow. "We were saying that you may be able to find out what the werewolves are planning."

Anastasia frowned. "How?"

"Through your friendship with Ostana," Celia intoned. "The two of you are very close."

Is that how it seemed to them? She met her father's warm brown eyes. He knew she and Ostana weren't close, but he didn't know the reason. She'd elected not to tell him, knowing that if he knew what Ostana had done, he'd be obliged as King of Jacqueline to arrest her. Though she detested Ostana, with a rage she hadn't thought herself capable, she couldn't let Ostana go to jail, not when she was pregnant with Vlad's child.

She'd vowed, as soon as the child was born she would turn Ostana in for her crimes. She would finally face consequences for spying for the Shadows, for poisoning Anastasia to suppress her premonitions, and for the death of Aatu. But now, she couldn't tell them what Ostana had done.

Elliot eyed Anastasia. "The Princess of the Werewolves has been living in Castavo with Sona and her family since the end of Anistes Droun. I doubt she knows much of anything about her family's dealings."

"All the same." Celia rolled her eyes. "It can't hurt to see what the girl knows."

Looking through the windows, Anastasia gasped. She was going to be late for dinner with the princes of the realms. "Please excuse me. We can resume this tomorrow morning."

Her family simply stared at her as she gathered her skirts and rushed from the room.

"Anastasia!"

Turning, she again met Calla's eyes. Not for the first time, she wondered who Calla's father was, the man her grandmother, Analie, loved more than she could ever say. She and Calla had never spoken of it, and if her aunt knew, she never said. Not surprisingly, Analie had been mum when they'd spoken of it in the alternate universe. It seemed secrets ran in their family.

Looking over her shoulder, Calla whispered, "There may be a way for you to save William Dinas."

Anastasia blinked. "What are you talking about?"

"You love him, yes?"

She remembered when they'd fallen from the Sky Temple in the elemental realm, hidden up in the clouds: *William held her gaze, his hazel eyes blazing with an emotion she couldn't quite place. His words were torn away by the wind, but she could read his lips: I love you.*

Her heart ached at the thought of him, at what she'd sentenced him to. "I do."

"Then you can save him." Calla glanced over her shoulder again, pulling Anastasia into an alcove around the corner. "You must make the Head Warrior Vow."

"Excuse me?"

"As a Head Warrior, he cannot be grayed out. But he must pass the trial of the Gods and Angels."

Calla couldn't be serious. William would never accept becoming Head Warrior just to keep from being grayed out. He had too much honor for that. She'd already asked him to become her Head Warrior once, to keep him from being drafted to the Realm Guard, and he'd rejected her. Besides, he hadn't participated in the original Head Warrior trials. The people wouldn't accept him, much less the Representatives, who'd charged him with treason.

Even so, she couldn't help but think of the William from the alternate universe, the one who excelled at his mastery examination right before he went out in a blaze of glory. She knew *her* William was twice the warrior he was; there was no doubt that he'd succeed at the Head Warrior trials. But she could never ask that of him.

"Do you doubt him?"

Anastasia frowned. "Never."

"Then why do you hesitate?"

"William would not accept this way out. He would demand to prove himself worthy."

Calla considered her words for a moment, pursing her lips. "Then we shall test him, the privy council. Who better than your family?"

"As much as I want to keep him from being grayed out, it would not be right."

"You're sure of your decision?"

Anastasia nodded. His breaking orders to join her in the Sky Temple in the elemental realm had been what got him into this mess. She wouldn't put him in another predicament like that. He'd been sentenced, and he was going to go through with it this time. On that, they both agreed, no matter how much it hurt. William Dinas would be grayed out for treason.

Calla inclined her head. "Very well. You'd best get ready for this evening."

Troubled, Anastasia hurried down the corridor. When she made it to her chambers, Lili was already waiting for her, her dinner gown draped across her knees.

"You're late, my Princess."

Anastasia stripped off her dress as she kicked the door closed behind her. "Yes, I know."

As Lili helped her into her gown—a beautiful summer dress with a structured bodice, decorated with swirling gold vines, and loose, flowing skirts—she thought about the night she had in front of her. She was going to have to sit through a dinner with a room full of people who either openly disliked her, or thought her responsible for the mess with the Shadows. And Niboki would be in attendance. She wondered how he would be. The last time she'd seen him had been at her wedding to his brother.

Standing in front of her looking glass, she eyed her bare arms. Had she grown up in Jacqueline, she would have a tattoo on her right bicep, a colored band that would name her the Princess and future ruler of Jacqueline, just as William had a tattooed band that named him a warrior apprentice. But she'd never received her tattoo. Yet another thing that set her apart from her people.

"You will get them, my Princess," Lili murmured.

Anastasia sighed. "But will it be in time?"

"Tattoos will not convince people you are a strong ruler. Only you can do that."

"But it would make it easier for them to accept me as one of their own, instead of as the girl that grew up in the human realm." Turning from the looking glass, she met Lili's eyes. "Would you want to join me for dinner?"

Lili smiled. "I would, but I have made plans with my family. It has been too long since we have been together."

Anastasia nodded her understanding.

"Are you ready?"

Turning from her reflection, Anastasia murmured, "As ready as I'll ever be."

Her guards took up their positions on either side of her as she stepped out into the hall. Lili stayed behind, offering a wave of encouragement as Anastasia made her way down to the banquet hall. Just beyond the door, she heard the murmured voices of her peers. Her stomach fluttered uneasily. Maybe inviting them all to dinner had been a rash and unwise decision. But, either way, they were here. Hopefully, she wouldn't live to regret it.

She nodded to the servants and they opened the doors. Every eye turned to her, but, thankfully, the princes didn't cease their conversations. Spotting Mohan at the side table, pouring himself a goblet of wine, she quickly went to him.

"Hey."

He smiled sadly, kissing her on both cheeks. "I know better than to ask how you are, love. I heard what happened to William."

"Yes, well, as far as anyone knows, he was only my guard apprentice, nothing more."

Taking a sip of wine, he motioned to the room. "What brought this on?"

"I thought, perhaps naively, that it was far past time for us all to reconnect. There's too much going on in the realms for us to be silent."

The door to the room opened again, and they both turned. When Vlad strode through, Anastasia relaxed. Seeing who was on his arm, however, her stomach quickly soured. It seemed, impossibly, like Ostana's belly had grown in the two days since she'd shown up in the Queen's study. Mohan fell into a coughing fit upon seeing Ostana, choking on his wine.

Anastasia narrowed her eyes. "What is she doing here?"

"I don't know." Mohan cleared his throat. "When I left, Vlad said she wasn't coming."

They both watched as Ostana approached her little brother, Niboki. Anastasia hadn't even seen him, so keen was she on avoiding the dinner she'd created. Niboki took one look at Ostana's pregnant belly and turned away from her, ignoring her attempts to talk to him. Eala, who was talking with Niboki, gave Ostana a pitying look, but said nothing to the little werewolf prince. Despite herself, Anastasia felt sorry for Ostana. Upon hearing of her unmarried state, her family practically disowned her, much like Euaristos, the King of the Demigods, had done to his daughter, Isidora, when she'd confessed her love for a vampire stable hand.

Looking away, Anastasia greeted Vlad. His vampire fangs flashed as he gave them a quick grin, shaking both of their hands.

"We've told everyone that we eloped," he said in lieu of greeting.

Mohan pursed his lips. "Any particular reason why you felt the need to elope?"

Vlad narrowed his eyes, but ignored him. "I'm sorry I didn't tell you I was bringing Ostana. I just thought—"

"You've made many mistakes, Vlad," Anastasia said coolly. "What's another among friends?"

Steeling herself, she marched away. Nearing the table, she surveyed the room. Nalin, Prince of the Elementals, stood with Eala and Niboki. His white hair—in a long braid down his back, as he was unmarried—lifted in a magical breeze, while his all-white eyes flitted between the mermaid and werewolf princes. He wore a traditional black jeogori coat that started with a high white collar, and hung loosely down to mid-calf. The long, puffy sleeves, chest, and back were decorated with gold thread, depicting the traditional nine symbols of his kingdom for wisdom, strength, and kindness when ruling.

Across the room, Prince Zeathus, of the Demigods, conversed with Prince Hughie of the ghosts. While Zeathus was dressed in the linen chiton toga-like gown of his home realm, with polished gold fasteners embossed with lightning bolts, Hughie was dressed in the simple shirt and pants he'd died in.

Behind them, the Prince of the Giants, Dammek, stood with Prince Rokker of the Trolls. They shared a plate of hors d'oeuvres, murmuring together.

These were the future rulers of the High Council, the Princes of the realms. It felt surreal to be with them all again, after so long. How they'd all changed over the years. She remembered when Dammek, now well over seven feet tall, had been shorter even than Rokker. Or when Eala had played ball games in the Sehirian gardens with Anastasia and his now-wife, Diriara. The only somber part was Aatu's absence. He would have loved this reunion of sorts, nearly as much as he would have enjoyed making poor puns at the transparency of Hughie's spectral form.

A servant stepped into the room, clearing his throat. "Dinner will now be served."

They all took their places at the long table, Anastasia at its head where her mother usually sat. Mohan took up the seat at her right, while Vlad and Ostana thankfully sat further down the table. Eala sat on Anastasia's other side, offering a reassuring smile.

"Good to see you again, so soon," he intoned.

She grinned. "I'm glad it's under better circumstances."

"As am I."

Servants entered, carrying bowls of iced fruit soup. When they left, murmured conversations began again.

Nalin nodded to Mohan and Anastasia's proximity with a wry smile. "Why is it that sorcerers and Nadmilise are so close? It seems you cannot have one without the other nowadays."

Hughie leaned forward. "It is because they are the two most ancient races. The Nadmilise were created as spiritual leaders and are the great ancestors of the human race. What they lacked in magic was put into the sorcerers, who were created as their counterpart. They were literally made as two halves of a whole."

Mohan snorted. "Thanks for the history lesson, love."

"I didn't know that," said Vlad.

From down the table, Zeathus cleared his throat. "So why are we *really* here, Anastasia?"

All other conversations ceased as the future rulers of the realms turned their eyes to Anastasia. She resisted the urge to squirm under the weight of their gazes, and instead wiped her mouth with a napkin while she collected her thoughts.

"Long ago, the future rulers of the realms would gather regularly." She looked between them. "They would discuss politics, trade, their lives, knowing that they would all, someday, make up the High Council. They understood that they would need to at least be friendly with one another, if nothing else, to rule effectively."

Zethus rolled his eyes. "Yes, yes, that's all well and good. But you don't want us to be friends. You want to know if we're going to leave Jacqueline to its own mess like the werewolves."

"We did not do that!" Niboki exclaimed.

"So what was it, *cub*?"

Ostana pursed her lips. "Our father is not the same after Aatu's death. He is not thinking clearly, which is why my mother stepped in—"

"They are not your family, *veyisha*."

Veyisha certainly was not a word said in proper company. In fact, Anastasia had to think of what it meant; her mother definitely wouldn't have taught it to her. Wincing at Niboki's harsh language, Ostana lowered her eyes. Vaguely, Anastasia wondered if this was truly how Niboki felt about his sister, or if those were his father's words coming from his mouth. She doubted the ten-year-old was capable of such blind hatred.

Mohan whistled softly, leaning close to Anastasia. "It's like our very own Opera."

"Either way," Nalin said into the stunned silence, "the werewolves *did* pull out of the Realm Guard."

Zethus started up again. "Yes, but none of this explains why Anastasia felt like getting us all together in one room. Unless…" He peered into his soup. "Wasn't someone poisoned here a few months ago?"

The other princes looked into their own soups, suddenly disinterested in eating. They couldn't honestly think she'd poison them, could they? It didn't make any sense. Gods and Angels, Anastasia forgot how much she detested Zethus. He was crude, just like his father. No wonder his sister Isidora wanted to get away.

"The food isn't poisoned, Zethus," Vlad said.

"Unless you're in on it, too. You, Mohan, and Anastasia are oddly close."

Vlad narrowed his eyes. "We're friends."

"Yes, well, so were you and Ostana, until, you know, you weren't." Zethus nodded to Ostana. "How was your *wedding*, by the way?"

Anastasia put down her spoon. "Enough!"

All eyes turned again to her, but this time, she didn't waver. They were nothing but frightened children hiding behind their parents' bravado—even Vlad. They'd never truly witnessed war. They'd never witnessed famine, or Shadow attacks, or mass imprisonments. None of them knew how to act, towards themselves or to each other. To get through this, they would need each other. They couldn't fall to squabbling amongst themselves, especially if their parents were lost along the way.

"We were all friends, once upon a time," she finally said. "And I believe we should work towards that, once again. My main reason for calling this meeting was to share information. Our realms cannot withstand us acting like individual realms any longer. We must merge, if we are to survive."

Dammek tilted his head. "Merge?"

"Freely share information and advice, integrate our policies and our people."

The servants came and cleared away the soups before bringing the next course. Anastasia was glad to see that most of them finished the soup, in spite of Zethus' poison claim.

Dammek spoke first in his low, slow tone. "I see the castle has fared well despite the Shadows."

"We are thankful it has been restored to its previous beauty," said Anastasia.

"And the refugees?"

"The lists change by the minute. It has been difficult, but we have managed to reunite forty-three-percent of people with their families."

Zethus snorted. "Only forty-three? The Demigods have ninety-eight-percent reunited."

"Yes, well," Mohan interjected, "only five of your men were displaced, so those really aren't very high odds."

"We lost more than five men."

"Oh, I'm sorry. Seven. Seven men. My apologies."

Before Zethus could retort, the servants cleared the table for the next course. Anastasia took a sip of cold ale, sitting back in her seat. It was at that moment she realized Niboki wasn't at the table. Confused, she excused herself and headed out into the hall. She found him, a moment later, standing at the door to the kitchens, holding a tankard of ale.

"Niboki?"

He turned, his face falling into a comically shocked expression as he recognized her. "A-Anastasia."

"What are you doing out here?"

"I don't like ale."

"Alright."

He held out the pitcher. "I added some honey, like Aatu used to."

She felt a pang of grief. Hearing Aatu's name coming out of his brother's mouth—his brother who looked like a miniature version of him—was surreal. It felt like ages since she'd lost him, and yet, it could've been yesterday.

"I know I've never said it to you, but I am sorry about Aatu."

Niboki nodded. "I know it wasn't your fault."

She started. Surely Tamo was just as upset about losing Aatu as he was about Ostana's pregnancy. So why wasn't Niboki shouting at her as he had his sister?

"Niboki, I—"

"And I know it isn't your fault we aren't getting married." He shrugged. "You were married to my brother. That would've been *weird*."

She laughed at the disgusted look on his face. "I agree."

"I liked you, you know, when we met."

"I liked you, too."

Together, they returned to the banquet hall. Wordlessly, she finished her ale and held out her goblet to take some of the honeyed ale, as Aatu had liked it. Niboki met her eyes down the table and grinned, raising his own goblet.

"No, I don't agree," Nalin was saying. "We shouldn't be punishing deserters so severely."

Zethus scoffed. "They do it once, they'll do it again. You can't trust a man at your back with a sword if he's just as likely to turn and run with it. They're cowards!"

"Following orders doesn't equate heroes."

"No, but you're less likely to die."

Rokker amiably slammed his fist on the table. "I agree with thine Council. Thine deserters should be punished to thy fullest extent."

"Thank you," Zethus said.

Eala speared a piece of meat and waved his fork around as he talked. "There are a number of reasons people don't follow orders. Cowardice is one, but it is not the sole reason."

"Again, it comes down to percentages." Zethus shook his head. "Cowardice is the most common reason, regardless."

Anastasia thought of William and Chris. Chris deserted the Realm Guard to help her get to Jumba among the Sehirian refugees in the Sky Temple. William had ignored his draft summons to help her find her grandmother. Neither was cowardice. But she couldn't share that information with Zethus.

"How easy your life must be," Mohan said, "that you can live in black and white."

Zethus frowned. "There is right or there is wrong. No in between."

Hughie pursed his lips. "So where do you stand on the draft? Should women be included for every realm?"

"If you are able-bodied, you should defend your realm."

Vlad dropped his fork. "How can you expect women to fight alongside men? They are the fairer sex!"

A guard slipped inside and approached Anastasia. She leaned back in her seat so she could hear the whispered message, covered from eavesdroppers by the buzz of conversation.

"William Dinas has escaped custody, Your Highness."

Anastasia didn't outwardly react, but inside she felt like she had a stomach full of snakes. "Thank you."

The guard exited. Anastasia thought back to the conversation with Calla and a silent anger ignited within her. Calla couldn't have honestly broken William out of prison, could she? What did she think would happen? That her family would pass judgement on him and he would just step into the role Head

Warrior? Did they care not for the fact that William was now a fugitive as well as a deserter? Gods and Angels, what had they done?

"There are examples from this last battle," Dammek murmured. "Of strong women."

Mohan continued, "Nadmilise, sorcerers, elementals—"

"All very well," Vlad replied. "But they have advantages. The sorcerers and elementals have kinds of magic, and the Nadmilise are stronger."

"Thine lasses can be trained," Rokker said.

Vlad scoffed. "I'd like to see you try to give a vampiress a weapon."

Anastasia's mouth twisted in a wry smile as she remembered the band of vampiresses that attacked her and William outside of Miruna's cottage. Surely Vlad would've sang a different tune had he met those women.

Ostana's fork clattered against her plate a moment before she gave a small cry of pain. They all turned to look at her. She had her hands on her belly and breathed raggedly. Immediately, Anastasia understood; Ostana was in labor. It took Vlad and the others a moment to realize. Once they did, they all leapt to their feet, quite unsure of how to handle themselves. Vlad recovered first.

"Someone send a message to my father. We need to portal to Viire!"

Nalin shook his head. "She can't portal in her condition; look at how close her pains are."

The men all stared at Ostana again, trying to figure out how best to handle the situation. Anastasia stepped up, all of her conflicted feelings about Ostana vanishing as she tried to remember what she knew of birthing a child.

"She'll give birth here." Turning to Mohan, she instructed, "I need a bucket of water and some cloths." To the others, she instructed, "Clear the table and help Ostana lie down."

As the princes leapt to follow her instructions, Anastasia spoke soothingly to Ostana. "Just breathe slowly and hold tight to Vlad's hand. It's going to be all right."

Once Ostana was on her back, and Mohan returned with the water and cloths, Anastasia knelt between Ostana's legs. It seemed the baby was ready to come into the world. Absently, Anastasia realized Ostana must have been in labor since before dinner. A grudging respect bloomed within her; she didn't think she'd be able to sit though dinner with contractions. Anastasia was thankful, either way, as she remembered very little about the correct way to midwife.

"By the Gods!" Ostana swore. "Make it stop!"

Vlad smoothed her hair back from her face. "It's almost over."

"This is your fault! Yours! You hear me?"

Anastasia did what she could to coax the baby free, pressing the warm cloths around Ostana's thighs. Mohan pressed a fresh cloth to Ostana's sweaty forehead. She screamed, gripping Vlad's hand. The other princes stood in a semi-circle around Ostana and Vlad, watching with equal parts mystification and fear.

When, at last, the baby was free, Anastasia took a knife from the floor and cut the umbilical cord. She cleaned the child and passed him over to Ostana.

"Dear God," Vlad breathed and started to cry.

Ostana stared at the pale infant in her arms as though shocked it had actually come from within her. Zethus wordlessly distributed everyone's goblets.

"To the baby!"

Anastasia raised her goblet in a toast, feeling suddenly very tired. "To the baby."

As she took a sip, she marveled at the strange taste of the ale. It was sweet and a little sour, along with the yeasty flavor of the ale itself. No wonder Aatu had liked adding the honey; it brought out dimensions in the flavors.

Mohan put his arm around her and pulled her close. "Life's a beautiful thing, love."

She leaned into him, watching Ostana and Vlad with the baby. Standing there with her friends—for it seemed that was what they were—her issues suddenly seemed miniscule.

She couldn't agree more.

CHAPTER FIVE

When Lili came to rouse her that morning, Anastasia was already awake, seated at the small desk in her chambers. She held a stick of violet wax over a candle, watching the wax drip onto the letter she'd just written. After it pooled, she pressed the seal to it, watching with tired fascination as it dried, the tiara and voluptuous swirls of the Jacquelinian royal crest embossed in the purple.

"Did you sleep at all, my Princess?" Lili questioned, throwing the curtains wide.

Anastasia winced in the sudden brightness. "Enough."

"Hmm."

Lili moved to the wardrobe, choosing the gown Anastasia would wear for the day. Placing her letter on the pile she'd accumulated that morning, Anastasia rose.

"I called on Master Glude."

Taking Anastasia's dressing gown, Lili nodded. "For?"

"I don't want to call the Representatives back for William's escape. I'm sure they'd do something drastic. But I can't do nothing, or else it looks like I just let him go."

"Did you?"

Anastasia shook her head. "How could you ask me that?"

"I'm sorry, my Princess."

As Lili dressed her in a light summer gown, Anastasia mulled over what she knew. Calla had come to her after the privy council meeting, basically telling her that she would break William out of prison. But did she actually?

Would she have gone behind her back like that, after she explicitly told her aunt she didn't want William to be freed that way?

"Do you know where he is?"

Anastasia sighed. "No. Which is why I contacted Glude. He'll be kinder in his search than whoever the Representatives would send."

Ready for the day, Anastasia glanced at her reflection in her looking glass. She'd removed her marriage necklace from Aatu on the day William had been arrested. Her neck had felt empty for weeks after, and she'd often caught herself reaching up to touch the golden rings. Now, however, she'd gotten used to only wearing her moonstone pendant. It sat along her collarbone, glittering in the sunlight, reminding her of her grandmother every time she saw it. A pang of longing went through her.

Turning away from her reflection, she straightened her shoulders. Following Lili out into the hall, she found her aunt Celia already waiting for her; she'd taken her position of Chamberlain seriously since Anastasia stepped in for her mother.

"Good morning," she said, offering a curt nod to Lili.

Anastasia forced a smile. "Good morning."

Without another word, Celia strode purposefully down the hall, expecting Lili and Anastasia to follow. Rolling her eyes at Lili, Anastasia followed. Gath and Mortam took up their positions alongside them.

"Today we have a lot to cover," Celia said.

Anastasia hurried to catch up. "What is first on the agenda?"

Celia seemed to not hear her. "I sent for your page. He should be picking up your letters now and delivering them to the sorcerer messenger."

"Good."

"Now, Master Glude is waiting for you. After that, you have a meeting with the Court. There are some things we need to discuss." Celia looked up from the list in her hand. "Is that what you're wearing?"

Anastasia furrowed her brow. "For?"

"Oh, it'll do."

Celia snapped her fingers and the guards in front of the throne room opened the doors. Anastasia strode inside hoping that this time she sat in the throne, the outcome would be drastically different than the time before. As she settled down, Celia snapped her fingers again. A guard escorted Master Glude into the room. He stood there, dwarfed by the distance between them, his bushy moustache rippling with displeasure.

Master Glude bowed. "Your Highness."

"Good morning, Master Glude."

"You called for me?"

Anastasia's skin crawled at the iciness in her own voice. "As you know, William Dinas was arrested for desertion and charged with conspiracy to commit treason."

Master Glude's expression gave nothing of his thoughts away. "Aye."

"Last night he escaped custody."

"I see."

She wished she could read Master Glude's thoughts. He had trained William from the time he was ten-years-old, watched as he surpassed his peers, his teachers. He couldn't believe what the Representatives had charged him with, could he?

"I would like you to dispatch warriors to find him. As portals are being watched closely, it is unlikely William left the city. As such, he is under your jurisdiction."

Master Glude nodded. "I have a few good men I could spare for the task."

Anastasia wondered just what that meant. Good men as in good warriors? Or good men he trusted to know the truth about William? Why did it feel like everything everyone said had double meaning?

"I shall start by putting out some wanted posters."

Anastasia nodded. "That sounds wise."

Master Glude bowed again. "Thank you, Your Highness. I shall begin right away."

He left the throne room and Anastasia sagged in her chair. She was sending warriors to hunt William. How had life become this? She didn't have long to dwell, however, before Celia prodded her with her quill and began reading from her list anew. Groaning inwardly, Anastasia made to follow her aunt, but the door to the throne room burst open. William's father, Dolan Dinas, marched inside.

Celia cleared her throat. "You do not have an appointment with the Princess."

Completely taken aback, Anastasia merely stared as Dolan approached the dais. She waved away the guards, letting William's father stand before her. He didn't speak at first, but looked up at her with an unreadable expression.

"Nothing," he finally said, his voice thick with emotion. "The night the Shadows attacked, I said nothing as my son ran off to find you. I wasn't even angry when I didn't see or hear from my son for six months. Because I knew he was doing the job he'd dreamed about."

Anastasia's heart twisted but she remained silent. Her aunt seemed too stunned to speak. It felt like the entire room held its breath.

"I said nothing when my son became an apprentice for the royal guard. He came home exhausted, but thrilled, knowing he was protecting the woman he'd wanted to protect since he first held a dagger." Dolan shook his head, his eyes wet with tears. "I didn't even say anything when his dagger was taken from him, or when he returned after almost dying, or the night he was arrested, because I knew that the person he'd dedicated his life to would at least try to repay the kindness given her.

"I knew in my heart that William would be looked after, because my son is no fool. He was raised to be better than that. And I could see it in his eyes that he knew exactly who he was throwing his lot in with. But I never thought of this ending. I never imagined you would do this to my boy."

Anastasia swallowed. "Master Dinas…"

Dolan cut her off. "I didn't say anything about William, and now you have my daughter off on some secret mission."

"I—"

"They are not your playthings that you can cast aside when you're finished. They are my children. And you have taken both from me."

Celia's pale cheeks reddened. "How dare you speak to the Crown Princess that way?"

But William's father merely turned away with a scowl. As he left, Anastasia felt as though her resolve would go with him. But now was neither the time nor the place to cry. She hadn't once broken down over William, or Chris, or her mother. And she wouldn't let herself, not when there was something to be done. She'd cry later, once her people were safe.

Celia rested a gentle hand on her shoulder. "What a horrible man."

"He's a father grieving for his wife and children."

Saying nothing, her aunt led her from the room. They made a silent walk to the Council chambers, where the royal Court waited to meet her. She'd never met the entire Court before; her mother always did, though infrequently. She didn't even know what they all did.

When they stepped into the Council chambers, Anastasia hesitated. It seemed like they were already mid-meeting. Her uncle, Graham, motioned her over with a silent wave. She took the empty seat beside him, in the seat her mother usually took in High Council meetings. Lili stayed with Gath and

Mortam just outside the door. Anastasia met her eyes, shooting her a pained look, before Celia slammed the doors closed. The Court glanced up, apparently used to Celia's dramatics, before turning to Anastasia.

She met their unfamiliar eyes. "Uh, good morning."

"It's never acceptable to begin a sentence with 'uh,' Anastasia," Celia admonished. "Try again."

Embarrassed, Anastasia clenched her fists under the table. How was she expected to rule in her mother's absence when everyone insisted on treating her like a child? She understood she was young. She knew her age. But she was still the acting ruler of Jacqueline. How could anyone look to her for guidance if they saw her as a kid?

"Good morning."

Celia nodded. "Better."

"It is wonderful to finally meet you all."

A man dressed in a dirty tunic and worn trousers scoffed. "That's all well and good, but I have things to do. Shall we just get to the point?"

Celia motioned to Anastasia. "As Anastasia is now the acting ruler of Jacqueline, I thought it best for her to know the Court. You should all introduce yourselves and explain your positions. You are *her* Court, now."

Anastasia worked to keep from frowning. She didn't like the finality with which her aunt spoke. This was her mother's Court, the people her mother chose to be a part of the extended royal family. They should all be serving her mother, not her. It felt wrong to claim them as her Court, a sentiment which a few members clearly shared by the looks they gave her.

The man in the dirty tunic spoke first. "I'm Yorren Argrave, Your Highness, the royal groom. I tend the caprases. Or I would, if I weren't stuck in this meeting."

Celia gave him a sharp look. "Bite your tongue if you have nothing kind to say."

"I have a job to do. I don't need to sit around and listen to people introduce themselves to a girl who is just as likely to return to playing dolls than she is to keep this position long-term."

His words stung, but Anastasia understood. She was just six months past her coming of age. To them she was still a child. But her grandmother hadn't been much older when she'd become Queen, having lost her mother to illness when she was nineteen-years-old. But she'd done everything in her power to prove she was worthy of taking on the task. It was they who had the problem.

Anastasia offered a saccharine smile. "Master Argrave, I would be honored if you would show me how you tend the caprases sometime. In fact, I would be delighted to learn from all of you, to better understand how the Court functions."

Celia looked down at her list, a frustrated expression on her face. Clearly, she was trying to see how she could fit all of them into her schedule, alongside the other daily necessities they had to attend to.

Grumbling some sort of response, Yorren fell silent. Anastasia was introduced to Rodsen Fuller, the royal falconer, and his wife, the royal huntsman, Gaela; the Court judge, Sira Vellen; the royal bard, Naay Spiritlight from the riverlands; and the two door keepers, Huln Dardek and Curno Cassade, before they needed to return to work. Yorren joined them, leaving Anastasia alone with the handful of people she recognized.

Her uncle Graham, the royal diplomat, waited until the door closed behind the others before he turned to his sister. "We have some items of importance to discuss. Celia?"

"The tattoos and the signet."

Anastasia's mind was still spinning with the names of the other members of the Court. Under the table, Celia passed her a rolled parchment. When she opened it, she found a small diagram of the people of the Court and their official titles. She thanked her aunt with a small smile

Belatedly, she realized what her aunt had said: the tattoos. Did they mean *her* tattoos? Was she finally going to get them?

Annek Sophine, the religious advisor, leaned forward. Anastasia had met her once before, when she'd returned from the Shadow compound with her sister, Representative Sophine. Then, she'd been too wracked with grief at Aatu's death to have much conversation with Annek. Now, she studied her. She had the same tanned skin and indigo eyes as her sister, but where her sister's hair was dark, Annek's was blonde as the sun.

"The tattoos should have been granted years ago," she said. "To wait so long is an affront to the Gods and Angels."

Graham nodded. "As you've said before."

"The summer solstice is a week away. The Crown Princess should have them by then."

Anastasia sat back in her seat. It felt odd to be referred to by her official title; most people called her Your Highness. But even stranger was the thought that in a handful of short days, she would have her tattoos. The ones that named her the official future Queen of Jacqueline. While it was obvious that was her eventual destiny, the tattoos made it real in a spiritual sense, granted by the magic of the Gods and Angels.

Every Nadmilise received their tattoos upon their tenth birthday, learning what their trade was to be. She'd missed out on that. Her tenth year, when she and her parents were in the human realm, she'd waited and waited for them to show up on her arm, not realizing sorcerer magic was needed.

Celia took to scribbling on her list. "The family should be in attendance, the Representatives, the High Council and their children... there is not appropriate time to send out invitations."

"Keep it simple," Graham said. "Invite the family, and Valdon will perform the ceremony."

Annek nodded. "That would please the Gods and Angels."

The other members of the Court agreed. Anastasia was shocked by how little excessive talk there was. In the High Council and privy council, all there seemed to be was talk. The Court, however, seemed to get right down to business. She supposed it had to do with everyone having duties outside these meetings, like Mistress Miglune, the Court physician.

Seemingly pleased with Graham's decision, Celia looked up from her list. "Now, the business of the signet."

Anastasia's stomach clenched. They meant her mother's signet. There was no way she'd take the signet, not while her mother still lived. She *couldn't*.

Mistress Miglune steepled her thin fingers. "Her Royal Highness Queen Anarose does not appear to be recovering any time soon. As the acting ruler of Jacqueline, it is Anastasia's job to take the signet, as I have said."

The Commander of the Royal Guard, Marya, shook her head. "Anastasia is only *acting* ruler. While Anarose still lives, she is the Queen. By rights, the signet is hers."

Anastasia watched Marya warily, remembering all too vividly the last time she'd seen her: *Warrior Worris, the leader of the Royal Guard, lay on the ground, unmoving. A large splinter of wood from her shattered lance stuck out of her side. Deep crimson blood pulsed from the wound.* Thankfully, she seemed to have recovered well enough.

"Let's give it some time," Annek intoned.

Mistress Miglune narrowed her grassy eyes. "We have given it time."

Marya pursed her lips. "It is clear Anastasia is the acting ruler. Should something happen to Queen Anarose, we shall reevaluate then."

"Queen Anarose is not—"

Graham cut Mistress Miglune off with a sharp look. "I agree with Marya."

"Fine."

Celia returned to her list. "It seems as though that is all we needed to discuss. This meeting can adjourn."

The remaining members of the Court disbursed, leaving Anastasia alone with her aunt once more. Looking down at the diagram her aunt had given her of the Court, she wondered about the royal judge, Sira Vellen. Could she possibly help William? Undo what the Representatives had done? Or protect him once he was found? Because, surely, he would turn himself over. He was too honorable to be a fugitive.

Her aunt nudged her, bringing her from her thoughts. "Let's go."

Lili approached as they exited, handing Anastasia a stack of letters that had arrived during the meeting. Knowing better than before to leave them unopened, she unrolled them as they walked. Most were correspondences that should be delegated to the Court or privy council. But one letter stood out from the others. It was sealed with the white, wind-like curl of the elementals. Anastasia cracked it open and as she read, she slowed to a halt. It took her aunt a moment to realize she wasn't walking beside her anymore.

"Anastasia? Come along, now."

Lili caught the stunned expression on Anastasia's face. "What's happened, my Princess?"

"There has been another body found, in Azire." She shook her head. "It's the same as the mermaid Eala contacted me about."

"With the note...?"

Anastasia nodded. "Yes, my name was pinned to the body again."

"A warning or a promise?"

"I fear it is both."

Her aunt impatiently returned, motioning to her list. When she caught the look on Anastasia's face, she refrained from mentioning their other tasks for the day.

Anastasia considered her options. She needed to go to Azire, just as she'd gone to see Eala when Ourla was found. But what did the bodies mean? They were killed in the same way, with their fingertips burnt. Were the deaths a sign, or was there more?

"Tell Nalin I'm coming," she told Lili.

As her handmaiden hurried off, her aunt protested. "You cannot go running off every time someone dies around here!"

"Whoever is doing this needs to be stopped. If I am involved somehow, I need to understand why."

"We have preparations to make, Anastasia."

Anastasia shook her head. "They can wait."

As soon as Lili returned, Anastasia went with Gath and Mortam to open a portal to the elemental realm. The last time she'd been there, she'd fought Adrian and the Shadows in the Sky Temple, hidden high among the clouds. She'd met Jumba, learned of his involvement in her grandmother's grand scheme, and told William she loved him. It was surreal to enter the Temple once again.

As the portal closed behind them, Anastasia found herself standing in a grand foyer. The crystalline ceiling rose three stories high, prisms of light filtering through from the ruby sun. Gilded floors depicted the four symbols for the elements, interspersed with veins of silver and bronze. Men in all white jeorgori shirts, baggy baji pants, and jokki robes rode atop Chinese-dragon-like jujhas, flitting through the halls. Anastasia watched as they flew by, the jujhas' tails flicking as they slithered serpentine-like through the air.

Moments after their arrival, Nalin arrived. He bowed respectfully and led them down a narrow hallway. "I am shocked by this occurrence."

Anastasia nodded. "Did Eala speak with you of what happened in Seathium?"

"Briefly."

They entered a small room, and Anastasia saw a body hidden beneath a sheet. It was uncannily similar to how Ourla had looked; Anastasia shivered.

Wordlessly, she approached. Just like Ourla, the fingertips were blackened, and there were wounds on the ankles, where the body had hung upside down. Lowering the sheet, she gasped as she recognized the young woman underneath. It was the elemental woman from the Center Realm, the one who had tended to the warriors.

Nalin furrowed his brow. "Did you know her?"

"She was a healer of sorts." Turning away from the young woman, she faced Nalin. "My name was pinned to her."

"It was."

She shook her head. "I don't understand."

"You knew the other girl that died, yes?"

"In a way."

Nalin shrugged. "Perhaps this is a message for you? Perhaps someone is trying to say something."

49

Anastasia considered his words. It had to be a message of some kind. Why else would her name be on these women? And what did it mean? There was no connection between them. As far as she knew, Ourla and this elemental woman had never met. What was the reason they were killed? Why them? And why burn the fingers? Why hang them upside down? Again, she felt a strange sense of déjà vu, as though she'd experienced the sensation before.

"If they are, I don't understand what it is."

Nalin moved closer to the young woman. "My physicians found a strange marking on her back. It looks like a puncture wound."

"Was it before she died, maybe some kind of sedative?"

"We aren't sure. But after speaking with Eala, it seems the mermaid woman had a similar mark."

Gods and Angels, what did it all mean? Three wounds, in the same places on both bodies. She knew she was missing something, an important piece of information, but she couldn't put her finger on what. Sincerely, she hoped she figured it out before there was another body.

"Thank you for telling me of this," she finally said.

Nalin inclined his head. "Of course."

They moved from the room together, silent. When they reached the foyer, Nalin turned to her and took her hand. "Be careful, Anastasia. The Shadows may be indisposed, but that does not mean your enemies are gone."

"Would that they were."

CHAPTER SIX

Dani loosed a bolt from her crossbow as she swung around the Shadow statue she'd marked. The last hooded figure dropped with a satisfying thud, and Mira wriggled out from underneath the body. Holding out her hand, Dani helped the sorcerer to her feet. Hooking her crossbow behind her back, she pushed back the hood on the attacker. It was a young man, perhaps a year younger than she. He was Nadmilise, with the red hair and fair skin of the riverlands.

Hayde sheathed his battle axe, his eyes wide. "Why did they attack us?"

"Soster," Dani grunted, dragging the body to the others.

"What?"

Mira dusted her hands on her skirt. "Soster. They're a faction of Nadmilise that have sworn to protect the Shadows."

Hayde's expression darkened. "Why would anyone do that?"

"You know the stories of the Shadows, how they used to live in the Gardens of Luas, the Nadmilise afterlife?" Hayde nodded. Mira continued, "Shadows and Nadmilise are both sides of the same coin, so to speak."

Dani stood. "Sometimes something happens to their brains when they've been possessed by Shadows. It's like they're indebted to the Shadows, connected to them somehow."

Hayde looked like he was about to vomit. Dani understood. She could never imagine feeling such a strong connection to the monsters. It must've been worse for Hayde, however, as he'd once been possessed by the Shadows. He made a reflexive movement, rubbing the scars on the back of his neck. She looked away, piling the bodies together. In a way, death was better for these people. It was unnatural to live in servitude of such beasts.

"Someone would've heard the shouts," Dani said. "We need to get out of here."

Mira stripped the bodies of their cloaks, tucking the fabric away for later use. Hayde stood by and watched, obviously unnerved by the whole thing. Unfortunately, Dani knew he would get used to it; the Soster were a surprisingly large group.

Checking to see the way was clear, Dani led them away from the carnage. They tagged their last Shadow statue, avoiding the guards that marched through the narrow streets. Turning back, they snuck through the city, heading to their tent among the sand dunes. It wasn't until they were far enough away that the city looked like a speck that Hayde spoke again.

"How can the realms ever return to normal?" he wondered aloud.

Mira shrugged. "They have to. They've done it before."

"What happens when the Shadows unfreeze?"

"We kill them all."

To Dani, the solution was clear. They kill the Shadows, and the man in charge of them, and the Chaos would dissipate. Things could return to normal. She just hoped it wasn't a wishful resolution.

Hayde objected, "But that's genocide."

"You really want the monsters to live?" Mira demanded.

"You said so yourself that the Shadows once lived in the Gardens of Luas, there was once peace between our peoples. Why couldn't the solution be something like that, instead of murdering thousands on both sides."

"Because the Shadows aren't the guardians of the afterlife anymore. They've changed too much, and so have we."

They reached their tent and the conversation ended. Dani pondered Hayde's words. Inasmuch as she'd heard talk of what to do with the Shadows, she'd never heard of a peaceful solution. The problem was, the Shadows had broken free from Luas, refusing to play their part in the ferrying of the dead any longer. She doubted they would so quickly return to their previous post. While a peaceful solution would be nice, it was unrealistic.

She left Mira and Hayde to their discussion, rolling up in her bedroll. Just before she drifted off to sleep, however, a flash of smoke brought a letter from Anastasia.

Her chest tightened as she read the words over and over. William had escaped prison and was a fugitive of Jacqueline. It didn't seem possible. Her brother was the last person to break out of jail, but even less likely to live life on the run. And from what she assumed about him and Anastasia, he wouldn't leave her behind.

"Any news?" Mira asked.

Dani tucked the letter under her pillow. "Just my father."

She hated lying to Mira, but she couldn't say anything about her brother. It was hard enough knowing he'd been convicted of conspiracy to commit treason. Besides, if it had been important, she would've said.

That night, she dreamed of Shadow sentries. It was still early morning when she woke, startled by the sound of boots outside their tent. She had a split second to wonder before guards burst inside.

Mira screamed, magic exploding from her fingers. Hayde grunted, rolling to his feet as a guard lunged at him. Dani reached for her crossbow but was halted by irons closing around her wrists. She stumbled forward, her face hitting the ground, hard. When the guards hauled her to her feet, she saw Mira and Hayde had been caught as well.

"What is this?" Hayde demanded. "What's going on?"

The guards said nothing as they dragged them from the tent. They were dressed, head to toe, in roughspun clothes, their faces covered with cowls.

They were unceremoniously tossed onto the back of a wagon, five guards holding them down with swords. Another two guards sat up front, snapping the reigns on a set of humped, capras-like beasts Dani had never seen before. They lumbered slowly, their droopy mouths dripping strings of drool.

"Who are you?" Mira demanded. The sorcerer was trembling, though from rage or fear, Dani didn't know.

Dani looked at Hayde. He followed her gaze, understanding instinctively what she wanted to do. Nodding once, he rolled over, giving Dani enough room to kick one of the guards square in the chest. The guard doubled over, and Hayde headbutted him. The guard crumpled, and Mira scooted out of the way as he fell. The other guards tightened their grips, pressing their blades hard enough against them that they drew blood.

In the scuffle, one of the guards had lost his cowl. Dani gasped as she recognized him. She hadn't seen him since before the Shadows' attack, but she'd recognize his dark hair and flinty eyes anywhere.

"Durse Follant."

CHAPTER SEVEN

The week leading up to the summer solstice was filled with feasts and bonfires. Anastasia didn't think she'd ever seen so much food in her life. Every night, just as the sun went down, all the people of Sehir followed a torch-lit pathway out into the west fields where massive banquet tables surrounded the largest fire Anastasia had ever seen. People fed the fire with logs larger than Anastasia was tall and ate until their stomachs were distended.

It all led up to the actual summer solstice at sunrise, where all the residents of the royal city would gather for a party that was to last until the following sunrise. There were games and rituals, jewelry and food, but the only thing Anastasia could focus on was getting her tattoo.

Dressed in a traditional gown, she followed Lili to the throne room. Her family—minus her mother—gathered on either side of the dais, bathed in the late afternoon light. Valdon stood on the middle step of the dais, wearing his drape-like sorcerer's clothing. His eyes followed her as she entered; she shivered with anticipation.

"Are you ready, my heart?" her father asked.

Graham chuckled. "I daresay she's waited long enough, brother."

Anastasia smiled, nerves fluttering in her stomach. She understood the gist of the ceremony, having learned about it from her mother as a child. Thinking of her mother sent a pang of sorrow through her. Her mother had been present for all other important days in her life; it didn't feel right that she wasn't here to see her get her tattoos. But she couldn't wait any longer.

Stepping up to Valdon, she knelt before the dais. He placed his hand over her arm, where her tattoo would soon sit. His fingers were cold, despite the warmth in the room.

"Do you, Crown Princess Anastasia Jacqueline Piliar Moneth, swear to uphold the dignity and reverence of your position, granted upon you by the Gods and Angels?"

Every inch of Anastasia vibrated with excitement. "I do so swear."

Valdon's hands crackled with magic. Anastasia felt it race across her skin, burrowing deep into the muscles in her arm. Her body thrummed with the energy of it, and warmth flooded through her. She closed her eyes against the strong sensation. Her mind seemed to separate from her body, soaring high above everything in her realm. When she opened her eyes again, she stood in the middle of an oak tree. Six empty thrones, carved from the trunk of the tree, sat off to the right, beside a round, glassless window.

On the other side of the window, she spotted pale green grasses and small, pastel flowers. But the light filtering through was too bright, making it painful to look at.

She turned away, glancing around the tree. Behind her, she found a table lined with a number of objects. Instinctively, she knew she needed to choose one of them. Vaguely, she wondered if all tattoo ceremonies were like this. Did every ten-year-old Nadmilise face the same choices? Or were they different for each one?

Her hand hovered over the table. There was a scallop, a crystalline star, a gold lamp, a brass key, and a small hourglass filled with white sand. She had no idea what they all meant. What was the point of taking the objects? What did they mean? Could she take more than one? Glancing around again, she determined she was alone in her decision. This was her trial, her choice to make. There was no one offering guidance or advice, only herself.

Closing her eyes, she focused on the objects in her mind. Her hand seemed to move of its own volition, guiding her to the star. Wind surged as she touched the crystal.

She shielded her eyes against the gale. When she opened them, she found herself looking up into her father's face, once again back in the throne room. She blinked to clear her vision, finding that she no longer held the star.

Her aunt Celia drew an astonished breath. "Elliot, *look*!"

She followed her aunt's gaze, looking down at her right arm. A three-finger wide violet tattoo wrapped around her bicep, naming her the heir to the Jacquelinian throne. But that wasn't what shocked her aunt. Beneath it sat a thin black band. She stared, speechless, as her father, uncle, and great-uncle fluttered around her.

"What does this mean?" Celia demanded. "Did something go wrong?"

Elliot shook his head. "I—I don't know."

Anastasia wordlessly turned to Valdon. It had to be because of her age, didn't it? No Nadmilise royal, as far as she knew, had ever gotten two tattoos. No *Nadmilise* had ever gotten two tattoos.

Valdon started to laugh. "Of course it wouldn't go right."

Looking down at her tattoos, Anastasia cracked a smile. Since when had anything ever gone the way they'd expected? They should've known something would go wrong; that's just what happened to their family. Her father and great-uncle joined in laughing, shaking their heads. Within moments, only Celia stood, stony-faced, her arms crossed over her chest.

"I'm glad you think your daughter's malformation is something to laugh at, Elliot," she said shrewdly.

Calla wiped her eyes. "Come, Celia. What's done is done."

"My niece has an abnormality! What's done is not done!"

They all turned to look at her arm again. Anastasia followed their gazes, lightly running her finger over her tattoos. The skin felt slightly raised, but smooth to the touch. It hardly seemed real.

Elliot turned to Valdon. "But what does it mean?"

"To hazard a guess, the Gods and Angels deigned to show us that Anastasia is both royal and warrior."

Royal and warrior. Anastasia grinned. That definitely suited her. Silently, she sent up a thank you to the Gods and Angels. She *was* the direct descendant of the warrior angel, after all. Looking over at her aunt's disgruntled expression, she nearly started laughing again.

"Well," Celia said, ruffled. "What are we going to tell people?"

Bale chortled. "I don't think we need to tell them anything. The Gods and Angels made their decision clear."

Anastasia's neck grew warm. But instead of the warmth from flushing, it felt like someone was pressing a candle close to her skin. She grew uncomfortably warm, and then painfully so. Crying out, she dropped to her knees as the pain spiked. Tingles and electric shocks shot through her neck. She blinked, trying to clear her vision. Then, all at once, her body seized. She shook with tremors, seizures wracking her body. Everything faded around her, as she lost herself in the quaking.

What felt like seconds later, she came-to. Her father hovered at her bedside, holding her hand. When she opened her eyes, he breathed a sigh of relief.

"She's awake!" he called.

The door opened and Mistress Miglune strode inside. "How are you feeling?"

"What happened?" Anastasia croaked.

"You had a seizure."

Confused, Anastasia looked at her father. But he seemed as in the dark as she was. How could she have had a seizure? She hadn't seen anything, so it wasn't a symptom of her premonitions. And she'd learned to control her visions during her time in the alternate universe with her grandmother. No, this had been something else entirely.

Mistress Miglune frowned. "It seems Anastasia has developed epilepsy."

Anastasia and her father simultaneously exclaimed, "What?"

"Have you experienced any kind of trauma to your head, Your Highness?" Mistress Miglune questioned. "Any brain injury?"

Anastasia shook her head. "No! Not at all."

"I'm afraid my healing abilities have had no effect on your condition."

Her father stepped forward. "What are you saying?"

Mistress Miglune sternly met his gaze. "I am saying that the Crown Princess should think of finding a successor to the throne."

Everything else faded away as dread seeped through Anastasia. How could this have happened? She was fine! She was better than fine! She'd had no issues before, no signs of any sickness. They couldn't really force her from the throne, could they?

"Tell no one of this," her father instructed. "We shall see what we can do."

Mistress Miglune frowned. "You know I don't want this, but if Anastasia cannot get better, she will be ineligible for the throne."

"We understand."

With a last pitying look at Anastasia, Mistress Miglune left. Anastasia sat with her father in silence, unable to wrap her mind around it all. She had epilepsy. And healers couldn't help her. Gods and Angels, what were they going to do? How were they going to take care of this? *Could* they take care of this? From the worried look on her father's face, it was clear he didn't have much hope.

"If anyone finds out about this, they can remove me as the heir to the throne," she said softly.

"I know."

A tear slid down her cheek. "What do we do?"

Her father looked at her then, gripping her hand. "I will consult with any and all healers I can find. Until then, we go on as though nothing is wrong. We tell no one about this."

Anastasia mutely nodded. This was a secret she didn't mind keeping to herself. For the first time, she wished William was there next to her, holding her hand. She imagined the way he'd look at her. Not like she was going to break, but like he knew she would get through this.

This time, she didn't know if she would.

CHAPTER EIGHT

The early morning of the summer solstice came with Anastasia's recovery. She sat in her room, wrapping twine around the amulet she'd
made out of agate. It's healing properties would certainly come in handy after
what had happened during her tattoo ceremony, once the amulet was strength-
ened by the ceremonial balefire.

Incense of sage, mint, and lavender filled the room, alongside bowls
of potpourri and vases of summer runas flowers—as were the traditions for
the solstice. Sitting in her bed, methodically wrapping twine, she reminisced
on the solstice. It had always been one of her favorite holidays. Everything
was bright and floral and sweet-smelling, celebrating the fire of life. But this
year, she was wholeheartedly not in the mood.

A knock sounded at her door before Lili entered. She was dressed in a
traditional flowy blue and green gown, a crown of bright yellow flowers in
her hair. She looked ethereal.

"Good morning, my Princess."

Anastasia tied her amulet around her neck, feeling the stone fall heavily
against her chest. "Morning."

Closing the door, Lili proffered a garment box, a long match, and a large
white candle. Anastasia took the ceremonial candle and placed it on her win-
dowsill. Lighting it, she wordlessly asked the Gods and Angels for protection
and guidance through the following year. The candle would remain lit all
through the day, until the following sunrise, when the solstice would end.

Out of the garment box, Lili pulled a new gown of blue and green. Anastasia admired the handiwork; the bodice was decorated with pale yellow
thread, sewn in flower patterns. Wordlessly, Lili helped Anastasia into the

dress. She completed the look with a flower-patterned tiara with yellow diamonds.

Looking at her reflection, Anastasia frowned. At the time, her tattoos seemed incredible, a testament to her individual strength and uniqueness. Now, they served as a reminder of her illness.

"You will be well, my Princess," said Lili. "The people will see that."

Anastasia laughed derisively. "Will they?"

Turning from her reflection, she made her way downstairs. Her family was already there, waiting. Calla and Celia wore similar blue and green gowns, while her father, uncle, and great-uncle were dressed in bright yellow doublets. They all carried ceremonial torches, lit for the procession through the town. As she approached, her father handed her one.

"How are you feeling, girl?"

She gave him a wan smile. "Fine."

He didn't press her any further, though she knew he wanted to. But there was nothing else to say. She had epilepsy, and unless they found a way to fix it, she would never be able to become Queen of Jacqueline.

As the first rays of sunlight colored the sky, the procession began. She stepped outside with her family and Lili, joining the growing collection of people in the castle square. Every last one of them was dressed in shades of blue, green, and yellow, holding torches that lit up the early morning sky. The sheer number of people took Anastasia's breath away, despite her sour mood. She saw the dressmaker, Mistress Woodsman, who offered her a kind wave. Beside her were Chris' sister and parents. The sight of them made her chest tighten. She turned away from them, but not before she spotted William's father amongst them.

Tears pricked her eyes. Swallowing her sorrow, she moved away from them, joining Calla and Celia. As she moved through the townspeople, she noticed their stares. It took her a moment to remember that she had finally gotten her tattoos, and they were, indeed, quite different than anyone else's.

"Oh, poppycock," Celia was saying.

Hoping for a distraction, Anastasia turned to their conversation.

Calla shook her head, her deep blue eyes pensive. "Are you so sure it is?"

"Of course I'm sure! There is no way Anastasia will give up her throne. Nor should she, when there is a perfectly good course of action."

Anastasia frowned. "What are you talking about?"

Celia didn't even bat an eye as she turned to Anastasia. "You need to remarry."

"What your aunt means to say," interjected Calla, "is that this new illness caught us all off guard."

"I said what I meant. Anastasia needs to remarry. She has gone through the proper mourning period for Aatu, and in light of recent events, it is the right thing to do. For Jacqueline."

Anastasia stared at her aunt, hoping she misunderstood what she was saying. But by the stony look on Celia's face, and the guilty look in Calla's eyes, she knew she'd understood perfectly. Her aunt didn't just want her to remarry, but to remarry and birth an heir. They'd moved straight past her epilepsy, understanding that she would certainly be removed as heir-apparent, and picked the next best thing.

Gods and Angels, she never thought this is what her life would be. She married Aatu because it was the right thing for their people. And she agreed to marry Niboki back when they thought it would protect them from the Chaos. But she never imagined she'd have to do it again.

"You want me to have a child," she said woodenly.

Celia huffed. "You must find a husband first."

Calla scoffed. "Surely you are not debating semantics right now, Celia."

Before Anastasia could begin to formulate a response, the procession began. The people of Sehir strolled through the early morning light. Musicians played frolicking tunes, children darted about carrying streamers, and people linked arms and skipped. This was a time for celebration, and yet, all Anastasia could focus on was the frivolity of it all. Her time was over. She suspected it had been long before her first seizure. It was her future daughter's time, now.

"There are plenty of good Nadmilise men," her aunt was saying. "Should you want to marry within Jacqueline."

Calla shook her head. "Is now really the best time?"

"Gerrard Tomlin is just over there," Celia retorted. "His father is the cousin to the Representative of Menen. He comes from good, strong stock. His roots can be traced back to the founding of Sehir."

"Yes, because that is what makes a good husband."

"It will do Anastasia no harm to meet the boy! Honestly, Calla."

While her aunts bickered, Anastasia followed their gazes to where Gerrard walked with his friends. He was handsome enough, she supposed. Tall, muscular, and had a decent job as a carpenter, denoted by the royal blue band tattooed on his right bicep, and the cyan blue band on his left.

But he wasn't William.

Her Uncle Graham suddenly joined them, his hands clasped behind his back. He strolled beside his sister, his eyes mischievous.

"What are we discussing, ladies?"

Celia rounded on him immediately. "Anastasia's future husband."

"Ah. You mentioned Ericcen Ros, right?" At their blank expressions, he shook his head. "He's the new armorer from Pousa." Scanning the crowd, her uncle pointed. "There."

They all followed his gaze, finding a rather scrawny redheaded young man. Anastasia sighed. Did everyone in her family have a suggestion of who her future husband should be? Did it matter not what *she* wanted?

Falling behind them, she let herself get lost in the crowd of people. Most of them whispered about her strange tattoos, but she found them easy enough to ignore. Clutching her torch, she wound her way through the city, letting her mind wander and the lilting music fill her head. Thankfully, no one approached her. She was able to meander through the streets of Sehir wordlessly, taking in the beauty of her home.

As they passed the warrior training grounds, Anastasia tightened her grip on her torch. Wanted posters with William's likeness were nailed to posts, and even the smell of basil, rue, and rowan—from bundles strung up in doorways—wasn't enough to calm her. She pictured him, being hunted by his sister warriors, and she suddenly felt like she couldn't breathe.

It didn't matter that she had nothing to do with his disappearance, or that Calla hadn't, either. It was the plain fact that she had no idea where he'd gone, or if he'd even gone willingly. And the warriors wouldn't care. They didn't care that he was innocent. All that mattered was that he was imprisoned.

She wrapped her free arm around herself, as though she could hold herself together from the outside. It didn't help.

"Anastasia!" Celia called.

Turning, she made her way back to her aunt. At that moment, she realized they'd reached the west fields. A massive balefire was already burning, filling the air with the scent of sweet smoke. Fallen trees had been carved into tables, and people quickly set to putting food atop them. Everyone seemed to know their place, from the people gathering for a hunting party, to the children folding paper boats to float on the water. Anastasia felt supremely out of place.

Celia made an impatient noise. "Come along, now, Anastasia."

Hurrying, she joined her aunt. "What?"

"I've spoken with Mistresses Tomlin and Ros. They're expecting you to spend time with their sons today."

"Excuse me?"

Celia leaned close, so only Anastasia could hear her. "You need an heir, Anastasia. Or Jacqueline faces losing everything. With your illness—"

"I understand!"

She planted her torch in the ground and moved away from her aunt, ignoring the shocked expression upon her face. Catching a worried look from her father, she huffed. What kind of life was she supposed to lead if everyone treated her like she was made of glass?

Plastering a smile to her face, she joined the children. "Happy solstice!"

Most of the children hurried to curtsy or bow to her. All except a young boy, who was concentrating so hard on folding his boat, his tongue stuck out the corner of his mouth.

"And who are you?" she asked.

The little boy looked up, his eyes wide. "Haspen."

"Well, Haspen, your boat looks very nice so far."

He grinned. "It's the first one I've ever made by myself!"

"Will you teach me to make them?"

He scrunched his nose. "Do you not know how to make boats? Everyone knows how to make boats!"

It didn't matter that she could speak both Bashaa and Virrean, or that she'd memorized the steps to the traditional dances of Jacqueline by the time she was ten, or that she knew all the dining customs for the realms. No, to this little boy, she was odd because she didn't know the simplest tradition for the Sehirian solstice festival. Something about that filled her with sorrow.

One of the little girls took Anastasia's hand. "I don't know how, either."

Anastasia smiled. "Perhaps Haspen could teach all of us."

Thrilled at the prospect of an audience, Haspen set to fluttering around the table, tossing bits of parchment every which way.

"You're good with them."

The deep voice behind her startled her. Turning, she found Gerrard Tomlin standing behind her. Mentally, she rolled her eyes. Outwardly, she smiled. He stepped forward, joining her at the table.

"Gods and Angels, I haven't made one of those since I was their age."

Anastasia picked up a finished boat. "You're never too old to do it again."

"No, I suppose not."

He seemed gentle, soft-spoken, but even so, the idea of being around him felt wrong, like she was somehow turning her back on William. Thankfully,

Gerrard didn't seem to pick up on her detachment. He seemed perfectly content to just sit beside her and fold little paper boats.

"You have to put a wish inside!" Haspen instructed, holding out a quill.

Anastasia took the quill, looking down at her blank boat. There were plenty of things she could wish for. Her health, her mother's health, Joey's safe return from his Shadow encasement, the prosperity of Jacqueline, peace between Hullenia and Jacqueline... but all she could think of was: *let him come home*. She didn't even know who the *he* was, per se, or to what home she was referring, but it felt right.

She and the children took their boats down to the water, where Gerrard stepped onto the bank and pushed them away.

Haspen tugged on Anastasia's skirts. "What did you wish for, Princess?"

The little girl from before, Nally, waved her arms at him. "You can't tell your wish, or else it won't come true!"

"Nu-uh!"

As the children took to chasing each other around, debating the proper wish-telling etiquette, Gerrard stepped up beside Anastasia. He smelled like sawdust and soap, and though the scent wasn't altogether unpleasant, it wasn't necessarily welcome among the strong herbal incense and smoke.

"I know what I wished for," he said an in low voice.

Anastasia screwed her face into a chiding smile, hiding her inner unease. "You know what happens to wishes if you share them out loud."

He laughed good-naturedly. "I'm sure I'm willing to risk it if you are."

"I just don't know if I could take that chance."

"Come now, Your Highness, what's a secret among friends?"

Ordinarily, she would proffer a sarcastic remark or a joke, and ask him to call her by her given name rather than her title. That's what she'd done with William, and Chris, and their sisters. But in this case, it didn't feel right. *She* didn't feel right. It had nothing to do with Gerrard and everything to do with everything else in her life. No matter what her family expected of her, she would not be screening candidates for a new husband. Not today.

Shrugging, she stepped away from him. "Every girl must keep her secrets. Surely you understand."

"Of course, Your Highness."

A horn sounded behind them and they both turned. The children ceased chasing each other, huddling around Anastasia's legs, as a line began to form in front of a smaller fire. Recognizing her family at the front of the line, Anastasia turned to the children.

"I guess that's my cue."

Haspen took her hand. "Good luck, Princess!"

They walked together towards the fire, Gerrard and the other children trailing after them. As they neared, Gerrard stepped up beside her.

"I shall find you later, Your Highness."

She politely inclined her head. "Happy solstice, Master Tomlin."

"Please, call me Gerrard."

The irony of his turn of phrase wasn't lost on her. She offered a curt smile and joined her family in line, towing Haspen along with her. Though her aunt didn't mention anything about Gerrard, she pursed her lips to hide a smirk. Anastasia focused her attention on Haspen, who shuffled worriedly from foot to foot.

A second horn sounded, and Anastasia's great-uncle Bale stepped forward. As the eldest member of the royal family, it was his duty to go first.

He backed up a few paces, and everyone in Sehir held their breath, watching. Shaking out his hands, Bale raced forward, propelling himself over the flames. Cheers surged up, and then a second horn sounded. Celia was next, followed by Anastasia's father, and then her uncle Graham. At last, it was Anastasia's turn. She knelt down beside Haspen, catching the anxious expression upon his face. The horn announcing her turn to jump carried through the field.

"Are you worried about me?" she asked him.

Haspen shrugged. "It's a big fire. What if it burns you?"

"Then I shall have a burn."

"Won't it hurt?"

"For a little while, but the pain will fade. Most things that hurt you don't hurt forever."

Seemingly pacified, Haspen nodded. He screwed his small, round face into a grimace and stepped back, hands on hips. Anastasia nodded to him as she hiked up her skirts and faced the flames.

Blowing out a breath, she charged. The wind tore at her cheeks; her stomach lurched as she leapt. The heat from the fire seemed to bloom around her, carrying her to the grasses on the other side. As she landed, she hardly heard the cheers. A nearly overwhelming sense of clarity took hold of her, and she stood stock still, letting it wash over her.

She was the Crown Princess of Jacqueline. She would not be deterred by seizures or illness. She was the direct descendant of the Angel Razibelle and

Humurse the Warrior God. Strength coursed through her veins. She would not give in so easily.

With that realization, she threw herself wholeheartedly into the celebration. Music started up as the townspeople lined up to leap through the fire. Some couples began to dance, jumping and twirling to the raucous jig. Feeling as though her heart had grown three sizes, Anastasia embraced it all. She made flower crowns, drank honeyed wine, and chased the children through the fields.

There were fruit pastries and salads, sweet ciders and teas. Some people set barrels on fire and chased them down the hill to the water, where they fizzled out, ready to be lit again. All the while, music threaded through the air, carrying the warm, fresh scents of summer.

By the time the sun dipped below the horizon, and twilight settled over the field, she was breathless with excitement. Everyone put on sun-inspired masks, like dancing light spirits before the firelight. Hunting parties returned with meat they roasted over a smaller flame; people passed around a communal wine goblet fashioned from an overlarge tree trunk roughly the size of Anastasia's head. The children leapt over smaller fires, their giggles piercing the night. Off a ways, Anastasia saw the royal bard telling stories, illuminated by the flames.

Standing off to the side to catch her breath, Anastasia fingered her amulet. It sizzled with energy, ever since she'd leapt over the fire, filling her with a comforting warmth.

"Beautiful night, isn't it?"

Startled, she turned to see someone standing behind her. He wore a mask, and the same blue and green clothing as everyone else, but there was something familiar about him. It took her a moment, but she finally recognized him as Ericcen, one of her potential suitors.

"It is."

He smiled. "Might I have a dance with Your Highness?"

Seeing no way out without getting an earful from her aunt, Anastasia agreed. Ericcen led her to the fire, where they joined the dancers flitting around the flames.

They twirled and clapped, the women's skirts blooming around them like flower petals. Turning, Anastasia and Ericcen leapt in amongst them. They darted left and right, bobbing and weaving to the rhythm of the song. Part of the way through, they switched partners, and Anastasia found herself with a vaguely familiar young man in a mask.

Something about the shape of his face, the warmth of his hand was familiar. But he wouldn't look directly at her. A moment later, she found herself returned to Ericcen's arms, the scent of smoke and the waters of the Fire Lake lingering in his wake.

"William?" she breathed.

But Ericcen pulled her away, following the dance. She searched the crowd for the young man, eyes roaming every face. But it was no use.

He was gone.

When the dance ended, Anastasia politely excused herself. Ericcen didn't seem to mind as she moved away from him, pushing her way through the crowds. Faces swam before her, but she was gripped with a fevered sort of fervor. She *needed* to find him.

Reaching the opposite end of the field, she spun around hopelessly. She felt, ridiculously, on the verge of tears. Somehow, she'd forgotten how much she'd relied on having William in her life.

They'd spent months together with no one else around them and had only ever fought the one time. He'd stood by her when the Shadows attacked Sehir and she was forced to relive the most traumatic night of her life. He'd been there when Adrian found her in the elemental Sky Temple, had held her hand as they fell towards their deaths. He'd protected her and kept her secret when she'd had a premonition in the middle of a party. He'd dragged her to safety more times than she could count. And he did it all without a negative word.

And now? He was being hunted for his dedication for her, imprisoned for serving a higher purpose rather than the draft to the Realm Guard. But all she could think of was how much she missed him. How she missed his steady companionship, his warmth, his strength.

No one could ever replace that for her, no matter how many men her family forced upon her. William was the be-all and end-all. He was hers.

Wrapping her arms around herself, she sank into the grass. Merriment sounded all around her, but it didn't touch her. She let her eyes go unfocused as she stared at the fire, the flames blurring. Knowing she needed to put on a braver face, so as not to draw unwarranted attention, she let out a deep breath and stood. Grabbing her amulet, she focused on its healing energies. She would make it through this, too.

Getting up, she ran her hands over her skirts. A strange bulge at her hem gave her pause. Frowning, she felt around until she produced a crumpled paper boat. Her heart quickened as she recognized the handwriting within. *William.*

Unfolding the boat, she read and reread the words hastily scrawled across the damp parchment. *I wish to always come home to you.* It mirrored her own wish she'd written in her boat, but was also a declaration for their future. His intentions toward her hadn't changed. She bit her lip to keep from cheering. William Dinas was hers.

"Thank you," she said into the growing darkness.

Grinning, she started back to the celebration, renewed. But as she stepped forward, hot and cold sensations flushed her. She staggered back, suddenly unable to breathe. Uncontrollable trembling overtook her; she dropped to the ground like a stone. The world blurred around her as her body seized. The last thing she saw was a masked man hovering over her, with eyes that looked like William's.

CHAPTER NINE

Dani spat on the ground, rubbing the toe of her worn boot through the dirt. It was strange how normal it felt to wrap her hand around the iron bars caging her in, how used she was to the cries of other prisoners around her. It felt like any other day, waking up from her wooden bed, stepping to the side to relieve herself in the hole in the corner, waiting for her meal to be slipped through the slit in the door. But it wasn't just another day.

With a sigh, she settled back on her bed. A bug crawled up from the thin mat that sat atop the wood; she flicked it away from her. A small, square hole in the wall held a candle, the only light in the cell. It flickered, giving the impression that the walls were rippling around her.

"Help!" Mira's voice carried through the walls. "Help us!"

She's grown hoarse in the week since they'd been captured, using every waking moment to call for someone. But no one was coming for them. Dani had assumed as much when they'd been captured. Anastasia only checked in haphazardly, or when she had important news. And no one else knew they were out here. So who would come for them?

"Quit yer yellin' girl!" one of the other prisoners shouted.

Mira ignored him. "Help! Somebody!"

Dani closed her eyes, leaning back against the wall. It had been surprisingly quiet around here. Back on the wagon, the guards had thrown sacks over their heads and taken them across the desert. She knew they were still on the Sand Isles, as they had only traveled by land, but she wasn't sure where they'd stopped. But from what she'd felt being led into the building, it seemed to be an impressive place. At least size-wise.

There were at least a dozen cells, most of them full. They were all given regular meals, and enough water. The latrine holes led down to a sewer that was regularly flushed out, so smell wasn't an issue, and they were allowed to bathe every few days.

And yet, Dani still had no idea who captured them. She knew only of Durse Follant what William had told her—that he was an arrogant, selfish young man, a ward of Master Glude, and the son of the most powerful warrior in the realm. But she didn't know who he was working for, or why. Perhaps it was the guards of the Sand Isles, or the Realm Guard, or even the Soster.

Somewhere down the hall, a door opened. Dani listened to the footsteps, counting as they exited the prison. Twenty-three. So, at least fifty steps from her cell to the door.

A sharp rap on her door startled her. She sat up, peering through the bars. It wasn't feeding time yet, and she'd just bathed the day before… but there stood Durse Follant, dressed in the same roughspun clothes he'd been wearing when he'd captured her.

"Come on," he said, his expression eerily blank.

Dani got to her feet as he unlocked the door. When she stepped into the hall, he wrapped his hand around her upper arm, just over her healers' tattoo. She squinted as he led her outside, yet another deviation from the norm, and across the deep ruby sand to a large tent. To her utter surprise, Mira and Hayde sat inside, chained to chairs.

"Dani, thank God!" Mira breathed.

Hayde looked up, one of his eyes bruised and swollen shut. Vaguely, she wondered what had happened.

Wordlessly, Durse tied her to her own chair. Crossing to the other side of the desk, he sat and started at them. Mira started to tremble but seemed unable to use her magic. Hayde merely stared sullenly at Durse with his one good eye.

"I assume you know why you're here," Durse finally said.

Dani tilted her head. "Assume we don't."

A ghost of a smile tugged Durse's lips. He looked down at a sheet of parchment in front of him, his expression blank. "Daniela Catherine Dinas. Healing apprentice in Sehir. Daughter of Dolan Frederick Dinas, the master blacksmith, and Victorya Syla Dinas, the dance master. Sister to William James Dinas, the disgraced royal warrior apprentice."

Dani bristled. "William was not disgraced."

"Charged with treason, was he not?"

70

"You're one to talk."

He chuckled. "So I am."

She glared at him. "So you know my name, my family. You lived in Sehir for twelve years. It's not so hard to know who people are. I can do it, too, Durse Gallan Follant. Ex-weapons warrior."

Durse merely looked amused as he stared at her. Hayde glanced between them, nearly turning all the way around in his seat to look at them with his good eye. Mira, meanwhile, quivered in her chair, veins in her arms popping as she tried to use her magic.

"Let me guess," he intoned. "You're here on special assignment for Princess Anastasia?"

Dani said nothing, but she was certainly taken aback. No one was supposed to know of their work tagging the Shadows. Anastasia had been adamant about keeping the people of Jacqueline unaware of the fact that the Shadows had begun to unfreeze, or that they were being moved to remote locations so that there would be fewer casualties once they did. So how was it that Durse Follant, of all people, knew?

She studied him, the way his mouth curved into a smile, how his flinty eyes searched her face. She hadn't known him too well before everything had happened with the Shadows, hating him on principal because of his beef with William, but it seemed like something about him was off. She just couldn't put her finger on what.

"Don't deny it," he said. "I know all about it. All about your work tagging Shadows, breaking the curfew in the Sand Isles to do it. And I even know why." He put his finger to his lips. "But we shan't say."

Dani frowned. "What do you want?"

"What do *I* want?" He considered her for a moment. "Nothing. But my men, that's another story."

Hayde shook his head. "You're crazy."

"Am I?"

"I've seen your brand on your arm, and on your *men*. You're one of them, one of the Soster. Those psychos that feel indebted to the Shadows. It's disgusting."

At Hayde's words, Dani searched Durse's body. And there, sure enough, on his forearm right below the crease of his elbow was a brand in the shape of a clawed hand. Thinking back, Dani remembered seeing it on the guards that brought her food in the cells. Closing her eyes, she blew out a breath. They were screwed.

"Disgusting, you say?" Durse pursed his lips. "Hmm."

Something about Durse shifted and he leapt forward, wrapping a hand around Hayde's throat. With his other, he punched, his fist connecting with Hayde's jaw. Hayde's head snapped back with a sickening *crack*. Dani was revolted but said nothing. She'd seen enough violence to be able to stomach it. She didn't like it, but it didn't bother her nearly as much as it once would have. Mira, on the other hand, started screaming and didn't stop.

Crossing the room, Durse silenced her with a backhand to the face. She shrank back in her chair, whimpering, while Hayde groaned, floating in and out of consciousness.

Durse turned his attention to Dani. "Tell me you'll be more cooperative."

"As much as I can be."

He smiled again. "Good choice."

Smoothing his hands over his trousers, he sat once again behind the desk and peered at her. His gaze was unnerving, but she held it. She needed to show him that she wouldn't be easily cowed; it could be their only way out.

She paused momentarily. "What would you like to know?"

"Where are the Shadow statues being taken?"

Dani grimaced. She'd been expecting a question like this. But even so, she hadn't prepared an appropriate answer. She knew she could never tell Durse the truth; the Soster would take the Shadows and try and help them. They could wipe out the realms if they tried. But did she really have the strength to withstand him if he tried to press her?

"I don't know. All I was told was to tag them. A separate team comes in and takes the Shadows."

He frowned. "And who is on this team?"

"I don't know that, either. They were selected by the High Council."

"I don't know if I believe you."

"I don't know how to convince you otherwise."

He stared at her again, but this time pensively. She wondered what it was like, to feel such a bond to creatures like the Shadows. She wondered if he was aware that he'd changed, if he knew what was happening but was unable to stop it. She wondered if it hurt.

"All the same," he intoned. "I need to be sure."

He snapped his fingers and more Soster entered the room. They lugged Mira and Hayde to their feet, dragging them from the room. Others came and grabbed Dani, leading her back to the prison. Instead of going to her cell, however, they brought her upstairs. Inside a new room, she was strung up by her hands and suspended off the ground.

"I'll see you in a few days," said Durse.

Blowing out a breath, Dani pulled against her restraints, making a show of struggling to escape. As they left the room, she counted their footsteps—sixty-seven.

Thinking back to when William had been teaching her self-defense, she grabbed onto her restraints and swung herself back and forth, working to gain momentum. At the right moment, she swung her leg up and hooked it around the rope. Gritting her teeth, she slowly worked her way up the rope to where it was tied around a beam in the ceiling. Looping her legs around the beam, she pulled herself right side up and straddled the beam.

Catching her breath, she got to her feet and rubbed the heel of her boot back and forth over the rope, fraying it. It was slow going, but she finally managed to break the rope from the beam. Carefully, she worked her restrained hands over the edge of the beam, breaking free.

She hastily retied the rope around the beam, and loosely retied her hands with knots that she could easily break, on the off-chance the guards returned for her. Listening for guards, she leapt from the beam. Pain lanced up her legs as she landed. Scrambling to her feet, she tiptoed to the door and peered through the bars.

Growing up with her father, she'd learned a thing or two about ironwork. Unfortunately, she'd spent more time in her mother's studio learning the strange dances from the smallest towns in Jacqueline. She had, however, picked up a trick or two messing around with William in the smithy. Pressing her hands to the door, she closed her eyes and concentrated. Her healers' power swirled inside her chest, tingling as it raced down her arms and out through her palms. It searched through the door until it found the lock.

It was like she could see the inner workings of the door, every bolt and tumbler, like a blueprint. It was the same as if she was looking at a body, searching for internal injuries. When she'd first learned how to do it, she'd followed her family around for weeks, just looking at their insides.

Thankfully, it let her know that there were three tumblers in the lock that needed to be depressed, and that the topmost nail holding the hinge on the door was loose.

Carefully, Dani braced herself on the bottom hinge, hoisting herself up to the top of the door. Working the nail loose, she dropped back. It was a harder metal, but it was warped with age. Chunks of it had already fallen away, and it stood crookedly in her hand. It would be easy to fashion into a key of sorts. She just needed a couple of tools to do it.

Glancing around the cell, she found it to be empty of anything other than the rope, which wouldn't really help. Upon closer inspection of the door, however, she realized it was made of sturdy metal, covered with planks of wood. Squatting, she wedged the edge of the nail into a corner of the wood and kicked it. The rotting wood fell away, leaving a corner of the metal door exposed. Sitting cross-legged in front of it, she started to saw the edge of the nail against the metal.

It would be slow going, for sure. And she'd need something to chip away at the nail to fashion teeth. But what? There was nothing else in the room and they'd taken her crossbow from her when they took her.

But then she remembered the bolt she'd hidden in case she'd ever been captured. Reaching up into her headwrap, she unraveled the length she'd tied around her head. Sure enough, a crossbow bolt fell into her hand. *Thank the Gods and Angels.*

Settling back, she set to work on making her key.

And then? Just sixty-seven steps to freedom.

CHAPTER TEN

Anastasia stared down at the letter in her hands. Two more bodies had been found, their fingers burned, small puncture wounds in their backs, and her name pinned to their chests. Sitting in her mother's study, staring down at Zethus' spiky script, she nervously touched her pendant. The High Council was struggling to find a connection between the victims, a reason why they'd been killed. But she was pretty sure she had one—the alternate universe. They were all people she'd met there, and the realization that someone other than William and Valdon knew about the alternate universe was terrifying.

Setting down the parchment, she considered her options. She could tell the High Council of the connection, but that would mean revealing that the alternate universe existed, that her grandmother was still alive, that a second alternate universe existed where Shadows had eradicated the realms, and that the Shadows wanted to bring the universes together and destroy them all.

She could also keep it a secret and find another connection, a way to find the killer without revealing the alternate universe. But that seemed unlikely.

But if she didn't say anything, she ran the risk of more people being killed. Her only hope was to figure out what the killer wanted. Why the puncture wound? Why the burned fingers? Once she understood, she could piece together who was responsible.

A knock sounded at the door. Lili stuck her head inside. "Mistress Miglune is here to see you, my Princess."

"Let her in."

The Healing Master strode purposefully inside, her traveling cloak rippling around her legs. She looked pointedly at the door until Lili closed it behind her, leaving her alone with Anastasia.

"You've had a chance to examine the bodies?"

Mistress Miglune nodded. "Their cause of death is severe trauma to the neck."

"They were snapped."

"That isn't all." Mistress Miglune pursed her lips. "The puncture wound is from a needle. A syringe was used to remove spinal fluid. I was able to see the leakage from the wound, which means they were still alive when it was extracted. They moved, likely a spasm of pain, as it was being taken."

Anastasia breathed, "Gods and Angels."

So, one piece of the puzzle had been unearthed. The killer was taking spinal fluid from the victims. But why? What could it be used for? When she voiced the question to Mistress Miglune, the older woman's frown deepened.

"DNA. It can be used in many ancient rituals, especially if there is magic in the victims' blood."

Anastasia mulled the information over. Then, suddenly, the answer seemed shockingly obvious. The killer was hunting the Ancients. Somehow, they knew who was on the List, or at least expected who was on the List. It would make sense as to why they were prominent in the alternate universe, and why their DNA would have magic properties.

Logically, the first person she thought of was Tamo. But he was no murderer. He hadn't lost himself so completely that he would stoop to cold-blooded murder, had he? Yes, he'd pulled his warriors out of the Realm Guard, but that didn't make him callous, just angry.

Turning to Mistress Miglune, Anastasia inclined her head. "Thank you for your time."

"Of course, Your Highness."

"I appreciate your help with this."

Mistress Miglune got to her feet. "Please let me know if I can be of further assistance."

As she left, Anastasia pulled out a piece of parchment and scrawled a quick note. Lili stepped inside, hovering in the doorway as Mistress Miglune let herself out.

"Was she of any help, my Princess?"

Anastasia stamped the letter with the royal seal, handing it to Lili. "Have this sent, would you?" As Lili nodded, she added, "She helped me understand the killer better, I believe. When the response comes in, tell him I will be awaiting him in the throne room."

Lili nodded. "Yes, my Princess."

Getting to her feet, Anastasia exited the room. When she reached the throne room, she sat in her mother's throne and closed her eyes. Centering herself as her grandmother had taught her, she breathed deep, focusing on her premonition power. She reached out with her mind, grasping onto the violet thread in her mind's eye. It jerked her forward, drawing her into the future. She tried to focus her thoughts, tried to select the future she wanted to see, but still hadn't quite gotten the hang of it.

As she slumped back in the throne, an image exploded in her mind:

The blue-eyed sorcerer stands on the dais in the throne room. I watch him as he gently runs his fingers over the carved wood. He stares up at the violet-glassed windows as though transfixed. And though this is a seemingly beautiful moment, I am on fire. Rage floods through me, this time my own. I hold myself still, wrapped in chains, threatening to explode.

How could he have done this? He murdered countless people for his agenda and destroyed the realms in the process. For what? A throne? To be King? He could have it. Though, now, it really isn't mine to give.

He moves down from the dais, a grin splitting his face. If it wasn't so laced with malice, I would be happy for him. At least the parts of him I used to know. But he isn't that person any more than I am the girl he once knew. We both changed over the last few years. And I'm not completely sure for the better. But here we are, facing off once again. It feels like a loop we can't break. No matter how we try to get away from each other, something keeps bringing us face-to-face.

"Come now, Anastasia," he says. "Surely you can muster some happiness for me in this time of coronation?"

I spit on the floor at his feet. "You're crazy."

He grins, which only justifies my response. He isn't the man I once knew. He is long gone, trapped by the madness. And I'm not sure I can ever get him back.

Throwing his arms wide, he engulfs me in black smoke. I begin to choke. Then reality sets in. This could be it, how I die. Is it a fitting end, do you think? Suffocated at his hands, with the use of Shadow magic? I don't particularly think so, but alas…

Just as I start to blink out, unconsciousness clawing for me, a flash of red explodes in front of me. An arrow shoots forward, hitting him square in the chest. He crumples, contorting on the floor. I suck in a deep breath of fresh air as his magic fades. My eyes widen as I struggle to take in what is happening to him. He shudders and quivers, screaming as his body starts to rip in two. But he isn't dying. He's becoming something new, something—

Anastasia awoke, gasping for breath. She struggled to return to the vision, to see the end, but it was no use; it had faded, her magical connection to it severed.

Sitting back in her throne, letting the deep auburns and blues of her premonition fade, she mulled over what she'd seen. The blue-eyed sorcerer was back; she hadn't had a premonition about him in ages. And, it seemed, he would be taking her throne, taking over Jacqueline. And given her reaction in the vision, that meant that her epilepsy wouldn't be getting better.

She shivered, forcing herself not to think about it. She needed to figure out who it was that shot him, and what they shot him with. What could that red flash have been? A person, surely. But who? And how did they know how to stop him?

A knock sounded at the door. Lili stuck her head in to announce, "Knowledgist Woodsman, my Princess."

Anastasia had nearly forgotten she'd written to Chris' dad. She waved him in, smoothing her hands over her skirts. A moment later, Aleric Woodsman stepped inside the room. He wore plain trousers and a decorative tunic, the small, knowledgists' tattoos on his forearms hidden.

He bowed. "Your Highness."

"Knowledgist Woodsman, thank you for coming."

She studied him for a moment, wondering if he would be prone to the same outburst as William's father. Though he regarded her in a detached manner, he didn't seem overtly hostile. She wasn't sure if she should be glad for that or not. It was far easier to know her footing with someone when they shouted at her.

"I suppose you're wondering why you're here."

He inclined his head. "Yes, Your Highness."

"There have been some disappearances across the realms. There seems to be no connection between the victims, other than their age."

She didn't enjoy lying to him, but she understood that she couldn't outright say all of these people had been murdered and she'd met them in an alternate universe. Nor could she tell him about their DNA being stolen for a ritual. It would cause undue panic.

"I would like you to look into the List of Ancients. I believe there could be a connection there."

He nodded, pensive. "Especially after the botched Anistes Droun attempt."

She raised her eyes at him, surprised of his understanding. She hoped her flimsy lie wouldn't be too easily uncovered.

"Is there anything you would like me to look at in particular, Your Highness?"

"Yes. There is a person called the Vatis. They are a vessel capable of reading the List."

"I will see what I can find." He considered her for a moment. "But I must be honest, Your Highness, I have not studied much about ancient Nadmilise lore. I am not sure I am the right person for the task."

She frowned. "Your son has the List, Knowledgist Woodsman. It is what blinds him."

Though the news certainly caught Aleric off guard, his demeanor didn't change. He looked up at her, with an expression so much like Chris' it nearly hurt to look at him. But he didn't challenge her or seem off-put in any way. He simply nodded, once, and bowed again.

"I will return once I have the answers you seek."

She offered a wan smile. "Thank you."

As he left, Anastasia sank back in her throne. She wanted to forget about all of this, just run away and not look back until she felt capable of getting a handle on all the moving pieces in her life. She was sure Aleric would see through her lies, especially if word of the murders was spreading through the people. Plus, William was still missing, which didn't bode well for either of them. Her mother still hadn't recovered, and Mistress Miglune was still pushing for her to take the signet. And there was still the matter of trying to fix the realms after the Chaos, the werewolves pulling out of the Realm Guard, her epilepsy, Dani being off on the Sand Isles tracking Shadows...

She needed a serious break. But she knew she couldn't afford one. Instead, she settled for reveling in the silence of the throne room. No one spoke; the silence pressed in on her like a living entity. Even Gath and Mortam were silent beyond the doors.

For the briefest of moments, no one was asking her for anything. No one demanded anything. Letters weren't appearing on her desk; drafts weren't demanding her signature.

But then the door to the throne room opened and Celia entered.

"Come along, Anastasia."

Why did her aunt insist on calling her like an insolent pup? She was the acting Queen! But honestly, she didn't have the energy to muster any kind of argument against it.

Anastasia rose. "Where are we going?"

"You've got to ready for this evening."

"What's happening this evening?"

Her aunt blew out a dramatic sigh. "Honestly, Anastasia. When I leave a letter for you, make sure you read it! I don't know how you get anything done with your desk as messy as it is."

"What was in the letter?"

Her aunt led her towards her chambers, gripping her schedule and quill. Humoredly, Anastasia imagined it was welded to her hands. But then her aunt's next words drove all humor from her:

"Tonight is the ball to find your next suitor."

Anastasia halted. "I'm sorry, *what*?"

"We discussed this, Anastasia! You need to remarry."

"Yes, but I don't remember agreeing to this."

Her aunt rounded on her. "You need to get your head out of the clouds. You're sick, and you're not getting better. While you've been busy calling on warrior masters and knowledgists, the Privy Council decided for you. You need this. The family needs this. And it's time for you to step up and accept it."

Caught completely off guard by her aunt's tongue lashing, Anastasia mutely followed her back to her room. Lili stood within, a traditional gown in her hands. Though she was used to going all out for balls and celebrations, there were no holds barred for this evening.

Anastasia was dressed in a gown of violet. Cutouts bared her shoulders, while the scooping neckline showcased her pendant. The full sleeves were slit at the crook of her elbows and hung all the way down to the floor. Swirling designs, like those of the royal seal, decorated the structured bodice in silver thread. A girdle of silver silk was tied around her hips, draping down with the velvety skirts and short train. Her long hair hung free, bound only by her intricately designed amethyst and diamond circlet.

Facing her reflection in her looking glass, she stared. She looked like a medieval queen. Her aunt added a traditional silver sash, much like the one she'd worn for her coming of age ceremony.

"You look beautiful, my Princess," said Lili.

Anastasia blinked. "Thank you."

Steeling herself, Anastasia followed her aunt from the room. They stood together before the ballroom doors, Celia fussing with nonexistent lint on Anastasia's gown.

"I will be down just as soon as I'm dressed, of course," she was saying. "Most of the court will be in attendance as well."

"Alright."

"And be on your best behavior. Some of these men have traveled very long distances to be here."

Vaguely, Anastasia wondered how long her family had been planning this ball. It had only been a few weeks since the solstice, which meant they'd probably started that night. She absently touched her pendant. Just beyond those doors were her potential suitors, and not a one of them was William.

Her aunt ushered her forward. Anastasia recognized the royal door keeper, Huln Davdek, from that meeting she'd had with the Court. He tipped an imaginary hat at her and she smiled. When he opened the door, she heard music rise up from within. Her heart suddenly leapt into her throat. There was a room full of men her family had selected as suitors, as future Kings of Jacqueline. How had she gotten to this point in her life? Facing down an arranged marriage for the third time.

Huln stepped inside and to Anastasia's supreme astonishment, trumpets sounded, heralding her arrival. She flushed. Her family really had gone all out for this ball.

Clearing his throat, Huln said into the now silent ballroom, "Her Royal Highness Crown Princess Anastasia!"

She didn't miss that he hadn't said her surname. It was no surprise that it caused tension, seeing as she and Aatu hadn't even been married a full day before he'd died. She supposed it wasn't something they wanted to draw attention to when trying to set her up with a new husband.

Working to produce a smile, Anastasia stepped into the room. A bright red carpet led from the door into the room, flanked on either side by silver-clad trumpeters, the royal sigil hanging from their overlong instruments. Tall candelabra and chandeliers illuminated the arched walls and the carvings of the ancient Queens of Jacqueline. Up in a balcony, Anastasia could see her family, all dressed in immense finery as well. Her father wore a polished crown, one she hadn't seen since before they'd left Jacqueline.

Musicians struck up a song into the growing silence and Anastasia turned her attention to the crowd. She recognized a few faces—such as Gerrard and

Ericcen—but many were strangers. It seemed most were Nadmilise, too, all dressed to the nines, in clothing traditional to their home cities. For some reason, the knowledge put her a little at ease.

"May I have the first dance with Your Highness?"

She turned to find Mohan behind her. He had traded in his usual drape-like clothing for a ruffled tunic, cravat, woolen vest, brocaded frock coat, jodhpur trousers, and spats. His usually spiky hair was tamped by a top hat decorated with metalworking goggles, and he held a jewel-topped cane.

She giggled. "Only if I can hold the cane."

"You say one more word about my clothes and I swear I'll leave."

She sobered. Slightly. "I promise I won't mention your out-of-this-world getup." When he scoffed and turned to leave, she reached for him. "Okay, I'm done now, I promise."

"You're one to talk." He motioned to the room and donned a facetious tone. "All the eligible men in all the land are hereby invited to try their hand at winning the fair Princess's hand in marriage! You could be the next King of Jacqueline!"

She swatted him. "Shut up."

"Tell me I'm wrong, love."

She followed his gaze, looking around the room. There were a fair number of royal ladies within the ballroom, but the men far outnumbered them.

Mohan winked. "And they all know it, too."

Rolling her eyes, Anastasia moved away from him. A servant approached her, timidly offering a glass of champagne on a platter. She took it, quickly taking a sip. How in the name of the Gods and Angels was she supposed to get through this evening? She felt like a lamb heading to slaughter. Every eye was on her, even when it seemed like no one was watching. The women's eyes followed her, checking to see which eligible men were fair game and which ones they should stay away from. The men were more open about their staring.

Finishing her drink, she snapped her fingers at Mohan. "Might was well get this started."

He stepped up beside her and took her hand, leading her to the center of the room. The guests backed away, standing in a circle around them. The musicians played an elegant waltz; Anastasia and Mohan quickly fell into step.

"How do I get out of this?" she asked him.

He shrugged. "There's always eloping."

"Is there a way out that doesn't require marriage?"

He didn't answer. Which, she supposed, was an answer in and of itself. A tap on her shoulder told her the night had officially begun. Turning, she found Gerrard standing behind her. He wore Sehirian finery, complete with a fitted doublet with slashed sleeves, and dark hose instead of trousers. A jeweled girdle at his hips shimmered in the candlelight; an ornamental dagger hung from it.

Mohan leaned close, as though pressing a kiss to her cheek. "He's very handsome. Maybe you could use some of these poor boys for some fun."

With a wink, he stepped back, allowing Gerrard to step forward. "Treat her well."

Gerrard nodded sternly, as though he'd been charged with the highest order. "I will, Your Highness."

Hearing someone refer to Mohan by his title made Anastasia smile. No one ever really called him "Prince," much less bothered with any formalities. It made her realize just how long she'd been in the company of other royals.

"Are you having a good evening, Your Highness?"

She turned to Gerrard. "I am."

Which was half-true, at least. She didn't mind the dancing, or the food, or even the clothes. She enjoyed parties, especially ones with her friends. It was just the reason for the party that was upsetting.

"Are *you*?" she asked.

Gerrard considered her for a moment. "Despite the fact that my sister is my chaperone for the evening, I am."

He grinned and motioned to a young woman over at one of the banquet tables. She was dressed in a beautiful pink gown with slashed sleeves, complete with a coned hat and veil. The end of her veil was tucked over her arm, reminiscent of the way Ostana used to sling her long braid over her arm. This girl's face was softer than Ostana's however, and bright with excitement.

"Do you get along?" she asked Gerrard.

He nodded. "We're twins; it made for easy companionship as a child."

"Do you have any other siblings?"

"Two older sisters."

She smiled. "So you know how to treat a woman, do you?"

He shrugged bashfully. "I may have learned a thing or two from my sisters. They were always very… helpful in teaching me how to court someone."

"I bet they were."

They both laughed. As the song changed, they continued to dance, waltzing lazily around the room. A few other couples had joined them, but for the most part, people congregated along the walls, watching. Gerrard didn't seem phased by it in the slightest, his smile coming easy. She wondered just what *would* phase him. What would bring this soft-spoken man to anger? Would he be calm under pressure? What if they were attacked? Would he call for help or try to fight?

But then she caught herself. She was mentally wondering if he would be a good King, a good ruler! It felt wrong. She couldn't turn her back on William. And yet... if, or when, he was found, he would be grayed out, forced into servitude. He could never be her suitor then. And if he wasn't caught, they could never marry. He'd be a fugitive for the rest of his life. Their only chance would be proving his innocence. And what if they couldn't do that in time? What if her illness overtook her before then? She would have no heir, and Jacqueline would fall to its own sort of Chaos.

Gods and Angels, she wished her mother was around. Anarose would know what to say, what to do, to help her make this decision. As it was, her mother was unconscious, still recovering from Adrian's torture.

Anastasia's stomach soured. That was not the proper train of thought for this sort of evening. She needed to focus on the task at hand: getting through the night without snubbing her family's efforts.

Turning to Gerrard, she forced herself to focus on him. "What about your parents, are you close with them?"

"I am." He shrugged again. "We all have dinner together once a week. My sisters portal to town and we just get together and talk. It's been a family tradition for as long as I can remember. When I was younger, all of my cousins would come, too. But now, they live too far away for it to be plausible. They come when they can."

"That sounds lovely."

He gave her a sheepish smile. "Thank you, Your Highness."

A young man to their left cleared his throat. It seemed her next suitor was ready. Anastasia and Gerrard slowed, and Anastasia turned to her next partner. Gerrard bowed, pressing a hesitant kiss to her hand.

"Perhaps I shall see you again this evening," he said, and then moved away.

Her new partner, a young man she hadn't seen before, bowed gracefully. He was dressed in the traditional clothes of the east and wore his family's crest emblazoned on the front of his tunic. He was nice enough, but Anastasia quickly forgot his name.

And so the night went on in a barrage of young men. There was Durrik of the riverlands, and Samin of the Sand Isles, and Fen from Talrom. There were gardeners, armorers, musicians, and knowledgists; healers and tradesmen, dancers and potters. And then there were their sisters, cousins, and friends; an endless parade of names and faces, swimming along a background of food and drink. Anastasia struggled to keep them all straight in her head.

Taking a breather, she stopped at the banquet table. There were a number of Jacquelinian delicacies, but nothing really drew her eye. She absently picked at some fruit, just glad to be still for a moment.

"Anastasia Moneth."

She turned to see Zethus, Prince of the Demigods, standing behind her. A circlet of gilded leaves bound back his wild curls, matching the golden fasteners on his toga-like chiton and the bracelets on his biceps. He didn't seem too pleased to be standing in her presence, but, then again, Zethus was never too pleased about anything.

"I didn't realize you were here."

He eyed her. "I received an invitation."

"Sure."

Unsure of what else to say, she turned back to the table. Zethus came up beside her, plucking a honeyed fig from a platter. As he licked his fingers, he regarded her.

"Do I not get a dance?"

She rounded on him. "I wasn't sure you were my biggest fan."

"I don't dislike you, Anastasia. I never have. We just don't see eye to eye on politics. That can be easily remedied."

She tilted her head. "And what if *I* don't like *you*?"

He wagged his brows suggestively. "That, too, can be easily remedied."

A full-bellied laugh burst from her lips, much to her own surprise. Zethus chuckled, taking another fig. Shaking her head, Anastasia turned to him and held out her hand.

"Zethus Spiros, would you care for a dance?"

He shrugged. "I don't know if I'm particularly in the mood, now. I don't enjoy having to work for my affections."

She turned away, as though leaving. "That's fine. I don't particularly care for the chase."

He came up behind her, grinning mischievously. "Oh, but dear Anastasia, that's the best part."

She rounded on him and he faltered, stumbling back a step. With a grin, she reached around him to grab another piece of fruit from the table. She brushed his arm with her sleeve, stepping close so he was pinned between her and the table.

"Is it?" she questioned, her voice low. "Is it really the best part?"

With a playful wink she moved away from Zethus, popping the grape into her mouth. Another song played, and more couples littered the floor. She hoped at least one person found a suitor here tonight. Someone in this room deserved happiness. Just as she thought it, however, her aunt appeared. She'd certainly taken her time getting ready, and she looked it, draped in jewels and ice green silk.

As she descended the stairs from the balcony, moving toward her, Anastasia wondered at the likelihood of escape. But she was weighted down with skirts, and the guards at the doors had no such hindrance.

"Are you enjoying yourself this evening?" her aunt asked.

"Sure."

Celia frowned. "You don't have to look so surly about it. A lot of these men are quite handsome and have strong backgrounds."

"Sure," she repeated.

Her aunt frowned. "Just narrow down your pick, Anastasia."

Anastasia started. "What do you mean?"

"You need to offer a list of candidates to the Privy Council and the Court tomorrow morning. Those men will be invited back, and so on, until we pick an appropriate future King." At Anastasia's shocked expression, Celia added, "You really didn't think we'd throw this extravagant ball for no return, did you?"

Of course she had. She'd expected the ball to end, the suitors to leave, and for her to be firmly single until she figured out what to do about William. Turning, she looked up at the balcony. Her father chatted amiably with his brother, seemingly unaware of the position he'd put her in. Though they were giving her some say in her next husband, it wasn't much. The Privy Council had hand-picked these suitors, vetted their backgrounds, undoubtedly looked into their family histories.

Smoothing her expression, she scanned the room. One of the men here would likely be her husband, whether she wanted them or not. They would be the future King, the father of her daughter. The thought made her stomach roil.

"Narrow it down to at least twenty-five candidates," Celia murmured.

Twenty-five? She didn't even know twenty-five of these guys' names, much less anything of value about them or their character. Gods and Angels.

Disheartened, Anastasia moved away from her aunt. The band struck up another waltz; the sound suddenly grated on her ears. Closing her eyes, she allowed herself one brief moment. She could do this. She'd accepted an arranged marriage with Aatu, and that had turned out alright—for the most part. All she needed was time. If she went along with her family's plan, she'd get the time she needed.

She only hoped it would be enough.

Opening her eyes, she approached Gerrard. He stood with his sister and a handful of others, all of whom turned to stare at her as she approached. Only Gerrard didn't look. He kept his back resolutely turned to her, even though she was sure he knew she was there. She found that endearing.

Reaching out, she tapped him on the shoulder. He turned and genuine happiness touched his eyes. "Princess Anastasia."

She cocked her head, offering a smile. "How would you like that second dance?"

CHAPTER ELEVEN

Four weeks, two more balls, and three more seizures had come and gone. Anastasia's list of potential husbands was getting smaller and smaller, whittled away by her Aunt Celia's insistent needling. Now, only ten names remained, but Anastasia couldn't care less.

It felt like the realms were holding their breath. More bodies had been found, in exactly the same manner as the others. Homes were still being rebuilt, families reunited. Mass graves had been dug and filled; mourning clothes seemed to be a new uniform. William still hadn't been found, Chris was still in prison, the Shadows were still frozen, her mother was still unconscious, and more and more warriors were being rounded up as deserters.

Anastasia found herself in her mother's study, pouring over stacks of parchments, struggling to find a way to prove William's innocence and find a connection between the victims.

William had been found guilty of conspiracy to commit treason, but treason on whom? Surely not her, not her family. She reread notes she'd gotten from Sira Vellen, the royal judge. They weren't very conclusive. Which meant that it had been an inside job. One of the Representatives—or more—had decided they needed William out of the way, permanently. But who? And why? Because of what he knew of the alternate universes? Or because of his relationship with her?

She sighed. The victims weren't easy, either. She'd thrown her Ancients theory out the window as soon as the other bodies were found. Each one was from a different realm. From what she'd learned from Knowledgist Woodsman's studies on the Ancients, each realm wasn't represented. So that meant something else was connecting them.

Leaning back in her chair, she studied her list of potential husbands. They all came from old Nadmilise families, ones that could trace their roots back to the founding of old cities. Maybe she had a type, after all. The thought brought a bitter laugh to her lips. As well as—

Gods and Angels, why hadn't she seen it before? She returned to the list of the victims. Ourla, and the elemental girl from the Center Realm…these people all came from ancient families, ones with pure blood. They could trace their families back to the founding of *realms*, not just cities. That's why their DNA was special. That's why it could be used in a ritual, even though most of them couldn't do magic. Shuffling through parchments, she searched for her aunt's original list of potential suitors.

"Lili!" she called. "Lili, get the pageboy and my aunt!"

Circling the names of the men with ancient Nadmilise roots, she rifled around the desk for the list of families in Jacqueline. A census had been taken recently, as a way to reunite lost family members post-Chaos. It would have a list of the old families, and ancestral homes.

She was a quarter of the way through the census when her aunt hurried into the room, a pageboy on her heels.

"What is the meaning of this?" Celia demanded. "I don't appreciate being summoned like a dog."

Anastasia shoved the list of potential husbands at her aunt. "You need to round up these men and bring them to the castle."

Her aunt's face lit up. "Have you narrowed down your selections already?"

"They're in danger."

"What are you talking about?"

Anastasia turned to Lili. "Get Warrior Worris in here, as well. We need to—"

Celia grabbed her, forcing her to look over at her. "You will tell me what is going on here, Anastasia. Do not dismiss me."

She really looked at her aunt then. Her icy green eyes were shadowed with exhaustion, her usually pristine white blond curls disheveled. She was afraid. For all her bravado, for all her orders and rules and *lists*, she didn't know what to do. And she was looking to Anastasia for answers.

"The murders," she explained. Her aunt's nose wrinkled with disgust. "The killer is going after ancient families, ones with ties to the founding of the realms."

"Then why these particular people?"

Anastasia motioned to the stack of letters on the desk. "The Nadmilise are the only ones left. The sorcerers, werewolves, elementals, ghosts… a member of their ancient families, their pure bloodlines, has already been killed. Only the Nadmilise remain. We must do whatever we can to protect these people, to prevent the killer from finishing their job."

Celia nodded, her mouth a flat line. With a clear directive, she seemed to have composed herself. Anastasia was glad; she couldn't be the only one here holding it together.

Lili cleared her throat. "Shall I send for Warrior Worris?"

Anastasia nodded. "Then come help me go through the census. We need to round up all the ancient families."

Her aunt shifted her weight. "What shall I do?"

"Contact the men on this list and have them gather in the throne room."

Nodding, Celia hurried off. The pageboy, who Anastasia had even forgotten was there, stood huddled in the corner. If he had been nervous around her before, he was downright frightened now. She wished she had the time and patience to sit with him, help him feel more comfortable, but she didn't.

As it was, she wordlessly handed him a letter. His hand trembled as he took it. Lili ushered him out of the room, giving him instructions on where to have the letter sent once he reached the royal messenger. When Lili returned, she sat across from Anastasia and took the bottom half of the census, working her way through the names. Grateful, Anastasia resumed her own work, scrawling names on the parchment in front of her.

By the time Celia returned, having contacted all the men on the list, Anastasia and Lili had finished. Their compiled list was, thankfully, shorter than they'd anticipated.

"Would you send word to these families as well?" Anastasia asked of her aunt.

Celia nodded. "Of course. The others are awaiting you in the throne room."

A knock sounded on the door and one of the guards announced Warrior Worris. Her dark eyes took in their harried states, and the papers scattered across the desk, before they finally alighted on Anastasia.

"You asked to see me, Your Highness?"

Anastasia inclined her head. "There will be people arriving in the throne room today. They need to be protected at all costs. And I will need you to up the guard that escorts me."

"Of course, Your Highness."

"I cannot tell you of the threat we are under, for I don't know it myself. Just know it should be formidable."

With a nod, Warrior Worris exited the room. Anastasia was glad it was so simple with her, giving directions and having them followed. She only wished other parts of her life were the same.

Handing the list of names to Celia, Anastasia followed Warrior Worris from the room. Lili hurried along after her, shouldering her way through the guards. As they headed for the throne room, Anastasia wondered what she would say to the people. She didn't know how long they would need to be under guard, any more than she knew the threat they were facing. There were certainly enough rooms in the castle to house everyone, but that was no way to live a life.

They wouldn't be able to go to work, attend social occasions, see friends. They would, for all intents and purposes, be prisoners in the castle. Though it was rather posh, it was still imprisonment. They couldn't sustain that long-term.

As they rounded the corner to the throne room, they ran smack-dab into Vlad. Startled, Anastasia just stared at him. He looked tired, and rumpled, but that was to be expected with a new baby. Still, she'd only ever seen Vlad without a cravat once in all the years they'd known each other, and that had been at the pajama party of sorts they'd had with Mohan and Aatu.

"Anastasia," he said, surprise coloring his voice.

"Vlad."

"What are—what are you doing here?" He gave her a wan smile. "I mean, of course you're here. You live here."

She frowned. "Were you not looking for me?"

"I was."

She blinked.

He tried again. "Do you have a moment? I need to talk to you about something."

Turning, she waved Lili and her guards ahead. They made their way to the throne room without her. As they opened the door, Anastasia saw the men gathered within. It was almost humorous, seeing them all standing there waiting for her, like a ball without the dress clothes and music.

"What's going on?"

Vlad twisted his hands together. "There's something I—we—Ostana and I would like to ask of you."

Anastasia pursed her lips. She hadn't been naïve enough to believe that the dinner was the last time she'd see Ostana. She and Vlad were to get married—despite the lie that they'd already done so, to keep their son from being a bastard—and Anastasia and Vlad would be on the High Council together someday. Plus, they were *friends*. But she hadn't expected for Ostana to be back in her life so soon.

"What is it?" she deadpanned.

"We want you to be our son's godmother."

She flinched. "What's his name?"

"Aagney Vali Roza. With a double 'A' in honor of…" he trailed off, but Anastasia knew who he meant. *Aatu.*

Blowing out a breath, she turned away from Vlad. She was honored, flattered, that they wanted her to be the godmother of their child. And if life had panned out like they planned, she would be that little boy's aunt. But life hadn't gone that way, and Ostana was a big part of the reason why.

Could she put that aside for the sake of the child? Could she ignore Ostana's actions, her hand in her brother's death? And now that she'd had the baby, hadn't she said she was going to turn Ostana in?

"Look, I know—I know our families aren't close. But Aatu would've…"

"He would've wanted us to be in the baby's life."

Vlad nodded. "Will you consider it?"

"I'll *do* it."

"You're serious?"

Anastasia nodded, and Vlad wrapped her in an embrace. As he pulled back, he flushed. She knew how important it was to him in light of him being so emotional with her. Viireans were not known for their openness and emotionality, to say the least. A small part of her felt better about her decision to be godmother in light of it.

"There will be a formal ceremony day after next."

She huffed. "What would you have done if I'd said no?"

"Ostana was sure you wouldn't."

With that, Vlad turned to go. Anastasia watched after him, her stomach souring. Ostana had been a good friend to her at one point. Now, all that was between them was bitterness.

She made her way to the throne room.

The men gathered within turned to stare at her as she entered. They all had a hungry look in their eyes, knowing just how close they were to becoming her husband and the future King of Jacqueline. It saddened her to see it.

She couldn't help but think of William. He'd never wanted anything from her, other than honesty and companionship. He'd stuck by her not only because it was his duty, but because he wanted to. He believed in her, and not just because she was the Princess.

But none of these men saw that. All they saw was the throne, the title. Even if they had the best of intentions, which she was sure most of them did, they were overshadowed by the glory of it all. "Win the fair maiden's hand and become King!" It was like a fairy tale, come to life.

Reaching the throne, she sat and surveyed the room. Lili stood off to the side with Anastasia's new guards, whispering. The men had clustered together in the large room, staggered expressions of awe and mischief on their faces. Anastasia almost didn't want to tell them the truth. They were all so innocent now, trusting, excited. It didn't feel right to take that away from them. Even though she knew she had to, to keep them safe.

"Some of you might have heard of killings going on through the realms," she said, without preamble. "There is a murderer out there, hunting down individuals of pure bloodlines, with strong connections to their realm."

A few gasps went through the men.

"You all have ancient bloodlines, that can be traced back to the beginning of Jacqueline. As such, I am hereby placing you under royal protection. You will be moved into the castle immediately, and royal guards will escort you anywhere you'd like to go, so long as you remain on the premises. Your things will be sent here, and your needs will be looked after."

She expected an uproar. These men were being plucked from their homes, taken from their families, and moved into a strange location. Instead, they seemed to be treating it like an extended vacation.

"Who will be picking up our things?" one of them, Thores, asked.

Anastasia considered him for a moment. He was from Atil, down in the southeast of Jacqueline. She knew him to be staying in the inn in town, with at least two others, one from Eun, also in the southeast, and one from Girrun, in the north. They would need more than what they'd brought with them to Sehir.

"If you give a list of necessary provisions to the royal chamberlain, we will see that they are picked up from your homes."

Gerrard stepped forward. "And what of our families?"

"If you have any siblings, please also alert the royal chamberlain. They will need to be brought to the castle, as well. As for your parents, grandparents, or extended family, they are all safe. The killer is only going after young people."

Murmured discussions sprang up just as Celia entered the room. A few of the men made a break for her, rattling off their lists of needed provisions. The other men waited until Anastasia came down from the dais to speak with her. Gerrard caught up to her first and joined her as she moved through the room.

"Just how much danger are we in, Princess?" he asked.

She frowned. "The threat is serious, and we are backing the killer into a corner by taking away the final piece they need for their spell. You should not take it lightly."

Thores came up on her other side. "Just how long will we be staying in the castle, Your Highness?"

"Until the threat has abated."

"How will you know when it has?"

She sighed, and then raised her voice so everyone could hear her. "If you have any further questions about what I have just told you, please hold them until this evening. We will hold a welcome feast for everyone, and the floor will be open for discussion."

Offering a quick smile to Gerrard, she stepped out into the hall. Celia stayed behind to take down their provisions, shooting Anastasia an impatient glare as she left.

Ignoring the men's startled, anxious expressions, Anastasia moved away from the throne room. Her new guards surrounded her in the hall, making a kind of shield around her. She took them in, all wizened, older warriors, dressed in their violet doublets with slashed silver sleeves. Their presence reminded her of William, of his time apprenticing as her royal guard. Her chest tightened with sorrow.

Motioning to her regular guard, she addressed the newcomers. "This is Gath and Mortam. They have been with me for a year-and-a-half, now. If you should have any questions, they are the ones to ask."

The older warriors didn't look to pleased having to answer to younger men, but no one complained.

Turning on her heel, Anastasia headed back to her mother's study. The people from the census would be arriving at any time, all throughout the day. She needed to try and gather as much information about the killer before then, so she could answer as many questions at dinner that night as she could.

Gods and Angels, she needed a nap.

CHAPTER TWELVE

Dinner that night was an interesting event. Usually, Anastasia and her family ate together in the dining hall, but that wasn't large enough to house everyone. So, the servants set up the banquet hall, filling the room with food and drink. The twelve ancient families of Jacqueline gathered around the table, seemingly speechless in the presence of the entire royal family. Anastasia sat at the head, flanked by her aunts. Bale and Graham sat opposite each other, while her father sat at the other head.

"Did you manage to get everyone?" Calla conversationally questioned as the servants brought out the salad course.

Anastasia frowned. "There were a few I couldn't."

She hadn't been able to locate Durse Follant. Thankfully, he didn't have any siblings. She'd sent word to Dani and Hayde out in the Sand Isles, requesting that they return to Sehir as soon as possible, but she hadn't heard back yet. Chris was safe enough in the dungeons, and she'd brought his sister into the castle. But William was still missing.

"Not to mention," Celia interjected. "It gets a little hairy when you try to trace back marriage records. Just to be safe, we rounded up everyone that could possibly be related to the twelve ancient houses."

Which left them with thirty-three people staying in the castle. She'd rounded up Gerrard's three sisters and his four age-appropriate cousins, two Dinas cousins, six Woodsmans, one Toldens—a distant relative of Warrior Surreg Toldens—Ericcen Ros and his two brothers, her Great-Uncle Bale's three grandchildren, five Bellvies, four Cardens, and a Sophine. It was safe to say the room felt cramped. Thankfully, the castle had more than enough room to fit them all.

It was interesting to ponder. Anastasia had never before known about the ancient houses, nor had she really stopped to think about it. These people could trace their ancestry back to the very beginning of Jacqueline, and yet none of them had seemed to know it. Now they knew. Now they were marked. Vaguely, she wondered if any were Ancients. But without the List, she couldn't possibly know.

Thores, the young man from Atil, cleared his throat. "So."

He sat with his three cousins, all younger than he. Though they had a few similar features—such as the shapes of their noses and the fullness of their cheeks—they didn't remarkably resemble each other. Unlike the Bellvie siblings across them from who looked like they could be quintuplets.

"You said we may voice our concerns, or questions, rather, at dinner." He opened his arms. "Well, here we are."

Anastasia inclined her head. "Yes, you all may ask any questions you have."

Little Kane Woodsman, seated a few people down from Anastasia, popped up. "Is it hard being a princess, Princess?"

Thores made an exasperated noise in the back of his throat. "Are you serious?"

"I just wanted to know."

Kane shrank back. Beside him, Chris's sister, Alex, rounded on Thores. "Are you always so rude, or is this special because you're in the castle?"

As they fell to arguing, Anastasia blew out a breath. She'd severely underestimated what it would be like to have a group of people, their ages ranging from Kane's thirteen years to Ryke Toldens' twenty-four, gathered together in such close quarters.

Thores vehemently shook his head. "I want to know when we'll be able to return home!"

A few of the others nodded in agreement.

"I've been away from home for weeks, now."

Gerrard chuckled. "And what did you think would happen if you and Princess Anastasia hit it off and you became King? That you would both go live in Atil together in your parents' house?"

Thores looked uncomfortable. "Well, no, but—"

"You should be looking at this as an adventure," Ryke Toldens intoned.

"But this isn't an adventure! We're being hunted!"

Ryke shrugged. "Either way you're staying in the castle with a chance to not only spend time with the royal family, but also woo the Princess. I'd say, kick back and relax before she realizes you're not worth it and delivers you to the killer on a silver platter herself."

Thores turned fearful eyes on Anastasia, as though thinking she would actually hand him over to the killer. A handful of others joined him. It was at that moment that Anastasia realized that her people didn't know her, not really. She'd been gone for ten years, and in the time since she'd returned, she'd spent most of her time with other royals. Not a single person in this room, outside of her family, truly knew her.

She vowed she would change that. She'd make her aunt put it on her schedule if she had to. The royal family used to spend time amongst their people during celebrations, and she remembered a time when her grandparents would have people over for dinner. Why hadn't she and her parents reinstated that practice when they returned? True, the threat of Adrian and the Shadows, and her illnesses, and the attempted poisoning of her family during a feast had thrown a wrench into things. But this was *Sehir*, the royal city, their home.

Pushing back from the table, she addressed the room. "I know we pulled you from your homes, your families, but that is for your safety. We are working to identity and apprehend the person responsible for these murders."

Her father nodded. "Once we do, you all will be free to return to your homes."

Thores protested. "Yes, but how long will that take?"

"We don't know," said Anastasia. "But we are doing everything we can to make sure that it happens quickly. Until then, the castle is open to you."

One of Gerrard's sisters inclined her head. "We are very grateful for your hospitality and protection, Your Highness."

A chorus of others chimed in with their thanks. Though Anastasia smiled outwardly, accepting their gratitude, inwardly she felt odd. It was strange, having the power to pluck people from their homes without facing any real resistance. She was just glad her family was here to support her.

Anastasia frowned. "Are there any other questions?"

It seemed that they hadn't really comprehended that they couldn't return home yet; most of their questions were surface ones. Could they go out into the palace gardens? Of course. What would they do for meals? They could join the royal family; they ate at the same times every day. If they missed those, they could always speak to the servants about food. What would they do about their laundry? The servants could pick it up for them and return it, much like they did for the royal family. How could they spend their time? Any way they pleased, so long as they stayed within the castle.

When their questions finally died down, pleasant conversation filled the hall. Anastasia's family excused themselves. She supposed they didn't want to be in a room surrounded by thirty young people any longer than they needed to.

As he pushed back from the table, her father shot her a wink. She grinned, waving at him as he left. Everyone around the table shot to their feet as the royal family rose. It took Anastasia a moment to remember that that was customary. It then struck her as humorous that William and Chris hadn't ever done that when they were together. Perhaps, as warriors, they followed a different training?

Gerrard didn't miss the opportunity to move closer to Anastasia once her aunts had vacated their seats. He scooted closer, bringing his plate with him. She found herself smiling at the action.

"So," he murmured. "This is the castle."

She nodded. "It is."

"Is it uncouth of me to ask how this whole thing will affect your… husband search?"

"Not particularly." She shrugged. "I suppose we'll postpone the whole thing until everything is resolved. It doesn't seem right to continue in light of recent events."

"Right." He whispered conspiratorially, "Don't want to give anyone an unfair advantage."

She smirked. "Yes, that's it."

He sobered, reaching to hand her the decanter of wine. "Just how do you feel about all this? About your family gathering the eligible men of the realm to find you a husband? About the transparency of it all?"

She knew exactly how she felt about it. But she couldn't very well tell him that she had no intention of marrying any of them. She took the decanter from him, busying her hands to buy some time. But as her hand brushed his, her entire body froze. She had a but a moment for concern before an image exploded in her mind:

We stand together at the water's edge. The sun has barely risen, its soft light filtering through the clear sky. It's breathtaking. Gerrard takes my hand and warmth spreads through me. I look over at him, marveling at the way the light plays upon the stubble along his jaw, the way it makes his dark hair shine.

"What are you thinking?" he asks me.

I smile. "I love you."

"I love you, too."

A noise down the bank draws our attention. I watch, filled with a supreme sense of rightness. I feel whole, swollen with happiness. This feeling grows as Anabel races up the bank, holding a paper boat.

"Mommy! Mommy, look!"

She looks so much like my mother it astounds me. But there's a little bit of Gerrard in there as well, with the turn of her mouth, the slope of her nose. And when she careens into me, shoving her boat into my face, I see a little of my grandmother, as well. She laughs, and I nuzzle her neck, earning squealing laugher.

Anastasia came-to with a startled breath. She stared at Gerrard, alarm flooding through her. Had that been a premonition? It surely had been the future. They were married, had a child… did that mean she was going to marry Gerrard?

"Are you all right, Your Highness?"

She quickly shoved her panic away, forcing a smile to her face. "Fine."

Pouring herself some wine, she took a long drink, collecting herself. She needed to talk to Valdon. He could have an answer about this.

"As far as your question goes," she said, glad her voice didn't waver. "I don't mind the transparency. It gives us a chance to be honest with each other."

He considered her for a moment. "I guess you're right."

Seeing an open seat across from Anastasia, Ryke Toldens dropped into it, a grin on his face. He was muscular, with broad shoulders and thick, curly red hair. And though he didn't resemble his distant uncle in the slightest, there was a familiar gleam in his eye that was usually present in Surreg Toldens.

"I see you're monopolizing the Princess, Tomlin," he intoned.

Gerrard flashed a sly grin. "I saw an opportunity."

"Do you two know each other?" Anastasia questioned.

Ryke laughed. "We're neighbors. Our families have lived next door to each other probably since the beginning of time."

Though Ryke was joking, Anastasia figured it might be true. Both families were old. Come to think of it, most of the people around the table seemed to know each other in one way or another—even the ones that didn't live in Sehir. She wondered how much of it was because of their families. She didn't know the history surrounding the founding of the realms—having heard stories of Queens and magic as a child—but she supposed the twelve ancient families must've known each other at that time. Prior to the founding of Jacqueline.

Anastasia turned to Ryke. "So, what do you do?"

He smirked, pulling up the left sleeve of his tunic to reveal an orange tattoo. "Warrior strategist, Your Highness."

"Though why they let him plan anything, I'll never know," said Gerrard.

"You're one to talk! Your first building collapsed!"

"It was a blanket fort and I was seven."

Ryke shook his head. "We lost a good stuffed animal that day. Poor Giffy."

Anastasia raised a brow. "Giffy?"

"It was a capras whose fur would change colors with different temperatures. Tomlin, here, took it everywhere."

Anastasia chuckled. A little part of her was jealous, however. These people had childhood memories, stories of scrapes and pretend games, of sneaking out at night to play, of daring each other to try and climb the temple tower in town. Anastasia's childhood was filled with learning, of books and scrolls, of memorizing history passages and vocabulary words, of being groomed to take the throne.

She had memories with Vlad and Mohan, of course, but those ended abruptly the night her grandparents were killed.

Shaking herself out of her reverie, Anastasia looked around. Everyone seemed ready to turn in. She understood; it had been a long day. But she'd forgotten that they couldn't leave until she dismissed them. There were a lot of customs she didn't remember.

"Everyone," she called. Attention immediately went to her. "You are more than welcome to retire to your rooms if you wish."

Ryke leaned forward, a rakish smile tugging his lips. "And where are *you* off to tonight, Your Highness?"

"Sleep," she deadpanned.

He shook his head. "I sincerely doubt that."

But he didn't press her. Instead, he held out his hand. She took it and he pressed his lips to her fingers. Before she could pull away, her entire body froze again, like it had with Gerrard. Panic fluttered in her chest, but she was unable to do anything about it as an image exploded in her mind:

A dagger soars by my face, so close I can feel its wind upon my cheek. I lean away, avoiding the blade, just as another flies towards me. This one I catch, feeling the vibrations through the metal as I clasp it between my flat palms. A shout sounds across the field and Ryke launches himself at me. I barely have time to flip the dagger in my hands before he is upon me.

An expert strike to my wrist forces me to drop the dagger. I block his next assault with my free arm and turn to sweep his feet out from under him. He leaps before I make contact, but I land a square hit to his chest. He stumbles backwards and wraps a hand around my wrist, tugging me with him.

I jerk away and move back, gaining surer footing. We circle each other, and I catch my breath. My body is thrumming with adrenaline. I breathe deep, inhaling the rich scents of the damp forest around us. We're both slick with sweat, but neither of us particularly minds. Besides, taking a trip to the Air Lake afterwards is part of the fun. I can imagine him, shirtless, standing at the edge of the Lake, surrounded by the cottony banks; a thrill goes through me.

He lunges, and I nearly miss my footing avoiding him. He gets a few good hits in before he suddenly twists and goes down. We're tangled in each other, so I drop to the ground with him.

We roll through the mulch until finally coming to a halt. Gently, he runs a hand down the side of my face. I look up into his large brown eyes and feel my heartrate pick up as he leans towards me. He presses his lips to mine and it takes all of my self-control to not lose myself in the kiss. Instead, I feel around in the dirt until I unearth his dagger. Pulling back from him, I press the blade to his throat.

He concedes with a groan, rolling away from me. "You'll be the death of me, Anastasia."

Anastasia came-to with a gasp, unnerved that she was still looking into Ryke's eyes. Pulling her hand away, she offered a polite smile. Had that been another premonition? It couldn't have been, seeing as Ryke had had a tattoo of Anastasia's name over his heart—a token of marriage. She couldn't be married to both Ryke and Gerrard. So what was going on? Shaking her head, she pushed back from the table. She really needed to meet with Valdon.

CHAPTER THIRTEEN

The day of William's birthday found Anastasia in the castle gardens taking tea with fourteen other women. They tittered as they sat in the shade of the hedges, talking of nothing of importance. Anastasia was reminded of the time she and Ostana had tea outside. It had ended up with them splashing together in the fountain to cool off. The memory left a bitter taste in her mouth.

The ceremony that morning, for little Aagney's christening, had been lovely. It had been short and intimate, with only a handful of other royals in attendance. Ostana's family hadn't shown up, not even her sister Kanna, with whom Ostana was close.

Mohan had been named the godfather, and during the ceremony, he and Anastasia had both taken turns holding Aagney, who had slept through nearly the entire service. When he finally did open his eyes, however, Anastasia saw that they were the exact same shade of brown that Aatu's had been. She knew Mohan had noticed as well, by the way his face had tightened when the priest passed him the baby. The tears she'd cried then had been real.

"Your Highness?"

Anastasia looked up, shielding her eyes against the harsh summer sunlight. Gerrard's twin sister, the one she'd seen at the summer solstice, stood in front of her, holding a deck of playing cards.

"Would you like to play?"

She stared at the young woman. Today had been hard enough, simply being the day that it was, but then there was the added upset from seeing Ostana. She was in no position to be good company, understanding that nothing was likely to pull her from her sour mood. And yet, she owed these people, for uprooting their lives.

Offering a wan smile, she said, "Sure."

The young woman, Alviva, sat across from Anastasia. A handful of others gathered around, filling the small table. Alviva shuffled the cards and then handed them out, her thin fingers gently handling the hand-painted cards.

Grabbing her cards, Anastasia looked at the other women. She'd had Lili quiz her on all of their names, just to be sure she remembered correctly. Thankfully, the men were on the other side of the gardens—firing bows and arrows at targets—for Anastasia couldn't quite get the Bellvie names quite right. There was something about all their names starting with a "C" that completely threw her. She grinned as she imagined their parents calling them all by the wrong names.

"So," Alviva intoned. "Does anyone else think Ryke is the best-looking man they've ever seen?"

Joslyne, one of Great-Uncle Bale's grandchildren, snorted. She was one of the older young women, approaching her twenty-third year. "He may be the best-looking, but his attention span could use some work, if you ask me."

"So what if he has roaming eyes?" Alviva's sister, Ayvery, said. "You're not marrying the boy."

Alviva frowned. "But isn't that the point? To get married?"

"Not to Ryke Toldens it isn't."

Joslyne nodded. "Aelnold Ros is more my speed, anyways."

Ayvery wrinkled her nose. "Aelnold? Seriously? He looks like a stick with fur."

"Yes, well, he's still better than Thores Carden. Who, might I add, sounds like he's holding his nose every time he talks."

As the young women fell to discussing the various young men that were staying in the castle, Anastasia felt herself feeling a bit lighter despite herself. She'd forgotten what it was like to sit and gossip with girlfriends. The last time she'd done that had been with Ostana. But back then, she hadn't really had anyone to talk about except Aatu. And that was awkward, discussing someone's own brother with them.

It was mind-numbing, in a good way, and made great background fodder for their card game. Plus, it didn't seem like any of the girls were letting her win, which was nice. She ended up losing her first hand, which made her enjoy the experience all the more.

Towards the evening, the men joined them. Their card game grew ridiculously large, so much so that it took nearly fifteen minutes for them to get halfway round. But Anastasia found she didn't mind. They discussed normal things, like their jobs, or their pastimes—Ayvery and Joslyne were in the same dance class that William's mother used to teach. By the time darkness rolled in, they were sitting in the light spilling from the castle windows discussing what the Gardens of Luas looked like.

They'd all seen it when they received their tattoos, but all they'd ever seen was what they called the entrance hall, the inside of the tree trunk with the wooden thrones. They speculated what was beyond the hall, what kind of riches and beauty awaited them upon their deaths.

As a group, they headed inside for dinner. Anastasia excused herself, glancing at the moon. It was already almost too late.

Rushing up to her room, she grabbed a traveling cloak and the basket she'd prepared that morning before the christening. On her way out, she dismissed all of her guards but Gath and Mortam. What she was about to do didn't require an audience, and she didn't trust her newer guards the way she trusted Mortam and Gath.

Sneaking past the dining hall, Anastasia headed out into the city. She skirted the marketplace and the residential area, coming up on the forest. It was a short walk from there, and she quickly spotted the Small Hall at the warrior training grounds through the trees.

Turning left, she headed deeper into the forest. Mortam and Gath drew their swords, huddling close to her in the darkness. Though she knew this was a risk—as she was one of the ancient families of Jacqueline, and likely on the killer's list—she knew this was something she needed to do. As much for herself as for anything else. She needed this closure, the small sort of celebration, to move past the darkness strangling her insides.

Reaching the precise spot, she dropped her basket. Pulling out some bread and cheese, she lit a small candle and sat down in the dirt.

"Blessed day of birth, William," she whispered into the darkness.

Crossing her legs, she picked at her bread. Her stomach churned, thinking of where he could be. The wanted posters throughout the city certainly didn't help things. She wished she could pardon him, bring him home, but not only did she not have the power—as the *acting* Queen—but she also couldn't risk the questions it would raise. She needed to keep the alternate universes a secret for as long as possible.

She imagined what it would've been like if he *had* been pardoned. They could've had a small celebration with his family and friends, with food and games. It would've been simple, compared to her own birthdays, but it would've been all the better for it. She could've given him a new dagger, to replace the one he usually kept hidden in his boot but had lost during their last battle. Reaching into the basket, she pulled the dagger out.

"I had this made for you," she murmured, "while you were in prison. I was going to give it to you when you were released."

"That's very kind of you."

She whirled around, her heart leaping into her throat; she hadn't heard anyone approach. When she spotted the intruder, however, her heart jumped for a different reason.

William stepped out of the shadows, a smirk tugging his lips. A strangled noise left Anastasia's lips as she flung herself at him. His arms went around her, holding her in a fierce embrace. She breathed in the scent of him—smoke and the exotic spice of the Fire Lake—and relaxed for the first time in months.

"What are you doing here?"

He stepped back and cupped her face. She leaned into his touch. "A little birdie told me I'd find you here."

"You can't risk yourself like that! What if someone had been here to arrest you?"

"It was safe, Anastasia. I made sure before I came."

Anastasia. Her name fell from his mouth so easily. There was no formality between them, just mutual respect.

She shook her head. "Where have you been? What have you been doing?"

"Hiding, mostly."

"William," she chided.

He grinned. In the months since she'd seen him, he'd grown a beard and let his hair grow long. She reached out and ran her hands through the soft golden strands. He just stood, staring at her. Vaguely, she wondered if she looked any different to him. But before she could say anything, a flash of smoke brought a letter. It hovered between them, insisting Anastasia take it. When she didn't, William frowned.

"Are you going to answer that?"

"I'd really rather not."

Slowly, William reached out and grabbed the letter. It was sealed with the Jacquelinian royal seal, which meant it either came from her father or her aunt. Despite the foreboding feeling the knowledge brought, she still didn't take the letter.

William's hazel eyes scanned the parchment. His expression darkened within seconds and he handed the letter to Anastasia.

"What?" she asked. "What happened?"

Glancing down, she scanned the first few lines. She went hot and cold all over as the words sunk in. *The werewolves have declared war on Jacqueline. They are moving their warriors into the realm.* She looked up at William, feeling like someone had plucked her out of the real world and shoved her into a dream. It couldn't be real. The realms hadn't gone to war—without the effect of the Shadows—in centuries.

Stepping back, William unwrapped the dagger. Sliding it into his belt, he stepped up to Anastasia. Wordlessly, he pulled her to him, pressing his lips to hers. Anastasia tried to savor the moment, the feel of him against her, the scratch of his beard on her cheeks, but it was over too quickly. Her head spun. She tasted tears but didn't realize she'd started to cry. They were at war. Her realm was at war. Against the werewolves. Aatu's father had declared war and was moving to attack the city.

"I love you," William said.

Anastasia looked up at him. "I love you, too."

Abruptly, she turned away from him. She didn't look back as she moved away, knowing that if she did, she'd start to cry in earnest. Instead, she made her way to Gath and Mortam, marching through the forest. Thankfully, they'd stayed a good distance from the clearing, so they hadn't seen William.

They were in earshot now, and she overheard them discussing the guard surrounding the castle. She was about to comment when a hand clamped over her mouth. Thinking it was William, she didn't struggle. But then, she saw William picking his way through the trees some yards away. Shock shot through her, and she wrenched against the hands that held her.

"Don't struggle, Anastasia."

The voice was familiar, friendly even, but there was something twisted about it. Something that made the hair on the back of her neck stand on end.

Something pricked her neck. She tried to scream past her attacker's hand, but the forest swayed around her. She dipped and turned, stumbling, trying to fight back against the darkness closing in. But it was useless. It dragged her down, until she saw no more.

***

She awoke some time later, entirely disoriented. When her vision finally cleared, she struggled to make sense of her surroundings; it seemed the ground was the sky and vice versa. Otherwise, everything seemed fine. But then the pain came. She cried out as fire tore through her ankles. The darkness threatened to take her under again, but she fought it back.

Laughter reached her ears. It brought her back, grounded her in reality. Then, finally, it made sense. She was pinned upside down.

"You're faring better than the others."

Squinting through the pain, she saw a figure before her. It was distinctly male, but she couldn't see him well enough to discern his identity. Something about his words gave her pause. *The others.* He meant the others he'd killed. This was the person murdering someone from every realm, the person taking their DNA to use in a spell. Panic overcame her, until she realized that her back didn't hurt. He hadn't taken anything from her. At least not yet.

Another wave of pain crashed over her and she whimpered. What had he done to her ankles? Struggling, she lifted her head. What she saw drove the air from her lungs. Her ankles were a bloody mess, nails sticking straight through them.

Bile coated her throat. Her vision flickered. Again, his laughter brought her back. There was something eerily familiar about it. But where had she heard it before?

Something in her mind clicked and she thought back to one of the first premonitions she'd had, the one that made her think William was trying to kill her: *Excruciating pain. My vision falters, fading out and in. A flash of deep blue; a flash of red. Laughter, maniacal. I fade out. Agony shoots through my ankle. Iron grips me, caging me upside down.* This was the blue-eyed sorcerer, the one she'd been seeing since she arrived in Sehir. He was the killer.

"My preparations are almost complete," he said. "What do you think?"

She shook her head. "Where are we?"

"Surely you recognize your own city, Anastasia."

The way he said her name sent chills down her spine. She looked around, finally able to differentiate the ground from the sky, and realized they were in the town square. It was oddly devoid of people, as silent as the grave.

"What have you done to my people?"

He chuckled. "Absolutely nothing. It's late. Everyone *decent* is in bed."

She didn't miss the subtle dig at her being out in the woods so late. Had he seen William? Gods and Angels, William. Where was he? Had he gotten away? Had he seen her get taken? What about Gath and Mortam? Surely they would be looking for her by now. If they were still at the warrior training grounds, they might be able to hear her.

"Help!" she screamed. "Help me!"

"Help! Help!" her attacker shouted, mocking her. "It seems like no one's here to hear us."

She glowered at his form. "Who are you, you coward? Show yourself!"

"If that's really what you want."

He stepped into the light and all the fight left Anastasia at once. She drew a shaky breath, hardly daring to believe her own eyes. But it was him. He looked like he had the last time she'd seem him, but leaner, darker.

"Joey?"

He grinned. "The one and only."

Joey was the blue-eyed sorcerer that tried to kill her in her premonitions. But that didn't make any sense. Joey wasn't a sorcerer; he was human! How could this be? Were her visions wrong somehow?

All thought of her premonitions fled her mind, however, when she saw what he was doing. He held a large syringe in his hand, poised to plunge it deep into her skin. She wrenched against her restraints, crying out as agony tore through her ankles. Tears leaked out of the corner of her eyes, falling up into her hair.

"Don't to this!" she pleaded.

He shook his head. "I thought you were stronger than that, Anastasia."

With one hand, he tore open the back of her dress. Pressing his cold fingers to her bare skin, he probed along her spine. Each touch felt like ice.

Without warning, he plunged the needle into her back. A scream tore from her lips. Tremors wracked her body as a seizing sort of pain flooded through her. She could feel the needle inside her, pushing deep into her back. It felt like the small of her back was on fire.

And then the suction began. She screamed anew, feeling like he was pulling her skin off from the inside out. There was nothing to brace on, nothing to detract from the pain. All she felt was the needle in her back, and his icy hands pressed against her skin. Unconsciousness threatened to overtake her again; she fought it back with everything she had left. She wouldn't pass out. She couldn't, no matter how bad the pain was.

When, at last, he retracted the needle, she started to cry. The pain didn't lessen but continued to throb around the entry site. Joey stepped in front of her, holding the syringe up to his face. She could see her blood on it, along with the spinal fluid inside. Something about seeing it outside her body made her lightheaded. This was *wrong*. Every part of this was wrong. Her body was screaming at her to move, to do something, anything at all, but she found herself oddly immobile. Iciness stole up her legs, clawing for her chest. Vaguely, she realized she was bleeding out.

"This almost feels too easy," he murmured. "But it is necessary. I have just one more ingredient to add, and then the spell will be complete."

She licked her lips. "Are you going to kill me now?"

"You?" He laughed. "Never."

"I'll find you, wherever you go. I won't stop till I do."

"I'm counting on that."

There was a flash of black smoke and then he was gone. Anastasia blinked, wondering if she was delirious. People didn't just vanish into thin air. But then her mind quieted. This was a nice way to go, she supposed; quiet, gentle. Sure, the way she got to this point hadn't been, but that didn't matter, now.

Something jostled her, but she didn't have the energy to scream any longer. She just let the pain ebb and flow, coursing through her. Something gold flashed across her vision, followed by more pain.

"Stay with me!"

This voice was familiar as well, but she couldn't place it, either. It made her feel calm, though, despite the circumstances.

"You stay with me," it commanded.

And she wanted to. She really did. There was something so pleasant about the voice; she wanted to do whatever it told her. But she couldn't cling to awareness anymore. The pain was too much; the blood loss made her fuzzy. She tried to mumble an apology, but her mouth didn't respond. She supposed that was for the best; she tasted blood on her lips. Funnily enough, it reminded her of when Aatu died, when she kissed him. Now she was to do the same.

CHAPTER FOURTEEN

William ran. Cradling Anastasia to his chest, he pushed himself faster and faster, but it wasn't enough. He could feel her fading, her body growing limp in his arms.

He thought back to when she'd fallen unconscious after their fall from the Sky Temple. Then, he didn't think he'd ever been so afraid for her life, so worried about her. Now? This was undoubtedly worse. Then, she'd just depleted her energy using magic. Now, she'd been tortured, her ankles nailed to a post. And that was just what he'd seen when he ran up towards her. The back of her dress was ripped open, blood smeared her back.

Gods and Angels. Whoever did this was going to pay.

Reaching the castle, he sprinted up to the gates. Warriors blocked his path, barring his entry. He wanted to scream at them. Couldn't they see she was dying?

"The Princess is injured!" he shouted. "Someone help!"

The guards leapt forward. One ran towards the castle, while the other helped William with Anastasia. They hurried inside, halting in the foyer. Other guards came running, along with Valdon. Upon seeing him, William relaxed a little. Valdon wouldn't let her die.

"Anastasia!"

William looked up to see the King running towards them. The look on his face twisted William's heart.

Valdon motioned to William. "Bring her to my chambers."

"Get Mistress Miglune!" the King shouted.

Waving his hands, Valdon created a direct portal. On the other side, William recognized Valdon's rooms. They strode through and put Anastasia down on the bed. She'd gone so pale she looked like a ghost upon Valdon's brightly-patterned sheets. Blood trickled from her mouth. William swallowed bile. His heart threatened to break through his rib cage. She couldn't die. She couldn't.

When he reached out to take her hand, he realized his hands were shaking. Had he ever been so scared in his entire life? He didn't think so. The realization shook him to the core. *Save her*, he silently pleaded. *Save her.*

The door flew open and Mistress Miglune strode inside. Her eyes immediately went to Anastasia, assessing her injuries. William was grateful she didn't look at him, for he didn't think he was capable of speech in that moment. Bending over Anastasia, Mistress Miglune pressed her bony hands to her chest. Bright green healers' magic exploded forth, shrouding Anastasia's body. Closing her eyes, Mistress Miglune knelt, concentration making her body tight as a bowstring.

Behind her, Valdon clanked around his room. He went from table to desk, mixing herbs and pastes. King Elliot merely stood in the corner, his haunted eyes trained on his daughter.

The door flew open a second time. Ten guards marched inside, their weapons trained on William. He was so surprised, he actually staggered backwards. The frontmost guard stepped forward and secured manacles around William's wrists.

"William Dinas," she intoned. "You're placed under arrest in the name of the Crown."

Valdon stepped forward, his eyes flashing. "Just what do you think you're doing?"

"This man is a wanted criminal."

William just stood there, dumbfounded. None of this seemed real. How was it that Anastasia was dying, and he was getting arrested, all at the same time?

"He just saved the Princess' life," said Valdon.

The guard fixed a stony glare on Valdon. "I don't care if he saved the Queen. We have orders to arrest him on sight. He is a dangerous man who needs to be contained."

Him, dangerous? William felt surprise leak through him. He'd never considered himself particularly dangerous, unless there was a Shadow at the end of his blade. But, he supposed, that blade could easily be turned on another. He thought back to what it had felt like to wrap his hands around Anastasia's throat, back when he'd been briefly possessed by a Shadow, right in this very room. He would've killed her then, if she hadn't found a way to stop him.

How was it that they were always together when something serious happened? Of all the times Anastasia had nearly been killed in the last year, William had been present for nearly all of them. That didn't give him the greatest track record. But, a small voice reminded him, she had survived all of those encounters. She had to survive this one, too.

The guards jerked him around, dragging him from the room. William glanced back at Anastasia, lying, unmoving, on Valdon's bed. She looked so vulnerable; he just wanted to protect her.

"I'll keep her safe," Valdon vowed.

William nodded, unable to say anything. He wasn't sure what he would do if anything happened to her.

The guards marched him through the castle, towards the dungeons. Everyone they passed stopped to stare at him. A few servants uttered frightened shrieks at the sight of his face. But the whole spectacle only mildly irritated him. None of this mattered anyways if Anastasia didn't pull through. They could leave him to rot in the dungeons forever and he doubted he'd mind very much. Every part of him felt numb, which was probably for the best.

When they reached the dungeons, the guards split in half, guarding either end of him as they moved single-file down the spiral staircase. At the bottom, they frisked him. When they found the dagger Anastasia had given him, he wrenched against their restraints.

"Don't take that!"

The guard holding the dagger spat at his feet. "One such as you doesn't deserve a blade as fine as this."

Opening the door, the guards shoved him inside a cell. He leapt forward, hands curling around the bars. "Please!"

The guard only laughed, tucking the blade into his belt. Anger unfurled in William's chest, bright and raw. He threw himself against the door. The guard flinched back, scurrying from the room. William shook the bars, but it was to no avail.

A weak voice sounded through the darkness. "It's no use. The door is too strong."

William started as he recognized the voice. "Chris?"

"William?"

"You're still in here?"

"Gods and Angels, they caught you?"

William slid down the wall of the cell, shaking his head. "I'm so sorry. I wish we could've come back for you."

Chris let out a brittle laugh. "You were getting grayed out, William. You needed to leave."

Gods and Angels, that felt like ages ago. Had it only been a couple of months since he and Chris had been sentenced to imprisonment? It felt like another lifetime that he'd knelt before the Representatives of Jacqueline in the throne room. Another lifetime since he'd been rescued from being grayed out. And even longer still since he'd last seen Chris, or any of his family.

He ran a hand over his face. He couldn't imagine what this was all like for his father and Dani. They would have to watch as he was grayed out in front of the entire city, and then probably exiled. It was too much.

"How are you?" Chris asked.

William went cold all over. "Anastasia's dying."

"What?!"

"I—I saw her, nailed upside down, screaming. She—he did something to her, took something from her with a needle."

"Who did it?"

William shrugged, even though a wall separated them, and Chris was blind as a bat. "I didn't see."

"Gods and Angels," Chris breathed. "You're sure she's dying?"

William put his head in his hands. "Mistress Miglune is with her now, but she lost a lot of blood. If I had just gotten there *sooner*. If I had caught the guy—"

"There's no use to what ifs."

He was right, of course. But William couldn't shake the feeling. It was a habit, he supposed, after being alone with her all those months, searching for her grandmother. He had been the only one there to protect her; his only job had been to keep her safe. Now, it felt like he'd failed her.

Pushing all of that from his mind, he got to his feet. He needed to have a clear head for whatever happened next. Calling on his training, he compartmentalized his thoughts.

"How are you?" he asked of Chris.

"Still blind, still here."

Pity flashed through William, but he quickly squelched it. Chris had blinded himself in service to the realm. He didn't deserve pity; he deserved admiration. Besides, neither was sure the List had done any real damage to his sight. For all they knew, as soon as they found the person that could read it, he would be able to see again.

Chris cleared his throat. "What's the plan, William?"

"What do you mean?"

"About us? What are we doing, here?"

William sighed. "The same as before. We take whatever punishment the Representatives dole out. Once the Shadows unfreeze, you go free, and I go into servitude."

"This isn't right. We don't deserve to be here."

Though he was right, William knew they couldn't just up and leave. They couldn't live life as fugitives of the Crown. He'd had a taste of it the last couple of months. It was a prison, same as this. They'd be ostracizing themselves from everything they'd ever known. And as much as that didn't seem to matter now, it would later, when it counted. Not to mention, they'd probably never be able to see Sehir, or Anastasia, again.

"You still have a chance to be a warrior again. You won't if you go."

A crash sounded in Chris' cell. "You honestly think I care about that?"

Surprise flashed through William. "What?"

"Anastasia is dying, the Shadows are going to move on the realm, and what are we doing about it? William, we're the only ones that know what's really coming. We have to stop it, before everything we know is destroyed."

"And how do you suppose we do that?"

Steel threaded Chris' voice. "We get the person who broke you out the first time."

William blew out a breath. It had been risky the first time around, especially because William hadn't wanted to leave the dungeons. But he'd been convinced, knowing he needed to do *something* to protect the realm from the horrors he'd seen in the alternate universe. It just didn't feel right, going against the Representatives. But, part of him reasoned, they'd charged him with a treason he didn't commit.

Perhaps the Representatives weren't who he thought they were. Maybe there was more to meeting Representative Zand in the alternate universe than he'd originally thought. Even thinking it felt wrong, like he was turning against a vital part of himself. However, he knew that the part of himself that loved Anastasia, that needed to protect her above all else, the part of him that was a royal warrior, would always win out against anything else within him. That was who he was; not even a graying out ceremony would change that.

Getting to his feet, he went to the door and peered into the dim hallway. Their escape would be complicated, with Chris' inability to see. But they were more than capable of making up for it. Especially with their person on the inside. He only hoped she would be up for the task a second time.

"Alright," he finally said. "Let's do it."

Chris' voice was fainter when he said, "What?"

"We're breaking out of here."

CHAPTER FIFTEEN

Dani just managed to get herself retied to the rope hanging from the ceiling before the door opened. Her feet dangled above the dusty ground, but she knew if she pulled just so on the rope, she'd go tumbling free.

Durse Follant and a handful of his Soster fellows stepped into the room. She tried to read their expressions but found them to be disturbingly blank. What did they want from her? It couldn't just be the locations of the Shadow statues, could it? That seemed too simple, too mundane. Durse Follant was the son of the most powerful warrior in the realms. He had to have another motive for capturing them. Didn't he?

"Dani Dinas," he said, slowly moving around the perimeter of the room.

Dani tried to follow him with her eyes but couldn't turn her body all the way around. "Durse Follant."

"Tell me you're in a cooperative mood."

Dani did the closest approximation of a shrug that she could manage. "I can't say that I am."

"Gods and Angels, you sound like your brother."

A pang of sorrow shot through Dani at the mention of William. The last she'd heard of him, he'd broken out of prison in Sehir. Had he been found? Had he been captured?

Thankfully, no one had been around when she received Anastasia's letter, summoning her and Hayde back to Sehir. Vaguely, she wondered what the necessity was. It couldn't be about William, or Anastasia would've said. Something else must've happened. But what?

She grinned. "I take that as a compliment."

"You shouldn't."

His holier than thou attitude was really starting to get on her nerves. "Either torture me or let me go, Follant. I grow bored of your games."

"I'm not going to torture you, Dani. I don't have a taste for it. But neither will I let you go."

Dani groaned. "So, what? You're just going to leave me here, hanging like a piece of meat?"

"Until you comply, yes."

"Great."

Durse pulled up a chair and sat in front of her. His goons fanned out around the room, leaning against the walls. Dani glared at him. Her arms were starting to ache. When was he going to leave? She'd finally gotten the key finished. All she needed was the chance to use it. But she wouldn't get that with them in her cell. And there was no way she could fight them all off by herself. Besides, she needed to figure out how to get to Mira and Hayde. She couldn't just leave them here.

She needed to do some recon. She'd be lucky if her key fit the locks on the other cells, but she highly doubted that was the case. And the only other thing she had on her was her one crossbow bolt. As satisfying as it would be to pierce Durse's chest with it, it wasn't enough.

"You could just tell me where the Shadow statues are."

Dani frowned. "I could, if I knew where."

"Don't feign ignorance."

Two of Durse's men stepped forward. One menacingly cracked his knuckles. The other just tilted his head and looked at Dani with an expression so calculating it made her shiver.

Dani flicked her eyes to Durse. "I thought you said you weren't one for torture."

"I may not be, but that doesn't mean that *they* aren't."

With a quick breath, Dani clutched at the rope over her head. As the bigger of the two men neared her, Dani moved quickly. Planting her feet firmly on the man's chest, she pushed outward. The larger man stumbled back, while Dani swung backwards. Using her momentum, she knocked the second man to the ground. Durse's other men leapt forward, trying to grab her.

She gave her rope a firm yank; it pulled free from the ceiling beam. She fell, taking the larger man down with her, while she used the rope like a whip and snapped two of Durse's men back. Bending down, she threw dirt into the eyes of the last man. He staggered, clawing at his face with a cry.

Turning, she pulled her crossbow bolt from her headwrap. Durse's men were lying around her, groaning. Stepping forward, she pointed the bolt at Durse.

"Let me out."

Durse considered her. "That's your only bolt. It would be a shame if you wasted it on me."

She worked her jaw. "I said let me out, Follant."

Instead of moving to the door, Durse smiled and got to his feet. Dani took a step back, weighing her options. His men were already recovering. She needed to get out of there. But Durse just moved towards her, a strange look in his eyes.

Dani raised her hands, taking up the fighting stance William had taught her. She ran through the things she remembered about self-defense. Never let your opponent get your back. Use your surroundings to your advantage. Go for the softer parts of the body. Don't aim to maim; just get your opponent on the ground and run. But there was nowhere for her to run *to*.

Before she could say anything, Durse swung at her. She narrowly avoided his punch, leaping aside at the last second. But then all she saw were a flurry of fists. She struggled to block him, feeling herself getting pushed back towards the wall. It was a messy, uncoordinated fight. He punched and kicked, while Dani blocked, working to get a hit in. When she finally saw an opening, she swung out as hard as she could. Durse grabbed her wrist and pulled her towards him, throwing her off-balance. She quickly recovered, kicking out at his knee. He staggered, and she saw an opportunity to move away.

Heaving, Durse held up a hand to his men. "Leave her to me."

Emboldened by his words, Dani wiped blood from the corner of her mouth and leapt forward. Her fist connected with his side, then her foot with his chest. He drew a shaky breath, and she knew she'd winded him.

And then, the miracle of miracles happened: Durse left his side open. Dani lunged, glancing up just as her blow landed. Durse's side was braced for impact, but he grunted as though she'd caught him unawares. He flicked his eyes downward, and Dani realized he was guiding her towards the keys hanging at his belt. All it took was a split second, and she understood.

She reached for the keys just as Durse kicked up dust around them. Her fingers closed around the iron hanging from his belt. He hesitated just the briefest of moments before he swung at her. She braced herself just before his blow landed square in the middle of her chest. Flying backwards, she slid through the dirt and slammed into the wall behind her. Rolling towards the wall, as though in pain, she tucked the keys into her belt. Durse roughly pulled her to her feet; she feigned injury.

"Please," she murmured.

Durse just shoved her towards his men. "Tie her back up. Maybe next time, she'll be more forthcoming."

She hung limply as the men tied her rope to the beam. As they left, she watched them through half-closed eyes. For some reason, Durse was pretending to be a part of the Soster. She didn't know how or why. But what she did know: Durse Follant had given her a way to escape.

CHAPTER SIXTEEN

Anastasia sat in bed, glowering. An Obzymian Medicine Man prodded her, while a Viirean doctor listened to her heart with a stethoscope. Not even twenty-four hours after Joey's attack, King Tamo had put the High Council to a vote, forcing them to evaluate Anastasia's health and her ability to rule. She knew precisely what they would find, and the look on her father's face confirmed it. But it was more than just her epilepsy that ailed her. Her closest friend had nailed her upside down to a post, plunged a syringe into her back, and left her to die.

Her father and Valdon hadn't taken *that* news well, either. In fact, Valdon hadn't said much since, while her father's anger was never far from the surface. They were all frustrated.

The Viirean doctor cleared his throat and stepped back, letting Mistress Miglune step forward. Though she'd been able to heal what Joey had done to her, at least physically, Anastasia knew the royal physician would be unable to cure the problem in her brain.

She wanted to scream. First William had been arrested, and now this. She'd be deemed unfit to rule, she knew. And she had no husband, no heir. Rule would go to Sona, and, in turn, Mohan. For the first time in all of history, a Nadmilise wouldn't be on the Jacquelinian throne. She swallowed back tears at the thought. Now wasn't the time to wallow. No, now was the time for anger, bright and all-consuming.

"Tell King Tamo I demand to see him," she told the Hullenian jhakri.

As he left, Anastasia looked at Valdon. He met her gaze, and she saw her own hopelessness reflected in his dark blue eyes. She swore under her breath.

Pulling away from the Medicine Man, she demanded, "Are you quite finished?"

The Medicine Man inclined his head. "Yes, Princess."

Crossing her arms, she glared at them as they left. She knew she was acting like a child, but, honestly, she didn't care. These were the final moments she had left as the Crown Princess of Jacqueline. She didn't want to spend them surrounded by healers.

"Tamo will call the Council tonight," Valdon said.

Anastasia nodded. "Alright."

"We can fight this, my heart," her father intoned. "There must be another way."

"Tamo has wanted me removed since I first started having premonitions. And, this time, he's right. I have seizures. It is unsafe for me to rule."

"Don't say that."

Valdon lowered his gaze but didn't contribute anything. Anastasia wrapped her arms around herself, sinking back into her pillows. What would become of them when she was found unfit? Would they have to leave the castle? Leave Sehir? Sona and Mohan were their friends. They would give them as much leniency as they could. But would it be enough?

Before she could voice any of her concerns, however, a guard entered and drew her father outside. Valdon just stood silently at the foot of her bed. She wanted a reaction from him, anger, sorrow, despair... but there was only silence.

"Why didn't I see this?" she asked him.

He shook his head. "I don't know."

That was such a fitting answer. For as long as she'd known him, Valdon had always held all the answers. He knew how to find her grandmother, he knew all about the premonitions, he knew the right herbs and remedies to heal. But he didn't know how to fix this mess. It seemed his reign of wisdom had finally come to an end.

Her father's voice carried through the door as he shouted angrily. Confused, Anastasia threw back her covers. Valdon helped her to stand, leading her to the door. She opened it and stared at her father.

She'd seen Elliot Piliar livid only four times in her life. One was when she was really little, and she'd gone missing outside. The second was when she'd snuck out of the house and nearly been captured by a Shadow. The third had been the night they returned to Sehir. And the fourth was the day they'd been attacked by rebels during the Head Warrior tournament. But this?

She'd never seen him like this before. He paced back and forth, looking ready to throttle the guard beside him. Anastasia was so surprised, she took a step back.

"You cannot be serious!" Elliot thundered. "Who does he think he is?"

The guard cowered. "I don't know, Your Majesty."

Valdon braved Elliot's wrath, putting a hand on the King's shoulder. He hardly even registered the touch. "What's happened?"

"Tamo is claiming Niboki is to succeed Anastasia."

Anastasia sucked in a breath. "What?"

"The High Council voted, almost a year ago, to give Aatu partial control of Jacqueline. When he and Anastasia were married, a clause was put into their marriage contract that stated if anything should happen to Anastasia, rule would fall to Aatu."

Valdon nodded. "We knew this. As he was her husband, he should have the right to rule."

"Yes, well," Elliot seethed, "apparently, Tamo has made it so the clause remained in effect, even after Aatu's death. As Niboki is succeeding Aatu, and he was engaged to Anastasia—"

"He can take the throne," Anastasia breathed.

A sharp ringing in Anastasia's ears blocked out whatever her father and Valdon said next. Niboki was taking the High Council *and* Jacqueline from her. No. That wasn't right. *Tamo* was taking them from her. As retribution for Aatu's death. She shuddered. She knew he would show them no mercy. She and her family would be cast out; everything they ever had would be taken from them. He'd backed them into a corner. Vaguely, it dawned on her that this was perhaps the reason Aylen made it easy for her to call off her engagement to Niboki. But she'd never thought her to be so callous before.

Turning, Anastasia made her way down the corridor. She didn't stop, even when her father and Valdon called after her. She just kept walking, putting one foot in front of the other, until she reached the dungeons.

At the bottom of the staircase, the guards stood at attention, bowing to her. If they knew anything about Tamo's plan, they didn't say. They just stared at her, their eyes quickly flicking to and from her ankles. But there was nothing to see, nothing left over from Joey's attack. No, those wounds were internal, wringing her heart until she was sure there was nothing left.

"Open William Dinas' cell," she commanded.

The guards traded surprised looks. "Are you sure, Your Highness? He was arrested for—"

"I know full well why he was arrested."

She didn't ask again. One of the guards stepped forward, unlocking the door. Anastasia strode inside, tears already stinging her eyes. William turned as she entered, surprise filling his face. Wordlessly, Anastasia threw herself into his arms. He held her tightly, not saying a word.

"Niboki is going to be named the Crown Prince of Jacqueline."

William swallowed. "I get grayed out in a week."

"I have epilepsy."

"The guards took the dagger you gave me."

Stepping back, they looked at each other. So many emotions flooded Anastasia, she couldn't understand how she felt. Instead of speaking, William drew her to him. Tucking herself under his arm, she sat. He slid down the wall beside her, holding her close. They said nothing. Anastasia wasn't sure how long they sat like that, wordlessly staring at the door to his cell. But she didn't think she'd felt so peaceful in quite a long time.

It was dark when her father came for her. He looked between them as they stood, brushing hay from their clothes. Glancing between them, he held out his hand. William shook it, a mutual understanding passing between them. He had Elliot's blessing.

Trying, and failing, not to cry, Anastasia followed her father from the dungeons. They made their way to the High Council chambers, where everyone was already seated, waiting. She took a look at their faces, taking in the way none of them met her eyes, and *knew*. Tamo had succeeded. Niboki was the next ruler of Jacqueline.

"Anastasia," Sona murmured.

But Tamo cut her off. There was no preamble. "You have been declared unfit to rule."

Sona wiped a tear as she got to her feet. "It is hereby this Council's duty to remove you of your title and position. You are no longer the Crown Princess of Jacqueline."

Hearing the words felt worse than imagining them. She felt hollow on the inside, carved out, her insides on display for them all to see. But she didn't cry. She didn't do much of anything. Even when guards stepped forward and grabbed her, even when her father resisted them, even when Tamo shouted that they were all to be confined to their chambers, she did nothing. She let the guards lead her back to her room. She let Lili help her into bed.

Curled on her side, eyes trained on the lamp on the far wall, she didn't even pray to the Gods and Angels. Her mind turned with images of Tamo and

Niboki sitting in her parents' thrones, of them sitting at their dining table, in their studies. And yet, still, she didn't move.

She wasn't sure she'd ever move again.

CHAPTER SEVENTEEN

The week went by in a haze. Servants came and went, bringing food and water, but no one else entered. Even Lili stayed away. But none of it mattered to Anastasia. She sat, staring out her window at what had once been hers, watching the days slip away. She hadn't so much as uttered a single word since Tamo had her locked in her rooms, but her mind turned constantly. It felt like waiting for the other shoe to drop, wondering what his next move would be. Where would they go if they were exiled from Sehir? Nothing was certain. But it was only a matter of time before she and her family were made an example of.

What did that mean of her premonitions? She hadn't paid enough attention, then, but she'd always pictured herself as the Princess of Jacqueline still. Thinking back, she remembered seeing her reflection standing in the throne room, but that didn't mean anything. In fact, none of her premonitions gave her any impression that she was still the Princess.

Wringing her hands, Anastasia stared down at the gardens. She traced the hedges of flowers with her eyes, lost in her thoughts. When the door opened, and a number of Hullenian guards strode inside, she hardly paid them any mind.

"Anastasia, you must come with us."

It took her a moment to realize they were speaking to her. Slowly, she turned, taking in their rust-colored trousers and brown, calf-length kurta tunics. It was so strange to see them in her home, to have them hold authority over her. She just blinked, struggling to understand why they were standing in her chambers.

"King Tamo demands it."

At the mention of his name, Anastasia's stomach clenched. She grimaced, stepping forward, feeling herself slowly fill with a simmering rage; it paled in comparison with the hopelessness inside.

After a week of being confined to her chambers, Anastasia was allowed to leave. She let Lili dress her in a beautiful summer gown. But there was no tiara. When the guards came and unlocked her door, they didn't meet her gaze. She held her head high, despite her shame and sorrow. They led her down the corridor. There were already subtle changes within the castle, such as the vases and tapestries from the Hullenian castle. Anything to do with Anastasia's family or their history had been removed.

When they rounded the corner to the throne room, realization dawned on Anastasia. "No, please."

The guards showed no mercy. "You will join us."

"I can't."

"You will."

The head guard pulled his dagger from his belt and leveled it at her. She was so stunned by the movement that she complied, moving towards the doors. She'd never before been threatened in such a manner within her own home. The startling reality made her head spin. Was this to be Niboki's rule? Threaded with fear and intimidation? Was that how her people would be treated?

Working not to cry, she followed the guards into the throne room. Most of Sehir was in attendance, their eyes trained on where Tamo sat on the throne, Niboki by his side. But their gazes were hostile, their silence radiated tension. She caught their furtive glances and wondered, was it anger for what was happening today, or for what had happened to her family? Perhaps it was both. Today was certainly a difficult day for Sehir.

When her people saw her, they resolutely rose and bowed to her. She was emboldened by their loyalty, and this time, she did cry.

"Be seated!" Tamo demanded.

Her people didn't oblige. Instead, they turned to her. Only after she nodded to them did they take their seats. A little thrill went through her at the sight. But it lasted about as long as it took the guards to seat her at the front of the room beside her father and Valdon. She would get a front row seat for the happenings.

At a wave of Tamo's hand, the doors to the throne room opened with a clang. More guards marched William inside; Anastasia's heart plummeted.

When they reached the end of the room, the guards forced William to his knees. Anastasia couldn't help but remember when he'd been there for his sentencing. Then, he'd refused to meet her gaze, staring defiantly ahead. Now, all he did was look at her. She wanted to go to him, protect him from this, but she'd never felt so helpless, not even when her premonitions were taken from her. Her hands were tied.

"William James Dinas!" Tamo's voice was uncomfortably loud in the silent room. "You have been found guilty of desertion and conspiracy to commit treason against the Crown of Jacqueline! As punishment for your crimes, you shall be stripped of your title as a warrior apprentice."

He waved his hand and Valdon rose. But William didn't look away from Anastasia. He seemed desperate to not break eye contact.

"Just look at me," she mouthed. "Keep looking at me."

Valdon raised his hands; his fingers crackled with dark blue magic. Anastasia's stomach clenched. It wasn't fair. This was the end of William's dreams, all because he'd gone with her to find her grandmother. None of this was right.

Steeling herself, she leapt to her feet. At that moment, three things happened simultaneously: Tamo shouted for guards to apprehend her, Valdon reached for William, and an explosion shook the castle.

Everyone within the hall halted. As one, they turned towards the windows, and Anastasia knew they were expecting the invisible shields to be crumbling away once again. But this time, it looked as though the sky itself was falling, large chunks dropping to the ground. It didn't make logical sense. How could the sky fall? How could it crumble like fractured stone?

Another explosion, this one much closer, rocked the castle. People stumbled and yelled. Anastasia fell backwards, her mind struggling to come to terms with what was happening. William reached for her but was held back by his manacles. The ceiling above them cracked, flecks of rock and dust trickling down. A third explosion rocked the castle; more screams rose up from the people. The floor beneath them rumbled ominously. Anastasia pushed herself to her feet, grabbing at her father.

The rumble beneath their feet grew. Everyone froze, looking down at the floor as a crack fissured its way through the room. A moment later, it crumbled beneath them, plummeting them into darkness below.

A scream tore from Anastasia's throat as she fell. The landing was hard. She jarred herself, rolling unceremoniously through the rubble. Cries of pain and fear filled the room below. Dust clouded the air. Anastasia coughed, struggling to draw breath. People called out to one another. More explosions shook the castle, making it near impossible to gain any footing.

"Dad!" Anastasia yelled. "William!"

The walls around them shook, large chunks falling away. It looked just as it had outside, their surroundings disintegrating into nothing. For a moment, Anastasia considered that she was simply asleep upstairs in her room, for what she saw defied logic.

A loud *boom* sounded, and it was like someone had taken a hammer to reality, shattering it like glass. The walls, the floor, the windows cracked and melted, raining down into nothingness.

And then the people started to shatter.

She screamed again in earnest, but her voice was lost among the thunderous rumbling. Turning around and around, she struggled to see, to orient herself in her surroundings. Everything was crumbling, breaking, falling away until nearly nothing remained. Panic fluttered in her chest, threatening to overwhelm her. What was this? What was happening?

"Anastasia!" William shouted.

She spun, reaching for him. He staggered across the uneven floor, stumbling in his haste to get to her. But they were too far apart. She cried out in horror as he fissured, chunks of him breaking off. He melted before her eyes, melding with the ruins around her.

Unadulterated fear gripped her. All reason left her mind as she looked at the utter nothingness around her. Blackness creeped into her vision. Looking down, she saw herself cracking like dropped china. Falling to her knees, she shrieked. It was a sound of complete terror. But that was no use against the vanishing world. She seemed to break into a thousand pieces, ripped through reality.

CHAPTER EIGHTEEN

There was fear, worry, and confusion. There was cold and wind. Waves crashed. Anastasia rolled over. A cry escaped her lips as pain lanced through her back. It felt like she was dislocating her arm, but they were both in front of her. She opened her eyes.

It took a moment for her surroundings to solidify around her. Stone swam before her, interspersed with flashes of color. Sitting up, she clapped a hand over her mouth. Nausea bubbled up and she vomited everything in her stomach. It was then that she realized she was utterly naked. Rustling sounded behind her. Covering herself with her hands, she turned. But there was no one there. A flash of white in her periphery drew her attention. When she realized what it was, she froze. This couldn't be real.

Getting to her feet, she took stock in her surroundings. It seemed she was in the middle of a gathering hall of some sort, within a castle. Through the high-paned windows, she could see water extend around her in every direction. Wind rushed through the windows, making the room chilled. She glanced around, wrapping her arms around herself.

On the opposite wall, she found a looking glass. Though it was warped and colored with age, she could still make out her reflection. What she saw drew a cry from her lips.

Violet swirls, like those on the royal seal, colored her body from head to toe. Her tattoos were gone, as though they'd never appeared. But most startling were the gossamer feather wings on her back. They rose from between her shoulder blades, tucked neatly around her body. As she turned her body to look at them, they stretched. Startled by the movement, she leapt back. The wings unfurled and carried her backwards with one powerful stroke. Staring at herself in the looking glass, she realized she looked like the Angel Razibelle.

"Gods and Angels," she breathed.

As soon as she thought of closing the wings, they obliged, snapping back around her. Jostled by the sudden movement, she staggered on her feet. What was all of this? Had she hit her head when she fell through the floor? Was this all an elaborate dream?

But then, dawning realization flooded through her. This was Joey's spell. This was what he'd done with the spinal fluid.

Looking around, she made a second startling discovery: small wooden crests, labeled with the names of the twelve ancient families of Jacqueline, lined the tops of the walls. She spotted the crossed swords of the Dinas family, and the plumes of feathers of the Piliar family… this was somehow a Nadmilise castle. What was this place?

Turning, she headed through the main door. A large foyer opened before her. Furs lined the entrance; a circular iron chandelier hung from long chains. A worn tapestry depicted some sort of battle, with an angel-like figure wearing a crown at the head. Vaguely, Anastasia wondered if it was her family pictured. Rough iron sconces held rotted wood torches, leading the way further into the castle. Anastasia followed them, working to ignore the rustle of the wings.

"Hello?" she called. Her voice rang hollowly through the empty halls.

A winding staircase took her up to a floor with rooms. They were sparsely decorated with furs and trunks. At the top floor, she found but one door. Inside was a bed with furs and knit blankets. Old wax hung from alcoves where candles must've burned at one time. A large trunk sat at the foot of the bed. When Anastasia looked inside, she found dusty gowns in the fabrics and designs of ancient Nadmilise. What stunned her, however, were the openings in the back. They were large enough to accommodate wings.

"What is this place?" she breathed.

Selecting a gown that seemed her size, she dressed. It was a simple off-the-shoulder gown, with fabric that pooled at her feet, in faded gray and gold colors. Finding a pair of slippers, she slipped them on. They were a little small, but they would do for now.

She needed to find someone or something to tell her where she was. If this was Joey's spell as she suspected, there should be a reason behind it. So far, she didn't understand.

A noise sounded downstairs. Gathering her skirts, Anastasia raced down the staircase. At the bottom, she stepped off carefully, tip-toeing towards the crashing sounds coming from the gathering room. Peering around the doorway, she found it to only be a bird that had come through the open door.

Breathing a sigh of equal relief and frustration, she shooed the bird out of the castle. As she approached the entrance, she looked out into the fading light. There was only water as far as the eye could see, turning to marshland in the feet surrounding the castle.

She was utterly alone.

Darkness was rapidly approaching. She needed to find light, some food, and search the castle for some indication of her location. Working quickly, in one of the rooms she found a candle that wasn't completely used. Using the top layer of her skirts, she gathered the remaining wax hanging from all the mantles.

Piling it all on the table in the kitchens, she ransacked the cupboards. Thankfully, she found a jar of some dried sort of meat cake wrapped in cheese cloth, hidden beneath a pile of rotting wood. It reminded her of something she'd had in the giants' realm, Obzym. Something called pemmican.

Sitting at the table, she took to fashioning candles. With flint from the fireplace, she managed to light the existing candle. She worked swiftly, taking intermittent bites of the pemmican as she went. Heating the leftover pieces of wax she'd salvaged, she formed them into cylindrical shapes, molded around twined pieces of cotton cloth she tore from the hem of her gown. Conserving the rest of her meal, she tucked the newfound candles into her bodice, grabbed her one lit candle, and headed back into the main floor of the castle.

Darkness settled on the castle. Thankfully, it was nearly a third the size of the castle in Jacqueline, making it less frightening to be alone. Her small candle provided just enough light to see.

She found that keeping herself busy kept her panic at bay. She didn't think about the fact that she'd been removed as ruler of Jacqueline, or that Niboki and Tamo had taken her throne. She didn't dwell on William's imprisonment, or Joey's attack. She didn't think about her family, or the fact that she was stranded in a strange castle on an island. All that mattered was finding information.

Ironically, she discovered an old map in the bedroom where she'd found the clothing. Unfurling the ancient parchment, she blew dust from the pages. A kingdom appeared before her, expertly diagramed.

There were eleven lands, denoted with colors and coats of arms. The most familiar, and the one Anastasia seemed to be in, was Irichat gol Naingeliar. It's coat of arms had the tiara from the Nadmilise royal seal, made with a laurel leaf circlet, as well as a flaming torch, all on a silver and violet background.

Spotting other familiar coats of arms, realization dawned on Anastasia. These were the first realms, back before the creation of the realms as she knew them. This was the time Before, back when magic still lived among peoples, back when Nadmilise were the spiritual leaders of the worlds. Joey had brought them back to an ancient place full of old power and superstitions. But… was it just her here in this place? Or had he brought everyone back with her?

She pictured the way the world had crumbled, the way the people melted. They had to be here somewhere, she just needed to find them.

She needed a boat.

Looking at the other kingdoms, she familiarized herself with the lands. All the realms were represented, but there was an eleventh realm, one she didn't recognize, smack dab in the middle of the continent she was on. And seeing as she didn't speak the ancient language the map was written in, and she didn't recognize the coat of arms, she had absolutely no idea what it could be.

Pushing back from the table, she stood. If everyone else had been brought to this world, as she suspected, they could be anywhere in these lands. The first thing she needed to do was get to the mainland of where she was. The castle was depicted on the map; if she traveled westward, she'd hit land in a matter of hours. But what to do once she found people was a separate question altogether. They needed to return to their home and stop whatever it was Joey wanted from this place. But how?

Absently, she looked over the crests on the edges of the map. It took her a moment to realize that they were decidedly *not* the crests in the gathering room. They were unlike anything she'd seen before.

Seven in total, they depicted strange things like vibrant phoenixes and chains wrapped around crowns. Anastasia studied them, trying to understand what they meant. Beneath them were what appeared to be titles. Seeing one she recognized, she understood.

"The Vatis," she breathed.

These were the crests of the Ancients. She supposed they were not considered so ancient here, in this ancient place. They were probably the predominant families of the kingdoms. She wondered how they coincided, or didn't, with the twelve ancient families of Jacqueline, for these were far older. There were too many questions that needed answering. But how was she to get answers?

Lightning flashed, making Anastasia jump. She looked through the windows, finding a storm rolling in. Quickly, she went around latching all the windows in the castle. By the time she finished, the rain started to come down in heavy sheets. She sat at a window, looking out, watching the way the storm churned the water. Her mind turned to the people that had once lived in this castle—her ancestors, she presumed. The clothes were made for wings. So, had all her people had wings in the past?

Turning, she studied the wings. They seemed to answer her instincts, moving as her other limbs, without any sort of provocation. It was strange, to say the least, and she couldn't quite think of them as hers. She wondered if the Angels felt this way.

Either way, some ancient Nadmilise had lived in this place, probably a distant relation of Anastasia's. It was surreal to imagine that she wore some great-grandmother's gown, sleeping in the same places she had, and yet she knew nothing of the woman. Who else had lived in these walls? Why had they built their castle on an island? What had their lives been like?

She'd studied history with her mother when they were in the human realm, seeing as she'd need the information to rule. But she'd only learned as far back as the founding of the realms. In fact, none of their historical scrolls had any knowledge of the time before the realms; that was why it was so difficult for Knowledgist Woodsman to find anything out about the Vatis. The map was the first piece of information, outside of the List in Chris' head, that gave them any inclination that the Ancients were *real*.

Suddenly, Anastasia made a connection. She didn't need a boat to get to the mainland. She had wings! In response to her thought, they rustled behind her, as though restless.

As soon as the storm cleared, she'd *fly* to the mainland and find her people.

CHAPTER NINETEEN

Daybreak brought about the end of the storm. Anastasia awoke, groggy and stiff, in the main bedchambers. She stretched, and her wings unfurled, startling her. She gave a small yelp, before she remembered what they were. Catching sight of them, and the violet swirls upon her skin, she sighed. Everything in this place was different.

Gathering up the map, she ate a small breakfast of pemmican and headed for the door. The overcast morning gave off pale gray light, but it didn't seem like another storm was imminent.

Clenching her fists, Anastasia steeled herself. Her wings unfurled with a loud flap, nearly twice as long as her arms. Facing west, she took off at a run. The wings caught air and lifted her, carrying her into the air. Elation and nausea warred within her. There was something primal about flight. It struck a chord within her, filling her with an intense sense of *rightness*. Yet, at the same time, it was wrong. She wasn't supposed to fly. Nadmilise didn't have wings.

She squelched both feelings, turning her attention west. Her wings carried her without much thought, and she scanned the water below for any signs of life. There wasn't much to see, other than the occasional tower. She supposed those were to alert ships nearing land. But they were empty.

A feeling of fear started to trickle through her, but she didn't understand why. The further west she flew, the more intense it became, until she didn't have to work not to focus on the feelings her wings induced. It squandered all other emotion, but she was distinctly unafraid. Other feelings, of panic and worry, flooded her, making her stomach roll. What was happening? Why did she feel this way?

She managed to ignore it, and the trembling it caused in her hands, as she spotted land. It came into view through the clouds, shrouded in a thin mist. The houses were mostly whole, like the castle, though showed signs of age. The stone walls around the town were crumbled, some with entire chunks missing. Boats sat along the shore, bobbing up and down on their ties. They were makeshift things, and distinctly old, with rotted flags and deep crevices on their decks.

A little further inland, she spotted people. At last! But as soon as her feet touched ground, she was overcome with warring emotions. Anxious. Frightened. Nervous. Curious. Horrified. They twisted through her. It felt like she was trapped within herself, peering through the haze of feelings, unable to assert her own amongst them. It was then she begun to realize that they didn't feel like her own emotions. But how could that be? How could she feel something other than what she felt? As she struggled to make sense of it all, people called her name.

She looked up, spotting familiar faces. But as they neared, the emotions furrowing inside her intensified. The panic drove her to her knees, while the fear blurred her vision. She cried out, wrapping her arms around herself, begging to make it end. Darkness dragged her under.

***

When she awoke, she found herself on a bed, lying on her stomach. Pushing herself up, she looked around. The inside of the house looked much like the castle, sparse with clear signs of age.

"Your Highness."

Turning, she looked up into Gerrard's eyes. He was covered in swirls as well, though his were the cyan blue his mastery tattoo had been. Thick brown wings stretched from his shoulder blades, nearly brushing the floor as he moved.

"Are you all right?" He grunted and shook his head. "Of course you're not. You're confused."

She blinked. What was going on? Thankfully, the strange emotions seemed lessened, though they buzzed inside her still. A sense of protection vibrated through her, stronger than the rest.

Gerrard sat beside her. Slowly, he touched her hand. The feeling of protectiveness exploded through her, threaded with caution and wanting. Anastasia pulled away from him as though he'd burned her; the intensity of the feelings faded. She stared at him in confusion, her mind struggling to keep up with what was happening.

"What was that?" she gasped.

"We can feel the feelings of others."

"I'm sorry, *what*?"

But the explanation made sense. She wasn't feeling everything that was inside her, and she had no other way to explain it. So… the Nadmilise were empaths. She tasted the thought, turning it around in her mind.

Gerrard looked at her, and she realized he knew what she was feeling. "It's a struggle at first, but within the hour, you should be able to ignore them."

"Who else is here?" she asked.

"The other ancient families."

"My parents? Valdon?"

He shook his head. "It seems this was where our ancestors lived. We found our surnames on things inside the homes."

"Where could everyone else be?"

Neither had an answer. Anastasia took in the room again. So, this part of town was where the twelve ancient families lived. Perhaps further inland they would find others. But it still didn't answer what Joey wanted by using this spell. What was his motive? And how was the man with the black eyes, Adrian, involved?

"We only just arrived here a few hours ago," Gerrard explained. "Perhaps others will arrive later in the day?"

"Where did you come from?"

He frowned. "Sehir."

"You mean you only woke up here a few hours ago?"

"How long have you been here?"

"Since yesterday."

Gerrard sat back. "Gods and Angels."

So, perhaps others would arrive. Could some still be trapped in Sehir? Who had Joey brought here, and why? She shook her head. She was no closer to finding any answers than she was the night before.

"We need to set up food and shelter," she said. "And then we need to go further inland and find others. If we have a central location, we can help everyone."

Gerrard nodded. "There are fish in these waters, and a grove of fruits and vegetables not far."

"Good."

Rubbing the back of her neck, Anastasia stood. How long would it be until everyone arrived here? *Would* everyone arrive here? They could set up a registration center, like they had throughout Jacqueline, to reunite families separated by the Chaos. They could log families, assign housing, hand out rations. Someone else would need to scout the land, find supplies.

She turned to Gerrard. "Who of those with you do you trust?"

"My sisters, and the Ros brothers."

Nodding, she turned everything over in her mind. Absently, she realized her wings unfurled slightly and tightened as she paced, seemingly as restless as she. Those that were less frightened by the current events would be good to forage and fish, others could search the nearby homes. Three groups would need to head north, west, and south—as the castle was the easternmost point—searching for others and taking stock of the town buildings and innards. They needed a more detailed map.

She hoped against hope that William, Chris, and her family were nearby. But, she remembered, there were ten other kingdoms. They could've ended up anywhere in the realm. Surely Nadmilise could not fly those distances?

"Do you have a portal tool?" she asked Gerrard, feeling stupid for not considering it before.

Gerrard frowned. "They do not work here. We tried."

Anastasia swore. It seemed their only choice was to fly. She guessed that would be a good time as any to test the limits of their travels.

"Call everyone together," she commanded.

Nodding, Gerrard headed through the door. Anastasia paced. She had no idea how long they would be in this place. It would take time to set up crops, to hunt whatever wildlife there was, to establish trade. They would be restarting their civilization. Unless the Ancients were the key to ending Joey's spell. There had to be something around that could give her the information she needed.

Gathering her skirts, she headed outside. The ancient families stood in a clump, eerily avoiding touching each other. It seemed that touch intensified a person's emotions.

Thirty-three people stood staring at her. Thirty-three frightened people, some no more than children. All that fear was focused on her; she struggled to see through it, to assert her own emotions among them. Letting out a breath, she worked to remember that she wasn't frightened, only concerned.

"I'm glad you all are safe," she said into the silence.

Thores scoffed. "Safe? You call this safe? We have no idea where we are or how we got here. By the Gods and Angels, we have *wings*!"

Anastasia shut out his panic, keeping her voice gentle. "We are in the Old World before the founding of the realms, the place where our ancestors once lived. And as far as I can tell, it was a spell that brought us here. Which means it can be broken."

"So break it and bring us home!"

"It is not that simple."

Thores' frustration seemed to leech into others. Those nearest him fixed Anastasia with the same hostile glare, clenching their fists. She needed to get control over the situation. Centering herself, she focused on feeling calm, on radiating a sense of peace. When no one else shouted up at her, she felt safe enough to continue.

"I will need to break you up into groups," she said. "Those that feel well enough to travel will join scouting parties. Those that wish to stay here can gather clothing, shoes, food, necessary items from the homes nearby, while others can help gather food from the fields and water."

Thores narrowed his eyes. "And what will *you* be doing?"

"Cataloging everything you bring back to me."

"So we work while you sit around?"

Gerrard stepped up beside Thores. "She is our Crown Princess. You will show her the respect she deserves."

"She is no longer our Crown Princess. King Tamo had her removed from the throne!"

All eyes turned to her. The memory of watching the High Council remove her flashed through her mind. Hurt and sorrow flooded through her. Thores was right; she was no more in charge here than he. But strength and determination trickled through the shroud of upset. As Gerrard neared her, it grew stronger, until it blocked the other emotions. She was the Crown Princess by blood. Divinity flowed through her veins.

"I was removed due to my health," she explained. "So long as I am well here, I will continue to rule."

Gerrard nodded. "All hail Princess Anastasia!"

Nearly everyone around him joined in the chant. All except Thores and his siblings. Anastasia didn't pay them any mind. They were scared and confused. Once they had a good meal in their bellies, and a decent night's sleep, all would be well.

Thankfully, the people divided themselves up for scouting. Gerrard went with his three sisters north, while three other Tomlin women headed south. The Ros brothers set off to the west, all scouting for other people. It was a sight to see their great wings unfurl, sunlight shimmering through their feathers. Anastasia and the others stared as they took off, lifting into the sky with effortless grace.

When they faded from view, the remaining members of the ancient families took to scrounging around the homes and nearby estates. Anastasia sat in the center of the town, scrawling on a piece of parchment.

As the day wore on, she catalogued everything the people brought to her: pemmican, clothing, shoes, blankets, the number of homes. She even managed to sketch a rough map of the city. It was circular, with the castle acting as a tip at the bottom. The further inland, however, the worse condition of the homes. It seemed poverty radiated outward, the wealthier families sitting closer to the castle's island. With a frown, Anastasia noted that on the map, as well, the homes of the ancient families were labeled.

The foragers returned with baskets full of fruit, vegetables, and seafood. It was all wild-looking, but safe to eat. Anastasia rationed them based on an estimated number of people.

At dusk, the scouting parties returned. They were disheveled and travel-worn, but otherwise unharmed. At least twenty others flew in with each group, all tight with nervous energy. Thankfully, they seemed neither surly nor hostile. They had questions, she knew, but they were just glad to have the food she handed out.

"How was it?" she asked Gerrard.

He shrugged. "They were scattered all across the inland. Some were in caves up in the mountains."

She thought it odd that there was a lack of wildlife, but she didn't voice her concerns to Gerrard. Were there no predators here? She'd seen the bird the night before, and certainly the fish in the water, but nothing larger, no game. That could prove problematic in the future.

Someone nudged her. "Your Highness."

She turned to see Ericcen standing behind her, holding out a makeshift torch. "It will be dark soon."

"Right. Thank you."

As they brushed hands, an image exploded in her mind:

Ericcen's head is bent over his work, his sweaty hair falling into his face. As I watch, he impatiently brushes it away with a swipe of his hand. His fingers are grimy, coated with dirt and grease, but it doesn't bother me. In fact, it's a little thrilling, a showcase of his dedication to his craft. I can imagine him scrubbing the dirt clean at the water pump outside, methodically washing away the day. It's soothing.

He doesn't lift his head as he says, "Are you just going to stand there and watch, or are you going to come inside?"

I shrug, though he can't see me. "I haven't decided yet."

Turning, he gives me a brilliant smile. I go to him and he wraps his arms around my waist, pulling me close. I'm not at all concerned that he's getting dirt on my gown.

"To what do I owe this nighttime visit?"

I grin. "I enjoy seeing you work."

"Is that so?"

He pulls me down into his lap and I laugh. His fingers tickle my sides, leaving me breathless. I wriggle away from him and leap to my feet, darting through the smithy. He gives chase and catches me round the middle, lifting me into the air.

A loud cough at the door makes us freeze. "Ericcen?"

Turning, we see his father staring down at us. Ericcen flushes. "Father."

"Have you finished yet?"

"Nearly."

His father gives us a disapproving look. "Better get to it, then."

"Yes, sir."

As Master Ros leaves, I fall to a fit of giggles. Ericcen shushes me, wrapping his arms around me again. I lean into him, breathing in his scent of oil and leather.

"I'll be home when I'm finished, my love."

I press my forehead to his. "You'd better."

Coming-to with a gasp, Anastasia stared at Ericcen. What in the world was that? It was just like the visions she's had of Ryke Toldens and Gerrard. Could it be some sort of premonition? It was good to know that her premonitions still worked in the Old World, but it was a small comfort. Especially given the way Ericcen was looking at her.

"Are you alright, Your Highness?"

Anastasia nodded. "Quite."

Turning, she planted the torch in the ground beside the table she'd erected in the center of town. Looking at her lists, she worked to shove the strange vision from her mind. There were no weapons to be found, but they had enough food to last their numbers for a decent time. She supposed the fields were what supported the majority of the town when their people had lived there in the past. So there would be no shortage of food. But they needed to find everyone beds.

Consulting her list, she thought again of William, Chris, Valdon, and her family. Where could they be? She felt too idle, like she wasn't doing enough to help her people. Sure, setting up supplies was the best thing to do first, but she needed to be proactive.

She waved at Gerrard and he whistled loudly, calling everyone's attention. They gathered around her, filled with trepidation and mild panic.

"Good evening," she said, her voice sounding hesitant to her own ears. "I know things have been strange, but believe me when I tell you that I am doing everything I can to understand what happened to us, and how we may reverse it. For now, we should make the best of our situation." She met their guarded gazes. "Find those that you feel comfortable with and pick a dwelling to bed down in for the night. In the morning, we can pick up where we left off today."

A young woman in the back of the group raised her hand. "What will we do for protection?"

"Yeah!" her friend called. "What will we do if we're attacked?"

Anastasia felt stupid for not even considering attack. Just because it had been quiet since her arrival didn't mean it would stay that way. Mentally, she kicked herself. She hadn't even thought of the Shadows. Would they be unfrozen here in the Old World?

"We can sleep in shifts," she said.

"I can guard first," Gerrard offered.

Ericcen nodded. "I will join him."

Thores scoffed. "That's all well and good, but what do we have to defend ourselves with? A melon?"

"Anything can be fashioned into a weapon if you try hard enough," said Anastasia.

A few people around her tittered. Anastasia wondered if Thores was going to prove to be a problem. It was a new feeling for her, facing a subject that didn't trust her. Which she found ironic, considering Thores had been vying for her hand in marriage. She wondered what had changed so greatly between them for him to consider her a threat. Or, perhaps, he'd always been that way, but was caught up in the excitement of it all?

Thankfully, others offered to take shifts guarding the city. Anastasia took down their names and shift times, trying to stay as organized as possible. If she'd learned anything from her aunt in the last few months, it was that you could always keep a level head if you had a comprehensive list of tasks to complete. It also helped to calm her nerves.

Taking her seat at the table, Anastasia watched the people split off and head into their respective homes. Gerrard and Ericcen, with a handful of others Anastasia didn't know, took up sentry in a half-circle around the city center, guarding the entrance to the residential area. Anastasia stared at their unmoving forms for a moment, letting herself momentarily dwell on William. Not for the first time, she wondered what he was doing, who he was with. Thank the Gods and Angels he hadn't been grayed out. It would give them time to find out who was framing him with treason.

She added that to the list of tasks to accomplish. Alongside discovering Joey's plot, finding her family, and bringing everyone back home.

As the night wore on, and the guard shifts changed, Anastasia felt her eyes drooping. Surprisingly, she found herself wanting for the large room in the castle, the sound of the wind whistling through the windows, the smell of the water thick in the air. It felt like… home.

A loud *crack* sounded through the city center. The guards turned towards the sound, their makeshift weapons—really nothing more than sharpened sticks—aimed at the whirlwind gathering behind them.

In a flash, a handful of figures appeared where the light had been. They stood in a circle, windblown and clearly disoriented. Anastasia rose, reaching for where her dagger would've been sheathed on her thigh, had it come with her to this realm. She swore under her breath wondering why it was that her dagger was always missing. As it was, she grabbed the quill and held it high.

The torchlight flickered and dimmed as the wind dissipated. Trepidation—and fear from the guards—flooded through Anastasia, but she didn't move. The figures approached, until the torchlight threw them into sharp relief.

Anastasia gasped. "Mohan?"

The man standing before her, with snowy white hair and icy blue eyes, opened his arms wide. He wore a majestic sort of robe in rich blues and silvers and held a gnarled cane. "The one and only, love."

Rushing forward, she threw her arms around him. Shock, apprehension, and frustration exploded within Anastasia and she flinched, pulling away from him. The emotions faded, leaving her feeling more like herself. Turning, she took in the others with Mohan. Chris stood behind him, eyes still tightly bound, with rich black swirls spotting his pale skin, and ebony wings stretching from his back. He cradled a baby in his arms, the only natural-looking being among them.

Anastasia hardly recognized Vlad as he stepped up beside Mohan. His skin was ruddy and bloated, his eyes all-black slits. He carried no shadow, and shrank back from the torchlight, fear radiating off of him. A decent ways away, Ostana stood, arms wrapped around herself as though in great pain. Her brow was a long, thick line above her narrow eyes. Her ears sat low upon her head; her curved, yellowed fingernails dug into the skin of her arm. They barely looked like themselves, and they all seemed keenly aware of that fact as they stood, huddled in the street.

"How did you get here?" she asked, avoiding the obvious question of what had happened to them.

Mohan held out his cane; there was a large orb at its crest. "This ugly little thing. Apparently, sorcerers can only do magic using talismans? It's a whole, long explanation."

"Alright."

Mohan took Anastasia's hand and pressed two rings into her palm. Nodding to Ostana and Vlad, he intoned, "They asked for you to hold onto these while… well, while they're not quite themselves."

Anastasia looked down. Ostana's engagement ring and Vlad's family ring sat in her palm, glinting in the torchlight. What in the name of the Gods and Angels was going on? What could make them take off these rings? She knew how much the engagement meant to Ostana, and what Vlad's family meant to him. Clearly, they'd changed just as she and the other Nadmilise had. And from how it looked, it wasn't for the better. Was this Jocy's plan? To weaken them?

"Clarell!" she called.

The nineteen-year-old Bellvie brother trotted over. "Yes, Your Highness?"

"Have the guards return to their posts. I need to speak with Prince Mohan and the others privately."

He bowed once. "Yes, Your Highness."

Turning, Anastasia led Mohan, Chris, Ostana, and Vlad to the ancient Dinas house, the dwelling she'd temporarily taken while she stayed in the city. It was elegantly decorated, with hand-carved tables, and what had once been overstuffed armchairs. Elaborate sconces held fresh torches, providing light in the smaller parlor.

Anastasia could picture William here, walking through these patterned walls. It fit him and his family, which she supposed made complete sense, as this was their ancestral home. Vaguely, she wondered what the castle said about her, about her ancestors.

Mohan led Chris to a chair beside the fire before pulling one over for himself. Ostana and Vlad stood in opposite corners of the house, discomfort and anger radiating from them.

Mohan looked out the window. "Your Highness?"

Anastasia shrugged. "As long as I am well, they continue to have me reign."

The baby in Chris's arms squirmed and let out a cry. Instantaneously, Ostana reached for the baby and then recoiled as though she'd been slapped. Vlad reacted similarly. They both gave off an unmistakable feeling of revulsion. What was going on? Instead of asking, however, Anastasia took the baby from Chris' arms and bounced him until he calmed.

Suddenly, she realized it was little Aagney. Why was he not with his mother? Why did it seem like Ostana couldn't even *look* at her child?

Holding Aagney close, Anastasia turned to Mohan. "What is going on?"

"It seems we are in the Old World."

"I've noticed."

"Yes, but not only are we in the world, but we have gained the attributes of our people of the time."

Anastasia's wings ruffled in response, as though agreeing with him. The Nadmilise were empaths and had the wings of the angels. But what did that mean for the sorcerers? The werewolves? The vampires? Obviously, it wasn't all good.

Chris drew a hand through his overlong hair. "Your rage is cloying."

"Sorry," Vlad and Ostana simultaneously muttered.

Anastasia eyed them, confused. "What's happening here? What is this?"

"They can hardly be in the same room with each other," Mohan explained, for Ostana and Vlad seemed utterly incapable of doing so. "Vampires and werewolves are notorious arch enemies in this time. Their instincts are driving them apart."

"Gods and Angels," Anastasia breathed. Looking down at Aagney, realization dawned on her. "He is part of both…"

Vlad clenched his fists. "I cannot bear to even look at my own son."

"We're monsters," Ostana sobbed.

Shock slammed through Anastasia. Chris turned his head in her general direction, apparently picking up on it. Blowing out a breath, she sat at the rotting table, gently rocking Aagney. Serenity flooded him; Anastasia clung to it like a lifeline. Gently, she brought Chris' hand to the baby, so he could draw from the peacefulness.

If the werewolves and vampires were this bad, she could only imagine what shape the other realms were in. They needed to find a way to return to their world, as quickly as possible. Despite her inner turmoil regarding Ostana, Anastasia couldn't bear to see her like this, torn apart from her family. And they hadn't even stopped to discuss the ramifications of Mohan and the sorcerers' magic. It would take weeks, months, to get between kingdoms, without Nadmilise wings.

"I have some food," she said. "You should stay here for the night and we can revisit this all in the morning."

Mohan nodded. "Sounds good, love."

"Have you seen anyone else?"

Chris shook his head. "We found each other somewhere north of here. There was no one else around."

"People seem to be showing up at different times."

"What do you mean?"

Hesitantly, she told them everything she knew about their predicament, about Joey's spell, about the use of spinal fluid, and of her suspicions about the Ancients' part to play in all of this. When she finished, they sat in stunned silence for a moment.

Chris cleared his throat. "I'd like to see the castle."

"Sure," said Anastasia.

Though she didn't remind him he couldn't really *see* it. She wasn't sure what good it would do him to go there, but she wasn't about to argue.

"If I knew what kind of spell it was, I could try and break it," Mohan grumbled. "Do you know where Joey's got to?"

"I don't."

Chris sighed. "If we could just find the Vatis, we could get the List and bring the Ancients together, to end this."

Anastasia agreed. But it seemed unlikely without any resources. What they needed was Chris' father. He'd been looking into the Ancients, searching for a way to free his son. Unfortunately, it would be like trying to find a needle in a haystack. Their usual methods of communication wouldn't work without sorcerer magic to send them, and portals were tricky without the right ingredients and incantations. Plus, it seemed to weaken Mohan more than before.

A shout outside drew their attention. Leaping to their feet, Mohan and Vlad raced for the door. Ostana caught at Anastasia's sleeve, holding her back.

"You're his godmother," she hissed. "I need you to look after him."

Anastasia looked down at Aagney. She couldn't imagine not being able to be around her own child. Her heart ached for Ostana. Nodding gravely, she met Ostana's pained eyes. "I promise, I'll guard him with my life."

Satisfied, Ostana let her go. Anastasia hurried outside. The guards surrounded a young man, holding him with their pointed sticks. Mohan and Vlad tried to break through their ranks, to no avail.

Clarell glanced over his shoulder at Anastasia, a wicked gleam in his eye. "We caught the treasoner, Your Highness."

Treasoner? As Anastasia approached, she took in the figure of the young man. His silhouette was disturbed by the curve of his long black wings, obscuring his identity. She knew him to be a warrior, by the black swirls across his skin, identical to Chris'. But when he shifted, she immediately recognized him. She knew that stance. And the calm protectiveness and calculating caution emanating from him felt as familiar as her own.

"William."

Anastasia pushed through the guards. As she passed, Mohan wordlessly took Aagney from her. Racing forward, she threw her arms around William. His emotions surged through her, mirroring her own. It was difficult to tell where his ended and hers began. A gasp went through the guard.

"Your Highness," Clarell protested. "He's committed treason—"

"William Dinas is an innocent man," she said.

Chris came around Anastasia's side and held out a searching arm. William grasped his hand, pulling him close.

Clarell stepped forward. "Your Highness, he's dangerous."

"You and the others are relieved of your duties tonight, Master Bellvie," Anastasia intoned.

He looked ready to argue with her, but seemingly decided against it. Instead, he turned and motioned for the others to follow him back to their respective dwellings. Anastasia just stood in the circle of William and Chris' arms, feeling as complete as she had in far too long. Judging by the sense of rightness flooding from them, they felt the same.

Standing there with Mohan, Vlad, and Ostana, Anastasia watched over her small town of people. It was the best night of lost sleep she'd ever had.

CHAPTER TWENTY

It had been a fortnight since Joey had brought them to the Old World. A little more than half of the population of Sehir had arrived in the city called Bahail, and yet Anastasia's parents were still nowhere to be found. Anastasia felt like she was floundering. It was different, when it had just been Gerrard and the others of an age with her. But now, there were adults, people looking to her for guidance. She was just a seventeen-year-old ex-Crown Princess; she felt woefully unprepared for the task.

She wanted, more than anything, to find someone, anyone, to help her. Her first thought was of her parents, or Valdon. She had no idea how long they would be in the Old World, which meant they needed to start preparing for the chance they were stuck here. The second option was to uncover what spell Joey had used and figure out a way to get them home. Searching for her family or the High Council would be moot if they returned home in a week and would have full communications and travel. But, if not, some decisions needed to be made.

Which was why she found herself sitting in the old inn in town. Gerrard and the other carpenters had fixed it up rather nicely. The inside was all dark wood and stone, filled with enough worn wooden tables to seat the entire town. Sunlight filtered through the shattered windows, illuminating the layers of dust and grime.

The twelve ancient families sat to the left side of the room, complete with William, his father, Chris, his sister, and their grandmother, Mistress Woodsman. It seemed Chris' father hadn't arrived, either.

The other side of the room sat the rest of the town. Anastasia faced them from where she sat with Mohan and Aagney. Ostana and Vlad sat on opposite sides of the room, glaring at each other. Their rage at being near each other was palpable; it made the Nadmilise in the inn irritable.

"Let's call this town meeting to order," Anastasia said over the din. Everyone quieted. "There are a few things we need to discuss about the running of the city. First and foremost, I want to make it clear that Prince Mohan is working day and night to find a way to break the spell that brought us here, so we may all return home."

Mohan gave the room a wave. Everyone just looked at him, mild hostility flashing through them. Many were wary of him, considering it was magic that brought them all to the Old World.

"I want to be plain," she continued. "King Tamo and the High Council removed me as the future Queen of Jacqueline. As such, I am no longer the Crown Princess. For all intents and purposes, I am the same as you all."

Mistress Woodsman cleared her throat. "I make a motion to reinstate Anastasia Piliar Moneth as the Crown Princess. Royal blood is in her veins, and we need a tried and true leader during these times."

Shock flooded Anastasia. She didn't think anyone would support her, given her epilepsy. The High Council—the most powerful people in the realms—had removed her title. She didn't think anyone would dare to argue against that.

An older man at the back of the room shook his head. "Tried and true? Bah! She is but a child!"

"She is a warrior and ruler by nature," Mistress Woodsman argued. "I think that is the sort of leader we need during these trying times."

"She let a treasoner free from prison!"

All eyes flicked to William. Dolan Dinas growled, "My son did not commit treason!"

"Pardon me, Dolan, if I don't readily believe you."

"My wife gave her life fighting alongside Princess Anastasia, fighting to free our home from the Shadows. She trusted the Princess' rule, and so do I. I second Jelina Woodsman's motion to reinstate her as the Crown Princess."

Anastasia cleared her throat, overcome by their words. "We shall put it to a vote, then. All in favor?"

The older man at the back of the room got to his feet. "Who's to say we even want to continue with a monarchy? What if we want something different for ourselves?"

"Would you like a democracy, Myris?" Mistress Woodsman demanded. "You want a republic?"

"I wouldn't turn down the option."

"We don't know how long we'll be here. Is now really the best time to destroy everything our people have known since the beginning of time? You're talking about starting over, of foregoing the Gods and Angels, of overlooking the *Book of Order*."

Myris glowered. "It's the only thing our people have ever known. What if we could greatly improve our world, our people?"

"Do you really want to gamble on what ifs?"

"Aren't we gambling as it is, putting a child in charge? A child with a severe illness?"

Anastasia flushed. There it was, the truth of who she was to them. Optimistically, she'd figured her people saw her as Mistress Woodsman did, as the strong, capable, natural future Queen of the Nadmilise. But the reality of it was that her people saw her as Myris did, broken, ill, inexperienced. She hung her head.

Mistress Woodsman frowned. "She hasn't been ill the entire time we've been here. And so what if she is? She is still the most capable of us all."

Dolan Dinas nodded. "All those in favor of reinstating Anastasia Piliar Moneth as the Crown Princess?"

Two-thirds of the people voted in her favor; Anastasia was stunned. They wanted to not only keep the monarchy, but also keep her as their ruler? In her mind, she hadn't truly connected with the people, at least not the way her grandmother did. But, somehow, they trusted her. It filled her with gratitude.

"Thank you."

Mistress Woodsman skewered her with a look. "Lead us well, Your Highness."

Nodding, Anastasia cleared her throat. "Now that that's been decided, we must discuss our next moves."

The people murmured their agreements.

"We don't know how long we'll be here in the Old World. As such, we need to start putting down roots, in case we're here longer that we anticipate. First, we need to instate a Guard. As most of the Royal Guard isn't here, it will have to be on a volunteer basis."

William cleared his throat. "I can work with Warrior Gerris on the Royal Guard, if you'll have me."

His father clapped him on the back. "I can outfit the Guard with weapons."

"Great," said Anastasia. "The next thing is building the marketplace, establishing a bartering system until currency can be made, so we can turn Bahail into a functioning city."

"I can help with the marketplace," said Mistress Woodsman.

Mistress Couland, the master bottler, said, "The Mistresses and Masters can meet to discuss town necessities and report to you, Your Highness, like our own Council of Representatives."

Anastasia nodded. In the early days of the realms, the Representatives met with the crown face-to-face, while the cities established themselves. Now, they just sent letters to her mother, detailing the goings on in Jacqueline. She knew other realms relied on much the same system, though with governors or dukes rather than Representatives. Though it was on a much smaller scale here in Bahail, it would work well.

"That sounds good," said Anastasia. "But the most important thing we need to focus on is sending people in search of the High Council and Representatives. They will have the most resources, and provide guidance through our time here in the Old World."

Lili produced a sheet of parchment and a quill. "You may sign up here to volunteer for either the Guard or the search parties."

Ericcen Ros was the first to sign up for a search party, offering to go forth with his brothers to search for the members of the High Council. It didn't surprise Anastasia; he had a protective air about him.

Despite William naming himself a part of the Royal Guard, a number of young men and women signed up to be warriors. Never in the history of the Nadmilise had people *chosen* their own paths. It was exhilarating to see healers and knowledgists and tradesmen all sign up to become guards.

Chris got to his feet. "I'd like to volunteer to search for the royal family."

Anastasia looked up at him. He'd gotten a haircut since arriving in Bahail, and had shaved his beard, but he still had a length of cloth tied around his eyes. He looked frail, despite the strong wings stretching from his back.

His sister leapt to her feet. "Chris, no!"

"I can go with Prince Vlad, seeing as he cannot travel during the day and will, therefore, be slower and more amenable to my condition. He can guide me."

Anastasia looked at Vlad. "What say you?"

Vlad shrugged. "I don't see why not."

"He's *blind*!" Alex cried.

"His other senses have heighted since he was blinded," Vlad explained. "He will be able to follow me without trouble when we are in the air."

Considering this, Anastasia looked to Chris' family. His grandmother just pursed her lips, watching him. The woman beside her, who had to be Chris' mother, was resigned, her bitter understanding coiled around her like a shroud. Anastasia wondered what she thought of her son's work, of how he always seemed to be in dangerous positions. Perhaps she was used to it, as the mother of a warrior? Somehow, she didn't think so.

Ericcen awkwardly shuffled his feet. "I can leave at first light, Your Highness."

Anastasia glanced at him. "Alright."

The others that volunteered for search parties quickly filed out of the room. Chris remained standing, his fists clenched at his sides, while Alex stood beside him, looking close to tears.

Alex seemed like the only one that truly grasped what these search parties meant. These people could be gone for weeks, for months, if they remained in the Old World. There was no telling what dangers they would come across, or what state the other kingdoms were in. For all they knew, they were alone here in the Old World, trapped within Joey's spell.

She frowned. "Christopher is a royal warrior. If he feels he is capable of searching for my family, then he may go."

Alex glared up at her brother, but, of course, he didn't see her. "How could you?"

Turning on her heel, she stormed from the inn, letting the door slam closed behind her. They all just sat in silence for a moment longer, while Chris' mother and grandmother took his hands.

Ryke Toldens broke the silence by approaching Anastasia. "Your Highness, I've volunteered to be one of your personal guards. Though I am a weapons warrior, I am more than capable of protecting you during this time."

She beckoned William over with a wave. He stood a few inches taller than Ryke but was slimmer than the muscular redhead. "This is William Dinas. He will be your partner."

"So," Ryke mused. "You're the infamous William Dinas."

William frowned. "Infamous?"

"You bested your masters when you were only twelve-years-old. You're the youngest warrior to have ever been accepted into the Royal Guard. Your prodigal work as a warrior is legendary."

Anastasia could feel the embarrassment radiating from William. But she didn't intervene. It would do him some good to remember the kind of warrior he was, the reason she'd wanted him to be her Head Warrior all those months ago. It would do them all good to remember just who he was, to overshadow the dark accusations the Representatives had roped him with.

"Toldens spoke highly of you, as well," William intoned.

Ryke nodded. "Taught me everything I know."

"He's a good man."

As they fell to discussing shifts, Anastasia turned her attention of Myris. He stood at the back of the inn, his arms crossed over his chest. She noticed Thores was with him, radiating anger and discomfort. Something about the two of them together didn't sit right with Anastasia, but she let it drop, knowing they needed to put aside their differences for the betterment of the people.

When the rest of the people filed out of the inn, Lili brought the parchment of names to Anastasia. Nearly forty people had volunteered to search for the High Council and Representatives, including Ostana. They'd all selected quadrants of the ten other kingdoms, leaving Irichat gol Naingeliar for Chris and Vlad. Those that volunteered for the Guard, meanwhile, had indicated their skill level next to their names. Thankfully, Warrior Gerris had offered to give lessons, to bring everyone up to speed.

Now that the marketplace would be taken care of, and Dolan had spoken to another blacksmith about creating coin currency, it seemed life in Bahail was looking up. It filled Anastasia with warmth, that not only had her people *chosen* her to lead them, but that it seemed like they would succeed.

Cradling Aagney in her arms, Anastasia followed Mohan and Lili from the inn. The realization that she was again the Crown Princess of Jacqueline, and she hadn't had a single seizure, hit her. She stopped in her tracks and looked out at the town around them, at their ancestral home, and flooded with excited anticipation. Things were getting back on track, despite the spell.

William bumped her with his arm. She let hers fall to her side, brushing her fingers against his. After declaring their love for each other in the Sky Temple, they hadn't had a chance to discuss what it all meant. And then he'd been arrested. Now, since she'd sort of pardoned him, they were free to be together. At least until they returned home, and her being reinstated as Crown Princess, and William's pardon, would disappear.

For a moment, she considered what the people would think of her being with a man who was convicted of conspiracy to commit treason. Surely her mother could pardon him. But when she did, would the people accept him? Would they respect him as their king?

It was then that she realized for the first time that she thought of William as the future King of Jacqueline. The thought twisted her stomach with both nerves and excitement. She'd never thought of anyone that way before, and the new emotions felt raw and all-consuming.

And yet, she wasn't quite sure what to do with herself.

She loved him, of course. But he was the first person she'd ever courted. Outside of Aatu, but that didn't really count, seeing as it had been an arranged marriage. With William, there were no contracts, no rules. She had no idea how to proceed. Did they hold hands? Did they go on dates? Did she sit down with his father and declare her intentions? And she was sure *he* wasn't sure, either, because he'd never courted a Princess before. Somehow, everything between them had gotten seriously complicated when neither of them had been looking.

Glancing up at him, she was enthralled by the small changes that had occurred in him during their time apart. He'd shaved the beard he'd grown in prison, but had let stubble grow along his jaw. He had a scar, at the top of his left cheekbone, that she realized she didn't know what from. He smiled less, now, but when he did, it was captivating.

His mouth turned up in a smirk as he laced his fingers through hers. A strange, sweet heat flared in her stomach at his touch.

There was something natural about their being together, like a part of each of them recognized the other. Though it wasn't something she tended to dwell on, she thought of killing him in the alternate universe, of the way she'd felt afterwards. It had been soul-shattering. Did that mean they were... soulmates?

It wasn't a word she threw around lightly. But, somehow, it seemed fitting for them. Like they were preordained, two pieces of a puzzle fitting together. The thought filled her with elation.

As they strolled through the town, an image flooded her mind:

Dani flutters around me, her hands smoothing invisible wrinkles from my skirts, my hair. I look at her through my veil; it shrouds her in silver. She looks resplendent in a violet gown, her green healer's tattoo bared. Even with the scars on the side of her head, she's an ethereal beauty.

"You can still say no, you know."

I smile. "I know."

She shakes her head. "Gods and Angels, this is really happening."

A guard rounds the corner and beckons to her. She squeezes my hand before she goes, leaving me alone in the hall. I look down at my hands, down at the engagement ring on my finger. It was his ancestor's, some great-grand-mother down the line. It feels like it connects me to them, to where he comes from.

Footsteps sound; the guard returns. "Ready, Your Highness?"

I nod and follow him to the doors. Music swells from within the throne room. My father hesitates in the doorway, staring at me with a misty-eyed smile.

"You look beautiful, my heart."

It takes everything within me not to start crying. As it is, I take his hand and approach the door. Everyone within the throne room rises, turning to face us as we begin the walk down the aisle. There are familiar faces in the crowd, but I don't even notice them. Representative Sophine stands at the head of the dais, beautiful in her white gown. Chris and Mohan stand on the steps of the dais below her, with Lili and Dani standing across from them.

But all I can see is William. He meets my eyes as I approach him, his face split with a grin.

Anastasia came-to with a gasp, still holding William's hand. It was jarring to look into his face as it was here, colored with the voluptuous obsidian swirls of the Old World, compared to how it had been in the vision. But more startling was having seen their wedding. It had felt so real, like she could reach out and touch it.

William looked at her. "Are you alright?"

She nodded, afraid to speak. Standing with him after seeing their wedding felt momentous, but she didn't pull away. If these visions of the future were true, did that mean she married William? Or were they fragments? Possible futures? Gods and Angels, she needed Valdon!

Thankfully, Gerrard approached them. Anastasia moved away from William, stepping ahead of Mohan and Lili to meet him. He didn't appear to have seen her and William holding hands, for which a part of her was grateful; she didn't want to hurt anyone's feelings, especially not Gerrard's. He was kind, and caring, and deserved better than that.

"The repairs to your chambers have been made," he said, holding out a small, leaf-shaped vial filled with a silver liquid. "We found this hidden in one of the walls during our work."

Shock shot through Anastasia; both William and Gerrard narrowed their eyes at her, feeling her surprise. She took the vial, her mind spinning. This was the vial the Fairy Queen had given her, the one her grandmother had requested all those years ago. She'd thought it had been lost. But, somehow, it had been sent here when even her dagger had not. Strange.

"Thank you."

Gerrard frowned. "Do you want me to bring it to Mistress Miglune, Your Highness? Perhaps it is an old healing remedy?"

"No, thank you. I can do that myself."

With a nod, Gerrard headed down the corridor. Anastasia felt uneasy. There was something about this vial that was important. If only she knew where the Fairy Queen was, so she could ask her. Instead, she tucked the vial into her bodice and turned back to William.

An overwhelming need propelled her forward. Grabbing his face in her hands, she stared into his familiar hazel eyes. "I love you."

Slowly, he leaned down and kissed her. Warmth spread from her lips down to the tips of her toes, filling her with determination and strength. For the briefest of moments, she didn't care if anyone saw them. She didn't care about needing to find a husband for when they returned home, or even if they did return home. All that mattered was William, and the way he made her stomach flutter with butterflies.

When they broke apart, she grinned. "I could get used to this."

He chuckled. "So could I."

CHAPTER TWENTY-ONE

The volunteers left at first light the next morning, taking along a copy of the map Anastasia had found in the castle. Mistress Woodsman made slings out of fabric scraps, which they strapped to their bodies and filled with as much pemmican and water as they could hold. Anastasia shook all of their hands, thanking them for their help, before they unfurled their wings and took off into the morning sky.

Standing at the water's edge, Anastasia watched them until they were mere specks on the horizon. Lili stood with her, crossing names off her list. William and Ryke hovered a few feet away, crude daggers William's father had made in the night strapped to their hips.

"That only leaves Chris and Prince Vlad, my Princess," Lili intoned.

Anastasia nodded. "And the Guard?"

"Those that are better trained are standing sentry around the edges of the city. The rest are training near the water."

"How does the town center look?"

"My sister said Master Blue is giving out food at the inn, while the other Mistresses have makeshift carts and are bartering their wares. Master Dinas is hard at work on weapons for the Guard, while his partner, Blacksmith Ferry, is forging coins as we speak."

It seemed things were finally coming together. She hoped Mohan was having the same luck with his search for the Vatis and the end to Joey's spell.

Aagney yawned in her arms. She turned her attention to him, stroking a finger down his soft, round cheek. Welcoming the calmness that washed over her at his touch, she turned and strode with Lili back towards the castle. William and Ryke took up positions on either side of her, chatting amiably about nothing of consequence. It was nice to hear a conversation that didn't center around certain doom.

A flap of wings alerted them to an approaching presence. William and Ryke drew their daggers, looking up as a young boy landed in front of them. He was out of breath, and ragged, his hair sticking up all around his head.

"Lower your weapons," she commanded of Ryke and William. "This is my page boy, Fommen."

He flushed, embarrassment and anxiety radiating off of him. Dropping into a quick bow, he said, "Your Highness, I have found something."

"Already?" Ryke said.

"There is a large building that's filled with scrolls a little ways north from here."

"A library!" Anastasia gasped.

Fommen nodded. "It could help Prince Mohan break the spell!"

Before she could stop herself, Anastasia grabbed Fommen in an embrace. He squirmed before a sense of calmness washed over him and he settled. As she put him on his feet, he looked up at her for the first time and smiled.

"I did well?" he asked

She nodded. "Very well."

"Could you show us where this library is, Fommen?" Ryke asked.

"Yes."

Anastasia turned to Lili. "Get Mohan. Tell him we'll leave as soon as Fommen's gotten some rest and something to eat."

Lili curtsied and hurried off. With one hand holding Aagney, and the other resting on Fommen's shoulder, Anastasia led the group towards the inn.

It was amazing what twenty-four hours could accomplish. The inside of the inn was spotless. People littered the tables, eating sweet porridge. The buzz of their conversations filled the room, making it feel comfortably close-quartered. Lili's sister, Melina, stood behind the counter, serving bowls of porridge to waiting hands. Back in the kitchen, Anastasia could just make out the rotund Master Blue as he slaved over a hot stove.

"Good morrow!" Anastasia called.

Melina froze, her eyes widening; Anastasia felt her surprise and timidity. "G-good morrow, Princess."

"Do you think I could get some food for my page, here?"

Melina nodded. "Of course."

Hurrying to the back, Melina bustled around. A moment later, she returned with a bowl of porridge, sprinkled with dried currants. Fommen grabbed it hungrily and fell into a seat, shoveling food in his face. Catching what Master Blue was working on in the back, Anastasia frowned.

"Still no game?"

Melina shook her head. "Only birds too scrawny to eat. But we have more than enough grain, vegetables, and fruits. And fish. Plenty of fish."

There hadn't been any game at all in the city or the surrounding areas. Anastasia wondered if it had to do with Joey's spell, or if it was the nature of the Old World. Did their ancestors not have meat? Did the other kingdoms have game? She supposed they'd find out from their search parties. She only hoped they would have enough fish to hold them over. If not, she wasn't sure what substitute there would be.

"Would you or your warriors like anything to eat?"

Anastasia shook her head. "I'm fine."

William grunted. "No, thank you."

As Melina flushed again, Anastasia remembered how she and William had been having an affair in the alternate universe. The sudden realization made her lose any appetite she might've had. But the flustered look seemed reserved for Chris, who had just walked into the room. And given the way she tried to hide her feelings, in a room full of people that could all sense them, made Anastasia lose any doubt that Melina had a thing for Chris.

"Hi, Christopher!" she chirped.

Irritation flashed through Chris, but it vanished as quickly as it appeared, replaced by cordiality. "Melina."

"Would you like some breakfast?"

"Please."

He tapped around with a long stick until he found the seat across from Fommen. As he sat, Melina hurried over with a bowl of porridge.

"Spoon's to your left," she said.

Chris grunted his acknowledgement, before digging into his food. Anastasia stood in companionable silence, waiting for Fommen to finish. She "eavesdropped" on the feelings of the people around her, taking in their contentedness, or their irritation, or their excitement. It was odd to know she could feel other's feelings, but, somehow, just like flying, there was a part of it that felt natural.

As Fommen finished, Anastasia rested a hand on Chris' shoulder. "We'll see you before you and Vlad leave tonight."

He tilted his head. "Where are you headed?"

"Fommen found a library north of here. We hope it might help—"

"—Mohan find information about the spell, of course!"

Anastasia smiled. "Yes."

"I'd offer to come, but..." He grinned sheepishly and motioned to the cloth around his eyes.

"Of course."

With a wave to Melina, Anastasia led Fommen back outside. William and Ryke followed at a leisurely pace. When they reached the town center, they meandered through the makeshift marketplace. Mistress Woodsman repaired clothing discovered in houses, while others offered herbs, tonics, or carved wooden toys. As it was, a few children darted about, their laughter ringing through the streets.

Their happiness filled Anastasia with warmth. She was glad they were able to find a bright side to the darkness that surrounded their people.

A few moments later, Mohan and Lili joined them. There was a brightness to Mohan's eyes that Anastasia hadn't seen since they'd arrived in the Old World. And, thankfully, there was a spark of hope burning within him, shining through his inner cloud of resentment and stress.

"What's this I heard about a library?"

Anastasia offered a small smile. "I guess we'll see when we get there."

Turning, she unfurled her wings and lifted into the air. Lili, William, and Fommen followed her, while Ryke—the strongest of them all—looped his arms under Mohan's and carried him upward.

Anastasia flapped her wings a couple of times, rising higher. In her arms, Aagney giggled, enjoying the wind on his face. She held him tighter, following Fommen as he took the lead. While flying wasn't as instantaneous as portal travel, it was still quick. It wasn't long before they'd flown past the edge of the city, out past a forest, and into what looked like an abandoned city. It was smaller than Bahail, with two large stone structures interspersed with small wooden huts.

Fommen brought them to the smaller of the stone structures, which was still a massive building. The glass dome in the center was shattered, leveling it to the same height as the open arches around it. Some of the walls had collapsed, with gaping holes leaving the inside open to the elements. The sunlight illuminated the dust motes within, making it evident that the place was abandoned.

Landing, William and Ryke took the lead, marching inside the building. Anastasia, Mohan, and Lili followed, leaving Fommen to catch his breath outside.

Ceilings, decorated with beautiful tile, stood at least six people high. Dusty, moldy shelves lined the walls, from marbled floors all the way to the tops of the arches. Cobwebbed scrolls sat within them, in organized disorder.

Anastasia's footsteps echoed as she walked further inside. She could imagine how breathtaking it must've looked in its prime, with the sunlight filtering through the large dome, and the tile and marble shimmering like gold. Knowledgist Woodsman would've been beside himself. As it was, Anastasia was flooded with awe. Here were scrolls upon scrolls of her people's history and literature, nearly untouched by time. The pages were yellowed, and many waterlogged, but they were still well-preserved considering the state of the building.

Lili frowned. "Do you think this was a Nadmilise building?"

"Must've been," Mohan said. "There aren't any ladders."

William nodded. "Just perches in front of each of the shelves."

Kicking off the ground, Anastasia flew up to the top of one of the shelves. A few feet of marble jutted out from the shelves, giving her a perch to stand on. The pressed metal label on the shelf had long since faded, so Anastasia just grabbed a scroll.

Sitting on the perch, she unrolled it. To her dismay, the scroll was written in a language even more ancient than the ancient language of the realms.

Mohan called up to her. "Well?"

She flew down to him and handed him the scroll. "Can you read it?"

He swore. "It's not the same language as my grimoire."

Just as Anastasia was about to return the scroll, she recognized the name of the Nadmilise kingdom she was in: Irichat gol Naingcliar. Perhaps this scroll spoke of the history of the city? If only she knew how to read it. But it was unlike any language she'd ever seen.

They all spread out, perusing the shelves. But William didn't stray too far from Anastasia's side. She felt safer with him there, looking out for her.

Pulling out another scroll, Anastasia found the same strange language. As a child, she'd learned the languages of the realms while living in the human realm with her parents. As such, she should have no difficulty learning another. But where could she start? No one she knew spoke it, unlike how she'd learned with her mother. Perhaps there was a scroll on it?

Pushing off from her perch, she started skimming the scrolls in the shelves. She flew from perch to perch, searching one level before moving on to the next. It was long going, especially considering the library was as wide as it was tall.

Around noon, she stopped to feed Aagney. When they'd first arrived in the Old World, Ostana had tried to nurse him. Unfortunately, she couldn't bear to be near him long enough, and her milk had made him ill. They'd figured it had something to do with Aagney being half-werewolf-half-vampire. And when they'd tried to use a Nadmilise wet nurse, Aagney hadn't eaten. Thankfully, Mohan had discovered a tonic that would mimic the milk he needed for sustenance. Anastasia always carried bottles of it with her.

As she sat, William came up beside her. "Want a hand?"

She passed Aagney to him and rooted around in the purse at her waist for a bottle. When she produced it, William surprised her by taking it and feeding Aagney.

Wordlessly, she watched William with the baby, a strange feeling of bittersweet happiness stealing over her. Though she knew he could feel how she felt, he didn't say anything. He just cradled Aagney's head and murmured to him while he drank.

"You're good with him," she whispered. It felt wrong to talk loudly in this moment.

William shrugged. "I had practice with Dani."

They sat together in silence. Anastasia tried to imagine William as a child, a toddler caring for his infant sister. She could picture their parents, so happy together, chasing them around their home. Dolan would be grimy from his work in the smithy, while Victorya would try to teach her son to dance. It pained her to think of all they'd lost since she'd returned to Sehir.

After burping Aagney, William returned him to Anastasia. She placed him back in his sling, cradling him close. Though it had only been a couple of weeks since he'd been placed in her care, she realized she felt his absence. She'd grown fond of him. Vaguely, she wondered what sort of implication that would have when they returned home. It was a difficult situation all around; she was glad Ostana and Vlad had both chosen to join search parties, so they could be distracted from their loss.

William and Anastasia pushed off from the ground together, flying up to a new shelf. There, they lost themselves among the scrolls, looking for anything that could help them return home.

Dusk found Anastasia perusing a scroll with what looked like an alphabet in it. Thankfully, it used the same runes as the ancient language. Just as she was about to sit down to study it, Lili flew to the center of the library and called out to them.

"Chris and Vlad will be leaving soon."

Chapter Twenty-One

Anastasia sighed. "Right."

Tucking the scroll into her bodice, Anastasia joined the others in the lobby of the library. Together, they kicked off from the ground and flew back to Bahail. The return flight to the city was quiet, everyone lost in their own thoughts. Anastasia could feel the collective frustration, however, and knew that though the library was promising, it hadn't given them the answers they were seeking.

They arrived at the castle just as Chris and Vlad were getting ready to leave. They were hopeful, determined, which lifted everyone's spirits.

Gingerly, Vlad approached his son. But as he neared, he instinctively recoiled and bared his teeth in a feral growl. Shame radiated off of him, and he backed away. Anastasia longed to comfort him, but knew there was nothing she could say that would help.

"Tell him I'm sorry," Vlad murmured.

Anastasia nodded. "Of course."

Chris stepped forward. "We'll bring your family home, Anastasia."

She couldn't help but think of the months before, when Valdon promised to find her family so she could find her grandmother. For months, they were tortured at the hands of Adrian and the Shadows. She knew, or hoped, that this time was not the same. She didn't think she could handle their torture on her conscience again.

Reaching out, she squeezed Chris' hand. He returned the gesture before stepping back and unfurling his wings. The jet-black feathers blotted out the glittering evening sky.

Vlad shook himself and closed his eyes in concentration. In a flash of dark smoke, he transformed himself into a pale vampire bat. He'd discovered the ability to shift one night at dinner, quite accidentally. As he'd darted around, they'd stared at him, completely stunned.

"Well," Chris intoned.

William cleared his throat. "Be safe."

"You, too."

"Always."

Vlad squeaked and flapped his wings, rising higher into the air. Chris tilted his head, listening, before he did the same.

As she had with the other search parties, Anastasia watched until they disappeared on the horizon. Then, she, William, Ryke, Lili, Mohan, and Fommen made their way into the castle. Melina was bustling around the gathering room, setting up bowls of stew for dinner. Seeing as they didn't have a cook in the castle, Anastasia was grateful Melina managed to bring them food from the inn.

She looked up, her cheeks wet with tears. "Christopher's left?"

Anastasia nodded. "Yes."

Grunting noncommittally, Melina finished setting the table. They all wordlessly filed into seats. What a strange sort of family they made, a hand-maiden, a baking apprentice, two warriors, a page boy, a sorcerer, a princess, and a baby. But they *were* family, in a sense. Seeing as none of their parents, outside of William's father, had arrived in Bahail, they were all they had. It usually made for interesting meals, but tonight's was somber.

Anastasia wondered what they would do if they couldn't read the language in the scrolls. How would they ever find anything out about the spell or how to return home?

As she fed Aagney, she pushed such thoughts away, instead focusing on the positive. They'd found a library filled with scrolls. Something was bound to give them a history of the kingdoms, or information about the Vatis. There had to be *something* they could go off. All they needed was some time to find it.

After dinner, they all cleaned their dishes together. When they were done, Anastasia took Aagney up to her room to put him down for the night. When she returned, Fommen was asleep at the dinner table, Melina and Lili had taken the dishes back to the inn, Ryke had gone home for the evening, switching shifts with Anastasia's evening guards, and Mohan was outside smoking the pipe he'd discovered in the castle. That left William and Anastasia alone.

She found him standing in the gathering room, staring up at the worn wooden shield with his family's name on it. Anastasia's two night guards hovered behind him in the doorway.

"What are you thinking?" she asked.

He pursed his lips. "I never knew my family was prominent."

"They're one of the oldest Nadmilise families in recorded history."

"What do you think it was like back then? I mean, they lived in this grand house near the other ancient families. Did they consort with other people in the town, or did they stick with their peers? Did they know your ancestors that lived in this castle?"

Anastasia stepped up beside him. "Well, your name *is* in my home, so I would hope they knew each other."

He chuckled. "It's just so different here. I can't imagine how they lived."

"But this place has got an odd sort of beauty to it. I mean, picture what the city would look like with a blanket of snow. Think of what a winter solstice celebration would be like."

"Breathtaking, I'd imagine."

He moved away from his family's crest and stepped underneath Anastasia's—the Piliar family. They sat right next to each other, their facades equally as faded. Anastasia followed his gaze, looking up at her last name, carved into an ancient piece of wood. Not for the first time, she wondered what the purpose was for the crests. Why gather them all in this room? Why emblazon these particular names for all eternity? What was it about these twelve families that made them so special?

With a sigh, William put his arm around Anastasia's shoulders. She snaked her arm around his waist and leaned into him, breathing in his familiar scent of smoke and the spicy waters of the Fire Lake. It was so odd that he smelled the same, despite the fact that they were so drastically far from home.

"I don't like leaving you," he finally said.

She nodded. She didn't like watching him leave, either. It was hard to part each night, but she knew it was necessary. "You need to be with your father. Especially with Dani not being here."

"Where could she be?"

"I'm not sure."

Which was true. There was so much about the Old World and Joey's spell that they didn't understand. She only hoped that wherever Dani was, she was safe.

William sighed. "I love you."

She turned to him, resting her chin on his chest. "I love you, too."

He leaned down and pressed his lips to hers, flooding her with warmth. Reaching up, she cupped his face, holding him close. When they broke apart, he trailed his thumb across her cheek. Standing on her tip-toes, she gave him a quick kiss.

"I'll see you in the morning."

"Yeah."

"Good night, William."

He playfully groaned. "Good night, Anastasia."

As he left, she felt his absence like a physical blow. But she'd insisted he go, in spite of it. They'd have plenty of time together in the future. Right now, his father needed him.

Her guards flanked her as she went to her chambers. They took up sentry outside her door. She was bone tired, nearly too tired to undress, but she worked the ties of her gown, regardless. Pulling on a nightgown Mistress Woodsman had fashioned for her, she blew out the candles scattered about her room. After drawing the curtains, she fell into bed.

She was asleep before her head even hit the pillow.

CHAPTER TWENTY-TWO

Anastasia rubbed her eyes, staring at the ceiling of her room. For the last three days, she'd been flying back and forth between the library. So far, she and Mohan had both managed to learn the alphabet of the strange old language, but they didn't have anything to go off for meaning, so it left them frustrated and strained.

Rolling out of bed, she stretched. Her back ached from being hunched over for hours at a time, and her eyes felt like they'd never re-focus. Thankfully, Aagney was in good spirits; he helped lift them out of their funk.

A knock sounded at the door before Lili stuck her head in. "Good morning, my Princess."

"Morning," Anastasia yawned.

Deftly, Lili dressed Anastasia in a fresh gown. As soon as she was free, Anastasia took a bottle from her nightstand and fed Aagney. While he drank, she and Lili made their way to the gathering room.

Melina had set up breakfast for them before her shift at the inn. The smell of sweet porridge and fruit was welcome, even though they'd had it nearly every day since Master Blue's arrival. It would still be some time until he was up to preparing his scrumptious feasts, seeing as he was still familiarizing himself with the foods growing in Bahail. But Anastasia didn't mind; food was food. And something was certainly better than nothing.

William and Ryke stood on opposite ends of the room, Ryke watching the only entrance, and William keeping an eye on the water through the windows. As Anastasia burped Aagney, Mohan trudged downstairs, still dressed in his nightshirt. He yawned, and blearily started eating.

"What's on the agenda for today?" Anastasia asked Lili.

Her handmaiden had taken up the mantle of royal chamberlain, and she was much gentler than Anastasia's aunt had been.

It was a pity that Lili wouldn't be able to hold that same position in Sehir. As she'd been grayed out from her mastery examinations when she was seventeen-years-old, and forced into servitude, all she'd ever be was a handmaiden. It pained Anastasia that that was her role. Maybe she could overturn it when they returned home?

"You have a meeting with the Mistresses about the state of affairs. And winter is quickly approaching. We'll need to make some decisions regarding the fall equinox and winter solstice, as well as what to do about the frost."

Mohan chuckled darkly. "When did we start living such pedestrian lives?"

"What do you mean?" Anastasia questioned.

"I remember when I went to a different ball every weekend. We always threw such grand parties. It feels like a lifetime ago."

Anastasia sat up, struck with an idea. "When my family returned to Sehir, we threw a feast, to unite the people and show goodwill. Why don't we do the same here? To put the people at ease, make Bahail feel a little more like home?"

Mohan lit up. "Oh, yes!"

Anastasia turned to Lili. "Do you think it's possible?"

"You could propose it to the Mistresses at the meeting today, see what their reactions are. But I don't see why not."

For the first time since arriving, Anastasia was actually *excited* to be in Bahail. A feast would do everyone some good, take their minds off their troubles.

She scarfed down her porridge and hurried out the door with a wave to Mohan. He just grunted his acknowledgement, practically asleep at the table. William and Ryke flanked Anastasia and Lili as they stepped out into the morning light. The air was crisper, signaling the oncoming autumn. Vaguely, Anastasia wondered if the seasons in Bahail were the same as in Sehir. Or if it was like Hullenia, where it never snowed.

It was a short flight into town; they touched down in the town center, where the vendors were just starting to open their carts in the marketplace. Anastasia and Lili passed them by, making their way to the inn.

The Mistresses of the city gathered on the main floor, passing around a tankard. As Anastasia entered, Mistress Couland, the master bottler, hurried forward.

"Your Highness, the first batch of ale is ready!"

Dolan passed Anastasia the tankard, giving his son a nod in greeting. Anastasia swirled the little bit of ale left in the tankard, breathing in the yeasty smell. It was lighter than the one they usually had in Sehir but seemed otherwise much the same.

As she took as sip, Mistress Couland continued, "And I've started fermenting grapes for wine. They should be ready by the fall equinox."

Anastasia grinned and passed the tankard to Lili. "That's great news!"

"I can have some bottles sent to the castle once they're ready."

"That's part of what I wanted to discuss today." Anastasia motioned to the tables. "Shall we begin?"

The Mistresses all sat, facing Anastasia and Lili at the head table. In her years in Sehir, Anastasia didn't meet all the Mistresses. Sure, she knew them from seeing them in the marketplace, or conversing with them in their shops or at gatherings. But this meeting was new, a council of the people, rather than the monarchies. It felt auspicious.

"When my family returned to Sehir after out ten-year absence, they were advised by the High Council to hold a feast, to gather the people of the royal city together to show a united force. Though not the same circumstances, I think it would be good for the community as well."

Gerrard leaned forward. "You want to hold a feast?"

"Yes."

Dolan rubbed his chin. "We're only just getting our bearings, here."

"And just how long do you think we'll be here?" Master Blue questioned. "Surely we'll be back home in Sehir before too long?"

Anastasia shook her head. "There's no way to know."

"I think a feast sounds like a great idea," Mistress Couland said. "What warms the heart better than good food, great ale, and generous company?"

Anastasia couldn't agree more. Looking back on her childhood, the best memories she had were in the company of friends and family, celebrating. There was something comforting about bringing people together for a happy occasion, especially during dark times.

"When would you want to hold the feast?" Gerrard asked.

Anastasia shrugged. "What seems reasonable?"

Mistress Couland pursed her lips. "The fall equinox works for me."

Master Blue nodded. "I could work with that, as well."

"Shall we put it to a vote?"

Dolan grunted. "I don't think that's necessary. We'll have a celebration of sorts during the fall equinox, try to bring as many of our traditions from Sehir here to Bahail."

With that settled, Anastasia listened as the Mistresses regaled her with the goings on in the marketplace and town—the volunteer warriors were learning quickly, taking up shifts around the edge of town; Master Blue had convinced a few other people to waitress at the inn, to relieve Melina; Dolan had made nearly enough daggers for the Guard, and was working on other metalwork throughout the town; the coins were almost complete, and it was decided that they would be embossed with the royal seal of Jacqueline.

Most importantly, the Mistresses had decided to hold mastery examinations for those that were ready. Which meant that William could finally be tested and named a Warrior, instead of apprentice. The only concern was about the tattoos. Though Mohan could perform the ceremony, there was no telling what his magic would be like, or if it would even work in the Old World. Did they even really need them with the colored swirls on their skin?

Anastasia figured the tattoo was superfluous at this point; they could always get them when they returned to Sehir. What *was* important was consistency, and recognizing the students for their talents. They needed structure, tradition, to keep from losing themselves in this foreign land.

As the meeting adjourned, Anastasia took Aagney out into the fresh air. She supposed it was time to return to the library, to see if she could find anything that could help her and Mohan learn the language.

She turned to Lili. "I'll probably be back from the library late tonight. Will you be sure to tell the warriors?"

Lili inclined her head. "Of course, my Princess."

William stepped up beside Anastasia. "Ready?"

Instead of responding, Anastasia unfurled her wings. William and Ryke followed her, and they took off into the sky. It felt like mere moments later that they arrived at the library. Anastasia resumed her searching from the day before, while Ryke took to wandering around. Two days ago, he'd discovered a tunnel that split off into all different directions. Anastasia was hoping they'd learn enough of the language to find something that could tell them what the tunnels were for.

Settling down on the perch, Anastasia flipped through the scrolls. William joined her and they passed the hours in amenable silence. At noontime, she fed Aagney again, and paused her search to stretch her legs.

Fluttering sounded down near the entrance of the library. She was about to wave it off as a bird having flown into the room when she remembered that Nadmilise had wings.

William was on his feet in an instant, his dagger drawn. He motioned for Anastasia to stay behind him as he flew forward. She crept behind him, clutching Aagney close. Ryke brought up the rear, his eyes trained on the room behind Anastasia. For the first time that she could remember, Anastasia felt vulnerable, felt unprepared to fight back. She supposed it had to do with the very fragile infant in her arms.

To everyone's utter surprise, Chris' father stood on one of the perches near the entrance. He looked up as they approached, apparently unsurprised to see them.

"Good afternoon."

Anastasia started. "Knowledgist Woodsman?"

He dropped down to the floor and headed towards them. "I see you've found the Royal Library of Anarelia."

Orange swirls spotted his pale skin, in contrast to his dark eyes and soft gray wings. He brushed past them to a lopsided table with only three legs and spread out the scroll he'd grabbed. Anastasia stared after him. The Royal Library of Anarelia? As in the very first Nadmilise Queen *ever*? This was her library?

As he faltered, Anastasia reached out to steady him. But instead of taking her proffered arm, he shied away from her.

Ryke put a hand on her shoulder. "He hasn't been around any people till now."

It took Anastasia a moment to understand. She remembered what it had been like to feel all the emotions of those around her when she first ventured into town. It had been so overwhelming she'd fainted. Understanding, she, William, and Ryke gave Knowledgist Woodsman some distance and waited for him to recover. When he did, Anastasia joined him at the table.

"Incredible," he breathed. "And I thought the wings were impressive."

"Knowledgist Woodsman, what are you doing here?"

"Please, call me Aleric." He gave her a small smile. "I woke up a short distance from here and quickly found the library. I started studying everything about this place, trying to understand what happened. I didn't know there was anyone else here."

"Gods and Angels," Anastasia breathed.

William frowned. "The city's a short ways south of here. Your mother, wife, and daughter are there."

"And my son?"

"Currently out searching for my family," said Anastasia.

Knowledgist Woodsman nodded, as if this made perfect sense. Anastasia studied him. He didn't seem injured or malnourished. In fact, he was clean-shaven and well-rested. And he was studying the scroll as though he could read what was on it.

"How long have you been here?"

He considered her. "Oh, roughly seventy-two days."

Anastasia started. "Over two months?"

When Aleric nodded, Anastasia felt like she'd been sucker punched. How was that even possible? She'd been the first to arrive in Bahail, and even that hadn't even been a month ago. What had Joey's spell done to them? And why? What was the purpose of sending people sporadically? And where had they all been during that time?

Ryke nodded towards the scroll. "You can read the language."

"I spent my first week here learning how," Aleric explained.

Excitement bubbled in Anastasia's chest. "Could you teach us? We're trying to learn as much about this place as possible."

"Of course."

She slid into the seat across from him, while William and Ryke resumed their guarding positions. They spent a few moments sharing their goings on, Anastasia telling him of the meetings, and the feast, and the construction, while Aleric regaled her with fairy tales and fables he'd come across about monsters called Galaens. It seemed they were the precursors to the Shadows. They were described as demonic beasts with skin the color of the sky and eyes as white as the clouds. They could fly and were practically invisible when in the air.

Then, they moved on to the language. It seemed it was spoken only by the Nadmilise. As it turned out, there was no common language amongst peoples as there was in the realms.

By the time evening rolled around, Anastasia had learned basic vocabulary words. Aleric took them to the cabin he'd been staying in, offering them dinner. It was a quaint, homey place, with two bedrooms and a kitchen. Surprisingly, it had largely survived the test of time.

"I believe the library's caretaker and her family would've lived here," Aleric explained.

Chapter Twenty-Two

Anastasia glanced around. "It's nice."

They ate in relative silence, eagerly dining on a stew Aleric had made of wild root vegetables and herbs from the garden in the backyard. Though simple, it was delicious.

As they watched the sun set over the mountains in companionable quiet, Aleric glanced at her. "I think I discovered something of interest." When Anastasia gave him a curious look, he explained, "There is a children's tale of ancient beings with people that had the power to create worlds. At first I thought it was a simple version of the Gods and Angels."

"But now?"

"Now I think they might've been about the Ancients."

Anastasia failed to keep the excitement off her face. "Why do you think so?"

"Well, for starters, there were seven of them, not six. But they also had different powers, like the ability to withstand the powers of others."

"You think it could be true?"

"It's a children's story, so it's hard to tell."

She leaned forward. "Does it say how to find them?"

He shook his head. "There was very little information, other than the story of them recreating the world."

Anastasia sat back. Why would there be a children's story about the Ancients recreating the world? She thought back to the stories she'd heard as a child. Before they'd left Jacqueline, her grandmother used to tell her tales of warriors and princesses, which she now realized were to help with her premonitions. And when they'd been in the human realm, her mother had told her mythologies and creation stories of the realms.

William seemed to be following her train of thought, for he said, "Are you sure it was a children's story?"

Knowledgist Woodsman raised an eyebrow. "What are you thinking?"

"What if it was a history? Some seem juvenile, considering the lack of knowledge people had at the time. It could've been a recording of what the people knew of the Ancients."

Aleric considered this. "The Ancients *have* been rather mysterious, even in our time."

Hardly daring to believe the theory, Anastasia grinned. Maybe they'd finally found an answer. And once Mohan found the spell to unearth the Vatis, they'd be one step closer to getting back home. She couldn't believe they were making progress; it had seemed like such an impossible task.

"Tomorrow, we can return to the library and see what we find."

Anastasia frowned. "Aleric, why don't you return to the city with us? I'm sure your family will be glad to see you."

He nodded. "Yes, of course!"

Their return to Bahail was quick. Aleric's reunion with his family was tearful, and Anastasia, Ryke, and William gave them their space; it felt wrong to intrude on their emotions.

Shortly after William and Ryke escorted Anastasia home, she was in bed. But her mind just wouldn't shut off. She kept turning the children's story over and over in her mind, flush with exhilaration. It could be the key to everything they'd been looking for. She couldn't believe she had to wait until the next day to find out.

She woke from a dreamless sleep the next morning before dawn. After feeding and changing Aagney, and scarfing down some toast and jam, Anastasia and Mohan joined Aleric and Alex in town. Anastasia carried Mohan, and they flew to the library to resume their work. Anastasia worked on teaching Alex and Mohan everything Aleric had taught her of the Old Language, while Aleric searched the scrolls for more information.

A flapping sound near the entrance drew their attention. Thinking it to be another Nadmilise, Anastasia braced herself. Ever ready, William and Ryke took up defensive positions. But, as it turned out, it was just a pigeon.

It fluttered and cooed, bouncing around in the doorway. It looked like the same bird she'd shooed out of the castle the night she'd arrived. As she headed over to shoo it out once again, it flew to her arm. Cooing softly, it held out its small leg. A scroll, no bigger than her pinky finger, was tied around its foot.

As soon as she took it, the pigeon flew up to the shattered dome where it sat, watching them with dark eyes.

"Is that a letter?" Aleric questioned.

Unrolling it, Anastasia found a seal she didn't recognize. "It seems like it."

Returning to the table, she sat between Mohan and Alex and opened the letter. The writing inside, written in the Old Language, had nearly faded completely, the paper crumpling beneath her hands.

She handed it to Aleric. "Can you read it?"

"I can certainly try." Glancing at the paper, he read, "'Anastasia, the vision you saw is coming true. You need to round up the Ancients and do what you can to leave this place. The pendants are your only hope, now. But, alas, they might also be your downfall. This is all just the beginning.'"

Anastasia frowned. At the mention of pendants, plural, she couldn't help but think of the premonition she'd had back in Sehir, when she'd been thinking of William: *As one, the doppelgangers grab their pendants and smash them. The beautiful stones shatter, sending flecks of colored gemstone skittering across the floor.* It couldn't be a coincidence, could it?

"Do they mean you?" Alex asked Anastasia.

Mohan shook his head. "Couldn't be. This letter is easily a thousand years old."

"They must be writing to Anastasia Futurebringer," Anastasia said. "My namesake."

Ryke frowned. "Does that say visions?"

"It could be vision, or dream, or story," Aleric said. "I am not entirely sure."

Anastasia turned away. Someone had written to her ancestor about the Ancients. Anastasia Futurebringer had told someone of the premonitions, someone who was warning her to heed them. It seemed everything nowadays led them back to the Ancients.

She looked up. "Who wrote the letter?"

"It says, 'From Anastasia'."

Shock flooded through Anastasia, but she quickly tamped it down. There were no other Anastasias in Nadmilise history. She knew that for a fact, having studied the names of the Queens her whole life. So, either Anastasia Futurebringer was crazy and writing to herself—which she sincerely doubted, seeing as her parents would never name her after a nutcase—or this was somehow connected to her.

Still, to be sure, she needed to find out more about her namesake.

"I think we're overlooking the obvious," said Ryke. "We can use the pigeons to communicate."

"Homing pigeons can only travel to one destination," said Aleric. "In ancient times, pigeons were transported in a cage to a destination, tied with messages, and then released to find their way home. This must be where the pigeon originated."

Anastasia's hopes fell. "So we can't find where the bird came from?"

"Afraid not."

Anastasia frowned. Maybe Anastasia Futurebringer had seen a premonition of her arrival in the library, and sent her a letter? But how could that pigeon have survived all that time? Surely it would've died in the thousands of years since the Old World? Then she remembered the strange way time had operated since their arrival. Maybe time worked differently here.

"What is our next move, love?" Mohan questioned.

"We need to focus on learning the Old Language, so we can sort out the business about the Ancients. Our primary goal is getting back to Sehir."

Alex furrowed her brow. "But the letter—"

"Is meaningless right now."

Turning, she resumed memorizing vocabulary words. The others quickly followed her lead, having no real connection to the letter as Anastasia did. But William could tell. He hovered near her, radiating worry. She felt like snapping at him, but knew it wouldn't do anyone any good.

Growing frustrated, she pushed back from the table and studied the family trees she'd discovered on one of the shelves. There was one for each of the Sehirian ancient families, and she wondered again what their importance was in this time. Perhaps it was simply because they were gentry? Or did it have to do with their careers? Which sent her down a rabbit hole of wondering about the culture in Bahail, and if the Nadmilise of the time got tattoos like in Sehir.

What drew her attention back to William's family tree, however, were the stars next to some of the names. There weren't any keys to tell her what the stars stood for, but she imagined it was some sort of special award—most of William's ancestors had been warriors. Curious, she studied the other trees. Except for the Woodsman and Piliar family trees having similar stars next to some of their names, there was nothing. It was exceedingly frustrating, being blocked at every turn. All she wanted was to find a way to bring her people home.

She found herself wishing more and more that her mother was there. She knew Anarose would know exactly what to do in this situation. Alas, it was just the six of them and little Aagney, slowly combing their way through the scrolls.

She only hoped the search parties were having better luck.

CHAPTER TWENTY-THREE

Ostana slowed her pace, wiping the sweat from her brow. The kerchief one of the Nadmilise girls she was traveling with had given her was already soaked through. Ever since she'd woken that morning, she'd felt *off*, almost like a sickness. Which would just be perfect. Not only was she trapped in this prison of a world, unable to have a relationship with her fiancé and son, but she couldn't shift into a wolf. And now, to top it all off, she was getting sick.

She was mildly concerned, considering there were no jhakris here to care for her. And she wasn't sure how much her anatomy had changed since their arrival. Was she now… human? The thought revolted her. She'd always prided herself on the power that coursed through her as a wolf. Without it, she felt like a shell of who she used to be, made worse by the absence of the people she loved most.

Turning her face to the sky, she breathed deep. The scent of the sea raised her hackles. She'd hoped going off on a search for the High Council would've proven a decent distraction from her current problems. But, instead, it only made her more and more irritable.

The kingdom they were in—Irichat gol Dhaiten, according to the map— rose up from the sea on a high cliff, bringing with it the sounds of crashing waves and crying seagulls. Both of which were not pleasant to the headache pounding at Ostana's temples. She closed her eyes and tried to focus her breathing, but the cries felt like needles piercing her eardrums, and the cool sea breeze made gooseflesh erupt across her heated skin.

"Oh!" one of her travel partners exclaimed. "Olives!"

Ostana opened her eyes and glared at the young blonde woman as she flounced over to a neighboring tree. Her sister, equally as blonde and loud, joined her.

While they fawned over the olive tree, Ostana made her way to the top of the hill. At the crest, she looked down at the town nestled at the bottom. There were towering columned structures interspersed with lush greenery. Nearly everything was under construction, with groups of people looking to restore the once-beautiful city.

Ostana frowned as she watched them. She was a Crown Princess, and the future Queen of Viire. And where was she? Off on a quest, trekking through dusty towns. By the Gods, this was pathetic. And yet, she had nothing else to do.

Without a backward glance at the blonde sisters behind her, Ostana started the descent into town. The people on the outside of the wall surrounding the city shot her curious looks as she passed them, but then quickly looked away. At first, she figured it was her dress—she still wore the gown from Bahail, in ancient Nadmilise styles. But they weren't staring at her long enough for that to be the case. There was something strange about the them. While they talked, it was quiet, somber. There weren't any children darting around; there was no laughter. What in the world was this place?

But then she reached the entrance to the city, and all curiosity left her mind. A line of armed guards blocked her path, dressed in short, dress-like chitons, with thick shawl-like chlamyses wrapped around their shoulders. Everything was hemmed with sky-blue cloth embroidered with small lightning bolts. It matched the sigils branded on their shields. They all brandished spears.

"Who goes there?" one of the men called.

Ostana pursed her lips, considering. Should she tell them the truth of who she was? There was no telling what the politics were like in these towns. Sure, Bahail had voted to keep Anastasia and the monarchy in power, but that didn't mean the other kingdoms would've done the same.

But then the blonde sisters stepped up beside Ostana and made the decision for her.

"I'm Ayvery Tomlin," the elder blonde said. "This is my sister, Alviva, and the princess Ostana Moneth. We have come on behalf of Crown Princess Anastasia Piliar Moneth, on a search for the High Council of the realms."

So much for anonymity. Ostana watched the guards carefully. They didn't seem eager to cut them down, which was good. They shared a glance, before one of the guards broke off from the pack and raced into town. The rest of the guard split down the middle, opening the way into the city. As Ostana and the sisters stepped forward, one of the guards inclined his head.

"I am Doro. I will be your guide through Pasilikí, the royal city."

As they stepped through the guards, Ostana studied the young man. He was younger than she, but not by much. Going by the look of their clothes, and their overall appearances, Ostana figured they were demigods. Great.

"So," Ayvery asked. "What's it like here in Pasilikí?"

Doro frowned. "It is very different from home."

He didn't elaborate, even when prompted. Instead, he took to pointing out parts of the town as they passed. There were the two large temples of Zeus and Hera, towering structures at least ten people high, with crumbling columns and steepled roofs. Ten other, smaller temples sat throughout the city, dedicated to the rest of the twelve Olympians. People moved in and out of them, carrying baskets of food and drink—offerings to the Gods, as Doro explained.

Then there was the sacrificial altar of Hera, a smaller building held aloft by statues of a beautiful woman. Within, sat a stone slab carved with a cow, lion, and peacock. Blood dripped over it, from the neck of a sacrificed animal.

Down the road sat two gymnasiums, which were really nothing more than fields of dirt enclosed by more columns. Ostana could hear people yelling within, but Doro led them in the opposite direction.

They moved through the marketplace, where people sold honeyed figs, and olives, and sweet grapes, and breads, and cheeses, and dried salted fish, and stewed beans. Ostana's stomach rumbled, but they didn't stop. Doro led them to the other side of town, where an immaculate palace was built atop a cliff. Hundreds of stairs led up to a columned entrance, complete with shimmering tiled roofs.

"What is this place?" Ostana asked.

Doro didn't look at her as he replied, "The Royal Palace."

Three mules sat at the bottom of the stairs, waiting for them. Doro motioned for them each to take one, so they wouldn't have to walk the stairs.

"What about you?" asked Alviva.

Doro shook his head. "You are guests of the royal family. To make you walk such an expanse would be rude. But I must walk."

And so, Doro trudged along beside them as the mules carried them up the massive staircase. It was strange to Ostana, riding another animal. Sure, she'd been in carriages before, but werewolves didn't need to ride anything else for travel; they could do it themselves. Again, she felt a sad sort of helplessness wash over her. Was this what all people felt like when they rode animals? What about the blonde sisters? They could fly in this land. Did it feel as superfluous to them?

When they reached the top, they were greeted by what seemed like the entire royal family of the demigods. It was at that moment that Ostana remembered she'd threatened the King of the Demigods, Euaristos, back during Anistes Droun. To her utter surprise, however, he wasn't among his family.

Instead, Queen Theophania stepped forward to greet them. She was a slight, regal woman, with fiery red curls, bound back from her face with a gilded circlet, and large blue eyes. She wore a beautiful peplos gown, tied with a gilded belt. Gold fasteners, embossed with a stalk of wheat, glimmered at her milky shoulders. She hurried forward and took Ostana's hands.

"Ostana, dear, you are well?"

Ostana remembered meeting Theophania many times over the years, whenever she'd had the distinct displeasure of spending time with her son, Zethus. But she'd always thought her to be kind.

"Yes," said Ostana. "And you?"

She couldn't help but notice that they looked remarkably the same as they did back home. Whereas Ostana was stuck with clawed nails, low-set ears, long-swinging arms, and a unibrow. Envy flared in her chest. How was it that everyone had a better lot in this world than her?

Theophania inclined her head. "Well, we can thank the Gods for our bounty." She turned back to the palace. "Would you please join us for a repast? You must be tired from your journey."

Sharing a look with Ayvery and Alviva, Ostana followed the queen. Her six children—Zethus, Isidora, Makedon, Klymene, Sotiria, and Adrastus— followed after her in a line. Spotting a familiar face, Ostana paused. The last time she'd seen Isidora Spiros had been when Ostana had set fire to the barn in Viire, and Isidora had run off into woods, disowned by her father for choosing to marry a stable hand. Guilt gnawed Ostana's insides; her actions had caused that stable hand's death. But what was Isidora doing here back with her family?

The inside of the palace was elaborate, even by Ostana's standards. Every surface was colored with bright tiles, all displaying renditions of the twelve Olympians. The light from round cutouts in the ceiling bounced off the polished marble floors and reflected over the glittering surfaces. A large fountain in the shape of a peacock spewed clear water, filling the room with gentle, bubbling sounds. Servants darted all around, weaving around the people leisurely strolling through the palace. They all stopped to bow to Theophania and her family.

It was all so strange. It looked like the demigods had lived in this world for centuries, not for mere weeks. How were they so much farther along than the Nadmilise? What had happened to them in their time here?

As they entered a banquet hall, they all filed into seats around the table. Servants brought out beautiful trays of food, placing them in the center of the large, rectangular table.

Theophania's youngest son, Adrastus, took a healthy portion of each of the dishes and piled them onto a plate. Crossing the room, he put it down on an altar, next to a candle, a bundle of incense, and a goblet of wine. Everyone else at the table grabbed hands. Ostana hesitated, before taking Isidora's hand.

"We give thanks to you, dear Gods," said Theophania, "for all that you give us. It is by your grace that we have such wonderful food to eat, and the wherewithal to appreciate what we have been given. It is by your hand, alone, that we live in such beauty. We are eternally grateful."

Zethus inclined his head. "Thank you, Zeus, for your just rule, and Hera, for allowing our conception."

Isidora cleared her throat. "Thank you, Poseidon, for the water that graces our food and our throats, and Hades, for protecting us in the hereafter."

"Thank you, Apollo," said Makedon, "for the sun that graces our world, and Artemis, for teaching us to care for and respect the animals we hunt."

"Thank you, Ares," said Klymene, "for giving us the strength to defeat our enemies and protect ourselves, and Aphrodite, for teaching us to love."

Sotiria leaned forward. "Thank you, Hephaestus, for giving us the tools to reap the things that sustain us, and Hermes, for protecting us during our travel to this world, and every place we go therein."

Adrastus returned to the table and took his mother's hand. "Thank you, Hestia, for giving us the fire and hearth to sustain us and our food, and Dionysus, for the fruit of the vine."

Finishing the circle, Theophania concluded, "Thank you, my dear ancestor, Demeter, for granting us a beautiful harvest and bountiful prosperity. And thank you, Athena, for your never-ending guidance and wisdom."

They all bowed their heads in a moment of silence. Ostana shared a surprised look with the blonde sisters. Never once, in all the years she'd known Zethus and his family, had they ever prayed to the Gods. They'd never even mentioned the Gods, unless they were boasting of their ancestral powers. What had made them change their ways? When had they become so devout?

But then they started passing around food, and Ostana didn't care. Everything was heavenly, from the creamy goat cheese on warm bread, to the crispy, salted fish, to the oil and olives, and the figs, and the grapes, and the lentil stews. But most welcome was the wine; all Ostana had had in Bahail was icy water from the river. The sweet wine hit the spot in a way nothing else could. It reminded her of the vineyards in Viire, which saddened her. But she didn't have long to dwell, before Theophania started up conversation.

"So, the guards tell me you came on behalf of Anastasia?"

Ostana nodded. "We did. It is her hope to locate the High Council, establish some sort of communication."

"And just where are you all hailing from?"

"South of here."

Theophania nodded. "Ah."

Isidora lowered her goblet. "And she is well?"

"Anastasia?" Ostana shrugged. "As well as she can be, I suppose."

Zethus narrowed his eyes. "The High Council removed her from rule. How is she still using her title? I thought she was unfit."

"The people voted to reinstate her."

They all fell silent after that, turning their attention to their food. For the first time, Ostana wished she had the Nadmilise ability to feel others' emotions. Their expressions were so reserved, it was difficult to tell what they were thinking.

This was also the first time in quite a while that Ostana remembered seeing all the Spiros children together at a table. Zethus was usually with whatever girl he was courting, while Isidora had been disowned by Euaristos. The two younger girls tended to eat in their rooms, while Makedon spent most of his time weapons training. It was strange seeing them all together. They seemed more docile than she remembered.

Ayvery cleared her throat; everyone's eyes went to her. "Excuse me, Queen Theophania. My name is—"

"We know who you are," Zethus said curtly.

"Alright." Ayvery glanced at him. "I hope this isn't overstepping my boundaries, Your Majesty, but where is King Euaristos?"

The tone of the room shifted palpably; the hair on the back of Ostana's neck stood on end. Had something happened to Euaristos? Surely, if she and her sister, Kanna, hadn't accidentally killed him when trying to get him to stop Anistes Droun, then the man was nearly indestructible. But there was something in the expressions of his family that made her think otherwise.

"He is not here," is all Theophania said.

The clang of a bell reverberated through the palace. Everyone froze. Taking in their shell-shocked expressions, Ostana frowned.

"Is it some sort of alarm?"

Sotiria pursed her lips. "It is, but not the kind you think."

"Hush," said Theophania.

Zethus looked to Theophania. "They'll have to join us, Mother."

"We would be glad to join Your Highnesses anywhere you wish," Alviva said with a grin.

Isidora pushed back from the table. "You might change your mind when you see where we're going."

Though her words sent a chill down Ostana's spine, she still rose and followed the demigod royal family from the banquet hall. They retraced their steps back through the palace, and down to the entrance. But this time, they started down the steps on their own, without any aid from the mules.

As she joined them, reluctantly trudging down, Ostana realized that every single person in the palace was doing the same. Looking out at the city, she saw everyone moving en masse towards the gymnasium. Was it some sort of prayer gathering? Was that why Isidora said they wouldn't want to go, because it was boring? Or was it something else altogether?

Either way, she was covered in sweat by the time she reached the bottom of the stairs. It seemed her illness from earlier was back with a vengeance. She slowed and wiped her brow, letting the others go ahead of her. What was she going to do if she was ill in this world? Her stomach squirmed, like live worms were trying to burrow their way out through her skin. She doubled over, heaving. Had it been something she'd ate? Was it the pemmican from Bahail? It was rather old.

Alviva hovered beside her. "Are you alright?"

"I'll be fine."

"Are you sure?"

Ostana nodded. "Just go on ahead. I'll catch up."

Reluctantly, Alviva joined her sister. People streamed past Ostana, until she was alone at the base of the palace. She lowered herself onto one of the steps and turned her face to the sky.

Dusk was upon them, shooting the sky through with shades of deep indigo. The moon looked like a ghost, hanging there in the still-lit sky.

Something about it calmed Ostana, despite the fact that every inch of her skin was on fire, and she was fairly certain her eyesight was blurry. She didn't remember ever feeling so awful in her whole life.

As the night grew darker, Ostana heard cheers and shouts rising up from the gymnasium. So, perhaps, it wasn't a temple. Unless it was a newfangled sort of temple. But she doubted it. The demigods here didn't seem the type.

Steeling herself, she forced herself to get to her feet and head towards the gymnasium. It took everything she had to put one foot in front of the other, to walk through the empty town.

But, as darkness enveloped the city, and the moon illuminated the sky, Ostana slowed. Then, very suddenly, searing pain tore through her abdomen. It remined her of when she'd given birth to Aagney, and she'd been writhing on the table in the Sehirian castle. The pain had completely outweighed her embarrassment at going into labor in front of all of her peers. And then, holding her little baby in her arms had driven every other thought from her mind.

Now, however, she knew she wasn't in labor. This was something else entirely, something that scared her. It felt like her blood was boiling, like her skin was cracking and falling away.

A cry tore from her lips as the pain intensified. She focused on the leaves of a tree some feet away, trying to center herself, but it was no use. Pain drove every thought from her mind, until she was just a whimpering mass on the ground. She could hear her bones cracking, shattering, tearing through her skin. It felt like needles pushed through every inch of her, like her teeth were too large for her mouth.

She fell forward, every inch of her on fire. As she looked down at her hands, she saw fur sprouting, her nails elongating into claws. Fear gripped her. What was happening to her? Was she shifting? But how? And why did it hurt so much?

But then, a primal instinct overtook her. She threw her head back and howled, an earsplitting sound that came from deep in her chest.

And then, everything went dark.

***

Ostana awoke, naked and covered in blood. She rolled over in the pale pre-dawn light. Her mouth tasted like ash, and her whole body felt bruised. Opening her eyes, she found herself in the middle of the gymnasium, surrounded by bodies.

Turning, she retched into the sand. Seeing what looked like blood spew from her lips, she recoiled. What in the name of the Gods had happened to her?

"Don't move!"

Sitting back, she realized she wasn't alone. Nearly a dozen armed demigods surrounded her, the serrated blades of their spears trained on her. They were looking at her like a feral dog. But why? She couldn't remember anything that happened to her after she left the palace. There was just the searing pain, her illness, and then nothing. But then she realized they thought she'd killed all those people lying around her. To her horror, she couldn't say for certain that she hadn't.

What was happening to her? Had she turned into a wolf? If she had, why couldn't she remember? By the Gods, it didn't make sense! She'd never hurt anyone as a wolf before, unless she'd meant to. And she'd never lost time before. Was it something to do with being in the Old World? Had it somehow changed the way she shifted?

Isidora raced in front of Ostana. "Stop!"

"Princess," said one of the guards. "She is dangerous. Please move."

"I will not!"

Closing her eyes, Isidora raised her hands and dropped to her knees. Ostana watching in fascination as she began to pray.

"O mighty Zeus, please let me call on an infinitesimal fraction of your tremendous power!"

Nothing happened. Isidora opened one eye and glanced around. Ostana was dumbstruck. If she was trying to save her, she was doing a terrible job. All Ostana wanted was to return to Bahail and hide. She was so ashamed.

Isidora tried again. "O gracious Demeter, I ask to use a sliver of your incredible power!"

This time, a wind whipped through the gymnasium, filling the area with the scent of hay and wildflowers. When Isidora got to her feet, her eyes were glowing with pale green light. She raised her hands and shoved outward. Wind tore through the gymnasium, sending sand stinging across Ostana's bare skin. When it dissipated, a field of poppies engulfed the guards. A heady scent rose from the petals, and the guards dropped, one-by-one, knocked unconscious by the flowers.

Placing her hands together, Isidora intoned, "Thank you, great Goddess. I owe you many bounties."

When she turned to Ostana, her eyes were again their usual color. She hauled Ostana to her feet and led her from the gymnasium. Only when they were a safe distance away did Ostana speak.

"What was that?"

Isidora didn't look at her as she spoke. "Demeter is my mother's ancestral mother, while Zeus is my father's. Therefore, my siblings and I all have access to their powers when they choose to grant them. Usually, it pertains weeks of praying in their respective temples, and giving numerous offerings."

Ostana halted. "I meant about me. What happened?"

"Every week, we hold a fight to honor the Gods. They select their champions, give them access to their powers, and have them fight each other till only one champion remains."

"Why do you fight?"

"We don't have a choice. We're slaves to the Gods, at their beck and call."

Ostana frowned. "And I... attacked during the fight?"

Isidora nodded. "You killed a lot of good men."

A harsh ringing sounded in Ostana's ears. She'd *killed* men in cold blood. But she hadn't wanted to. She hadn't even known that's what she was doing. And yet, that didn't matter. It was still her, just like it had been her that helped Adrian, fed him information about Anastasia, and ultimately got her brother killed. She'd have to live with all of those lives on her conscience.

"I'm so sorry," she breathed.

"Hear me when I say it isn't your fault, Ostana."

Perhaps Isidora was right? She hadn't meant to kill anyone. But how could she distance herself from what she did as a wolf, when she could still taste the blood on her tongue?

"Will it happen again? Will I... kill people again?"

Isidora started walking again. "The knowledge from the Gods tells us this will happen to you every full moon. But only on the first night of the moon."

"By the Gods."

"Look, Ostana, one night a month isn't too much to ask for freedom the rest of the time, trust me."

Ostana wasn't comforted by the haunted look in Isidora's eyes. Vaguely, she wondered if the demigod Princess had fought in the gymnasium. She'd have to fight thirteen other champions to win, to earn a break for her family.

As they rounded a corner, they ran smack into Ayvery and Alviva. As they looked at Ostana, she was glad to see their eyes were devoid of fear.

"I can hide you here until it's safe for you to leave. If you flew off now, our people would surely hunt you down."

Ayvery pulled a gown from a knapsack and passed it to Ostana. She gratefully dressed, brushing sand and grime from her skin.

When she was dressed, Isidora led them down a narrow street. They quickly moved from building to building, seeking cover in the shadows. On the outskirts of town, Isidora led them down into a cellar. It was dank, and smelled of mold, but it was certainly better than being killed.

Isidora motioned to Ayvery's knapsack. "You should have enough food and wine to last till I return."

"Thank you," said Alviva. "For all your help."

Isidora nodded. "Be safe."

As she left, Ostana sat back in the dirt with a frown. She really hoped that Isidora could get them out of the city before the next full moon.

CHAPTER TWENTY-FOUR

Ericcen Ros dropped down into the city in Ha'ae gol Sima, the sorcerer kingdom, just after sundown. His bothers, Aelnold and Norden, landed beside him, peering through the foggy night. They hunched their shoulders against the brisk wind, heading for the lights they spotted at the end of the forest.

A leaf-strewn pathway led through the skeletal trees and into the small town. All the homey stone shops and brick buildings were illuminated by candles flickering inside strange carved pumpkins that covered every door-step. They had grotesque features and seemed to glare at Ericcen wherever he moved. The streets between them were eerily silent and empty; the whisper of wind through the trees was the only sound. If not for the pumpkins, Ericcen would've thought the town deserted.

"Where is everyone?" Norden asked.

Crossing the street, Ericcen peered into the nearest shop window. The inside was empty, the door bolted. What would make an entire town of people leave their homes at the same time?

Then, a faint, strange sort of chanting sounded through the silence. Aelnold frowned. "Sounds like it's coming from the forest."

They followed the chanting to the other side of town where a line of more carved pumpkins created a path into the forest. At the end of it, three large tables sat what looked to be the whole town. Just like Prince Mohan, all the sorcerers had stark white hair and icy blue eyes. They were dressed in flowing black or orange clothes, with large obsidian and sapphire amulets around their necks.

As Ericcen and his brothers watched, a woman at each table led the other sorcerers in a chant, each reading from a grimoire similar to Prince Mohan's.

"Spirits of my fathers and mothers, I call to you, and welcome you to join me for this night," the women recited. "Your blood runs in my veins, your spirit is in my heart, your memories are in my soul. Tonight, I thank you."

Each table was filled with stewed apples, bowls of pomegranate seeds, porridges, rice, pies, roasted hazelnuts, cakes in the shape of skulls, corn, cranberry muffins, and tankards of ale. There was also an extra place setting, complete with food and wine, though no one sat before it. But that wasn't even the strangest part. A large altar, complete with white and black candles, gourds, apples, a bowl of smoking heliotrope, nutmeg, and sage, and a chalice of wine sat at the far end of the gathering.

Norden whispered, "What is all this?"

"Looks like a feast of some kind," said Ericcen.

"Maybe we shouldn't intrude," Aelnold murmured.

But as they stepped back, a branch snapped beneath their weight. The sorcerers whipped around, fixing them with harsh glares.

Ericcen blanched. "Seems a little too late for that, now."

"Nadmilise!" one of the women hissed.

Another woman stepped forward, holding a metal scepter aloft. It was carved into the shape of a stag, whose antlers caged a large opal.

"Hístalek!" she shouted.

A wave of magic exploded forth from the scepter, engulfing Ericcen, Norden, and Aelnold. They flew backwards, harsh wind tearing at them. When it dissipated, they were once again standing in the middle of the empty town, entirely disoriented.

"What in the name of the Gods and Angels was that?" Norden cried. "I thought they couldn't do magic here!"

Ericcen got to his feet, dusting his trousers. "I think it's safe to say Queen Sona isn't here."

"She did magic!"

"Sorcerers can do magic, Norden," said Aelnold. "It just takes a tremendous amount of energy, and requires a talisman, like that woman's scepter."

Norden shook his head. "But why did she attack us?"

Ericcen frowned. "I think it's safe to say the Nadmilise aren't that popular around here."

"They must blame us for coming to this Old World," said Aelnold.

Ericcen agreed. If he'd had magic, and it was abruptly taken from him, he wouldn't be too pleased with whoever caused it, either. But they didn't realize that the Nadmilise weren't to blame; every single realm played a part in the spell to bring them here, even if it was unwilling. Princess Anastasia had been doing everything in her power to stop it from happening. And yet, she was again under scrutiny for something that was out of her control, like the Shadow attacks on Sehir all those months before.

Shaking his head, he turned to face the task at hand. He knew from the last time he'd checked the map, that they needed to head westward. He supposed if they finished searching their section of the kingdom, and wound up empty-handed, they'd simply return to Bahail and hope the others had more luck. But he couldn't imagine returning to the Princess without any information.

In the last month or so, he'd gotten to know Princess Anastasia pretty well. She was poised, and wise, and, of course, very beautiful. But there was something about her, like she wasn't being entirely honest about herself. It wasn't sinister, but it did intrigue Ericcen. He wanted to earn her secrets.

He supposed that was why he'd agreed to join the confluence of men vying for her hand in marriage. It had been fun, beating the competition simply by having easy conversation with her. But now? Now they were in the Old World, and she hadn't so much as looked at any of them in a romantic sense since. He wondered if she was biding her time, waiting until they returned to Sehir. Or if, perhaps, she wasn't interested in a husband any longer? She hadn't been sick since their arrival, so maybe this was all moot?

With a sigh, Ericcen turned to his brothers. "It's time to move on."

Norden rubbed his stomach. "I'm starving!"

"We could stop into the tavern," Aelnold suggested, motioning to the building across the street.

Ericcen frowned. "We haven't any money."

"But we have some pemmican left. It could be a trade."

Though Ericcen wasn't convinced, he was just as hungry as his brother. They hadn't had a proper meal in days. And though the sorcerers were sure to be upset if they found out, it was better than eating pemmican for the sixth day in a row.

So, the three brothers hurried across the street and ducked into the open tavern. In the kitchens, they found bread, vegetable stews, and lots of cakes. They dug in hungrily.

"What are you doing in here?"

Startled, they all turned to see a sorcerer standing behind them. He was dressed like all the others and carried a small satchel. Ericcen swallowed nervously. They'd been caught. But a cursory test of the man's emotions found him to be simply curious, rather than angry.

"We meant to make a trade," Ericcen explained.

The sorcerer laughed. "I'm sure you did."

Eyeing the satchel, Aelnold frowned. "What are you doing here?"

"I came to make a trade of my own."

The four men considered each other. Ericcen furrowed his brow. Was this sorcerer taking food as well? What about the feast in the forest? Surely they had enough to feed the whole town twice over.

The sorcerer held out his hand. "Balan."

Aelnold took his hand. "Aelnold Ros, and my brothers Ericcen and Norden."

"A little bold for you Nadmilise to be in this kingdom, the way things are now. Might I ask why you'd brave the wrath of the sorcerers?"

Ericcen cleared his throat. "We're searching for Queen Sona."

"Ah, you're from Princess Anastasia." At their surprised expressions, he explained, "Word of your search has spread. It is the young princess' hope to establish communication with the High Council, correct?"

Norden frowned. "How do you know this?"

"I've come across members of your search parties in my travels."

Ericcen shared a look with his brothers. If this sorcerer knew of their search, surely the members of the High Council would, too. They just needed to find them.

But it seemed Aelnold followed a separate train of thought entirely. "Your travels, you say?"

Balan nodded. "I've been all over the kingdom."

"So you know whether Queen Sona is in this kingdom."

Balan grinned. "You're a sharp one, friend. Aye, I do know. Queen Sona is, in fact, in this kingdom. And I can take you to her."

"What do you want in return?"

"What say you to making a trade of sorts?"

Ericcen looked between his brother and Balan. From a read on the sorcerer's emotions, he seemed genuine. There was nothing backhanded about this. He knew Norden was concerned, but Aelnold was certain.

Ericcen stepped forward. "What do you want to trade?"

"My sister's been taken captive. I'll need help rescuing her."

Aelnold held out his hand. "We help you rescue your sister, and you take us to Queen Sona."

Balan shook. "We have a deal."

CHAPTER TWENTY-FIVE

Anastasia sat at the table in the gathering room, eating lunch with Lili while they discussed plans for the upcoming feast. Aleric had found some scrolls in the royal library detailing traditional customs in Bahail, and they were working on incorporating them into the feast. Thankfully, Master Blue had familiarized himself with most of the foods that grew in the city, so his fare had much improved.

As the door to the castle opened, the two guards stationed at the door to the gathering room barred the entrance. Upon seeing Mohan rushing forward, they stood aside. He barreled into the room, breathless and radiating excitement. Anastasia looked up at him, surprised.

"I've got it!" he exclaimed. "A way to find the Vatis!"

Anastasia was speechless. After all this time, they were finally taking definitive steps towards going home. She couldn't quite believe it. It felt like she'd been searching for the Vatis her whole life.

Mohan headed for the door. "Come on."

Getting to their feet, Anastasia and Lili hurried after him. William and Ryke followed. They all made their way out into the crisp autumn air, made bitter by the wind rising from the water. Hunching their shoulders, they headed round the side of the castle, to where Mohan had been working. To Anastasia's surprise, there was his old, leather-bound grimoire, a crumpled map, a chalice, and a rather large, navy-colored apatite crystal.

"What is all this?" Anastasia asked.

Mohan grinned. "The things needed for a locator spell."

"Gods and Angels," Lili breathed.

Anastasia hesitated. Here was the chance to locate someone. And while she knew they needed to find the Vatis, to take the List from Chris, find the Ancients, and use their magic to return home, a part of her just wanted to find her mother.

As though Mohan knew her train of thought, he gave her a sad smile. "I only have enough ingredients to find one person. And I'm not sure if I'll be able to find everything I need a second time."

Anastasia understood; the Vatis was the priority. "How does it work?"

"Here is a map of the kingdoms. In the chalice, I've added the ingredients needed for the spell. The last one I need is the blood from a Nadmilise with an ancient bloodline. As the Vatis was a product of the Gods and Angels, anyone with a line to them should be connected to the Vatis, too."

William held out his hand. "Take mine."

"Are you sure?"

"My family line can be traced back to the Warrior God, Humurse."

Anastasia couldn't help but smile. She knew he was being chivalrous, offering to give his blood so that she wouldn't have to. It was endearing.

"Once the blood is added," Mohan continued, "I read the incantation from the grimoire and we hold the amulet over the map. When it stops swinging, we should have the location of the Vatis."

Anastasia nodded her understanding. "Let's do it."

Mohan turned to William. Gently, he pressed a ceremonial knife to his finger. Blood welled beneath the tip, and Mohan squeezed until enough blood gathered. When it dropped into the chalice, smoke puffed up from the swirling liquid within. Mohan breathed it in. After a moment, his eyes flew open, the icy blue irises clouded over by all white.

He begun to chant in an ancient sorcerer tongue, holding the amulet over the map. "Elu gedulah, l'azor lanu l'matzo et h'matus ha'elohí. Azor lanu l'atar utu."

His body grew rigid and the amulet stopped swinging. Directly beneath the amulet, a navy-blue dot appeared on the map. Anastasia peered at it; it was still in Irichat gol Naingeliar, but farther north. The Vatis was in the Nadmilise kingdom.

Mohan stopped chanting; his eyes returned to their normal color. "So, the Vatis is in a city called Armol."

"Well?" Anastasia got to her feet. "Shall we go?"

Ryke frowned. "We have no idea what this city of Armol is like."

"But the Vatis is there."

"We need to prepare before we go, my Princess."

William frowned. "He's right, Anastasia."

Groaning, Anastasia relented. She knew they were right, but the less time they spent here in the Old World, the less time Joey had to accomplish whatever he wanted. They were so close to the Vatis she could taste it. But she knew it wouldn't do any of them good to go blindly into a possibly dangerous situation. For all they knew, the Vatis was with Joey. Ryke and William were right, they needed to prepare.

As Mohan tossed the contents of the chalice onto the rocks, Anastasia headed back inside. Rubbing her hands against the chill, she entered the gathering room. To her surprise, Aleric stood within, waiting for her.

He inclined his head. "Afternoon, Anastasia, Lili."

"Afternoon, Aleric," Anastasia replied. "What brings you here?"

"I have news, about the Vatis."

Mohan chuckled. "As a matter of fact, so do we."

"We found a location," Anastasia explained.

Aleric nodded, taking this in stride. "Well, I have some history that might be of use."

They all sat at the table, and Aleric splayed a number of scrolls on the table. Anastasia studied them, able to make out most of their contents after the weeks of studying the Old Language.

"You see, Bahail is not the ancestral home of Nadmilise royalty. A small part of the Nadmilise royal family moved to the castle in Bahail in the early thirteenth century. The rest of the family lived in the actual royal city of Armol."

Mohan leaned forward. "Armol."

Aleric nodded. "One and the same, I expect."

"Why did they move?" Anastasia asked.

"They were at war with the demigods. So, the Queen and her daughter moved here to Bahail, while the rest of their family remained behind in Armol."

Lili frowned. "What does this have to do with the Vatis?"

"The castle of Bahail was said to be inhabited by a woman with the power to communicate with the Gods and Angels and learn about the nature of reality."

"I don't understand."

"They called this woman the Vatis."

Anastasia gasped. The Vatis had lived in the castle. The Vatis would've needed to have been protected during the war, so it would make sense for them to come to this castle, to hide. Did that mean she was wearing the clothes of the Vatis? Sleeping in the Vatis' bed? Had the Vatis left something of theirs behind, a clue as to who the other Ancients were? It was all too much to consider.

"That's not all," Aleric said. "It was discovered that the woman was none other than Queen Anarelia's youngest daughter, Analynn."

Anastasia froze. "*Youngest* daughter?"

Aleric nodded. "Anarelia had *two* daughters."

Gooseflesh erupted across Anastasia's skin. Queen Anarelia had had the gift of premonitions; it was the only way a Nadmilise royal could have two children. Except, in the Old World, the people had known about the two children, instead of them being hidden as they currently were in the realms.

Could the Vatis be passed down through the bloodline like the premonitions? If so, they needed to find Princess Analynn's family tree. Perhaps, her current descendent was the person they were looking for, the one that was somewhere in Armol. She was frustrated that she knew nothing about the Queens of the First Realms. Their records didn't extend so far back, outside of exceptional Queens that withstood the test of time.

She pushed back from the table. "We need to go to Armol."

"We need to be prepared," said William. "We don't know what we're walking into."

"So grab some weapons, and let's go."

"It's not that simple."

Ryke nodded. "We don't know where the Vatis is within the city, nor do we even know *who* they are. For all we know, we might've sent them to Armol ourselves."

Anastasia shook her head. "If we wait, the Vatis could leave, and our chance will have gone. You do what you need to get ready to go. Grab whatever previsions you can carry, and whatever weapons won't weigh you down. We'll leave at first light."

With that, she made her way from the room. Heading upstairs, she pushed her way into her chambers. Aagney was within, napping peacefully. She just stared at him, hardly daring to believe that in twenty-four hours, they could have the Vatis and the List of Ancients. They would be one step closer to going home!

But then she remembered the feast, and the people that needed her here in Bahail, and little Aagney. She couldn't shirk her responsibilities. But at the same time, none of it would matter if they returned home. This was the right thing to do. And yet, she wasn't sure what to do with Aagney. She couldn't bring him along, could she? What if there was a fight, or some sort of attack? He could be injured, be killed! But she couldn't just leave him in Bahail, either. She was his godmother. His parents had entrusted her with him.

She resolved to bring him along, and at the first sign of danger, she would get him out.

CHAPTER TWENTY-SIX

Dawn found Anastasia sitting anxiously on the edge of her bed, staring down at Aagney. Pulling him from his crib, she held him close and rubbed his back. There was something about going to Armol that felt momentous, like if they went there, there was no going back. It worried her, to bring an infant into that, but the thought of leaving him made her feel worse. She just kept reciting her promise to protect him should anything go south. But she couldn't bear to put him down just yet.

Continuing to rub her hand gently over his back, she headed downstairs to find Lili. She was seated at the table, eating a breakfast of fruit and bread. As Anastasia entered the room, she looked up. Anastasia was surprised to see she had a bow and quiver of arrows slung across her shoulders. She also wore travel-ready clothing.

Across the room, Ryke and William wore tunics and trousers, with an extra dagger each at their belts. Anastasia hesitated in the doorway, a frown tugging her lips.

"Why is everyone dressed like we're heading into battle?"

"For all we know, we are, my Princess," said Ryke.

So they felt the strange foreboding, too. Sitting at the table, Anastasia helped herself to some bread and jam. She hadn't had a chance to alert the Mistresses yet that she was leaving Bahail. She'd hoped it would be a quick trip to Armol, where they could find the Vatis and return. Even though the feast celebrating the harvest equinox was in a few days, she figured they'd have more than enough time without needing to alert anyone.

William strode forward and held out a bundled package to Anastasia. "These are from my father."

Unwrapping the bundle, she found two daggers within. One was longer than she was used to, the blade roughly the length of her forearm. The other was the usual size. They fit into a belt that she strapped around her hips.

"I'll be sure to thank him," she said.

"I hope you don't need them."

"Better safe than sorry."

By the time Mohan came downstairs—dressed in a black robe with a large, gray hematite crystal around his neck, and a belt of vials—they were ready to go. Gerrard met them at the door, seeing as he'd volunteered to join them, after much prompting from William the night before. He and Ryke said he knew what he was doing with a hammer and would provide more protection.

Together, with Lili, they headed out behind the castle. There, Mohan upended the contents of the bag he carried. Upon seeing a dead bird and rat, Anastasia recoiled.

"What is this?"

"Portal travel," Mohan explained. "It will take us directly to the location from the spell."

Anastasia turned away as Mohan took to carving the bird and collected its blood in a chalice. He placed its heart and wings separate from the rest of its body into a bowl and added the rat's ribcage. Covering it all in anointing oil, he put the bowl off to the side. He poured the rest of the oil into the blood-filled chalice and traced a circle upon the ground, outlining four pentagrams and the crescent moon-shaped sigil he stood upon in the center of the circle.

He turned back to look at them. "Ready?"

Anastasia nodded, though the whole thing made her squeamish. Thankfully, everyone else seemed as off-put by it as her.

"Stand in the pentagrams," he instructed.

They all stepped into a pentagram. Mohan dipped his fingers into what was left of the bloody oil and drew a circle pierced by a triangle on the back of his hands.

The oil in the chalice burst into flames as Mohan chanted, "Ani korah lo, aleelah g'dolah. K'cha et hakurban hazeh uftach et hadelet l'olam habah."

The blood around the circle lit like a fuse, until the entire circle burned. Mohan snapped his fingers and the bowl of sacrificial items burst into flame as well. Anastasia watched on, fascinated and awed, holding Aagney close.

Mohan called, "K'cha otanu l'mamlechat harochot, aleelah!"

Wind whipped through the trees, extinguishing the flames. As it dissipated, they looked around. Nothing had happened.

Gerrard glanced upwards. "Did it work?"

But then, the wind tore through the trees so forcefully, it knocked them down. Anastasia reached for William, but she was trapped inside the pentagram. The ground rumbled, and then it felt like they were falling, tumbling down to the depths of the earth. A scream tore from Anastasia's lips; she clutched at Aagney. And then, just as quickly, it all stopped. They slammed into the ground, the air knocked from their lungs.

Gerrard turned and vomited. Mohan groaned, rolling onto his back. William and Ryke staggered to their feet, drawing their daggers. Sucking in a breath, Anastasia sat up and tried to calm a wailing Aagney. Fear radiated from him in waves, leeching into the Nadmilise. Holding him so close, Anastasia felt like wailing, herself.

Getting to her feet, Anastasia took in their surroundings, illuminated by pale moonlight. They stood within the square of a beautiful castle. To her left stood a high tower, but the flag flying wasn't a Nadmilise one, but rather blood red claw marks upon a black banner.

"Is this the castle in Armol?" Ryke questioned.

But before anyone could answer, a cry rang out, "Fire!"

An explosion sounded, and a moment later, a cannon ball impacted the stone at their feet, flinging them backwards.

Panic flared in Anastasia's chest. She needed to get Aagney out of there. William was on her in an instant, shielding her and Aagney with his body. She could barely see the others through the cloud of dust, before a second cannon ball hit. She and William rolled out of the way. They struggled to get to their feet.

"Can you see who's shooting at us?" she yelled over the din.

William shook his head. "No!"

Glancing behind her, Anastasia spotted a walkway. She grabbed William's arm and pulled him towards it. They squeezed through the narrow space between the buildings and climbed over a low wall. There, it was a short drop to the roof of a building below.

Another explosion shook the ground, flinging them from the roof. They tumbled down to the cobblestones below, Anastasia twisting painfully to keep from landing on Aagney. Through the dust, they could just make out a doorway. They crawled over on hands and knees and pushed their way inside.

Getting to his feet, William pushed the heavy door closed with the weight of his body. Anastasia, meanwhile, looked around.

Rows of black iron doors colored the bare white walls. A spiral staircase let up to a second and third level, where more doors stood bolted.

"What is this place?" she wondered aloud.

As her voice echoed, others rose up to meet it, begging her for release. Horror flooded through her as she realized it was some sort of prison. What if this was where the Vatis was being kept, by whomever carried the black flag with the claw marks? It couldn't be. Who were all these people? And who was living in the castle?

But all thought left her mind as William shouted, "Dani!"

He raced up the stairs, two-at-a-time. Anastasia ran after him, utterly bewildered. "William, stop!"

Reaching one of the doors, William threw himself against it. But it was no use; the door was solid metal. Anastasia held him off, peering through the small window in the door. To her utter surprise, Dani Dinas sat within, covered in grime.

"What in the name of the Gods and Angels?"

A click sounded behind them. "I see you've found me, at last."

Anastasia whirled around, finding Joey standing behind her. Dark indigo swirls covered his skin, while jet black wings jutted from his back. He'd cut his hair short, making him look older, but it was white as snow. And his eyes were ice-blue, as opposed to their normal deep sapphire.

"Joey?"

Her eyes flickered to the crossbow in his hands. She had just enough time to turn her back to him, and wrap herself around Aagney, before he fired. The pain never came, however. Instead, she heard William grunt, and she turned to see him crumpled on the floor, the bolt sticking out of his stomach. Rage flared within her, and she flung herself at Joey. But before she reached him, he struck her with a bolt.

She crumpled, feeling unconsciousness drag her under. The last thought she had was elation that William was merely drugged, and not dead. But then the drugs dragged her under, as well.

CHAPTER TWENTY-SEVEN

Ericcen frowned. They'd flown Balan all over the sorcerer kingdom, collecting the strangest ingredients he needed for his potions. They had a cage of birds and rats, a half-gallon of something he called anointing oil, a couple of bowls and chalices, and a number of herbs and spices. It had taken them a little over a week to find everything, and Ericcen was growing restless. The sooner they got Balan's sister, the sooner they could find Queen Sona and return to Princess Anastasia.

Rounding the corner of the cottage they were squatting in, Ericcen found Balan drawing a circle in the frozen ground with a carved knife. Seeing as that wasn't nearly the oddest thing he'd seen Balan do, he shrugged it off and entered the cottage.

Norden sat at the table slicing their dried fish into pieces. Ericcen dropped the water jug on the table with a thud. "Where's Aelnold?"

"Went to gather some more apples from the grove."

Nodding his understanding, Ericcen sat at the table. He drummed his fingers on the wood and jiggled his legs. He knew he was irritating his brother, but he couldn't help it. Every second they sat there was a second they weren't completing their mission. It might not be much, but it was something he could use to impress the Princess. And he wasn't so sure he'd get a second chance to do that.

Pushing back from the table, he peered at Balan through the grimy window. The crazy sorcerer was carving the wings off a bird. It was dead, thank the Gods and Angels, but watching it was still unsettling.

"Why don't you go help Aelnold?" Norden suggested.

Ericcen relented, pushing his way through the backdoor. The apple grove stood a few paces from the house, spreading as far as the eye could see. The apples within were bright and crisp, and tasted like he was eating fresh cider.

A few rows back, he spotted Aelnold circling the top of one of the trees, plucking apples and placing them in his knapsack. Unfurling his wings, he wordlessly joined his brother.

The quiet serenity didn't last long before Balan came rushing into the grove. "It's time!"

Aelnold landed. "Time for what?"

"Our travel! Come along!"

Sharing a look with his brother, Ericcen landed and followed Balan around the side of the house. He'd drawn three pentagrams around the circle, and a crescent moon within. Everything was outlined in blood. Ericcen wrinkled his nose. He'd known a couple of sorcerers back home in the realms. They hadn't been the strongest of magic users, but they'd never needed to resort to bleeding a bird and drawing in the dirt. The Old World was a strange place.

Norden stumbled out of the cottage, toting his and Ericcen's knapsacks. As he jogged over, Balan stepped inside the crescent moon. They watched in fascination as he methodically checked his chalice and bowl of ingredients. The whole thing was rather revolting. But Ericcen could feel Balan's excitement grow. He supposed the sorcerer would do anything to get his sister back, as he would for his brothers.

Balan motioned to the pentagrams. "Step up."

Ericcen and his brothers obliged. Then, Balan cut the edge of his palm, dripped the blood into the chalice, and began to chant in a strange, guttural language.

The circle and pentagrams lit up, and a wind stirred the leaves around their feet. A moment later, they were all falling. Just as suddenly, they came to halt, slamming into the ground. Ericcen groaned; his stomach roiled uneasily, threatening to lose his lunch.

A loud bang propelled him to his feet, however. Dust clouded the air, making it difficult to see anything. What he could make out were enormous stone buildings. Rock exploded to his left, and he shielded his face with his hands. He couldn't see his brothers or Balan anywhere. But a short distance away, in the sky, were Nadmilise, silhouetted by the moon. Archers were shooting at them, trying to bring them down.

Before he could move, however, Balan raced by him. "It's time to take on the Soster!"

Ericcen coughed. "What's the Soster?"

But Balan disappeared into the dust, cackling. An ear-splitting *boom* tore through the air. Ericcen turned, watching with wide eyes as a cannonball gouged the earth not three feet from him. He fell back, looking around wildly. What in the name of the Gods and Angels was happening here?

Movement to his right drew his eyes. A Nadmilise landed, drawing his wings close to his body. Beside him, some small flying creature shifted into a man with a soft squeak.

This was too much. Ericcen and his brothers were not warriors. And Balan was certainly insane. Sister or not, he'd knowingly brought them to a battle. He needed to find Norden and Aelnold, and get as far away from this place as possible. They needed to find Queen Sona and return to Bahail, their promise to Balan be damned.

A hiss stopped him in his tracks. The man that had been a small creature whipped around and called, "Werewolves!"

In a flash, he was gone, his movements so quick he was merely a blur. His Nadmilise partner hesitated before leaping into the air. Startled, Ericcen just watched as he circled in the sky. He supposed that would be a better place to search for his brothers than down here, where he couldn't see much of anything.

Another cannonball wracked the earth, sending bits of dirt flying through the air. Ericcen dodged it, rolling to his feet. Drawing a knife from his knapsack, he took to the sky. Unable to see, however, he ended up running into a balustrade. The men stationed there turned to face him and he worked to keep his emotions in check. They were Nadmilise, same as him. Fighting his sister Nadmilise left a horrific taste in his mouth. Especially because they all seemed to be trained warriors, and all he had was a puny knife.

Explosions made his footing precarious as the guards rushed him. One of the warriors managed to clip his wing with an arrow and he hissed in pain, pulling his wings in close. But why in the world were Nadmilise fighting him?

"I'm a Nadmilise!" he called. "Please!"

But they didn't seem to care. "Aelnold!" he shouted. "Norden!"

It was no use; the cannon fire and explosions were too loud. Backing down the balustrade, he felt the low wall press against his legs. Figuring it was safer to go than stick around the people that wanted to kill him, he threw himself over the side. His wings snapped open and jerked him upward. From this vantage, he could see that he was outside a castle. But he had no idea which kingdom he was in.

Below, he saw the shifting man from before fighting what looked like werewolves, but none of them had shifted into their wolf forms. Other people were fighting, all Nadmilise. But at the far end of the castle square, magic erupted.

"Balan," he murmured.

Angling himself, he shot downward. When he reached the mayhem, however, he found that it wasn't Balan, but Prince Mohan.

"Your Highness?" Ericcen called.

"Find Anastasia!" he shouted. "Joey's here!"

Joey was here, in the middle of all of this? And so was Princess Anastasia? Ericcen shook his head. None of this made any sense. But he didn't have time to sort it out. He needed to find the princess.

Spinning, he found Chris Woodsman behind him on the balustrade, battling a number of Nadmilise. He leapt forward, spinning a wooden staff over his head. A couple of the Nadmilise lost their footing and fell over the balustrade. He caught an archer in the wrist; she cried out and dropped her bow. As he kicked it away, he launched himself at another archer, using his body's momentum to drive her to the ground. His fist connected with her chin with an audible crack. As she fell, he whirled around and launched his staff, catching a third archer square in the chest. Flying up to meet it, he grabbed his staff and landed.

Awe flooded through Ericcen. Chris managed to do all of that without his sight! How was something like that even possible? He supposed that's what separated the warriors from everyone else. They were fighters, through and through, as opposed to him, who hardly knew what to do with his knife.

Turning away, Ericcen ran through the dust. "Princess Anastasia?"

No one answered him. How was he supposed to find her in this mess? Taking the stairs down to the next level, he peered over the side. Balan was down at the front gates, creating quite a raucous with explosions. He rent the air with the guttural sounds of his shouts. Ericcen flew towards him, but before his feet could touch the ground, a massive explosion rocked the castle.

He landed in the castle square, blown back by the cannon fire. Everything stopped as a large crack raced up the stone from the portcullis. Before Ericcen had a chance to brace himself, the rock crumbled away beneath his feet. He fell forward just as another explosion filled the air with dust and stone. Though he unfurled his wings, it wasn't enough to keep him from hitting the ground. He slid through debris, coming to a halt at the foot of the portcullis, bruised but otherwise unharmed.

Coughing, he sat up and peered through the dust. "Princess Anastasia? Balan!"

No one answered him. As he made to move, he found his leg was pinned beneath a large pile of stone. Slowly, he started to pull the stone away, struggling to free himself. No other sounds reached his ears, but he refused to let himself fear the worst. His brothers and the princess had to be fine. He wouldn't imagine otherwise.

By the time he freed his leg, he heard footsteps. Getting to his feet, he peered around the mound of rock. "Princess Anastasia?"

A figure appeared through the dust, carrying a long wooden tube. When they came into view, Ericcen frowned. They wore a long cloak, obscuring their features. Ericcen squinted, trying to see through the shroud created by the hood. But it was if nothing was there.

The figure raised the wooden tube and pointed it at Ericcen. Before he had a chance to react, the figure expelled a breath into the tube. A dart flew from the end, striking Ericcen right in the neck. He staggered forward, his vision flickering. His movements felt sluggish, as though he was moving through wet cement. Dropping to his knees, he glared up at the figure. What was happening here? And why? What did this have to do with Princess Anastasia?

But all thought left his mind as the ground rushed up to meet him and his vision went dark.

CHAPTER TWENTY-EIGHT

Anastasia groaned as she opened her eyes. Her head felt like someone had smashed it with a hammer; her mouth felt like it was filled with cotton. The last thing she remembered was seeing Dani in a cell. And then Joey had shot her and William with some kind of tranquilizer.

Raising her head, she took in her surroundings. It was pitch black, and smelled damp. A chair cushioned her body, with ropes tying her down, but she seemed uninjured, despite the aching in her head.

But then she realized Aagney was missing. Panic momentarily overwhelmed her, but she pushed through it, reaching out to take in the feelings around her. There were people she didn't recognize, their emotions foreign to her, all laced with malice. Aagney's signature serenity shone like a beacon among them. If he was peaceful, then he wasn't in any danger, he wasn't afraid. Further out, she felt fear, despair, and desperation, but they were too far for her to know to whom they belonged.

"Good morning, Ana."

She jumped; she hadn't realized anyone was in the room with her. But how was that possible? She felt the room around her again, but no emotions flooded her. It was as though she was alone. How could that be?

A match struck a moment before a lantern flared to life. Joey stood illuminated by the firelight, his icy blue sorcerer eyes trained on her. "Sleep well?"

"What is all this?" she asked.

"All in due time." He turned and picked up a small paring knife from a table beside him. Holding it to the lamp, he studied it. "I'd wager the last time I saw you was the most pain you felt. Am I right?"

Anastasia thought back to when he'd attacked her, when he'd nailed her upside down to a post, when he'd stabbed a syringe into her back. She shivered. None of her previous injuries compared, not even when a Shadow's claws pierced her chest. Perhaps it was because Joey had been the one hurting her, and there was an emotional component as well as physical.

"No matter," he said with a chuckle. "You will know worse pain. Like I did."

She looked up at him. "What do you mean?"

"All those months I was gone, did you ever wonder what had become of me?" He moved towards her, holding the knife aloft. "I was being tortured, for information about you and your precious premonitions."

She started.

"Oh, yes, I know all about your silly little visions, Anastasia. But they are *nothing* compared to the gift I've received."

"What gift?"

He smiled, an unnerving thing that sent a chill through her. "All in due time."

Leaning forward, he pressed the tip of the knife to the edge of her fingernail. A hot sweat broke out across Anastasia's skin. Reflexively, she jerked away from him, but her hands were too tightly bound; she couldn't move.

"Please," she whimpered. "Why are you doing this?"

He met her eyes; there was nothing but empty darkness in their depths. "If you make a sound, I'll kill all your friends I have captured here, starting with the baby."

With that, he wedged the knife beneath her fingernail. White hot pain burned like fire up her arm. She clenched her jaw, swallowing back a scream. In one fluid motion, he brought the knife up, tearing off her fingernail. She clenched her body, writhing, clenching her jaw to keep from shrieking in agony. Tasting blood, she gasped, trying to breathe through the pain. But Joey didn't give her a reprieve. He just worked the knife under her next fingernail and tore it off.

Her vision flickered. With her good hand, she dug her nails into the wooden arm of the chair. Bright red blood dripped down her fingers, pooling on the stone floor beneath. Anastasia focused on the sound, but the pain overwhelmed her, driving her into the darkness beyond.

She awoke with a start, dripping from head-to-toe. Joey held a bucket, which he apparently had just used to dump icy water over her head. She gasped, taking short, quick breaths.

"Did I say you could pass out?" he demanded.

Her vision flickered in and out; her head lulled to the side.

Joey slammed his hands on the arms of the chair. "Look at me!"

She dragged her eyes to meet his. He'd been tortured at the hands of Adrian and the Shadows for months, hidden away in the Shadows' world. That was enough to break anyone. But there was no trace of the Joey she'd grown up with, the young man who had earnestly learned the ancient language, and blushed when he talked about Alex Woodsman. That man was gone, replaced with a monster she didn't recognize.

"You will face what I faced, dear Anastasia, and then I will make dear William watch as I kill you."

Anastasia's breath caught. "William?"

But Joey just shoved the knife under her third fingernail and ripped it off. Her throat was raw with her swallowed screams. Her body convulsed under the pain; she slipped in and out of unconsciousness.

"Why?" she croaked.

He gently caressed her face. "Because I am the rightful King of Jacqueline."

She spat blood onto the floor. "You're crazy."

"Am I?"

He pressed both hands against her face, gripping so tightly she thought he meant to crush her skull. But then her vision flickered as though she was falling through smoke. She slumped back against the chair as an image exploded in her mind:

I stand in the castle gardens, my hands clasped behind my back. The moonlight filters through the runas bushes, bathing everything in pale pink light. Valdon leans casually against a pillar, his arms crossed. He looks far younger than I've ever seen him, still carrying himself with a youthful air.

He straightens as someone approaches. Shock slams into me as I see my grandmother. She can't be more than seventeen-years-old. Her hair is elaborately pulled back on the left side, as is the custom for married women, and she wears a beautiful summer gown of green and gold. As she glances behind her, I see our pendant glinting at her throat.

Valdon reaches out as she approaches, gently pulling her to him. "You're late."

Analie frowns. "We need to talk."

"Do we?"

Leaning in, he presses gentle kisses to her throat. She doesn't pull away from him, but neither does she return his affections.

She whispers hoarsely, "I'm with child."

Valdon stops immediately. "Do you know—"

"She will not be the Princess of Jacqueline, I have seen that." She lowers her eyes. "She is your daughter."

"And Brock?"

She hangs her head. "He does not know."

Stepping back, Valdon considers her. "I don't have to abdicate the throne, Analie. We could legitimize her, raise her as our princess."

Analie makes a scoffing noise in the back of her throat. As she moves to sit on the bench beside them, I see the tattoo over her heart: Brock. She's already married to my grandfather. And yet she's sleeping with Valdon? Valdon?

"She doesn't have the bloodline," Analie finally says. "She isn't going to be Queen."

Valdon nods. Slowly, he moves to sit beside her. She holds out her hand and he takes it, lacing his fingers through hers. They complement each other reflexively, both reacting to the other's movements. They're like mirrors of each other. And their love for each other is plain even from where I stand, hidden amongst the flowers.

Valdon looks over at her. "What does that mean for us?"

"We will follow the vision I've seen," she says, but it's clear she isn't completely convinced. *"I will go away for a year. Upon her birth, I will give her to Deera."*

"The Sterata woman?"

Analie nods. "Our daughter will be the mother of the next Sterata. She will need to learn."

This doesn't seem to please Valdon, but he doesn't say anything. Analie squeezes his hand before she pulls away.

"And… you will abdicate the throne, let your sister Sona become Queen. I will not take that dream from you."

"I am abdicating the throne to be your advisor, to follow in my mentor's footsteps."

Analie frowns. "That won't have to change."

They sit together in silence. None of Analie's words seem to surprise Valdon. I suppose he's used to hearing of her premonitions. It also feels like they've had this conversation before. Had they? Did they discuss the *ramifications of their actions? Surely, my grandmother would've seen this in her premonitions? What would become of them?*

"Will she be safe, our daughter?"

Analie smiles. "She will grow to be strong, and lovely, and kind."

"Just like her mother."

This saddens Analie. "I love you."

"I love you, too."

After a moment of silence, Analie gets to her feet. "Brock will return home in the morning. I will leave shortly after."

Without another word, she strides away from him.

"What is her name?" he calls.

She stops but doesn't turn. "Calla."

Valdon falls back onto the bench, staring after her as she hurries away. She passes me, and I can see her eyes shimmering with tears. I long to reach out to her, to comfort her, but black smoke obscures my vision. I struggle to stay where I am, to stay with this open, emotional version of my grandmother, but the smoke drags me back to my own reality.

Anastasia awoke with a jolt, breathing raggedly. Her mind spun, struggling to make sense of what she saw. But before she could sort her thoughts, the pain of Joey's torture sprang to the forefront. She bit back a scream, grabbing the armrest with her good hand.

"What was that?" she breathed.

Joey grinned. "My gift. You can see the future? I can see the past."

"That really happened?"

"That's the story of my mother."

The ramifications of Joey's words slammed into Anastasia. Valdon and her grandmother had been lovers. Their daughter was Calla, the woman who married Deera's son, the woman who gave birth to the next Sterata. Her son… was Joey?

It couldn't be. Joey was human. He'd lived in the human realm his entire life. How could he be Valdon's grandson? And yet he had the wings of the Nadmilise and the eyes of a sorcerer.

"Let me fill in a few gaps, *cousin*," Joey sneered. "Analie went off to have her baby, and your stupid grandfather never knew anything about it. After she gave my mother away to Deera, she returned to her pretty little kingdom and had your mother, the *Queen*. Meanwhile, my mother grew up with my father. They fell in love, got married, and had me.

"Everything was fine, but then Analie came back. She told Deera this story about my father, about what would happen to him. Together, she and Deera took me and my mother away from my father. Our loss drove him into the madness of his Shadow half, and he came after us. That night, eleven years ago, when the Shadows attacked Sehir? That was my father, exerting his power, trying to bring me and my mother home. But instead, my mother went with Analie and Deera to the alternate universe, while Valdon sent me to the human realm."

Anastasia shook her head. "That can't be."

"But that isn't all!" Joey cried. "My father found me. He knew I'd returned to Sehir and saw his chance. When the Shadows attacked Sehir those months ago and took your family? That was my father coming to collect me. He took me back to the Shadow universe and awakened me, showed me what *real* power can do."

"He tortured you!"

Joey's hand cracked against her face. "You shut up! No more of your lies, Anastasia! I am the rightful King of Jacqueline, and I'm going to take back what's mine."

Kneeling, he worked his knife under her fourth fingernail. Her entire body trembled with the exertion of trying to stay quiet. She focused on little Aagney's sense of peace, even as she slipped in and out of consciousness. Thankfully, when he ripped off her fifth fingernail, blessed darkness wrapped around her and she didn't return.

CHAPTER TWENTY-NINE

William awoke sluggishly. With a groan, he rolled onto his side. He'd been having the nicest dream. He'd been standing in the throne room in Sehir, dressed in elaborate finery. All of his friends and family had been sitting in pews, looking up at him. Chris and Mohan had stood to his right, while Dani and Lili had stood to his left. Flower petals had been strewn down the middle of the aisle, giving off a faint scent. But just as the doors had opened to reveal his bride, he'd awakened.

Wiping the sleep from his eyes, he looked around. He was inside a small cell, complete with a slab of a bed, a hole in the floor to relieve himself, and a small candle in a window no bigger than his hand. Getting to his feet, he rushed to the door.

"Anastasia!" he shouted. "Anastasia!"

But she wasn't by his side. He couldn't believe Joey was here, or that he'd been keeping his sister prisoner for months. Was this really the royal castle, the ancestral home of Anastasia's family?

Banging across the way drew William's attention. "Let me out!"

He'd recognize that voice anywhere. "Dani!"

"William?"

Peering through the window, he could see his sister's face pressed up against the glass. He grinned. By the Gods and Angels, it was good to see her alive. He hadn't realized just how worried he'd been about her. And she seemed relatively unharmed, save for a few scrapes on her cheeks. She still had fight left in her.

"Are you alright?" he called.

"Fine! You?"

"Fine. Just trapped."

She laughed. "When are *you* ever really trapped?"

A loud thump sounded farther down the hall. "I'm glad we've established you're both fine, but I'd really like to get out of here already!"

William frowned; he recognized that voice, too. "Zand, is that you?"

"Aye."

Hayde Zand was a prisoner here, as well? Who else was trapped in these cells? And why? What did Joey want with them all? And where was Anastasia? He knew Joey had nearly killed her some months before, back in Sehir. And William didn't doubt that he'd try again. If they weren't free from these cells soon, he was afraid Joey could succeed.

"Mohan!" he called. "Are you here?"

"Yes, love," came the soft reply.

"Can you get us out of here?"

"They took all my potions."

William swore. The doors were solid metal; he couldn't break through it. And there was nothing he could use in this cell as a weapon. Nothing protruded from the walls or bed, and the hole in the ground was too small for him to fit through.

Frowning, he sorted his thoughts. Master Glude had always taught him that he could turn anything into a weapon if he tried hard enough. In fact, he'd once won a training match against one of his sister apprentices with only a pair of spoons. But what did he have here? The clothes on his back, his shoes, a sheet and pillow, his wings, and a candle.

He supposed he could try sticking strips of the cloth into the door and lighting it on fire, trying to get the metal to expand and warp, allowing him to open the door. But there were no gaps large enough.

There was no metal he could break off and use as a lock pick on the door.

There were no other windows, no glass he could break.

The hinges were on the outside of the door, so he couldn't even try and pry those free.

They were good and properly trapped.

And then the door to his cell opened. He squinted in the sudden brightness, hesitantly stepping forward. He froze, however, when he saw who stood in front of him, holding a key. He had jet black swirls across his skin, and obsidian wings, but William would recognize him anywhere.

"Durse Follant."

Durse chuckled. "Fitting, isn't it?"

William glowered, until he saw his sister over Durse's shoulder. Pushing past Durse, he pulled his sister in an embrace. A split second later, a whip cracked across his back. He cried out, stumbling backwards.

"Back in line!" Durse commanded.

Wordlessly, William joined the others. Mohan was there, along with Dani, Lili, Gerrard, and Hayde. But so was Ericcen Ros and his two brothers, two sorcerers William didn't recognize, and Vlad and Chris.

"Chris?" William called.

He lifted his head. "William?"

"What are you doing here?"

"Vlad and I arrived shortly after the fighting started. We were coming to search this city for the royal family."

Durse cracked his whip in the air. "Silence!"

Cloaked guards led them forward, out into the pale moonlight. Durse patted each of them down as they exited. William found it preposterous. What could they possibly have taken from their cells? But as Durse patted him down, William felt the cool steel of a blade slide into the belt of his trousers. Had Durse given him a knife?

He waited until they were outside to covertly check. Sure enough, the dagger his father had made for him sat tucked into the top of his trousers. Why in the world would Durse have given him a knife?

Durse flicked his gray eyes to Dani. William followed his gaze, finding a similar blade tucked into the belt of Dani's skirt. The others around them all had blades, too. Why would Durse give them all blades? If he was a guard, working for Joey, surely he'd want to keep them prisoner. It didn't make any sense.

But then Durse let out a fierce battle cry and pulled out a battle axe, and William reacted instinctively. He pulled the dagger from his belt and launched himself at the nearest guard. They grappled before William gained the upper hand. Driving the Nadmilise to the ground, William hit him with the hilt of his blade. Hayde, Durse, and Chris moved swiftly, cutting down the rest of the guards. When they were gone, Dani strode toward Durse.

Before William could stop her, she punched him square in the face. "That was for before."

Durse stumbled back holding his nose. "Fair enough."

"What is this, Follant?" William demanded. "Why'd you help us?"

Before he could answer, a slew of guards rounded the corner, weapons raised. William ran forward, brandishing his blade.

Vlad darted forward, so quick he was merely a blur. Reaching the nearest guard, he sunk his fangs into the man's neck, drinking deep. As revolting as it was to see Vlad drinking someone's blood, William was glad Vlad was on their side.

Turning, he caught the next guard in the stomach. Hayde and Chris took down the next two, and Dani—to William's utter surprise—leapt onto the back of a guard, used her body's momentum to drive him to the ground, and cut his throat with one quick swipe. It seemed in the months since he'd seen his little sister, she'd become a formidable warrior.

As more guards descended on them, Durse turned to William. "Anastasia's in the north tower. You need to go to her."

Nodding, William unfurled his wings and leapt into the sky. A few guards pursued him, chasing him to the north tower. When he landed, he drove one into the stone wall, stunning her. The other two he quickly dispatched; they were reckless and untrained.

He kicked in the window to the tower and landed in the dark room. "Anastasia?"

A groan answered him. Even with the shattered window it was too dark to see. He felt his way forward, until he reached a chair in the middle of the room. Feeling someone tied to it, he quickly dropped to his knees and began cutting the ropes. Gods and Angels, what had Joey done to her? He pushed his panic aside and focused on freeing her.

Once the ropes fell away, he scooped her into his arms and returned the way he came. She felt limp in his arms, like the way she had when she'd been dying from Joey's torture in Sehir.

"Gods and Angels," he breathed. "Stay with me, Anastasia."

Landing on an empty balustrade, he put her down. Feeling her pulse, he began to panic. She was dying. But her body looked pristine. There was no blood, no scratches, not so much as a bruise. She looked as though she'd simply gone to sleep. But he knew this was one she wouldn't wake up from.

A sound behind him drew his attention. He found more guards running towards them. Leaping to his feet, he fought them back. Thankfully, the balustrade pathway was narrow, so they could only rush him one at a time. But each time one fell, and the next guard climbed over their fallen guards, they pushed William back towards Anastasia.

By the time he felled all the of the guards, he was covered in blood. Some of it his own. He dropped to his knees beside Anastasia and felt for a pulse. When he didn't find one, he shook himself.

Chapter Twenty-Nine

It couldn't be.

A crack sounded a moment before pain seared across the back of his head. His vision flickered, and he pitched forward. Had someone snuck up on him? It didn't really matter, he supposed. Anastasia was gone. He'd been too slow to save her.

As unconsciousness dragged him under, he pictured her face, smiling down at him. It soothed the heartache.

William awoke sluggishly. With a groan, he rolled onto his side. He'd been having the nicest dream. He'd been standing in the throne room in Sehir, dressed in elaborate finery. All of his friends and family had been sitting in pews, looking up at him. Chris and Mohan had stood to his right, while Dani and Lili had stood to his left. Flower petals had been strewn down the middle of the aisle, giving off a faint scent. But just as the doors had opened to reveal his bride, he'd awakened.

Wiping the sleep from his eyes, he looked around. He was inside a small cell, complete with a slab of a bed, a hole in the floor to relieve himself, and a small candle in a window no bigger than his hand. Getting to his feet, he rushed to the door.

"Anastasia!" he shouted. "Anastasia!"

But she wasn't by his side. Then he remembered, she'd never be by his side. Déjà vu struck him like a physical blow and he staggered back. He'd done this before. This exact thing.

Peering through the window on the door, he saw Dani. Down the hall, he knew Mohan would be there. As would Chris, Vlad, Hayde, Ericcen, Aelnold, Norden, Gerrard, Lili, and two sorcerers he didn't know. So did that mean they'd been caught, and he'd had the same dream about his wedding? Or did it mean that Durse hadn't come to free them? They hadn't battled the guards? He hadn't escaped?

A voice behind him said, "It's a little of both, really."

Whirling, he found Joey standing behind him. "What's going on?"

"I learned a lot of things in my time with Adrian. They really do come in handy."

"Where's Anastasia?"

Joey chuckled. "You mean you don't remember?"

William followed his gaze, finding Anastasia's body crumpled on the floor at his feet. Her blood coated his hands. He could see bruises on her neck that matched his fingers. He'd strangled her?

"This is a trick," he said. "I'd never hurt her."

Joey smiled. "Is that so?"

Unbidden, he thought of the time he'd been possessed by the Shadows, when he'd wrapped his arms around Anastasia's throat, trying to choke the life from her. If she hadn't found a way to stop him, he would've killed her.

But he hadn't been possessed. Not this time. And yet, a small voice in the back of his head wondered if he would know if he had? Would he remember? He shook himself. Of course he would. This was Anastasia they were talking about. He loved her more than anything in this world. If he'd done anything to hurt her, he'd remember. He'd *know*. This was all a mind game. He wouldn't let Joey break him.

"This isn't real."

Joey grinned. "You'll soon find out that reality is subjective."

He snapped his fingers and a cloud of thick black smoke engulfed William. He struggled to breathe, clawing at his throat, but, ultimately, the smoke won out and he fell into cloying unconsciousness.

CHAPTER THIRTY

Anastasia awoke for the second time tied to a chair. This time, however, someone was cutting her free. She groaned as pain lanced up her arm. Memories of her time with Joey flashed through her mind and she bit her tongue, worried he'd start hurting those she cared about.

"It's alright, Your Highness. Just stay with me."

Forcing her eyes open, she glanced down at the young man kneeling before her. He had dark hair, that matched the black swirls on his skin and the wings that stretched from his back.

"What are you doing?"

He looked up at her and she gasped, recognizing his flinty eyes. *Durse Follant*. The last she'd seen him, he'd broken out of the dungeons in Sehir and hidden in Ostana's chambers. How in the name of the Gods and Angels was he here? And why? Was he working for Joey? It wouldn't surprise her, considering he'd been arrested for letting Shadows into the city. But... she then remembered that it had been Ostana that let the Shadows into the city. So what had *he* been doing?

She winced, biting back a cry of pain, as he pressed a gel to her raw fingertips. Gently, he wrapped bandages around her hand. Sweet, blessed numbness stole up her fingers. She slumped back against the chair, taking a deep breath.

"I bet that feels better."

She glanced at him. "What are you doing here?"

"I have a lot to explain. But let's get out of here first."

Tying off the bandages, he grabbed his knife and sliced through the rest of the ropes tying her to the chair. Getting to his feet, he peered through the bars on the door.

"Come on," he murmured, stepping out into the hall.

Anastasia wordlessly followed him. They moved through narrow servants' halls, until they spilled out into a courtyard. Squinting in the darkness, Anastasia peered out at the castle yard beyond. They stood close to the wall, crouched low to the ground. Durse led her to a squat stone building just west of the tower they'd exited.

When they reached the door, Durse turned to face her. "You have a dagger on you?"

Reaching for her belt, she felt the daggers William's father had given her. It seemed Joey hadn't expected her to get free of his bonds.

"I'm good."

"Will you trust me?"

She looked him up and down. What other option did she have? If she ran, she'd likely get lost and stumble upon Joey accidentally. Besides, she doubted Durse Follant could be any worse than Joey had been.

"Yes."

Slowly, so as not to hurt her, Durse clasped her hands behind her back. Leading her forward, he knocked on the door in front of them. It swung open a moment later to reveal a Nadmilise with a crossbow slung across his back. He eyed Durse before inclining his head. It seemed Durse had some sort of sway over these people.

But then the guard's eyes slid to Anastasia. "Gods and Angels, I didn't know *she* was going to be held here."

"Change of plans," Durse grunted. "I'm to take her upstairs."

The guard stepped aside, letting them in. Rows of cells filled the room, and a spiral staircase led up to a second floor with more cells. Each door was bolted shut, the sounds of kept prisoners emanating from within.

In the center of the floor sat a table of weapons. Anastasia spotted daggers, a small knife, Chris' bo staff, Lili's bow and arrows, Gerrard's hammer, Mohan's belt of potions, and a scepter.

"I'll need to take these," the guard said, reaching for Anastasia's weapons belt.

Instantaneously, Durse dropped her hands. Anastasia reached back with her good hand, unsheathing one of her daggers. In one fluid motion, she flipped the blade and drove it into the guard's neck. He dropped to the ground, blood spurting from the wound. Durse leapt around her, running at the other guards that charged them. Anastasia yanked her blade free and dropped to her knees, searching the fallen guard for the keys to the cells.

Finding the key ring, she ran to the nearest cell and unlocked the door. It hardly mattered who was being held in these cells; whoever was a prisoner of Joey's deserved to go free, regardless of who they were.

When Durse finished off the guards, he circled back to help Anastasia. In a matter of moments, they'd opened every cell in the building. Chris, Ryke, Mohan, Vlad, Gerrard, Lili, Dani, Hayde Zand, Ericcen, Aelnold, Norden, and two sorcerers congregated together, while the other prisoners made a run for it.

"Anastasia!" Dani exclaimed.

Mohan turned. "Oh, am I glad to see you, love."

They all embraced. When they stepped back, Dani motioned to the female sorcerer standing beside her. "This is Mira. She was with me in the Sand Isles."

The other sorcerer held out his hand. "And I am her brother, Balan."

Dani glanced around. "Where's William?"

"I thought he'd be here with you," said Anastasia.

"Joey has him somewhere in the castle," said Durse. "As well as the baby."

Anastasia went cold all over. Joey had Aagney and William. She clenched her fists, rage flooding through her. If he harmed a single hair on either one of their heads, she'd kill him herself. The Nadmilise flinched back from her, clearly feeling her anger.

"What do you mean 'the baby'?" Vlad asked, an edge to his voice. "You can't possibly mean my *son*."

Anastasia deflated. She's willingly brought Vlad's son here. Gods and Angels, why would she have ever brought him along? She should've foreseen the danger, should've known what would happen.

"You brought my son here?" Vlad demanded of Anastasia.

Mohan rested a hand on Vlad's shoulder. "They have to be safe for now. Joey will be waiting for us to come find them, so he won't hurt them. They're bait. Right now, we need to focus on getting the Vatis."

Anastasia took a breath. He was right. That was the reason they'd come to the castle in the first place. The sooner they found the Vatis, the sooner they'd be free of Joey's spell.

Vlad skewered Anastasia with a look. "If he touches one hair on Aagney's head…"

"You found the Vatis?" Dani asked.

"Sort of," said Mohan. "We did a location spell that sent us here. But we aren't sure of the precise location or identity of the Vatis."

Gerrard stepped forward. "Could you do another location spell?"

Mohan shook his head. "I don't have enough ingredients."

"What do you need?" asked Balan.

While the two sorcerers bent their heads over Balan's collection of herbs, Anastasia studied the people with her. It was very possible one of them was the Vatis. And if Mohan was right about the Vatis being connected to ancient Nadmilise bloodlines, then it could easily have been Durse Follant, Hayde Zand, or Dani, who were all present in the castle when Mohan did the spell.

A moment later, Mohan and Balan were pulling out a chalice and apatite crystal. Ryke and Durse took up positions in front of the door, peering out into the evening. Hayde and Dani grabbed the weapons from the fallen guards, handing them to those that were unarmed.

Spreading out the map he'd brought, Mohan peered at his grimoire. Anastasia offered her blood this time, instead of William. Just thinking of him set her on edge; there was no telling what Joey could be doing to him, or to Aagney. Surely, he wouldn't hurt an infant? She'd been so stupid, bringing him here. And poor Vlad. His son was in the arms of a killer, one they all once called friend. And she'd been the one to bring him here. If only she'd known.

Mohan looked up at them. "It says the Vatis is in this room."

They all looked at each other.

Gerrard frowned. "Is that even possible?"

"Look," said Anastasia. "Only Dani, Hayde, and Durse were in the castle when we did the last location spell. They're the only choices."

Ericcen shook his head. "So how do we find out who it is?"

"We cast a circle," said Mohan.

Anastasia watched as he and Balan drew a circle in the dirt. Inside it, he drew four pentagrams. At the head, they drew a circle inside a triangle. Stepping back, Balan and Mohan shared a look.

"What?" asked Lili.

"We need physical representations of the elements," Balan explained.

Mohan considered them for a moment. "Dani, grab a handful of dirt; you'll stand in for earth. Hayde, take the chalice; you'll be water. And Durse, take the candle from inside one of the cells; you'll be fire."

"What of air?" Balan murmured.

"As the connection to the ancient bloodlines, Anastasia can stand in for air. Her pendant will suffice."

Slowly, Dani, Hayde, Durse, and Anastasia grabbed their totems and took their places in the pentagrams. Mohan stood in the triangle in the middle, flipping through the pages of his grimoire. Everyone else—except Ryke, who kept an eye on the door—stood around them, watching with wide-eyes as Mohan raised his hands and begun.

He strode three times around the circle before stopping in the center. Wind kicked up around them, swirling the dirt around their ankles. A tingle raced across Anastasia's skin.

"We call Earth to the circle, so we may be grounded," Mohan said.

The pentagram beneath Dani's feet lit up with bright green light. The wind blew harder.

Turning, Mohan continued, "We call Fire to the circle, so we may be unafraid."

The pentagram beneath Durse's feet lit up with red light. Anastasia swore she could smell the spicy waters of the Fire Lake. She felt the surprise and uncertainty of the people around her. Thankfully, she heard Lili faintly describing to Chris what was happening.

"We call Air to the circle, so we may open our minds."

As the pentagram beneath Anastasia's feet lit up, she felt a rush of cool air. Gooseflesh erupted across her skin.

"Finally, we call Water to the circle, so we may find our way."

As soon as the pentagram beneath Hayde's feet lit up, Anastasia felt a rush of energy. A bright light engulfed them all, blocking out the cells around them. Anastasia shielded her eyes, unable to move. The others' uncertainty trickled through her, making her uneasy. She centered herself, trusting in Mohan's ability.

When the wind died down, she opened her eyes to see she was standing in the atrium within the large tree, the one in which she'd gone to receive her tattoos. Just as before, the large circular window gave her a glimpse of vibrant fields, but it was too bright for her to look at for long. The thrones of the Gods and Angels were empty, as well, and the table of objects was gone.

Turning, she was surprised to see Chris, Dani, and Mohan standing with her. But they looked incorporeal, transparent like ghosts. And they were dressed strangely.

Chris was clothed in black boiled leather from head-to-toe, complete with thick gloves and forearm bracers. A thick belt held his batons at his waist, while a thinner belt slung across his chest held a dagger. Most strange was the crest on his chest: chains wrapped around a crown.

Beside him, Dani wore a simple orange gown and shawl, embossed with the image of a swan. Strands of beaded necklaces, gold rings, and a brightly-patterned headdress decorated her.

Behind them, Mohan was dressed in all green with polished metal accents. A long, flowing shawl hung over a fitted vest, geometric-patterned flared trousers, and metallic platform boots. A splayed hand was embossed on the front of his chest, which seemed to glow as he moved.

Looking down at herself, Anastasia saw she was dressed in a snow-white gown of tulle and lace, with a golden harp embroidered on the front.

"What is all this?" Mohan asked.

But before any of them could respond, bright light flashed through the room. When is dissipated, Isidora Spiros, Hughie Roth—the prince of the ghosts—and the Fairy Queen stood before them. They, too, were dressed strangely. Shock slammed through Anastasia when she saw them. What were they all doing there? And why?

Hughie looked down at his deep blue robes—embossed with a vibrant phoenix—and strings of beaded necklaces with a frown. "Where are we?"

"It seems we're in the realm of the Gods and Angels," said Dani.

Isidora twirled in her flowing gold gown with the image of a fox. "Why are we dressed like this?"

"All we know is that Mohan casted a circle, to try and find an ancient being called the Vatis. And now we're here."

"Isn't it obvious?" the Fairy Queen asked.

She was dressed in a resplendent silver gown, with an acacia branch circlet around her head. She looked more human than Anastasia had ever seen her, with pale skin and long, flowing hair. Instead of being roughly five inches tall, she now stood head-to-head with Anastasia.

"We're the Ancients."

Surprise flooded through Anastasia. *They* were the Ancients? How could that be? Wouldn't they have known?

"That means one of us is the Vatis, and can take the List from Chris," said Dani.

Isidora frowned. "I'm sorry, but what's happening here?"

"When this is all over, head to Síthe," said the Fairy Queen. "We shall discuss there."

Mohan looked between them. "So what do we do now?"

"Maybe we should all hold hands or something?" Hughie suggested.

Figuring it was worth a shot, Anastasia stepped forward. But when they all grasped hands, nothing happened. Frustrated, Anastasia swore. This was not how all this was supposed to go! They needed to find the Vatis, to get the List from Chris. It didn't matter who was on the List anymore, seeing as she knew now who the Ancients were, but he was still blinded by it. There had to be a way to unearth the Vatis and free him.

She had to admit, she wasn't so surprised she was an Ancient. She'd figured, when Tamo had hunted her all those months before, trying to imprison her for Anistes Droun, that he had to have some inkling that she was on the List. And, the more she'd thought about it, the more sense it made. Why else would she have the power to see the future, if not for being an Ancient?

But Dani? And Chris? Did it mean they had powers, too? Was there something each one of them could do that no one else could?

"Well," mused Mohan. "How do we get out of here?"

"We have to Awaken," said the Fairy Queen.

Hughie sighed. "And how do we do that?"

"The Vatis is supposed to Awaken us."

Dani threw up her hands in frustration. "Well, how are we supposed to figure out who the Vatis is?"

Suddenly, a circle of light rose into the air. They all stepped back, staring at it. It gave off a faint heat and wavered in the light emanating from the Gardens.

"What is it?" asked Isidora.

"Maybe some sort of Ancients magic?" Mohan offered.

"Or something from the Gods and Angels," suggested Dani.

Whatever it was, none of them moved towards it. Anastasia stared at it, wondering if it really was from the Gods and Angels, like a prompt, egging them forward. Not for the first time, she wished she better understood the Ancients and their powers. Perhaps she would've been able to figure out what to do now if she had.

Mohan nodded to Anastasia. "You're the descendant of the woman they called the Vatis. Why don't you go touch it?"

Anastasia frowned. "You're the second most powerful sorcerer in the realms. *You* touch it."

"I don't have permission from Zeus for any of this," Isidora said, backing away. "There's no way I'm going to touch it."

"I'm a ghost," said Hughie. "That thing could tear me apart."

Dani rolled her eyes. "Gods and Angels, I'll do it."

She stepped forward, reaching out a hand to touch the light. With a loud *crack* it flung her backwards. She rolled to a stop at the base of the round window, holding her injured hand to her chest.

"Let me try," offered Chris.

Stepping forward, he touched the light. When nothing happened, he stepped inside the circle.

"Great," said Isidora. "The blind guy can enter the lightning circle."

"Well, he's got the List," said the Fairy Queen. "If this is a way for the Vatis to take it from him, he's got to be able to enter."

With a sigh, Anastasia stepped forward. "I'll go."

Reaching out, she brushed her fingertips against the light. When nothing happened, she stepped inside the circle with Chris. Surprise shot through her; she hadn't expected to be the Vatis. If that were the case, why couldn't she have taken the List from Chris ages ago? What had stopped them?

But before she could think of an answer, the light intensified, lifting them both from the ground. Chris cried out, his body arching painfully. As she reached for him, she found she couldn't touch him. Suspended like she was, she felt like time had stopped altogether. It was like every moment of time happened at once, and yet not at all. Every past, every future, wrapped around her, displayed as her present. She comprehended nothing as it flashed before her, overwhelming her mind. And then, an indeterminate amount of time later, she dropped to the ground beside Chris.

When she opened her eyes, she found herself on the floor in the jail, surrounded by Durse, Hayde, Balan, Gerrard, and all the others. Beside her, Mohan, Chris, and Dani were stirring.

"What happened?" asked Gerrard.

Anastasia ignored him, rolling to her feet. "Did it work?"

"Did what work?" asked Vlad.

But all Anastasia did was watch Chris as he slowly reached up and removed the length of cloth binding his eyes. As it fell, he took a deep breath.

Then, for the first time in months, Chris looked up at Anastasia. Shock flooded through her at the deep color of his eyes; she'd forgotten just how green they were.

"By the Gods and Angels," Dani breathed.

"It worked," murmured Chris. "I can see."

Durse frowned. "As beautiful as I'm sure this moment is for all of you, we need to go. Joey won't wait forever."

"But wait," said Lili. "Did you find the Vatis?"

Anastasia shared a look with Chris. "We did better; we found the Ancients."

"Gods and Angels," Hayde murmured.

"We can go home," said Ericcen.

"Not just yet," said Anastasia. "We have to Awaken the Ancients, first."

Aelnold swore. "It's always another step, isn't it."

"Just the one more, then we can return to Sehir."

Vlad stepped forward and held his hand out to Anastasia. "Well, then, in the meantime, let's go get my son back."

Getting to her feet, Anastasia turned and faced the people around her. She was an Ancient. Not just any Ancient, but the Vatis, the vessel of the Gods and Angels. It was her job to Awaken the Ancients, to bring them to their power.

She couldn't help the smile that tugged her lips at the thought.

CHAPTER THIRTY-ONE

Durse stepped up to the door of the jail, peering out into the darkness. "Joey will have them in the Great Hall. He'll be expecting at least Anastasia to come for William and Aagney."

"So we'll need to take them by surprise," said Hayde.

"There's no telling how many guards he'll have on him."

Vlad growled, "It doesn't matter. No one will stand between me and my son."

Durse looked at Chris. "Are you well enough to fight?"

Chris nodded. "Aye."

Anastasia squared her shoulders. Now that she knew she was the Vatis, she felt a renewed sense of purpose. She was the thing standing in Joey's way. She would to whatever she could to keep him from achieving whatever he wanted by bringing them to this world. And she would do everything in her power to rescue William. Like Vlad said, there was nothing that would stand in her way.

Turning to the others, she surveyed them. They seemed grimy, malnourished, and exhausted. But they were strong; they could do this. After all, she, Dani, and Lili had managed to save Sehir from the Shadows. Then, they'd only had four others with them. This time, they practically had an army.

"Where is the great hall?" she asked Durse.

He pursed his lips. "First floor, fifth door on the right."

As one, they stepped out into the night. Candlelight spilled from the castle windows, giving them enough light to make their way up to the castle square. Anastasia pushed thoughts of William standing there with her from her mind.

Dani pulled her and Mohan aside. "You said you performed a location spell to find the Vatis, and it brought you here?"

"Aye," said Mohan.

"But if Anastasia's the Vatis, why would that have happened?"

Anastasia nodded. It didn't make much sense.

"We used William's blood!" Mohan suddenly said. "It must've brought us to you, Dani, since you're an Ancient. The spell must've not been specific enough."

Before either of them could respond, however, an alarm rang out. Anastasia gripped her dagger, leaping out of the way of an onslaught of arrows. "Run!"

Unfurling her wings, she took off into the air. Chris and Durse followed, while Hayde and Dani took on the archers. Mira and Balan huddled together for a moment, before they both released handfuls of liquid into the air. It hung there, as though suspended, little droplets shining like stars upon the dark night sky. As Nadmilise guards flew near it, Mira and Balan shouted, "L'tzrov."

The liquid burst into flames, dousing the guards. Ducking through the flames, Anastasia, Chris, and Durse landed on the main floor. Guards blocked their way to the great hall. Tightening her grip on her dagger, Anastasia leapt forward with a fierce battle cry.

Fighting one-handed proved difficult, but not impossible. She slashed out and lunged, cutting her way towards the doorway. The sorcerer guards stood on the perimeter, sending explosions through the air. Chris managed to take one out with a good swipe of his bo staff, while Durse took on three Nadmilise guards. He used his wings like weapons too, forcefully unfurling them and driving guards into the walls on either side of him.

Anastasia flung her dagger through the air, catching one guard in the shoulder. Pulling the second dagger from her belt, she cut the legs out from underneath the next guard.

Freeing her first dagger, she leapt onto the next guard and used her body's momentum to drive him to the ground. Rolling away from him, she sprang to her feet, drawing her dagger through another guard's belly. He dropped at her feet, freeing the way to the Great Hall.

"Go!" Durse yelled. "We've got this!"

Not needing to be told twice, Anastasia shouldered open the door to the Great Hall. The door slammed closed behind her, sealing off the sounds of battle out in the hall. Glancing around, Anastasia was immediately reminded of the premonition she'd had in Sehir: *When I open my eyes, there are two rooms reflected as though on opposite sides of a window. Three of my doppelgangers stand in the Sehirian throne room on the left, while the other three stand in an ancient throne room, complete with a checkered floor and pale red walls.*

The ancient throne room was here, in Armol. But there were no doppelgangers, no pendants. Just suits of armor lining the walls, up to where Joey stood with his back to her at the head of the room.

Between them, splayed on the cold stone floor, was William. It took her a moment to understand what looked odd about him, but once she understood, bile coated her throat. Joey had plucked all the feathers from his wings.

An acidic rage built within her as she looked up at Joey. "How dare you."

He shushed her. "Not so loud, dear cousin. You'll wake the baby."

Icy dread dripped down her spine as she understood. Slowly, Joey turned to face her. Cradled in his arms was Aagney. Thankfully, he was fast asleep.

"Don't you hurt him," she hissed.

Joey tilted his head. "That's entirely up to you."

"What do you want?"

"Give me your throne."

She needed to bide some time till Durse and Chris finished with the guards out in the hall, or till William woke. *If* he woke. No. She wouldn't let herself think that way. William would wake; he *had* to.

In one fluid motion, she flipped her dagger around and threw it. It embedded deep into Joey's forearm; he cried out and dropped Aagney. Flying forward, Anastasia caught Aagney before he hit the ground. He began to cry, his shrill screams echoing through the room.

Joey swore, pulling her dagger from his arm. She had just enough time to put Aagney down with William before Joey was upon her. Bringing her good hand up, she blocked his attack. He drove her back, until her back was pressed against the sword of one of the suits of armor. Bracing herself, she punched outward with her injured hand.

It connected with his jaw, driving him back. Thankfully, whatever Durse had used to numb her kept her from feeling any pain.

Wiping blood from his mouth, Joey raised a hand. Thick black smoke shot from his fingers and wrapped around Anastasia's throat, crushing her windpipe. It felt like thick fingers gripped her throat, sticking her with little pinpricks of acid. She gasped for breath, falling to her knees. Joey stalked towards her, a smirk tugging his lips.

"That's one advantage I have over you, Anastasia. I actually have access to my magic."

Her fingers pressed against the bare stone of the floor as she struggled to breathe. He was right. The only times she'd ever used magic was by accident, in times of danger. She only hoped now would be one of those times.

Closing her eyes, she focused on the feeling of magic in her veins, the way it had felt to make that door explode in the Shadow compound, the way it had felt when she and William were plummeting towards their deaths when they fell from the Sky Temple. She hadn't tried to use magic then; it had just burst forth from her when she'd least expected it. Maybe that was the trick? Try to not use it? But she was losing her sight. Joey was strangling her to death.

What had happened in her premonition? Her doppelgangers had smashed their pendants, and magic had exploded from them. But there were no other pendants here but hers. And there was no way she was going to smash her pendant, not until she was sure it would help. She needed something else, something to distract him enough for her to get away.

It was then she remembered the sword at her back. She reached behind her and worked the blade loose. With her last bit of strength, she drove it into Joey's chest.

He staggered back, but he didn't release her. She collapsed on the ground, clawing at the smoke around her neck. Joey just laughed and pulled the sword from his chest. Inky blood trickled from the wound.

"You think a piece of tin could kill *me*?"

She felt herself losing consciousness. As she choked, she looked over at William.

Joey laughed. "I told you I'd kill you in front of him."

The doors to the Great Hall burst open in a shower of magic and dust. Her friends leapt into the room and ran at Joey. He stepped back but didn't release Anastasia. She was losing consciousness, her vision darkening. There had to be something she could use against him. Something they could use to hinder him.

At that moment, she felt the vial from the Fairy Queen pressed against her chest. What had the Queen said when they'd talked about it? That it could save someone? Perhaps it could save Joey.

It took everything she had to pluck the vial from her bodice. But then it just sat there in her hand, utterly useless. What could she do with it, chuck it at him? She had no strength left; she was fading fast. This time, however, she wasn't ready to give in to death.

Struggling, she slid the vial across the floor. It hit the toe of Lili's boot. As she bent to pick it up, Anastasia collapsed. Then, in one fluid motion, Lili tossed the vial into the air, raised her bow, and shot the vial. It shattered, spraying the arrow with its silvery liquid as it rocketed towards Joey. It hit him square in the chest, and, for a moment, everything froze. Joey stared down at the arrow sticking from him with a bemused expression; Anastasia fell into the darkness.

But then, Joey staggered back, releasing Anastasia. She came-to, gasping, just in time to see Joey explode in a shower of gray dust. An unbidden shriek tore from her lips, mixing with Aagney's pained wails.

A moment later, the dust cleared. In its wake, were two unconscious men, one sorcerer, the other Nadmilise. Both looked like Joey.

No one moved. They, like Anastasia, were entirely unsure of what to do next. But then the sounds of guards reached their ears. Anastasia knew they needed to act, needed to get out of there. But what would they do about Joey? Better yet, what had she *done* to him? Why was he split into two people? And what was each individual like?

"Mohan!" she shouted, her voice hoarse. "Cast a circle!"

He quickly set to drawing one in the drops of blood from Joey's wounds. Balan and Mira helped him, while Lili dragged the sorcerer Joey over. Ryke, Durse, and Hayde faced the doors, ready to take on the guards. Behind them, Dani knelt beside her brother, her hands glowing with pale green healers' magic.

"William?" she murmured.

"Ready to go!" called Mohan.

Staggering to her feet, Anastasia scooped Aagney into her arms and headed for the circle. Dani looped her arms under William's and dragged him over, as well. The others all gathered together inside the circle. As Mohan took to chanting, the doors to the Great Hall opened and guards spilled into the room. Anastasia held Aagney tight, squeezing her eyes shut as the floor fell out from under her. A moment later, she felt soft grasses beneath her feet.

Opening her eyes, she found herself standing in a large meadow. Massive trees, larger even than the oaks at the Lakes in Sehir, spotted the beautiful grasses around them. They were carved with doorways and walkways, reminiscent of the fairy castle in Sehir.

Turning, she spotted William a few feet away, surrounded by beautiful white flowers. She turned towards him, drawing a painful breath. But before she could touch him, the Fairy Queen stepped into her path. She was dressed in polished silver armor, but looked much like she had in the realm of the Gods and Angels.

"Welcome to Síthe."

Sitting up, Anastasia looked around. There were beautiful meadows and large oak trees as far as they eye could see. Other fairies, similar in look and stature to the Queen, frolicked through tall grasses alongside short-legged, caramel-colored canines.

Turning, Anastasia took in her friends. They were all battle worn, but mostly unharmed. Awe flooded from them as they took in their surroundings.

"Why don't we get you all a bath, some fresh clothes, and something to eat?" offered the Queen.

"Yes," said Hayde. "Please."

Moments later, Anastasia found herself in a warm river, scrubbing away the grime and dirt on her skin. She could hear Lili, Mira, and Dani around the bend, splashing. But Anastasia was glad for the distance. She needed to clear her head, figure out their next move. Thanks to the Fairy Queen, she knew Isidora and Hughie would be on their way to Síthe, so she could Awaken them all.

But what would they do after that? Would they just return home? What would that mean for Joey? Would he still be separated into two people if they went back? And what about the Shadows? Surely, they'd be free from their stony encasements by now.

Rising from the water, she dried herself with a plush towel. It certainly felt nice to be clean after so long. It was calming, brushing out her long hair. She hadn't cut it in so long, it hung past the small of her back. She supposed she needed to cut it when they returned home. But thinking of home reminded her of her family. Where were they? Surely, Joey hadn't attacked them in Armol, tortured them like his father did? No. She had to believe they hadn't been in the castle but had escaped that fate altogether.

Turning to the clothing the Queen had given her, she dressed. It was a garment unlike anything she'd ever worn before. The violet-colored top started in a high neck and ended at the top of her ribcage, hemmed and tied by swirling metal filigree complete with amethysts and crystals. The skirts had the same filigree at her waist, from which the flowing, layered skirts draped down to cover her slippers.

She felt like a fairy, just wearing it. When she returned to the trees, she found Lili, Mira, and Dani dressed in different gowns, all with flowing designs and metal filigree. They looked like royalty.

Wordlessly, they filed into the largest tree, where the Queen had told them a feast would be held. There, they found the others, all dressed in loose trousers and tunics, with boiled leather vests. They were chatting amiably, while servants laid the table.

The Queen acknowledged them with a slight nod. Anastasia took an empty seat beside Mohan. It didn't take her long to notice that William wasn't among them. Vaguely, she wondered what Joey had done to him, if it was more than just pluck the feathers from his wings, if there was something internal she couldn't see. It seemed everyone close to her had been tortured at the hands of the Shadows. She vowed to make sure that never happened again.

"Shall we begin?" the Fairy Queen said. All eyes flicked to her. "Princess Isidora and Prince Hughie should be joining us within the next few days. But, until then, we have some things to discuss."

Anastasia nodded. "We do."

The Queen motioned to the table. "Let's eat."

There were buttery fruit tarts, and creamy squash pies; there were salads with nuts, and lentil stews. Carafes of pale, honeyed wine sat interspersed between savory casseroles and breads. But, like in Bahail, there was no meat. There wasn't even any fish at the table. But no one seemed to mind. Everything was so delicious.

But Anastasia hesitated. "What are we doing here?"

"I told you to keep the vial with you," The Queen replied.

"You also told me you'd dance to the sound of my screams."

"Trivialities."

The others stopped eating, glancing between them. It was an unspoken rule that the Fairy Queen's laws governed above all else. When she called, you went. When she gave an order, you followed. But Anastasia was tired of feeling like she was being jerked around without any guidance. She wanted her questions answered.

Anastasia frowned. "Who is *he*."

They all turned to look at the sorcerer that both was and wasn't Joey. Someone had propped his head on a pillow, but he hadn't been moved since they arrived. He slept, his chest rising and falling evenly. As Anastasia looked at him, she realized she could feel his emotions.

"The vial I made for you contained a potion," the Queen explained. "One that would split both halves of Joey into individual beings. For lack of a better explanation, here is the good half of him. The one we left behind is the evil half."

Anastasia stared at him. "Will he know who he is when he wakes?"

"He will have all of his memories, but his personality will be different."

"Where do we go from here?"

The Queen smiled. "Once we are all fed and rested, you, me, and the other Ancients will restore the realms and bring everyone back to their homes."

Dani gasped. "We can go home?"

"Yes."

Anastasia tilted her head. "And what do we do about… evil Joey?"

"One problem at a time, Anastasia."

Shaking her head, Anastasia pushed back from the table. On the one hand, she was immensely glad the Queen had welcomed them. It made it easy to unite the Ancients and find a way to return home. But on the other hand, she felt like she had no control over her actions. It was like she was just following in the Queen's wake, with no say in what she did. And after everything she'd been through, she wanted to exert some control.

Getting to her feet, the Queen motioned for everyone to follow her. "I will show you to your rooms."

Wordlessly, Anastasia filed out after the Queen. To keep herself calm, she grabbed Aagney from his place at the table. His innocence drowned out her inner lividity and helplessness. Around her, the others chatted animatedly, as though they hadn't all just been fighting for their lives.

The Queen motioned to a circular room. "Yours, Anastasia."

Wordlessly, Anastasia entered. Everything within was made of carved wood, including the base of the circular, mossy bed on the far wall. To her utter surprise, William was already on the bed, placed on his stomach. Finding a cradle by the bed, Anastasia put Aagney down and turned to William. Gently, she ran the fingers of her uninjured hand over the bare outline of his wings. Thankfully, the gel Durse had given her still numbed her hand, even after her bath. She figured she'd have to thank him the next time she saw him.

She couldn't imagine how painful it must've been for William, to have his feathers ripped out. Her heart ached for him. But, they would be returning home soon, and it would only be a pain of the past.

She supposed she should be glad for that, but something about it didn't feel right. They hadn't stopped Joey but rather created a concentrated version of evil in his dark doppelganger. Who's to say he wouldn't redo the spell when they returned, bring them all back to the Old World with the snap of his fingers.

Settling back on the bed, she took William's hand. She sat in silence, just staring at him, tracing the familiar outline of his face with her eyes.

"He's going to be just fine."

Anastasia jumped, finding someone standing in the doorway. As her eyes adjusted to the light, her heart leapt into her throat. It couldn't be. She had pale white wings, with rich violet swirls the same color as her eyes, eyes that were identical to Anastasia's.

"Mother?"

"It's me, darling."

Anarose opened her arms wide. Anastasia jumped off her bed and threw herself into her mother's arms. Burying her face in her mother's shoulder, she breathed deep. It had felt like a lifetime ago that her mother had stood before her. She hadn't realized she'd needed to feel her mother's embrace until she stood within it.

Pulling back, Anastasia looked up at her. "What are you doing here? *How* are you here? Are you alright?"

"I'm fine, darling." Anarose chuckled lightly. "The Queen brought me here and healed me."

Anastasia returned to her embrace. "I'm so glad you're alright."

"You will be, too, you know."

She pulled back again. "Where's father? And Aunt Celia—"

"Everyone's here. We're all fine."

They settled back on the bed and sat together silently. Anastasia had thought she'd had so much to say to her mother since her return from being tortured at the hands of Adrian. But, honestly, all she needed was to know that her mother was there, telling her everything was going to be alright.

Anarose smoothed her hair back from her face. "Just sleep, darling. I'll be here when you wake up."

And though she tried to fight it, tried to be present in every moment she shared with her mother, the toll of the last few days caught up with her. In moments, she drifted off to sleep, comforted by the contentedness radiating from her mother. That night, she had no dreams, no nightmares, no premonitions. She slept soundly for the first time in months.

CHAPTER THIRTY-TWO

Morning brought bruises and stiff muscles. Anastasia rolled over with a groan, rubbing sleep from her eyes. Her entire body ached. And though she knew she needed to rise, needed to face the Ancients and her mother and find out what to do next about Joey, all she wanted was to slip back into sleep. She wished she could pretend none of it was happening, that she was just a regular seventeen-year-old Princess, awaiting a bath and a party.

But she wasn't. She wasn't the Crown Princess of Jacqueline any longer. For so long, it had meant everything to her. She found, however, that what really mattered to her was the safety of her people, and how her title allowed her to help them. But she didn't need the title to fight for them, to protect them from Joey, Adrian, and the Shadows.

Opening her eyes, she found William staring at her. Reaching out a hand, she trailed her fingers down his cheek. He closed his eyes at her touch, turning his head to kiss her palm. But she saw he rested on his stomach, his bare wings bloodied and battered. An acidic anger flared in her chest.

"Stop," he murmured. "I'm fine."

She narrowed her eyes. "He hurt you."

"And if we went after everyone who has ever hurt us, we'd never stop fighting."

"It seems we never stop fighting as it is."

Leaning up on her elbow, she pressed her lips to his. He was safe now, that was what mattered. As she got out of bed, she reminded herself that they all made it out alive, that they were safe and well. That was what was important. Opening herself to their emotions, she let their relaxed, gentle happiness wash away the lividity.

Stretching, she turned to see William eyeing the tunic on the bed. It was good to see him on his feet after what he'd been through, and she allowed herself a moment to study the bare planes of his back, and the black swirls that colored his skin.

"Need a hand?" she questioned.

He gave her a wry grin. "I was thinking of foregoing the tunic altogether."

Rolling her eyes, she helped him fit his tunic and vest over his wings. She grimaced every time she felt pain shoot through him, wishing she could just take it all away from him.

It was at that moment, she realized her hand was healed. "What's this?"

"The Fairy Queen came in last night," William explained. "Healed the worst of our wounds herself."

Gratitude filled Anastasia. She clung to it as she and William exited the room, leaving Aagney to sleep soundly in his crib. Absently, she wondered what her family thought of her sharing her bed with William. All they'd done was sleep, just like they had those months together they'd been searching for her grandmother. In truth, it had felt odd, not having him beside her, after he'd been arrested. Now that he was by her side, she wanted him to never leave. And she could feel that he felt the same.

As they rounded the corner, however, she forgot her train of thought. Bright sunlight filtered through the tree's branches, bathing everything in a pale green glow. They followed the narrow hall to where it spilled out into a sort of dining hall. At a wooden table, seemingly carved from the tree itself, sat her family. They all looked up at her and William as they entered.

"Good morning, girl," said her father.

Her face splitting in a grin, she raced forward and threw herself into her father's arms. Aunt Celia, Uncle Graham, Aunt Calla, and Great-Uncle Bale all hugged her as well, until she was surrounded by their love.

"I'm so glad you're all safe," she said.

"And we you," said Bale.

They all looked well, safe, renewed. It was incredible to see her mother up and around. She hadn't realized how frightened she'd been for her. And now, she was glad she hadn't taken the signet, as Mistress Miglune had suggested. She was glad she hadn't given up on her mother and her recovery. It felt whole to be with them again.

"I think we have some things to discuss," Anarose intoned.

William politely inclined his head. "I'll leave you to it, then."

"No, William, stay."

Anastasia felt his surprise and gratitude at being invited to join a family conversation. Surely, her family did, too.

As they sat together at the table, Anastasia thought how strange it was to see her family with wings. It was at that moment, she realized that the swirls were the color of a person's trade, such as William's black as a warrior, and hers and her mother's violet. Bale's and Celia's were royal blue, for their trades as a candlemaker and a clerk, respectively; Graham's were silver, for his status as a diplomat; and her father's were rose pink for his work as a painter. Calla's were the same dark indigo as Joey's.

All were moot, now, as they hadn't worked their trades since they became members of the royal family. So, it was shocking to be reminded of who they were before they were royalty, to be reminded of how much their lives had changed.

"The Fairy Queen has told us some of what has happened," said Anarose. "Why don't you fill us in?"

And so, Anastasia told her mother of Joey's spell, of how it brought them to the Old World, and of her life in Bahail. She told them of the peoples' decision to reinstate her as the Crown Princess, and of her opening the inn, and of discovering the Royal Library. As she filled them in on the Ancients, and going to the castle in Armol, William stopped her.

"My sister's an Ancient?"

Anastasia nodded. "And Chris."

"So you're waiting here for Isidora and Hughie to arrive?" asked Calla.

"Yes."

Celia tittered. "Who would've thought that Hughie would ever be an Ancient? He's always been rather droll, don't you think? It'll be nice to see him put to good use."

"That isn't all," Anastasia said. "Joey has the power to see the past."

Her family glanced at one another, understanding the significance of what she was saying. He could see the past, just as she could see the future.

"He shared a vision with me." She glanced at Calla. "About his family."

Celia leaned forward. "And?"

"I think I can explain," said Calla.

They all turned to look with her, surprise flashing through them. Anastasia just grabbed William's hand under the table. She wasn't quite sure how her family was going to take the news about Joey's history, and Calla's keeping it a secret.

"I'm Joseph's mother, and Adrian, the man in charge of the Shadows, is his father."

No one moved for a moment. And then her family started speaking all at once. Anastasia shrank back, letting them get it all out.

"*You're* his mother?" said Graham.

Celia stuck her nose in the air. "I knew it! I knew there was something off about all of this."

"Why didn't you tell us?" demanded Anarose.

"Did you make it so Anastasia and Joey were friends as children?" asked Elliot.

Bale shook his head. "You should've said something!"

When they quieted, Calla said, "I struggled a long time with who my parents were, and why I wasn't raised by them. I was raised alongside Adrian, we were the best of friends as children. He wasn't always the evil man he is today."

"That doesn't change the fact that you lied to us," said Graham.

"Perhaps not, but I feel it will explain why." Calla took a deep breath. "My parents are Valdon and Analie."

Silence pervaded the table. William laced his fingers through Anastasia, clearly feeling her worry. Her family were filled with a range of emotions, ranging from Bale's quiet rage, to Anarose's concern.

"You lie," hissed Bale. "Analie would never—"

Anarose frowned. "What did Joey have to say about all this?"

"You *knew*?" demanded Celia.

"My mother was a woman of many secrets, but this wasn't one of them. She told me stories, growing up, about a sister I had, one that she had to give away to protect the future."

Bale pushed back from the table, radiating anger. Elliot just sat quietly, taking it in. Anastasia supposed her mother hadn't kept this a secret from him either. Celia, however, was red in the face, her eyes accusatory.

"How dare you keep something like this a secret?"

Elliot calmly replied, "You'd do good to check your tone, and remember that my wife is the Queen of Jacqueline."

"I mean, just look at the two of them," said Graham. "The resemblance is uncanny."

Everyone at the table turned to look at Anarose and Calla. Just as she had the first time she met Calla, Anastasia thought how greatly she resembled her mother. They had the same features, though Calla's hair was darker, and her eyes were now the ice blue of the sorcerers. There was no mistaking they were related.

"We could debate the rights and wrongs of this till we're blue in the face," said Anarose. "But there are more important things at hand."

Elliot nodded. "Such as Awakening the Ancients and getting home."

"And understanding what was done to Joey in Armol."

Anastasia had nearly forgotten about the vial from the Fairy Queen, how it had split Joey into two people, and how the good sorcerer half was somewhere in Síthe. It made her shudder to think of his evil half, still roaming free in Irichat gol Naingeliar.

"The Fairy Queen said this was his good half," Anastasia explained. "And the other side was his evil half."

Anarose pursed her lips. "He can't stay that way forever."

"No," said Calla. "We'll have to unite him eventually."

"Preferably once we return home," said Celia.

Anarose leaned forward. "But, until then, we will try and learn everything we can from the 'good' half about the other half's plans. Why did he bring us all here, and what does he hope to accomplish?"

Anastasia nodded. "I think we should talk to Durse."

"Follant?" William darkly intoned. "You shouldn't trust a word he says."

"All the same, he helped us escape the castle. He was one of Joey's men, he might know something that will help."

Anarose inclined her head. "I agree."

"Well, then let's go meet the others," said Celia.

They all rose and followed the winding pathway through the trees and down to where Anastasia had eaten the day before. There, the table was filled with similar delicacies from the previous evening. The large group they'd taken from the castle sat around it, chatting amiably. Warmth and contentedness radiated from them in waves, calming Anastasia and her family.

The Fairy Queen joined them a moment later, and they all took a seat at the table. Everyone else stopped eating, staring between the royal family and the Queen, all except Mohan and Vlad, who were royals themselves, and used to such a meal.

"Good morrow," said Anarose.

Norden dropped his fork, shock plain on his face.

Lili cleared her throat. "Good morrow, Your Majesty."

The Fairy Queen clapped her hands. "Well, now that that's all settled..." She turned to Durse. "You were one of the leaders of the Soster. What can you tell us?"

Anastasia had to appreciate the Queen's abruptness. She knew how to get right to the heart of a conversation. Her mother seemed to appreciate it as well, for a sly smile tugged her lips. Everyone else, however, needed a moment to collect themselves.

Mohan frowned. "If he was one of the Soster, he can't be trusted."

"Wait," Ericcen held up a hand, "what *is* the Soster?"

Dani leaned forward. "They're people that were previously possessed by Shadows who feel a sort of kinship with them. They serve them like masters."

"He also held us prisoner for months," Hayde grumbled.

"I told you you couldn't trust him," William said.

Dani shot him a look. "But he helped us to escape."

"Yeah, before we were brought to this world," said Hayde. "Once we were in the castle dungeons, he kept us there."

Anastasia narrowed her eyes. Durse Follant had kept Dani, Hayde, and Mira prisoner all this time? While Joey had been there? Had they been tortured? It hadn't seemed like it. And what would Joey have needed with them? Or Durse for that matter? Gods and Angels, they'd been prisoners before Joey had even cast his spell, and she'd had no idea they were in any sort of trouble. She hadn't been concerned when they hadn't reported to Sehir as members of the ancient families of Jacqueline, and they'd been prisoners the whole time! Guilt gnawed at her.

Durse splayed his hands on the table. "I feel like I should explain."

"You'd better," William growled.

Everyone turned to him, wearing varying expressions of distain. But Anastasia felt his conviction. Whatever his excuse, he believed in it wholeheartedly.

"Two years ago, I was reporting to Warrior Elken, then head of the royal guard."

Anastasia remembered Warrior Elken; she had seen her die in one of her first premonitions. It was how they'd known the Shadows were possessing werewolves. She'd gone to her funeral to pay her respects.

"I passed by the Hall of Rulers," Durse continued. "There, I saw a woman in the looking glass."

Anastasia froze. It couldn't be.

"It was Queen Analie. She told me all about what happened to her the night the Shadows attacked, and how she'd managed to escape. At first, I didn't believe her, but then things she'd told me started to come true." Durse shook his head. "So, I went back to her and she recruited me to help her. I've been following her instructions ever since."

Silence met his words. Anastasia couldn't believe it, but a part of her knew it had to be true. She thought back to the conversation she'd had with Durse in Ostana's chambers, when he'd escaped the dungeons: *I'm only following instructions, Your Highness. This is all a part of it, a part of the bigger picture. I wish you could understand.* He was following instructions—her grandmother's instructions. Just like Valdon had, and Turania, and Miruna, and Jumba, and the Fairy Queen. They were all strands in her grandmother's tangled web.

"Queen Analie is dead," Dani breathed. She looked to Anastasia's parents, to her brother, but none of them met her eyes. "Isn't she?"

Elliot inclined his head. "In a sense, yes. My mother-in-law can never return to our world."

Gerrard furrowed his brow. "So, where is she?"

"An alternate universe."

Taking in everyone's shocked expressions, Anastasia sat back. For so long, she'd been keeping more secrets than she could count. Now, one of the biggest was out here for them all to see. Somehow, the reality didn't frighten her. She trusted every single person at this table, even Mira and Balan. It was time the people started to learn the truth.

Mira choked on her drink. "I'm sorry, *what*?"

"That's why I had to distance myself from William, to let him and Chris go to prison," Anastasia explained. "We couldn't let anyone know about the alternate universes. But they are both innocent."

"Speaking of," Anarose got to her feet, "I hereby officially pardon William James Dinas and Christopher Jay Woodsman. You are no longer fugitives of the Crown."

Dani squealed, throwing her arms around her brother. Chris just sat, utterly stunned. All those months they'd sat in prison, the degrading trial led by the Representatives, William's charge of treason, it was all gone. Elation flooded Anastasia. They were free, finally, blessedly, free. They could live whole lives, without the darkness of their charges cloying at them.

Aelnold narrowed his eyes. "You don't expect us to believe that 'alternate universe' stuff, do you?"

"It's the truth," Elliot intoned. "There are three universes that we know of. Ours, the one Queen Analie is in, and the Shadow world."

Norden frowned. "The Shadow world?"

"It's where my family and I were held those months we were missing," explained Bale. "We were tortured at the hands of a man called Adrian."

"Where is this Adrian now?" asked Gerrard.

"We don't know."

Graham shook his head. "It seems Joey has taken his place."

"Which brings us back to the original point," the Fairy Queen said, turning to Durse. "What can you tell us?"

No one spoke for a moment. Anastasia took in their emotions. They ranged from Vlad's acceptance, to Dani's confusion, to Durse's resignation, to Balan's skepticism. But beneath it all was an underlying understanding. They believed her family and were willing to accept the idea of alternate universes and Queens that weren't truly dead.

"Joey was looking for something, some sort of source of power," Durse said with a sigh. "He still hasn't found it."

Gerrard frowned. "What would he need the power for?"

"Probably to take the throne," Anastasia said. "That's his goal, to assert himself as King of Jacqueline."

Looking up, Anastasia met Anarose and Calla's eyes. They understood, he was asserting himself as the true heir to the throne, the son of the firstborn daughter of the Queen. It made Anastasia's stomach clench, just thinking about evil Joey taking the throne and ruling over Jacqueline.

Mohan chuckled. "Well, there's not much to rule out here. Everything and everyone is so scattered. There's no High Council, no King of the Land. If he wants to rule, it will be over one city at a time."

Vlad nervously licked his fangs from where he sat, hidden from the sun. "Unless he starts a war."

"Prince Vlad is right," said Ryke. "If he starts to conquer the lands, he could build himself an empire. Especially if he has some immense power at his fingertips."

Balan worked his jaw. "Then we need to stop him."

"Now that we're all on the same page." The Fairy Queen rolled her eyes. "We will keep him from getting that which he seeks."

"How?"

The Queen motioned to Anastasia. "We are the Ancients. You think one such as him could defeat the most powerful beings of time? We were given the power of Gods, child. The power to restart entire worlds."

Chris nodded. "Once Princess Isidora and Prince Hughie arrive, you can Awaken us, and we can go home, where we will be stronger, have a home advantage."

"He's right," said Mohan. "Joey was not raised in our world. He doesn't understand it like we do."

Anastasia didn't mention that she wasn't raised in their world, either. Though, she supposed, six years surely trumped the months Joey had been in the realms. And while it would be good to return home, seeing as Mohan and Calla would have their magic again, the idea of leaving didn't sit right with Anastasia. What was to stop Joey from just bringing them back to the Old World, to get the power he sought?

"I agree that we need to Awaken the Ancients," she said. "But we should be focused on finding the power Joey's after." She turned to Durse. "Do you have any idea what it is?"

Durse shook his head. "He wasn't very open to talking about it."

"So how do we find what he's looking for?" Lili asked.

Anastasia wracked her brain. What could Joey have wanted so badly he needed to murder nine people and cast a spell to go to the Old World to get it? It must've been something that only existed here, something he couldn't find anywhere else.

"We can check the library here," said the Fairy Queen. "While we wait for Isidora and Hughie."

Graham nodded. "Good idea."

Moments later, Anastasia found herself again in a library surrounded by scrolls. This one, however, was high in the boughs of the tree. Long branches connected to hold a mossy, leafy canopy over them, bathing them in pale green light. The shelves were carved from the tree itself, as were reading alcoves, tables, and benches. While it wasn't as tall as the Royal Library in Bahail, it was long; it seemed to stretch across all the trees in the city.

Opening a scroll, Anastasia found that the words inside shimmered and shifted until they were in the ancient language. She'd never been happier for fairy magic than she was at that moment.

She and William filled their arms with scrolls and tucked themselves into a nook to read. Everyone else spread through the enormous library, the

Nadmilise flying about on their wings, and the sorcerers and Vlad strolling leisurely along.

If they hadn't been trying to find a way to defeat Joey, Anastasia would've been happy, seeing them all together this way. As it was, she was just glad to have something to do, something that made her feel like she was making a difference in ending what had happened to them. Settling back against William, she started on her pile of scrolls.

Slowly, William trailed his fingers over her hand as he read. She smiled up at him.

Regardless of the situation, she was still pretty happy.

CHAPTER THIRTY-THREE

Three weeks had found Anastasia and the others up to their elbows in scrolls in the fairy library. The Queen came and went, needing to run her kingdom, but she helped when she could. Otherwise, they were on their own. Occasionally, the fairies' dogs curled up with them while they read; Anastasia loved to pet them while she worked. They were soft and sweet, and radiated nothing but warmth and contentment.

Stretching, Anastasia turned to William. He dozed in the alcove they occupied, sunlight playing upon his face. Sometimes, she couldn't quite believe they were together. She often thought back to when they first met, and everything they'd been through since. He'd gone from the frightening warrior that held a blade to her throat, to the man she loved more than anything else. She'd never imagined she'd trust him the way she did, and yet, she still hadn't told him about her premonitions.

How did she even broach a subject like that, especially after the way Aatu had reacted, and the way the alternate universe William had called her an abomination? She couldn't bear it if her William looked at her like that. She wasn't sure what she'd do if he wasn't a part of her life anymore.

"He hasn't left your side since we got here."

Startled, she turned to see Gerrard standing in front of her.

"Sorry," he said. "Thought you heard me come up."

"I was lost in thought."

He motioned to William. "He must take his job as a warrior very seriously."

"He does." She faltered. "But that's not—it isn't really—"

"I get it," he murmured. "We can feel each other's feelings, remember? I knew how you felt about each other as soon as he arrived in Bahail."

She nodded. "I didn't want to hurt anyone."

"You needed a husband for an heir, so the throne wouldn't be lost. And he was in prison—not a likely candidate for the future King."

Anastasia nodded, turning to look at William again. She imagined what he would be like as a king, wearing a shimmering crown, sitting in the throne beside her. Perhaps, someday, a painting of the two of them would hang in her daughter's study, just like her grandparents did in her mother's. Maybe they would look as regal, as happy.

At that moment, she realized, regardless of the circumstances, she wanted William to be the future King of Jacqueline. She wanted him to become a part of her family, to pick up the mantle so many incredible men held before him. It was almost a physical need, to bring him into her home.

A voice carried from down in the library. "I think I found something!"

William jolted awake as Gerrard ran forward. As Anastasia leapt off the alcove, William grabbed her hand, pulled her back to him, and kissed her.

"What was that for?" she asked.

His eyes searched hers. "You are the love of my life."

Her heart skipped a beat; she was speechless. He sounded so serious, and a cursory read of his emotions left her overwhelmed by determination and love. Part of her wanted to step out of his embrace, to lessen the emotions, while another part of her wanted to step closer.

Gerrard called, "Come on!"

Slowly, Anastasia stepped out of William's arms. Keeping a hold on his hand, however, she followed Gerrard to the middle of the library, where Hayde sat at a table peering over a scroll. Everyone gathered around him, crowding the small table. The tension among them was palpable. Only little Aagney broke the strain, radiating joy from his perch in Celia's arms. Her Aunt had taken to the baby immediately, bouncing him on her knee and babbling at him incessantly. Anastasia was glad to have a reprieve.

"It says here that there is a power of the Ancients," Hayde said. "That each Ancient had an individual strength, used to repel the evil from their world and protect their people."

Anastasia frowned. So the Ancients were warriors? From what she knew of Anistes Droun, that didn't fit. The ancient magic cocooned the Ancients until a time when the world was safe, and they could use their magic to restart the realms. Was it different in the Old World? Were they a God-given weapon to protect the realms?

"How does that help?" Mira snapped. "We already knew the Ancients had power!"

"Yeah," said Hayde. "But the raw power they had was too powerful for them to handle, so they needed something to help them channel it."

Dani frowned. "And?"

"And it could store power in it. Whoever wielded it could wield the power of the Ancient it was from."

"While fascinating," Celia icily intoned, "I don't see how this helps."

Hayde flipped the scroll around so they could see it. "What does that look like to you?"

Collective shock went through the room. Anastasia looked down at the scroll and gasped. There, sketched among the words, was her pendant. But not just hers, there were seven of them, all identical save for their color.

At that moment, Anastasia remembered her premonition: *Six identical copies of myself stand around me on the line of the circle. They're dressed strangely, in anciently-fashioned clothing, but that isn't even the strangest thing about them. No, they're all wearing my pendant, but the stones are different colors.* They weren't different version of *her*, they were the Ancients! Wearing their pendants that helped them channel their power.

Gods and Angels, she'd had a tool of the Ancients since she was six-years-old. It had been passed down through her family since the very first Queen of Jacqueline. Which, of course, now made sense. The pendant helped her channel her premonitions, just as Valdon had told her. As the Fairy Queen said, they had the power of Gods. It was too strong on its own.

"That must be what Joey's after," said Graham. "Anastasia's pendant."

Anastasia shook her head. "There are seven pendants."

"And Joey wants all of them," reasoned Dani.

Balan shook his head. "If he gets all of them…"

Mohan frowned. "He'll have the power of all the Ancients, the power of the Gods."

"We'll just have to find them first," said Ryke.

"How do you suggest we do that?" demanded Mira. "In case you hadn't noticed, we can't just portal willy-nilly and start searching all the kingdoms. For all we know, they're not even here!"

"Joey wouldn't have brought us here if they weren't," Chris retorted.

As they fell to arguing, Anastasia stepped back from the table. If her premonition was to come true, the Ancients would throw their pendants to the ground and shatter them. It would render the stones useless and make it extremely difficult to use their powers. Not to mention, there was the bit about the Ancients turning to stone.

But then there was also the part where she grabbed the shards of the broken stones and used some sort of spell to go back to the castle in Armol and repair the pendants. But there was the concern that she was alone there. Did that mean the Ancients remained encased in stone?

Not for the first time, she wished Valdon was there with her. He'd provided so much guidance during her premonitions. She wondered where he was, where he'd ended up in the Old World.

"Is there a way to use a spell or something to find the other pendants?" Gerrard asked.

Mohan frowned. "I'm not sure a location spell works on an object."

Vlad went rigid all over a moment before he bared his teeth in a feral snarl. "Werewolf."

"What are you talking about?"

As footsteps sounded behind them, a voice Anastasia recognized said, "He's probably talking about me."

They turned to see Ostana striding towards them. She looked rather worse for wear, dressed in a torn peplos gown. Her hair was matted and tangled, her skin smeared with dirt. She looked like she hadn't slept in weeks. Gerrard's sisters, gathered behind Ostana, looked much the same. As Gerrard spotted them, he raced forward and wrapped his arms around them.

"I'm so glad you're both alright!" he said.

Alviva giggled. "You, too, brother!"

"What are you lot doing here?" asked Durse.

Isidora stepped around Ostana. "I think I can explain that."

She was pristine, shimmering with gold, including a bejeweled circlet that bound back her wild raven curls. She confidently put her hands on her hips, and Anastasia was surprised to see she wore the sigil of her family. Had she been with them the whole time, even though she'd been disowned months ago? Behind her, Prince Hughie of the ghosts hovered. He was spectral, like nothing more than a wisp. But Anastasia knew it was him, even though he had no face nor body, seeing as the Fairy Queen stood with him.

"By the Gods and Angels," Ericcen murmured.

Anastasia glanced at all their faces. All the Ancients were together in one room, along with her family and friends. She couldn't quite believe that after all this time, she'd found the Ancients, that they were finally just a few steps away from going home. It was so close she could taste it. Once they found their pendants, they could stop Joey once and for all.

Dani cleared her throat. "Well, what do we do now?"

Everyone turned to Anastasia. She balked. She didn't have any clue about what to do next. How was she supposed to Awaken the Ancients? There was no spell, no incantation. She'd thought she'd feel something once they were all together, but she felt nothing. There was no spark, no sense of inspiration. It felt like any other day with any other people. Was it too much for the Gods and Angels to give her a clue, like they had back in their realm? But she knew, she couldn't rely on the Gods and Angels for everything. She was an Ancient; she needed to figure this out for herself.

"Why don't we cast another circle?" she suggested.

Balan nodded. "Right-o. I'll get on it."

He and his sister hurried from the room, leaving them all to stare at each other again. Anastasia wished they'd find something to distract themselves. If she failed, she really didn't want an audience.

As it was, they all went outside together, save Vlad, who hid from the sun in the shelter of the library. Mohan joined Balan and Mira, helping them draw three identical circles. It looked like the circle Mohan had made back in Armol, though this time, there were items in each of the pentagrams—rocks for earth, broken glass for air, a chalice of water, and a candle for fire—instead of people. Empty pentagrams sat between each of the cardinal ones, outlined in salt.

"Everyone must pick a spiritual partner," Mohan explained. "To ground you to this reality."

Wordlessly, the Ancients paired off and stepped into their respective points in the pentagrams. Anastasia stood with William, Chris, and Lili in Mohan's pentagram, while Dani, Hayde, Isidora, and Durse filled out Mira's pentagram, and the Fairy Queen, Anarose, Hughie, and Alviva rounded out Balan's.

Everyone else stood by watching with wide eyes. Their expectant exuberance was cloying; it grated on Anastasia. What if it didn't work?

As one, Mohan, Balan, and Mira walked their circles three times. Returning to the center, they turned to each of the cardinal points and welcomed the elements. Each pentagram lit up, filling the circle with warmth. Feeling her father's uncertainty, Anastasia glanced back and gave him a reassuring smile. Please let it work, she prayed.

Turning his face to the sky, Mohan began to chant, "Alí, aleelah, l'ha'ir et haitzorim haetikim halah. Tabit otanu l'otzmah hagadolah shelanu."

The circles filled with light. Anastasia looked over at William, a grin tugging her lips. But then a sharp pain in her abdomen drove her to her knees. She cried out, her vision flickering as wind whipped around her.

William made to move towards her, but Mohan held out his hand. "Don't break the circle!"

Anastasia's eyes flew open and she arched her back in pain. Flashes of images flitted across her vision, reminding her of what it had felt like to stand under the Wishing Tree.

As the pain peaked, the images solidified, exploding in her mind:

I stand in a field as battle surges around me. A little ways off, I can see a Nadmilise royal. She's dressed in bright white battle armor, with the harp sigil of the Vatis emblazoned on her chest. My moonstone pendant glitters at her throat. Even as people fight around her, she scrawls a letter.

"Anastasia!"

We both turn to see another Nadmilise running towards us. She wears identical armor, though hers is black, and emblazoned with the same chain-wrapped crown as Chris' clothes had been in the realm of the Gods and Angels. Her skin is covered in black swirls, the same shade as her curtain of obsidian hair, and the wings stretching from her back. She wears a black moonstone.

"We must go!"

"Not yet, Evangeline!"

Evangeline? As in the woman from the story my grandmother told me as a child? The one who lived in the First Realms and was able to withstand the power of the Shadows?

"We must," Evangeline calls. "The others are waiting."

"I need to warn Anastasia of what's to come. If I don't, she won't understand!"

"The girl may never come here. You're risking us all on a whim."

I move forward and look at the letter she's writing. Shock slams through me as I see it's the one I received in the Royal Library, the one about the Ancients and the realms. Even as I watch, she signs it "From Anastasia". I stagger back as realization dawns on me. This woman, this Ancient, is Anastasia Futurebringer, my namesake. She was a Vatis, too.

As the battle nears Anastasia Futurebringer, Evangeline leaps into the fray, fighting them back. She wields a bo staff, just like Chris'. Vaguely, I wonder if she is an ancestor of Chris, just as Anastasia Futurebringer is mine.

Rolling and sealing the letter, Anastasia Futurebringer plucks a pigeon from the cage behind her and ties the scroll to its foot. As it flies away, she turns back to the battle.

"I'm ready!" she calls.

Spinning, Evangeline takes Anastasia Futurebringer's hand. Their free hands are held out, palms up. They begin to chant in a strange language. As their chant grows, I can see transparent images of the other Ancients—another Nadmilise, a ghost, a demigod, a sorcerer, and a Fairy, just like us, now.

As they chant, the Ancients yank off their pendants, all except Anastasia Futurebringer, and place them on the ground. A moment later, the ground opens up and swallows the pendants.

Evangeline and Anastasia Futurebringer drop each other's hands, and the other Ancients fade.

"Protect it, at all costs," Evangeline says to Anastasia Futurebringer.

Anastasia Futurebringer touches her pendant. "I will."

"You're the only one that can see what's coming, now."

"We'll be victorious."

Anastasia jolted awake, sprawled inside the pentagram. Wind whipped around her, tearing at her cheeks. Balan and Mira chanted while Mohan thanked the elements and closed his circle. Moments later, the wind dissipated. The light from the pentagrams faded, and William rushed to Anastasia's side.

Images still flooded Anastasia's mind; she struggled to make sense of them all. The pendant she wore was the only one the Ancients hadn't buried. All the others were gone.

"Are you alright?" William questioned.

Dani looked at her hands. "Did it work?"

"Well," the Queen intoned, "the circles were a bust."

Slowly, Anastasia looked up at William. "I know where the pendants are."

One thing that stumped her was why Joey hadn't taken her pendant when he had the chance. Surely, he'd had ample opportunity when she was his prisoner. And with his ability to see the past, it would be easy for him to unearth the knowledge of the pendants and their power. But she knew how erratic her premonitions had been, perhaps his were the same. That was something to hope for.

Before she could say anything, someone stepped into the clearing. "Ana?"

Turning, they all found Joey standing before them. She'd nearly forgotten about him, with everything that had happened. The fairies had kept him under guard while he'd been unconscious. But now that he was awake, it was safe to assume his evil counterpart was, as well. They needed to act quickly, to prevent Joey from getting the power he wanted. It was only a matter of time before he figured it out and came for her pendant.

William, Chris, Durse, and Hayde drew their daggers. "Not a step closer," Chris growled.

Joey raised his hands in surrender. "I mean no one any harm!"

Durse considered him a moment. "He's telling the truth."

"Or he's an exceptional liar," Hayde muttered.

Joey flicked his icy blue sorcerers' eyes to Anastasia. "Ana?"

"It's fine," she said. "He's fine."

Slowly, the warriors lowered their weapons. Joey stepped into the clearing, taking in their pentagrams and scattered appearances. It was strange to see him as a sorcerer. He was shorter, more youthful-looking. And though he smiled like the Joey she remembered, there was something not quite right about it, not quite complete.

"I know how this seems," he finally said. "But I'm here to help. Honestly."

Mira narrowed her eyes. "If that's the case, where is your other half going now?"

"I don't know, but you can bet it has to be for the pendants."

William frowned. "You think he's figured it out?"

Joey shrugged. "He was close before we… separated. I have no doubt he's redoubling his efforts as we speak. He's determined. He'll get what he wants."

"Then we'll just have to get there first," said Mohan. "Anastasia, where are they?"

"Buried, all over the kingdoms."

Durse swore. "You've got to be kidding me!"

Isidora went rigid all over. "Someone get me a map. I think something's happening!"

Hayde jogged back into the library and returned a moment later with a map of the kingdoms and a quill. Taking the quill, Isidora dropped down in the dirt and started to draw in a frenzied manner. When she stood again, she handed the map back to Hayde.

Peering at it, Anastasia saw that she'd marked six places on the map. Something inside Anastasia told her they were the places the pendants were buried. Excitement shot through her.

"What is this?" asked Hayde.

"The pendants," said Anastasia. "We're to go collect them."

Mohan snorted. "*We're* not going anywhere, love. *You're* going to stay right here in the fairy kingdom where you're safe and Joey can't get to your pendant. The rest of us Ancients are going to get our pendants."

Ryke frowned. "Is that really the best idea?"

"We'll split up and cover more ground. As long as we have a warrior or two with us, we'll be fine."

Dani nodded. "It's not like Joey knows precisely where they are."

"And I have a feeling, we're the only ones that can get them."

The Fairy Queen stepped forward. "Let us go quickly, before Joey has a chance to figure out where they're located." Turning to Anarose, she said, "You are in charge while I am gone."

Surprise flooded through Anarose. Anastasia grinned. It was an immense honor to be granted power by the Fairy Queen. No one was more deserving than her mother.

The Queen snapped her fingers. "Sorcerer, with me!"

Mira hurried forward. Anastasia watched as Mohan, Balan, and Mira all drew new circles into the dirt. The Queen sent servants off to gather the ingredients they would need to cast portal spells. While they worked, Anastasia returned to the library with her family and William. Gerrard and the Ros brothers offered to act as guards for the Ancients on their travels. Ostana, Lili, and Gerrard's sisters went to clean up.

When they reached the library, Vlad greeted them at the door. "Well?"

Anastasia relayed what was happening. He took the news in stride, turning back to the doorway to watch.

"Queen Anarose, King Elliot?" said William. "I was hoping I could speak with you privately."

Anarose inclined her head. "Of course."

As they went off, Anastasia tried to get a read on William's emotions. However, she found that he was giving off a sense of indifference. It seemed he could exert the same control over his emotions as he did his facial expressions.

While they were gone, Anastasia sat at the table with the rest of her family. She couldn't quite believe the note she'd received in the Royal Library had come from Anastasia Futurebringer herself! She'd gotten a letter from an ancestor, a thousand years in the past. And, on top of all of that, her ancestor had had premonitions of *her*, of her coming to the Old World. It was surreal. Not to mention, all the Ancients in the Old World had known of her premonitions. Anastasia Futurebringer had been open about her abilities. It made her wonder if all the other Ancients had been, as well.

Nightfall brought the departure of the Ancients and the warriors. Anastasia embraced all of them, wishing them luck on their journey. William spent some time with his sister, the two of them whispering animatedly. After a moment, she pulled a ring from her finger and gave it to him. He slid it onto his little finger and pressed a kiss to her cheek. As he stepped back, Balan, Mira, and Mohan started the incantations.

William, Vlad, Anastasia, and her family watched until they all disappeared. As soon as the wind died down, Anastasia joined her family for dinner. It was quieter than the previous days, but all the sweeter for it. They were able to talk about intimacies, to catch each other up. To understand where they'd all been in the past few months.

But then Anastasia remembered the fall equinox feast back in Bahail. She was sure it had happened already, and she sincerely hoped it was fun, a way to bring their community together. Surely, the people would be upset that she hadn't attended, but they would understand once they all returned home.

After dinner, Anastasia returned to her room to put Aagney down for the night. After gently rocking him, he was out like a light, nestled in his crib. She quietly snuck out of the room, so as not to wake him, and found William watching her from the hall. He grinned as she looked up at him, but there was something off about him. Nervousness fluttered through him. Immediately, she was alarmed. Had something happened?

He took her hand; his was shaking. "I was hoping I could ask you something."

She answered immediately, "Anything."

Did she mean that? She still wasn't sure about telling him of her premonitions. If he asked, would she tell him the truth? It felt like now, as deep as they were into their relationship, she'd need to.

"You know, I was never really afraid of much until I met you."

She gave him a look. "Oh, wonderful."

"I meant that you showed me what I could lose, showed me what I was fighting for." He took a deep breath. "That night we met, when you returned to Sehir, I vowed I would do everything in my power to protect the woman that had the gall to elbow me in the ribs."

She laughed. "Seriously?"

"I was impressed."

"Yes, well, I did end up stealing your dagger."

"And my heart."

Anastasia felt like she was going to melt. Even though she knew what he was saying was extremely sappy, she didn't mind. It made her want to throw her arms around him and never let go.

William led her through the trees. "You know the moment I knew I loved you?"

"When?"

"At Warrior Elken's funeral. See, I realized I had feelings for you when you attended the costume ball in Viire. I saw you slap Aatu and run off, and then I saw you collapse in the hall—I was worried, more worried than I should've been. But then at the funeral, we shared a cup of cider, talked about your grandparents. I felt so close to you."

"Before I collapsed again, you mean."

He nodded. "I wanted to run after you, to make sure you were alright. But you were engaged to Aatu, and it wasn't my place."

Anastasia looked away from him. Aatu. She hadn't thought about him in so long. But she no longer felt so guilty for it. If Adrian hadn't killed him, they would be happily married, building a life together. But that wasn't the life they'd had. There was no use feeling uneasy over what wasn't and could never be. There was no use in feeling guilty over her feelings for William. She wasn't being unfaithful to Aatu or his memory; she was living her life.

They reached the ground floor of the trees, strolling through the soft grasses. She could hear the fairies' canines barking in the distance, likely chasing fireflies. It made her lighthearted. They were in such a beautiful place, and they had the time to share it, together.

William cleared his throat. "What I'm trying to say is that I love you, Anastasia. In a way I'd never imagined."

She looked up at him. "I love you, too."

As they rounded the corner of the tree, Anastasia gasped. The meadow they'd landed in when they'd traveled from Armol was decorated with an elegant archway, wrapped with beautiful flowers.

"What is this?" she asked.

William didn't respond. When she turned to look at him, she found that he'd gotten down on one knee. Butterflies exploded in Anastasia's stomach. She felt like she was going to cry. He couldn't be doing what she thought, could he? There was no way. Her hands trembled as he reached out and took them. His face was so earnest as he looked up at her.

"Princess Anastasia Jacqueline Piliar Moneth," he said. "Will you marry me?"

She looked into his bright hazel eyes and knew, without a doubt, he was the man she wanted to spend the rest of her life with. He'd be an incredible King, and an even better father. She wanted to be everything with him.

A tear ran down her cheek. "Yes."

He leapt to his feet and grabbed her in an embrace, spinning her around. She cried and laughed, pressing her lips to his.

When they finally broke apart, Anastasia saw her family gathered at the archway behind them.

"What is this?"

William grinned. "I might've mentioned something to your parents."

Hand in hand, they stepped forward. Elliot and Bale were already crying, tears running freely. Anastasia started to cry harder as she saw them, wiping her eyes with the back of her hand.

When they reached her family, Anastasia saw her mother was holding a length of brightly-colored, braided cord. It was then that she understood, and her heart ached with happiness. William had gone through the trouble of putting together a traditional engagement ceremony. It was everything she'd ever wanted when she pictured her future.

"Your hands, please," said Anarose.

William and Anastasia obliged, holding out their left hands. Methodically, Anarose wrapped the cord around their hands, so it made an infinity symbol. As her mother knotted the cord, William spoke.

"I give myself to Anastasia Jacqueline Piliar Moneth for a year and a day."

Anastasia grinned through her tears. "I give myself to William James Dinas for a year and a day."

Anarose said, "It is considered that, as the hands are bound together, the couple are joined in love, trust, and mutual support."

"The rings?" asked Elliot.

Surprise shot through Anastasia as she saw William pull the ring from his sister off his little finger. Turning to her, he smoothly slid it onto her finger.

It was a burnished gold posy ring, carved with beautiful flowers. On the inside, "Love Eternal" was engraved in the metal.

"Oh," was all Anastasia managed to say.

But then Bale stepped forward and handed Anastasia a gold fede ring, complete with two hands clasped at the front.

"It was your grandfather's," Bale murmured.

Anastasia's eyes were so full of tears, it was difficult for her to put the ring on William's finger. But when she did, she saw it fit like a glove. She started to cry in earnest. She couldn't believe this was happening. It was all so beautiful.

"For a year and a day, you are hereby betrothed," said Anarose.

William turned to Anastasia, wrapping his free arm around her. She leaned into him, tilting her head up to meet him as he bent to kiss her. Her family applauded.

When they broke apart, William wiped away her tears with the pad of his thumb. Anastasia wasn't sure she'd ever been so completely thrilled in her entire life. She was engaged to William. Engaged. To William. She'd never imagined it would happen, especially not after he'd been arrested. But her mother had pardoned him, and her family approved. It was so utterly perfect, she nearly started crying again.

"This deserves a toast!" Celia cried.

Anastasia's family made their way back to the banquet hall in the tree, while Anastasia and William lingered under the archway.

"This was perfect," she whispered.

In response, William kissed her again. She didn't even mind that their hands would be bound for the next day. In fact, it would be fun to see what they had to do to get dressed in the morning. Which made her realize that it was all real. They would share intimacies she'd never shared with anyone before. And while the thought of doing so with Aatu had made her feel a bit queasy, the idea of doing so with William was exhilarating.

As though he could read her thoughts, William scooped her into his arms, a hungry look in his eyes. "Shall we go, milady?"

"Let's!" She giggled. "Though if we don't toast with my aunt, she's sure to be very cross."

Laughing, William carried her back to the banquet hall, where they shared a toast with her family. After, they retired to their room. Which was now *officially* theirs, as a couple. As soon as the door was closed, however, Anastasia realized just how difficult it would be to undress with their hands bound.

So, they took their time and helped each other. Anastasia reveled in feeling the smooth, bare skin of William's shoulders as she helped him with his tunic. She shivered as he unlaced her gown.

Then, they just held each other, staring into each other's eyes until they drifted off to sleep.

CHAPTER THIRTY-FOUR

Anastasia awoke to an explosion. She jumped violently, the cord tied around her hand jerking her back towards William. Before they could move, the door swung open, revealing a breathless Lili.

"What's going on?" Anastasia demanded.

"Joey," Lili breathed. "He's attacking the kingdom."

With coordinated effort, Anastasia and William got out of bed. Lili helped them dress quickly. Scooping up Aagney, she led the way from the room. Following the spiral staircase carved into the trunk of the tree, they made their way up to the library, where Anastasia's family, Alviva, Ayvery, Vlad, and Joey waited.

Upon seeing his son, Vlad hissed, backing away. Lili shielded Aagney, hovering near the doorway. Anastasia looked at her parents' faces. All revelry from the night before was gone, replaced with unadulterated fear.

Their warriors had all gone, leaving them alone amongst the fairies. Anastasia was sure Lili, Ayvery, and Alviva could hold their own in a fight, but her family couldn't, Vlad could only fight until the sun came up, and "good" Joey was a wildcard. That left her, William, and the fairies that could fight, to fend off Joey and the Soster. Whatever the cost, they couldn't let him have her pendant. He couldn't get even a single power of the Ancients.

"How does it look?" Anastasia asked.

"They're approaching from the west," said Elliot. "Their numbers are impressive, but we have the full might of the fairies."

"I've already dispatched the vanguard," Anarose intoned. "We're holding them off while those that cannot fight are evacuated from the city."

"Where are they going?" asked William.

"Farther north."

Anastasia nodded. With the innocents out of the way, there would be fewer unnecessary casualties. But her family remained here, instead of evacuating, which worried her. She couldn't join the fight while she worried for their safety.

"You need to hide yourselves here in the library," she told them. "It's the safest place in the city."

Celia narrowed her eyes. "What do you mean 'you'? You're coming with us."

"I can't."

"Anastasia—"

"You remember my tattoos better than anyone. I bore a warrior's tattoo as well as one of royalty. This is my fight."

Bale sighed. "At least we know that the others are safe, seeing as Joey's here."

He was right. It meant the other Ancients had a chance to find their pendants unmolested. All Anastasia needed to do was keep Joey occupied here, so they had enough time.

"We'll join you," said Graham.

Anastasia frowned. "You're not warriors."

"She's right," said William. "We can't risk you."

Anastasia met her mother's eyes. "Please, I can't lose you all again."

Anarose nodded tersely. "You're right. We'll take our leave. You just make sure you're safe, Anastasia. We can't risk you, either."

Wordlessly, Celia took Aagney from Lili's arms. Thankfully, the infant hadn't cried once since they'd taken him from his crib. Glancing at him, Anastasia turned to her mother. Blowing out a breath, she ripped her pendant from her neck and passed it to her. Anarose stared at it for a moment, before clasping it around her neck.

With a look, Anastasia knew her mother understood. She couldn't wear the one thing Joey wanted into battle. It was so strange, seeing the pendant on her mother. The last person who'd worn it had been her grandmother, mere moments before she died.

Resolutely turning away, Anastasia looked at Lili. "Where's Ostana?"

A resounding howl answered her. Alviva and Ayvery shared a knowing look. Anastasia furrowed her brow, confused. It had sounded like a werewolf, but the werewolves couldn't shift in the Old World.

Running to the door, she spotted a werewolf racing through the trees. It looked like a large, tailless wolf, but the eyes were human—Ostana's eyes. Holding her face to the full moon, she howled again. As the sound echoed, she turned and disappeared in the trees.

"How?" asked Anastasia.

"They shift every full moon," explained Ayvery. "She'll be like this until the sun rises tomorrow."

Alviva nodded. "She can't remember who or what she is while she's like this. She'll cut down everything in her path."

"So just stay out of her way, and you'll be fine."

Anastasia supposed a wolf that cut down everything in its path was a good weapon to have. Just as long as Ostana didn't accidentally turn on them before the sun rose.

Squaring her shoulders, Anastasia met William's eyes. "Let's suit up for battle."

They all hurried from the library, leaving Anastasia's family behind. The head of the Fairy Queen's guard met with Anastasia, giving reports on the situation. He led them down to the armory, where they grabbed extra weapons. Anastasia and William grabbed an extra dagger each, tucking them into their belts. Lili found an extra quiver of arrows, and Alviva and Ayvery found maces that suited them.

Joining Vlad outside, they hesitated at the base of the tree. Anastasia knew there was a battle raging out there, but all she could see was the flower-covered archway where she and William had their engagement ceremony mere hours before.

William squeezed her hand. They were still bound together, their left hands wrapped in the braided cord. Anastasia didn't have the heart to cut it off, knowing it would mean bad luck for their future together. And they needed all the good luck they could get. Besides, she and William had fought under worse circumstances before. They would manage just fine. Squeezing his hand in return, she drew on the strength radiating from him.

Running footsteps sounded a moment before Good Joey ran up to them. "I want to help!"

"Can you fight?" asked Vlad.

Joey shrugged. "I'm not quite sure."

"Just do what you can to distract the enemy, then," said William. "Your face might be enough to throw them off."

Joey nodded. "Okay."

Sounds of battle reached their ears. Joey flinched. Nerves fluttered in Anastasia stomach, but she quickly squelched them. She'd been in countless battles before and had come out alive every time. This battle would be no different. She would do anything to keep Joey from retrieving either of the pendants; there was no way she'd let him get his hands on that sort of power.

"Does it always feel like this?" Alviva questioned.

William worked his jaw. "Usually."

"Just don't vomit," Ayvery said with a rueful grin.

Vlad blew out a breath. "After this, I seriously need to find some new friends. I'm in desperate need of a perfectly boring life, where I grow peacefully into old age."

Anastasia clenched and unclenched her fists. They would wait for the battle to break into the clearing. Hopefully, the fairies would be able to hold off the Soster, and they wouldn't need to fight at all. But then Vlad bared his teeth in a feral snarl and leaned forward.

Narrowing his shark-like eyes, he murmured, "Blood."

Before they could stop him, he was off, moving so quickly his body was a mere blur. She worried for him, but figured a battle was the best place for him, giving him ample opportunities to feed.

On the horizon, the battle raged. Though it was too far off, Anastasia imagined she could see the fairies fight, see their silvery blades flash through the air. Alviva, Lili, Joey, and Ayvery moved restlessly around her. She understood. On the one hand, they were glad to be safe behind the might of the Queen's warriors, but on the other hand, they wanted to be out there, physically defending what was dear to them. But none of them were true warriors. It was safer to stay where they were, let the battle come to them.

A crash behind them drew their attention. A horde of the fairy dogs raced away from the tree, barking and growling. Anastasia followed them with her eyes, realizing what it meant; Joey had sent warriors from the east, as well. Yelps and shouts reached her ears. The battle was closer than they'd thought. Wordlessly, the others fanned out around Anastasia.

William drew his dagger. "Don't let them break the tree line."

They stood, on the tips of their toes, waiting for the battle to near the clearing. Anastasia couldn't help but think of the battle she'd been in with Deera and Calla, back at the Wishing Tree, when they'd turned all the Shadows to stone. She'd felt just the same way, twisted inside letting others fight for her. But she understood, it was the only way to keep everyone safe. She was the sole heir to the Jacquelinian throne, after all.

Just when it felt like the anticipation was going to kill her, the first few warriors burst through the trees. Ayvery, Alviva, and Joey sprang forward. As more warriors ran through the trees, Anastasia, William, and Lili leapt into the fray.

William and Anastasia stood back-to-back, their bound hands clasped. They mirrored each other as they ducked and lunged, flinging their daggers through the air. More of Joey's Soster fell beneath their blades, their blood darkening the beautiful grasses beneath their feet. Anastasia and William slid through it, cutting down anyone that sprinted from the tree line.

In the air, Lili fired arrows, picking off those that made it through their defenses. Alviva and Ayvery swung their maces like bats, felling those that neared Anastasia and William.

Joey had picked up a spear in the armory, and he spun it wildly, stabbing warriors clean through the stomach. Intermittently, Vlad or Ostana appeared through the trees, violently tearing apart their enemies with their teeth. They moved with a deadly synchronicity that felled everyone in their path.

Behind them, the Queen's forces were not as successful. Though made up of strong fairies with incredible magic, the Queen's army were not warriors. They'd never fought a day in their lives, and, as such, were savagely cut down by the Soster. In the west, Joey's forces broke through the vanguard and approached the clearing where Anastasia and the others fought. There weren't enough of them to battle the Soster back.

Wrapping her free arm around William, Anastasia unfurled her wings and launched herself into the sky. From above, they could see Joey's forces spilling into the clearing from all sides; the Soster had them surrounded. It was utter chaos, weapons and magic flying through the air on all sides. Even with Ostana—who was utterly merciless—it didn't look good.

Landing, Anastasia and William renewed their efforts. Together, they slid through the bloody grasses, rolling up under enemy warriors. They cut men down, slicing through their stomachs, their necks.

Up above them, Lili fired arrows with unerring accuracy. Alviva and Avyery picked up fallen daggers and raced through the fray, slicing anyone that crossed their paths. Joey just twirled his spear like a bo staff, whacking warriors back to where Vlad waited to tear at their necks with his teeth.

Finally, Anastasia looked around, and saw nothing but a field of bodies. She stood with William, drenched in blood, breathing raggedly. Somehow, they'd managed to defeat Joey's forces. But where was Joey? He wouldn't have sent his warriors after them to retrieve the pendant without him. And yet, he wasn't anywhere to be seen.

Fear slammed into her, a fear that wasn't her own. Her family. Joey had found her family! She turned to William.

"Hold onto me!"

He obliged, and she shot into the air. Mere seconds later, they'd arrived at the library. Anastasia flew through until she found her family, standing in a protective line in front of Anarose, while Evil Joey stalked towards them.

"Get away from them!" Anastasia shouted.

Joey turned to her. His eyes flicked to her bound hand; a dark grin twisted his mouth. "I suppose congratulations are in order."

Anastasia gripped her dagger. "Get away from my family."

Joey raised his hand. Black smoke encircled her mother's neck, lifting her into the air. She struggled, choking. "I don't really think you're in a position to make demands, dear cousin."

Anastasia could see the dark smoke curl around her pendant, as though caressing it. Anastasia's stomach twisted. He couldn't get that power, but one wrong move and he could kill her mother. Anarose's eyes flicked to Anastasia; she seemed to be trying to communicate something nonverbally, but Anastasia was too frightened to understand. The rest of her family huddled behind Anarose, staring at Joey.

Calla stepped forward. "Joseph, stop."

Joey faltered, his grip on Anarose slipping. She fell to the ground, where Bale and Elliot helped her to her feet and hurried her down the hall. Calla slowly stepped away from Graham and Celia, her icy sorcerer's eyes narrowed. As she neared Joey, Anastasia could see the familial similarities. It hurt her to think this was the first time Joey was seeing his mother in sixteen years.

Stepping forward, Calla threw up her hands. Light exploded over their heads, and Anastasia saw a circle and pentagrams drawn on the ceiling. As Joey tried to move away, he found he was trapped by the circle, unable to move.

"Let me go, you witch!" he shouted.

"Go, Anastasia!" Calla called. "Find the others. Get out of here."

Anastasia hesitated. "Calla…"

"Go! I'll hold him here!"

As much as it pained Anastasia to leave, she knew this was the only chance they'd have to keep the pendant away from Joey. With a last reassuring look at Calla, she ran the way her mother had gone.

At the end of the library, Anastasia caught up with her family. The first rays of dawn pierced the darkness. Vlad would be in danger outside, and Ostana would be shifting back. They needed to go as soon as possible. She only hoped Calla could hold Joey until she and the other Ancients could bring them all home.

"I got the ingredients for a portal," Bale said. "But it's useless now, without Calla."

Anastasia's eyed widened. "No. It's not."

She led them from the library, descending to the battlefield. Lili, Ayvery, and Alviva were cleaning off their weapons together, while Vlad went to each fallen body and checked they were really dead.

"Joey!" Anastasia called.

He bounded over to them, looking pleased that he'd managed to help during the battle. When he saw Bale holding a dead bird and rat, he paled. Anastasia ignored his expression and started drawing a circle in the dirt near the roots of the tree.

"What is all this?" he asked.

Graham flipped through Calla's grimoire until he found the page for a portal spell. "Just read this when we tell you."

"I—I don't know if I can do this."

"You're the grandson of the most powerful sorcerer in all the realms," said Anastasia. "You can do it."

As the sun started to rise over the horizon, Anastasia saw Ostana collapse through the trees. Ayvery and Alviva ran over and dragged Ostana into a pentagram. Lili shielded Vlad with a cloak, pulling him into a pentagram as well. Once Bale and Graham had the ingredients ready for the spell, the rest of them all stepped into pentagrams in the circle.

"Now!" yelled Graham.

Joey started to read, in a halting, unsure voice. "Tanu lanu l'nasoh, alilah g'dolah, l'matzo et eleh shanu m'chafashím!"

Wind tore through the clearing and then petered out. Opening her eyes, Anastasia saw they were still standing in the clearing in the fairy kingdom. Joey didn't have a good enough grasp on his magic to transport them. They were stuck.

Turning back to the tree castle, Anastasia only hoped Calla's spell would hold.

CHAPTER THIRTY-FIVE

Chris looked down at the crystal-clear waters in Eorrigon gol Peylee. He could see himself reflected in the smooth surface, for the first time in a little over six months. Somehow, he seemed older, with a scruffy beard and unkempt hair. But it was his eyes that did it really; they held a hardened sort of cynicism that hadn't been there before.

Turning away from the water, he looked back at where Dani sat, seemingly meditating, beneath a large palm tree. A few hornless cows spotted the mossy banks behind them, staring at them with strangely human eyes.

"It isn't working," said Dani.

Mira frowned. "Are you concentrating?"

"Obviously."

A splash behind Chris drew his attention. There, on a sandbar out in the water, sat a handful of mermaids. They had long, tangled green hair, and their bodies were covered entirely in scales, but they were still breathtakingly beautiful. Chris stared at them as they started to sing, a haunting, lilting melody that somehow sounded vaguely familiar. He listened for a moment, watching as the mermaids brushed out their hair.

A moment later, Dani and Mira ran across the beach and stepped into the water. They, too, were watching the mermaids.

"What are you doing?" Chris asked.

Neither responded.

A few feet from the sandbar, mermen treaded water. They were uglier than their female counterparts, with mossy teeth, beady, pig-like eyes, red noses, stubby, fin-like arms, and small, red ornamental hats.

"Dani!" Chris called.

But she hadn't seemed to hear him. She just pushed through the water, swimming towards the mermaids.

Chris could feel the malice radiating off of the mermaids. They weren't just there to entertain, they were there to harm. Steeling himself, he jumped into the water after them. Grabbing Mira's and Dani's wrists, he dragged them back towards the beach. The mermaids' song grew louder; Dani and Mira struggled against Chris' grip, trying to break free.

"It's so beautiful!" cried Dani.

Grabbing the girls around the waist, Chris managed to bring them ashore. Somehow, it seemed like the mermaids' song had possessed them. He needed to break it, or else they were never getting out of here.

As he looked around the beach for something to help them, he saw a couple of the hornless cows head towards the water. Moments later, they'd shifted into mermaids; they joined the others on the sandbar, adding to the haunting song. Dani and Mira redoubled their efforts, wrenching against Chris' grip.

"Gods and Angels forgive me," he murmured, before he hit them both on the temple with the butt of his baton, knocking them unconscious.

Once the mermaids realized their song was falling on deaf ears, they fell back into the water. Chris sat back on the sand, blowing out a breath. It seemed like everything in this Old World was out to kill them. They needed to get the pendants and get out of there, as quickly as possible; which led him to thoughts of the Ancients, and how he apparently was one. It was strange to think that he had some incredible power that he'd never known. And, to think, he'd once been unsure of the Gods and Angels' decision to make him a warrior.

But what could he do now? They needed to get the pendants, and Dani and Mira were both unconscious. Besides, Isidora had told them that this was the location of Dani's pendant, not Chris'. He'd only come along as protection.

Getting to his feet, he pulled his dagger from his belt and started to dig beneath the palm tree. Methodically, he shoved the dagger into the ground and pulled it out, over and over, marveling at how the grains of sand cascaded over each other. After not seeing for so long, he took pleasure in the little things, the way of nature.

Chris shed his vest and rolled the sleeves of his tunic, digging. He was nearly up to his shoulders, and parched and sweaty, but he kept digging.

When the sun was high in the sky, and blisters were forming on the palm of his hands, Chris struck something hard. He brushed away some sand with his hands, and tried to work his dagger around the edges; there was some kind of box around the pendant.

He pushed his dagger down again, and wind exploded forth, throwing him back across the beach. Bright orange light engulfed the beach, and Chris felt like he was being carried up into a tornado. He shielded his eyes as sand whipped across his skin. Peering through squinted eyes, he saw Isidora, Hughie, and the others. They were translucent, like Anastasia said the Ancients had been in her vision from the pentagram.

They all turned to look at him, shielding their eyes. As the wind picked up, and the light brightened, Chris felt himself drawn forward. Beside him, Dani got to her feet and joined him.

Grasping hands, they and the other Ancients began to chant. "Cuirimid ar ais chugainn a lorgfaimid, ionas go bhféadfaimis ár gcumhacht a aisghabháil!"

The sand swirled around them, creating a wall between them and the rest of the beach. Through it all, Chris could see the other Ancients, wrapped in similar lights and walls of dirt or leaves. They chanted louder and louder, until a *crack* sounded.

The earth beneath Chris' and Dani's feet opened up, and Dani's pendant rose through the air. Slowly, she reached out to grasp the pendant. As soon as the citrine-colored moonstone touched her fingers, she rose into the air, cocooned in bright orange light. Chris shielded his eyes and looked away, struggling to stay on his feet.

All at once, the light and wind faded. Straightening, Chris looked over at Dani. As she lowered to the ground, she looked like a completely different person. She was dressed in a flowing orange dress and floor-length shawl, her swan sigil emblazoned on her chest. Her eyes, once hazel like William's, were now the same deep orange shade as the pendant around her neck. As he looked at her, he had the distinct urge to bow.

"Dani?" he breathed.

She turned her fiery eyes on him. "I am Cordia."

She raised her hands; they were glowing with bright orange magic. A moment later, a number of portal-like doorways opened. Chris had never seen so many together at once.

The other Ancients strode through, looking much like Dani. They all crackled with power, their pendants at their throats. The other warriors stumbled through the portals after them, awe plain on their features.

The Fairy Queen stepped forward, looking like one of the Angels. She held out a rich black moonstone pendant. "Time to Awaken, brother."

"I thought the Vatis had to awaken us," he said, suddenly fearful.

"She will connect us to our mortal bodies."

Gingerly, Chris reached out to take the black moonstone. As soon as his fingers touched the stone, he felt a rush of power. Wind wrapped around him, warm and comforting. What felt like a mere fraction of a second later, he felt himself lower to the ground. But when he opened his eyes, he found that he was looking through his own eyes as though a stranger. There was a disconnect, like he wasn't in charge of his body any longer.

He heard himself say, "Let us return to Vatis."

But he hadn't told himself to speak, or to move. Then he realized this must've been what the Queen meant. The Ancients had taken over their bodies. And it was up to Anastasia to unite them both together. Until then, he supposed he was just along for the ride.

Dani opened another portal and they all strode through. They entered the fairy kingdom and shock went through Chris as he saw bodies everywhere. Had there been a battle? Was Anastasia alright?

"Gods and Angels," Aelnold breathed.

Gerrard raced forward. "Find the royal family!"

As the others ran into the trees, the Ancients remained behind in the clearing. As his body turned towards them, Chris studied them. They all had different colored pendants, the same shade as their ancient-looking clothing. He wondered what *he* looked like. Though, he supposed, given that his moonstone was black, he was dressed in all black.

"Vatis," said the Fairy Queen.

They all turned to see Anastasia striding towards them. Chris watched her as she took in their appearances, awe flashing across her face. He was surprised to realize he couldn't feel her emotions anymore.

"Time to Awaken, sister."

CHAPTER THIRTY-SIX

Anastasia stared up at the Ancients. They were beautiful, just as they had been in the realm of the Gods and Angels, when she'd taken the List from Chris. They each wore their pendants, shimmering in the autumn sunlight.

"We cannot stay like this much longer," said Dani. "Without being anchored to our mortal bodies."

Anastasia reached out to take the Fairy Queen's hand, to Awaken, but before she could, an explosion shook the trees. Joey. He'd broken free of Calla's circle. It had held him for a day, enough time for them to evacuate the city, but not enough for them to come up with a concrete plan of how to stop him. Thank the Gods and Angels the Ancients had arrived.

A second explosion threw Anastasia back from the Fairy Queen. The Ancients stumbled, flickering between their ethereal forms and their mortal ones.

"Anastasia!" William shouted, running towards her. "We need to go!"

Suddenly, they were surrounded. Warriors spilled into the clearing, and Anastasia had but a moment to wonder at where they came from, before she leapt into battle. Grabbing her dagger, she launched herself at the nearest warrior.

All around her, her friends fought. Lili launched herself from the tree, brandishing her bow and arrows. Ayvery, Alviva, and Gerrard ran in from the ground, felling warriors with their maces. Hayde, Durse, and Ryke flew through the air, holding battle axes, while the Ros brothers ran through the fray with swords. Mira and Balan threw potions through the air, shouting. They all wordlessly protected the Ancients, who were still flickering between themselves and their mortal bodies. They staggered back and forth; Anastasia knew she needed to act quickly.

Felling the warrior she fought, she threw herself into the sky. Three warriors followed, hot on her trail. She blocked their swords, tucking her wings close to her and rolling through the air as arrows barraged them. Unfurling her wings, she rose higher, flying towards the warriors from above. Catching one of the men unawares, she drove her dagger into his neck. Pushing off from him, she grabbed another warrior by the neck and wrangled him to the ground.

There, they grappled, the hilt of his sword catching her in the temple. She staggered back, seeing stars. The warrior ran at her. She raised her dagger at the last moment, spearing him through the chest. As he fell, she reared her arm back and launched her dagger. It tore through the third warrior's wings, forcing her to the ground.

Grabbing her dagger, she turned and shoved it through the warrior's chest. As she yanked it free, she leapt at a sorcerer. Coming up behind him, she drew her dagger across his throat. When he fell to his knees, she grabbed his belt from his hips.

Tying his vials to her own hips, she sprinted clear of the melee. Drawing a vial, she threw it as hard as she could and shouted, "L'fotzatz!"

Fire exploded, flinging people through the air. Grinning, she ran back into the fray. The battle raged on in a shower of explosions and blades, screams and battle cries renting the air. The cold heat of battle washed over Anastasia, forcing her forward. Blood splattered across her face, her clothes, and made the ground slick. And yet, her head was perfectly clear. She sighted her targets and took them down, avoiding their weapons as best she could.

But Joey's forces were immense. They drove her friends back to the oak trees, despite their valiant efforts. Concern flashed through Anastasia as she felt bark at her back. There was nowhere left for them to go, nowhere left to protect the Ancients.

She renewed her efforts, felling anyone that neared the tree's entrance. But then, an icy stillness overcame her. She glanced down to see thick black smoke winding up her legs. She jerked against it but froze when she saw Joey striding towards her. He was haggard, thin, his skin sallow, his eyes black as night. This was evil Joey, the part of him that was Shadow and Nadmilise.

He bared his teeth in a feral grin. "Anastasia."

He stalked towards her, his smoky magic holding her in place. She stared over his shoulder, watching as her family filtered into the clearing.

"You should know that nothing can hold me, cousin."

She glared at him. "It worked well enough."

In one fluid motion, he wrapped his hand around her neck and lifted her. Her feet dangled off the ground. Turning, he slammed her into the ground, driving the air from her lungs. She gasped out a laugh, staring up at him.

The look in his dark eyes told her that in that moment, he was ready to kill her. He flew forward on his obsidian wings and drove his fist into her face. Pain erupted through her body, but she just kept laughing at him. All around her, her friends battled, holding off Joey's forces. She just needed to hold out a little longer, till everyone was ready. She could do it. The Gods and Angels had named her a warrior, after all.

A scream tore through the air. A few feet away, Isidora—now in her mortal form—threw her arms wide. Lightning shot down from the sky and struck Isidora full in the chest. She exploded with electricity, her eyes glowing with power. Everyone around her halted, staring as she moved through the clearing. Joey paused, mid-punch, looking up at her.

"Get away from her," Isidora growled.

Clenching her fists, she raised her hands to the sky. Lightning exploded from her palms. Anastasia looked at her mother. "Now!"

Anarose tore the pendant from her neck and threw it. Just as Anastasia's fingers wrapped around it, Isidora's lightning struck. Anastasia screamed, feeling like her body was being torn apart from the inside out. But then, an intense warmth cocooned her. She rose into the air, wrapped in bright violet light. When she opened her eyes, she stood, flushed with power, the power of the Vatis.

Around the clearing, the other Ancients stood, fully Awakened. Joey looked between them, his face screwed into a grimace. His warriors stood, hesitating, quite unsure of what to do with themselves. Anastasia couldn't blame them; she was sure they looked quite imposing. But all she could think of was the power flooding through her veins. When she raised her hands, they were glowing with pale violet magic. She felt as she did when the Angel Razibelle had taken over her body, back in the Forest of Luas all those months ago. Except, now she was in control.

"Anastasia!" Dani shouted. "Do it now!"

Her body moved of its own volition, holding her hands out towards Chris and Dani. The other Ancients reached for each other, a bright white light stretching between them.

As one, they drove their hands into the ground, power gushing from their palms. The world trembled around them, forest trees falling around them as wind tore at them. Light surged from their bodies, bathing everything in white.

Anastasia felt like she was falling. She wasn't sure for how long, but after a time, she opened her eyes. A familiar hall solidified around her, one with high windows and a pair of carved wooden thrones. As she looked around, she realized she stood in the center of the throne room in Sehir. Tears welled in her eyes. They'd done it. They'd returned home!

A chuckle sounded behind her. She whirled around to see Joey seated on her mother's throne. "So, you think you've won."

She glared at him. "I *have* won."

"Oh, really?"

He held up a hand. Her pendant hung from his fingers, glittering in the sunlight. Anastasia gasped, reaching for her throat. But her neck was bare.

"This world, and everything in it, is mine."

She glared at him. "For someone who can see the past, you understand very little of it."

"I understand enough, dear cousin."

Whirling, he threw the pendant down. Anastasia shrieked as it shattered, feeling like a part of herself had been torn to pieces. She fell to her knees as pale white shards skittered across the stone floor. A wave of magic flew from the pendant, shattering the windows as it shot outwards. Anastasia threw up her hands to cover her face; shards of glass sliced her skin.

"There is nowhere you can hide," Joey cried.

Anastasia pushed herself to her feet, tears streaming down her face. "What have you *done*?"

"I got what I wanted, cousin."

"You wanted the power from the pendants! And now you've ruined it!"

"Have I?" He grinned. "See for yourself."

Turning, Anastasia sprinted from the room. Panic fluttered through her. He needed the power of the pendants for himself. Why would he break the pendant? In her premonition, the Ancients had broken their pendants themselves, not Joey. And then they'd all been turned to stone. She needed to find them!

Skidding around a corner, she ran smack into Deera.

"You're alright!" Anastasia cried, throwing her arms around her.

Deera cleared her throat. "Yes, I'm fine. Why wouldn't I be?"

But then Anastasia realized what it meant, if Deera was up and walking around. Horror flooded through her as she understood what Joey had wanted all along. He didn't need all the pendants to exert his rule as King of Jacqueline; he just needed one or two. But Anastasia's pendant served another, far more sinister purpose.

Even as Anastasia thought it, her blood ran cold.

Joey had unfrozen the Shadows.

CHAPTER THIRTY-SEVEN

Anastasia returned to the throne room, but Joey was gone. Anastasia turned around and around, struggling to figure out what to do next. The Shadows were free, which meant they would be moving on the realms. There was no telling where they were, seeing how the time between the realms and the Old World moved so strangely. They could be converging on Sehir as she stood there, thinking.

With trembling hands, she scooped up the pieces of her pendant. Tears streamed down her cheeks as she tucked them into the purse at her waist. Her pendant was gone. Joey had broken it. And now the Shadows were marching on the realms. Her mind just kept repeating those three things over and over again. She couldn't seem to move past it, frozen in place in the throne room. They'd lost. For everything they'd accomplished, they'd lost. Joey had succeeded in his plan. They were trapped.

"Anastasia!"

She looked up, but hardly understood what was happening as William raced towards her. But then he grabbed her in his arms and she melted into him. Her fiancé. William.

"Are you hurt?" he asked.

She shook her head. "Joey, he… the Shadows. They're coming."

"The High Council is here," he said. "They've held a meeting."

Vaguely, Anastasia wondered just how long everyone else had been back in Sehir. For her, it was mere minutes. But it seemed like William had had time to clean up, change his clothes. Gods and Angels, what had Joey been able to accomplish in the time she was gone?

"They're trying to enact Anistes Droun. They've imprisoned the Ancients. They're coming for you."

It took Anastasia a moment to understand. The High Council was coming for her. They were going to lock her up, just like Tamo wanted to do all those months ago. It was the only thing they could think of, seeing as they hadn't come up with a plan to stop the Shadows. They were outnumbered, and turning them to stone hadn't bought them as much time as they needed. And now Joey had the Shadows *and* access to the pendants.

But there was a place where Shadows didn't exist, a place where they could regroup and figure out how to save their home. A place where the High Council couldn't control the Ancients.

She grabbed William's hand. "Come on!"

They raced through the throne room, spilling out into the hall. Anastasia ran as fast as she could, taking the stairs two-at-a-time. A part of her wished she still had her wings; flying would certainly be much faster.

Finally, they reached Valdon's chambers. Anastasia pushed her way inside, not surprised to find the room empty. William bolted the door closed behind them, fixing her with a curious look.

"We can't barricade ourselves in here forever."

She turned to Valdon's bookshelf. "Not forever. Just long enough."

She tore through the books on the bookshelves, searching feverishly for what she sought. William hovered behind her, keeping an eye on the door. Anastasia knew that Valdon came from an ancient family, seeing as Mohan was an Ancient. And Valdon always had the answers, about things Anastasia had never understood. It would make sense that he would have the answers now.

With the very last book on the shelf, Anastasia found what she was looking for. She held it aloft, a cry of excitement leaving her lips.

"What is that?" William asked.

Sitting on the bed, Anastasia flipped through the pages. "A grimoire."

"From the Old World?"

Anastasia nodded. "There has to be a spell in here that can take us back, one that doesn't require spinal fluid and murder."

"You want to go back to the Old World?"

"It's the only chance we'll have."

A moment later, the door opened. Anastasia and William looked up to see Valdon. Elation flooded Anastasia, and she leapt up and threw her arms around Valdon. He returned her embrace, holding her tight.

"I'm so glad you're safe," he murmured.

She nodded. "You, too."

"You need to get out of here. The High Council is coming."

"We need to get back to the Old World." She turned and grabbed his grimoire. "Can you help?"

Valdon pursed his lips. With a snap of his fingers, the grimoire returned to his hands. He flipped through the pages for a moment, before handing the book back to Anastasia. She perused the pages, reading the spell. It had a number of ingredients, ones Anastasia wasn't sure they could get. But, it was a start.

She looked up at him. "What do we do?"

"You and William need to go to the elemental realm. I'll get everything else."

***

Moments later, Anastasia and William stepped through the direct portal to the elemental realm. As it was far from Jacqueline, it was likely that Joey's spell hadn't reached the Shadows gathered there yet, and there were still some encased in stone.

The thought of going near the Shadows, even as statues, made Anastasia uneasy. They were running out of time! What if they statues had already unfrozen, and they were too late? She was running from the High Council, once again, on a whim that they might have a way to return to the Old World. But, this seemed like it was their only choice, to keep everything they knew from being obliterated.

Thankfully, William didn't speak. He just stood by her side, silently offering his support. It filled her with a confidence she didn't really feel.

They reached the edge of the jungle, tumbling through onto the sandy beach. Anastasia stared up at the massive stone statue in front of them, covered in moss and vines. The Shadow's claws were extended, its razor-sharp teeth bared in a howl. Even though it was frozen, the sight still made her shiver. Perhaps it was because she knew firsthand how deadly the Shadows were in battle, or because the beast could come to life at any moment.

She knew of a tale that whoever managed to break a Shadow statue would become the next King of Jaqueline. It was something children made up, to cover up the fear of having these grotesque monsters so close to home, she supposed.

She understood the urgency with which they needed to work, but she just couldn't bring herself to touch the statue. Every inch of herself felt *wrong* without her pendant.

A soul-piercing roar forced her to step up, despite her uneasiness. The hair on the back of her neck stood on end as she turned. A Shadow raced across the beach towards them, its blood red eyes trained on her. Pulling out her dagger, she took up a fighting stance; the cold heat of battle washed over her, driving her forward.

"Figure out a way to smash that thing!" she called to William.

Racing forward, she met the Shadow. They collided in a clash of bronze against claws. Anastasia fell back into the sand and rolled out of the way as the beast's claws shot out at her. Still, it grazed her shoulder, drawing blood. She hissed in pain as she leapt to her feet.

Behind her, she heard clanging as William stabbed at the Shadow statue with his dagger.

Stumbling back, Anastasia ducked beneath the Shadow's claws. Coming up behind it, she sliced through its back. Inky blood splattered across her face. She wiped it from her eyes as the Shadow fell forward. Its claws raked against the statue, taking out a chunk of stone. Anastasia leapt onto its back, driving her dagger through its head. It roared once, bucking her. She tumbled to the ground as it died, soaking the sand with its dark blood.

Lying there, she stared upwards. Fluffy clouds moved slowly across the pale blue sky. Anastasia watched them, as William continued to hit the statue. Gathering herself, she sat up and sheathed her blade.

In one fluid motion, William cut one of the Shadow's claws from its hand and drove it into the statue. The stone fissured, cracking with a deep rumble. Leaping up, he kicked out his both legs, slamming his feet against the claw. It went clear through the statue as William dropped into the sand, making the entire beast crumble.

Wordlessly, they gathered the stones into a knapsack and turned back to the jungle. Hurrying forward, they stepped through the portal that awaited them.

They stepped through into the throne room, where Mohan and Valdon were grinding up ingredients with a mortar and pestle. Salt was sprinkled around a pentagram, and a chalice of blood sat inside it. Anastasia handed him the knapsack. He just gave her a slight nod in response.

Anastasia looked at the windows. Frigid autumn air filtered through, chilling the room. Glass crunched under her boots as she moved towards the thrones. It was nearly impossible to believe that mere months before, she'd sat there, condemning William to prison. And before that, her grandfather had been murdered by Shadows on these very steps. Such history this room had seen. And it would stand to see more history, long after she had been forgotten.

Her body vibrated with urgency. They needed to act, before Joey returned, and the Shadows reached the city, and the High Council locked her away.

At last, Valdon stepped back from the circle. "I think we're ready."

Anastasia held her hand over the chalice, drawing her dagger across her palm. Her blood dripped down, swirling through the cup. William quickly did the same, before joining Valdon in the middle of the circle. Their blood would count as the essence of an angel they needed.

A soul-piercing roar tore through the air. The Shadows had arrived in Sehir. As deep rumbling tore through the city, Anastasia thought back to when the Shadows had attacked all those months ago, when she and William had gone off on a quest to find her grandmother. Then, she'd run to warn the High Council. Now, she was running from them.

As she joined Mohan and Valdon in the circle, the door to the throne room burst open. The High Council, along with all of Anastasia's family, spilled into the room.

"Grab her!" yelled Tamo.

Anastasia stepped back within the circle as guards ran into the room, surrounding them. Anastasia met her mother's gaze, silently trying to convey what they were doing. If they returned to the Old World, they would all be safe!

William drew his dagger.

Valdon raised his hands and started to chant. "Elet g'dolah, bevakasha l'hachazir otanu el haolam ha'ishen. L'hachazir otanu el ma hashu ha'aber shelanu."

Nothing happened.

Panic fluttered in Anastasia's chest. It hadn't worked? Maybe there wasn't a way to return to the Old World. Maybe Valdon's magic wasn't the same as the sorcerers of the Old World. Maybe Anistes Droun would be the only way.

But then, she remembered her premonition: *I break free of my window and charge him, managing to take the shards back from him. Whirling, I drop them into a goblet of blood and shout words in a strange language. Light surges, once again, and the Sehirian throne room disappears, leaving us all in the ancient throne room.*

Taking the shards from her purse, the dropped them into the chalice.

"Try again!" she shouted.

The guards lunged forward. Tamo shouted, "Don't move!"

Valdon repeated his chant as the guards broke through the circle and grabbed William and Anastasia. Wind whipped through the room, tearing at their clothes. As it felt like the floor was dropping out from under her, Anastasia turned to William.

"I'll find you! I promise!"

But then, everything went dark.

When Anastasia awoke, she turned and vomited everything in her stomach. Once she could breathe again, she opened her eyes and took in her surroundings. A long wooden table was covered with maps and parchments, bright against the stone walls. Pops of color lined the wooden ceiling beams, carved crests proudly displaying house colors and sigils.

Turning, she rushed to the looking glass. Though it was warped and colored with age, she could still make out her reflection. Once again, she was utterly naked, but this time, she wasn't afraid. When she heard a rustling noise behind her, her smile widened.

They'd done it. They'd returned to the Old World.

Taking stock of her surroundings, she realized she was again alone. But then, she remembered the last of her premonition: *But when I turn, my doppelgangers are gone. It's just me, holding the six repaired pendants. But I'm unafraid by the sudden loneliness. Somehow, it gives me hope.*

They'd returned, they were safe. She wouldn't be alone for long.

As soon as she was dressed, she ran out into the frigid evening and threw herself into the air. Her wings unfurled with a snap, carrying her into the sky. Breathing deep, she crossed the water and landed on the opposite shore. Everything was just as it had been when she left, the houses built, the marketplace set up; there were even candles flickering in windows. Anastasia took it all in, feeling both excited and concerned. Yes, by returning to the Old World, they were protected from the Shadows. But they were also once again bound by the restrictions of it.

Crossing the street, she ducked into the inn. Chairs were scattered around carved wooden tables, topped with mugs and plates of food. Anastasia grabbed herself a blanket from upstairs, wrapping it around her shoulders to ward off the chill. Slipping behind the counter, she grabbed a tankard and filled it with Mistress Couland's rich ale.

She took a long drink. The next steps were clear: unite the High Council and the Ancients, find a way to defeat the Shadows, and return home to the realms. All she needed do to now was wait.

Grabbing a chair, Anastasia dragged it outside. Planting it in the center of town, she sat down and took a long drink of ale. Pale flecks drifted down around her, and she blinked in surprise. The first snowfall in Bahail. She wondered if it was as magical in the Old World as it was in Jacqueline.

Something told her it would be.

ACKNOWLEDGEMENTS

I have to thank my parents, Cat and Bernard, for their unconditional love and support. You guys are the reason I'm able to write books, much less share them with others. I'm not sure there are enough words to give my thanks. But I hope this is a step in the right direction!

To my editor and beta reader, Lissa. You have stood by me through all different iterations of these books and have given me such incredible advice and support. I'm glad I have someone like you in my corner, keeping me from using the same phrases 300 times in one book. I am truly grateful for your dedication and the way you treat my books like pieces of art. I feel like you often see the beauty in them before I do.

I want to give a shout out to Josh and Anna, who not only let me vent to them when I have writer's block, but who also give me imaginative ways to get out of it. You should see pieces of yourselves in these books. You inspire me.

Aaron Lambert, your cover art is phenomenal as always. Thank you for taking my ideas and turning them into incredible pieces of art. You're a phenomenal artist; I'm so glad to have you be a part of this journey!

Last but not least, I do what I do for you, my dear readers. If it wasn't for you, my words would be empty. You motivate me to be more, to grow, so that I can give you the best story my imagination can conjure. Thank you for reading what I write!

ABOUT THE AUTHOR

Jordi Burton grew up in Plantation, Florida, and graduated from the University of Florida in December of 2017 with a degree in English, and a minor in History. She started her first novel at age ten and has since worked on forty-six others. She is published in Virge Literary Magazine, and P'an Ku Literary Magazine.

An ardent science fiction and fantasy enthusiast, Jordi can usually be found geeking out at comic conventions, binge-watching anything Marvel or DC, and obsessing about her next creative project. Her hobbies include: showering her Boston Terrier with love, mentoring new writers, holding deep conversations about the real-world application of fictional characters, and searching for her next great written adventure.

Follow her on:
Facebook: /AuthorJordiBurton
Twitter: @Jordi_Burton
Instagram: @Author.JordiBurton

Visit Jordi online at www.JordiBurton.com

www.ingramcontent.com/pod-product-compliance
Lightning Source LLC
Chambersburg PA
CBHW060539180626
46817CB00002B/649